ALVIN LE
TEN YEARS AFTER

VISUAL HISTORY by Herb Staehr

FREE STREET PRESS

ALVIN LEE & TEN YEARS AFTER–VISUAL HISTORY

Published by Free Street Press - Hingham, MA
International Standard Book Number (ISBN):
0-9708700-0-0

Printed in the United States of America
by BookMasters, Inc. – Mansfield, OH

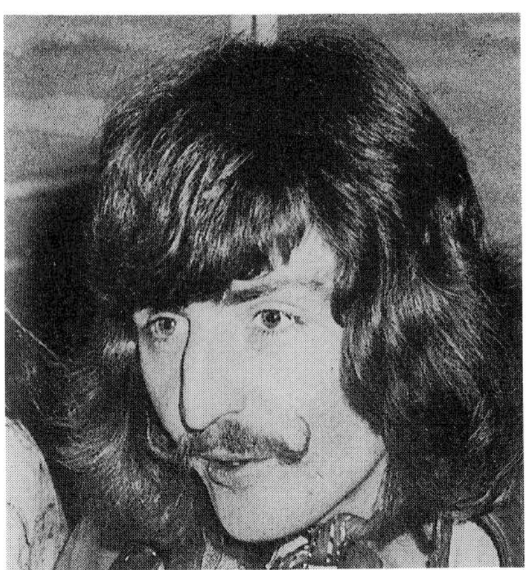

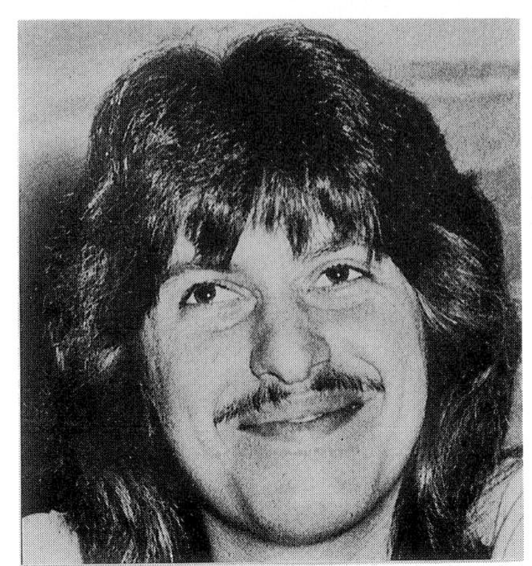

DEDICATION

This book is dedicated to Alvin Lee, Leo Lyons, Chick Churchill and Ric Lee in appreciation for Over thirty-five years of great music. Also to John Hembrow and in memory of Bill Graham for his unparalleled contribution to classic rock.

Very special thanks to Dot Barnes, Armand Basilico, Toni Franklin at the fan club (AlvinLee.com), Luky Schrempf and Joe Sia for being there with his camera.

Many thanks also to the following friends and fans for their inspiration and assistance in making this book possible: Steve Bander, Dr. Patrick Bellier, Diane Bolivar, Peter Brkusic, Dan Carroll, Henrik Christensen, Mark Felkins, Christian Fix, Mikael Gehrs, Adrian Goldwater, Barry Gruber, Hennie Banen, John Kenney, Henry Kiecman, Russ Levine, Benny Lundin, Brad Matisoff, Tony McKiernan, David McMullen, Greg Moebius, Antonio Abel Moreira, Ian Radburn, Claus Rasmussen, Matti Rekonen, Leon Rubin, Ian Russell, Dr. Thomas Schmid, Andy Seghers, Peter Smith, Rod Steanson, Izumi Tada, Mikael Uneman & Doug Vachon. Thanks to anyone we have missed and to all fans of Alvin Lee & Ten Years After around the world.

FRONT COVER

Alvin Lee at the Fillmore East in New York City September 1969 – photographed by Joseph Sia.

Note: Every effort has been made to contact the Copyright holders of the photographs in this book, but some were untraceable. We would appreciate it if the photographers concerned would contact us.

FOREWORD

Ten Years After *was one of the top blues/rock bands to emerge from the "Second British Invasion" of the late 60's. They were fronted by dazzling lead guitarist* ***Alvin Lee*** *and equally adept bass player* ***Leo Lyons****. The other members of TYA were* ***Ric Lee*** *on drums and* ***Chick Churchill*** *on keyboards. The Alvin Lee/Leo Lyons collaboration began in 1960 when they first played together in a Nottingham group called the Atomites. A succession of name changes followed - including the Jaymen, the Jaycats, the Jaybirds and Bluesyard, before the band ultimately settled on the name "Ten Years After" in the spring of 1967. As was the case with many other "2nd Wave" British bands of the period (Cream, Chicken Shack, Fleetwood Mac, John Mayall, Savoy Brown, etc.), Ten Years After's music had a solid blues base. But, early on, TYA also fused jazz and swing into their brand of the blues and this set them apart stylistically from the others. The result was a very energetic form of music played by four extremely skilled musicians. The excitement level that Ten Years After projected in their live set earned them regular work in the London clubs and well received appearances at national blues festivals.*

Following the release of their first album, it wasn't long before TYA caught the ear of American promoters like ***Bill Graham*** *and they were invited to perform in America. They immediately took USA venues such as the Fillmore West by storm when the American audiences, accustomed to the psychedelic noodlings of San Francisco Bay Area musicians, were blown away by the highly taut and accomplished playing of Alvin Lee and his bandmates. The solid following and respect that Ten Years After achieved brought an invitation to play at the* ***Woodstock Music & Arts Festival*** *in August 1969. Woodstock was only one of many landmark events of the period where TYA were among the featured performers. The movie that followed caused the band, and guitarist Alvin Lee in particular, to suddenly become* ***"Rock Stars"****. After the Woodstock film was released, it became increasingly difficult for Ten Years After to get their* ***other*** *music heard. The new and expanded audiences were mainly interested in seeing and hearing Alvin Lee perform the adrenaline-rushed fretboard acrobatics featured in the popular movie. Their elevated superstar status also brought pressure from management for Ten Years After to cash in on the increased popularity, and nearly constant touring resulted. Despite the tour pressures, Alvin Lee and the band managed to create a number of great albums that still sound fresh today.*

The following pages provide a history of Alvin Lee & Ten Years After by looking at their record releases, tour schedules, set lists, reviews & interviews - plus many rare photographs. Ten Years After has a rich concert history, having performed at many of rock's most memorable events and festivals, including: ***Windsor 7th National Jazz & Blues Festival, Bath Festival of Blues, Newport Jazz Festival, Woodstock, Texas Pop Festival, 2nd Atlanta International Pop Festival, Randall's Island New York Pop Festival, the 1970 Isle of Wight Festival, Deutschlandhalle Super Concert and many others****. It was not possible to list all Alvin Lee and Ten Years After performances in this book, but by the mid 70's TYA had already completed in excess of 28 American tours - more than any other rock band. They have, of course, also toured extensively in the U.K., Europe, Scandinavia, Japan and Brazil. Their 9th album title* ***"Rock & Roll Music To The World"*** *was most appropriate!*

In today's age, rock & roll performers usually draw media attention for their commercial appeal, fashion statements, off-stage antics, past or present addictions, or untimely demise - but not very often for musical integrity. In contrast, this book chronicles a band that has maintained an ongoing and uncompromising commitment to their music for over thirty years. TYA's only legacy is the music they have made. It can be found on their eleven albums and on several Ten Years After compilation releases. Many great Alvin Lee solo efforts are also available, as well as albums featuring Leo Lyons ("The Kick") and Ric Lee ("The Breakers"). Chick Churchill also released a solo LP ("You and Me") in 1973.

Of all the legendary rock bands from the 60's, there is only one that continues to perform today in it's original line up ....

Alvin Lee, Leo Lyons, Ric Lee & Chick Churchill - TEN YEARS AFTER !

I hope you enjoy their story.

PHOTO CREDITS

***Richard E. Aaron** - page 120 (Madison Square Garden, New York City 5/74).*
***Jorgan Angel** - page 10 top & 15 (Gladsaxe Teen Club, Denmark 2/68);*
Page 14 left & 17 (Gladsaxe Teen Club, Denmark 4/68); 48 & 49 (K.B. Hallen/Copenhagen, Denmark 12/69).
***Hennie Banen** - page 153 (Jubeck, Germany 8/86); page 154 (Amsterdam, Holland 2/87).*
***D.M. Barnes** - page 1 (Alvin Lee - age 15); 2 (Jaybirds 1962 - Leo Lyons, Alvin Lee & Pete Evans);*
page 3 (Jaycats 1961 - Pete Evans, Leo Lyons, Ivan Jay & Alvin Lee); 4 bottom (Jaybirds 1963:
Leo Lyons, Alvin Lee & Dave Quickmire); page 5 (left-Jaybirds 1964; right-Alvin Lee 1965).
***Ken Beken** - page 64 & 65 (Isle of Wight Festival, England 8/70).*
***Robert Bennett** - page 151 (Syracuse, New York 1987).*
***John Chappina** - page 47, 52 & 53 (TYA backstage at Fillmore East, New York 9/69).*
***Dagmar** - page 116 & 117 (Madison Square Garden, New York City 5/74).*
***Tom Englehardt** - page 181 (Esbjerg, Denmark 5/97).*
***Bruce Gebert** - page 25 bottom left (Fillmore East, New York 9/68).*
***Douglas Kent Hall -** page 50 top & 51 (Fillmore East, New York 2/70).*
***Larry Hulst** - page 81 (Leo Lyons & Alvin Lee 1971) & 129 top (Leo Lyons & Alvin Lee 1975).*
***Henry Kiecman** - page 182 & 183 bottom (Day In The Garden - Bethel, New York 8/98).*
***Lothar Krist** - page 147 (Marquee Club, London 7/83); 156, 158 & 159 (Ten Years After 1988-1990).*
***Jon Levicke** - page 103 (Alvin Lee 1972); 128 (Midnight Special/Burbank, California 3/75).*
***Vincent Lagana** - page 180 (Alvin Lee - Udine, Italy 6/96).*

***Jeffrey Mayer** - page 100 & 101 (Alvin Lee 1972); 118, 119 & 132 (Ten Years After 1974).*
***Brad Matisoff** - page 125 top right, 126 & 127 (Alvin Lee - Seattle 2/75).*
***Norwood Price** - page 21 (Alvin Lee, 1st USA Tour - Whiskey A Go Go/Hollywood, California 6/68);*
page 24 top right (The Bank/Torrance, California 11/68);
page 26 bottom left & 28 top (Shrine Expo Hall/Los Angeles, California 11/68).
***Steen Moller Rasmussen** - page 7 (left-Alvin Lee; right-Ric Lee & Jeff Beck, Brondby Pop Club 4/68);*
page 8 (Brondby Pop Club, Denmark 2/68); 23 (Ric Lee - Brondby Pop Club, Denmark 4/68);
page 28 bottom (TYA - Brondby, Denmark 2/69); 67 (Jimi Hendrix - Isle of Fehmarn 9/70).
***Joe Rizzo** - page 143 (Alvin Lee & Mick Taylor 12/81); 149 (Alvin Lee 12/81); 150 (Alvin Lee 1983).*
***Leon Rubin** - page 163 (Ten Years After - Ritz Club, New York City 11/89).*
***Joseph Sia -** page 34 & 35 (Newport Jazz Festival, Rhode Island 7/69);*
page 38 bottom right, 39, 42 & 43 (Woodstock Music & Arts Festival/Bethel, NY 8/69);
page 46 (Fillmore East, New York 2/70); 55 & 78 (Ten Years After - Publicist's Office, NYC 1969);
page 63 left & 73 top (Capitol Theater/Portchester, New York 8/70);
page 70 bottom & 71 (Madison Square Garden, New York City 11/70).
***Paul Skonieczny** - page 124 bottom left & 125 bottom (West Hartford, Connecticut 1/75).*
***Herb Staehr** - page 4 top (Star Club/Hamburg, Germany 1964); 137 & 141 (Miami, Florida 5/79);*
page 160 & 161 (Paradise Club/Boston, MA 11/89); page 183 top (Bethel, New York 8/98);
Page 185 (Hampton Beach Casino, New Hampshire 8/99).

PART ONE

"From Nottingham to New York"
Ten Years After – Band Biography

***Alvin Lee**, was born on December 19, 1944 in Nottingham, England. He had an early exposure to his father's collection of ethnic records. His parents, Sam and Dot, were avid jazz and blues fans and Alvin was raised in an environment that was filled with the music of Ralph Willis, Lonnie Johnson, Blind Lemon Jefferson, Leadbelly, Big Bill Broonzy, John Lee Hooker and Muddy Waters.*

When Alvin was twelve, his father asked him if he wanted to learn an instrument and he chose the clarinet, "only because my brother-in-law played one." He spent about a year taking lessons once a week and did not enjoy it very much but, by listening to Benny Goodman's clarinet work, Alvin heard Charlie Christian and he started getting into the guitar more than the clarinet.

After seeing him at a local club, his parents brought Big Bill Broonzy back to the house and he sat in the living room and played guitar - which made a big impression on Alvin. He soon traded his clarinet for an f-hole guitar ("an ordinary acoustic cello guitar called a plexon") and took a year of guitar lessons, doing jazz rhythm chords and listening to Django Reinhart, Barney Kessel and Tal Farlow. Alvin played all the old standards like 'A Nightingale Sang In Berkeley Square', "with all those minor sevenths and things."

He also became interested in Elvis Presley's guitarist Scotty Moore and followed his roots back to Chet Atkins and Merle Travis, which got him interested in finger style picking.

According to Alvin, "then I went into a bit of classical, when Chet Atkins started his classical trip it steered me into Juan Serrano - it was always a hobby, I never really thought I'd be able to get on stage and play when I was young, but it came naturally after a while."

About a year after he picked up the guitar, rock 'n roll hit England and Alvin heard the first exciting sounds on the Armed Forces Network (AFN) and Radio Luxembourg. Alvin also had another source, "I have an aunt in Canada who used to send me all the latest American records. It was a big deal in those days to get a Chuck Berry album before anybody had heard of it. When the rock 'n roll explosion hit England from America, I think Chuck Berry was the one for me - in a way it was all the blues I was used to, melted into rock 'n roll so I could understand it. I had learned to play along with Hank Marvin and I got a couple Buddy Holly songs off note for note, but what started to develop when I found Chuck Berry was that, rather than copy what he was playing, I would play along and imitate the style - not actually playing his licks, but applying my own licks to that feel.

Once I got the basic Chuck Berry rhythm riff, it was a revelation to me. It's such a big sound - the difference between playing one note at a time and playing two or three notes at a time. I kind of took that a bit further. I'm not a terribly clean player because I like to add extra notes. If it hadn't been for Chuck Berry, I'd probably have gone on to be another jazz musician. I still get off on what I originally got off on - ethnic blues, Chuck Berry and Jerry Lee Lewis. I don't think there is anything, for me, that beats it yet !"

Alvin's first band when he was only thirteen was ***Vince Marshall and the Squarecaps****. "It was a weird affair where this guy was planning it like a show and we all had completely different numbers. He just advertised in the paper for everyone to meet him at the Lyons cafe in Nottingham. He was in there and he waited an hour so that those who were not very keen would go, and he would keep the rest.*

It ended up with two drummers, five guitar players, no bass player, an electric accordionist and a country & western banjo player. We rehearsed about three times a week for six months. We played at All Souls Church Hall and we had little plywood stands to stand on, because it was his idea of professionalism. I played rhythm guitar with them and I used to watch 'Oh Boy' on the TV and see Joe Brown and Eddie Cochran. It was the first time I'd ever seen a Bigsby tremelo arm, so I went down to Dad's shed to make one ! I got this metal thing, stuck it on my guitar and went down to the gig that night at the church hall. We were doing 'Milk Cow Blues' and when it got round to my big tremelo solo, I grabbed the arm, shook it and broke all six strings ! Believe me, there is nothing more useless than a guitar with no strings. That was the end of Vince Marshall and the Squarecaps, but I learned a lot off the guitarist who played lead, I picked his brains and got to know quite a bit. Up until then I had been playing just on a hobby basis."

Alvin's next band at age fourteen was ***Alan Upton and the Jailbreakers****. "We used to play at the Palace Cinema in Sandiacre. The drummer that got me involved in the band was kind of like the manager. He was always hustling around and got us a gig playing a ten minute set between the B-movie and the main feature. It was an idea that the guy at the cinema thought would get a few more people in to watch the movie. I've still got one of the things in a scrapbook somewhere where we are on with Bridgett Bardot. We played sort of rock and roll because Alan played piano and liked Jerry Lee Lewis, and by this time I was into Scottie Moore and all those other rock guitarists. I played lead and got a proper electric guitar for my birthday - a Guyatone with crystal pickups. We had some fun, it was an experience. When we finally broke up we were playing at a lot of pubs and other low places."*

After the Jailbreakers, Alvin had no further involvement with bands for about a year and, when he turned

sixteen, he left school as soon as he could for a job in a factory. He soon became dis-satisfied at the factory and his parents said, if you want to get a band together and work like that, you had better leave your job. "So I left the job and I answered an ad in a Nottingham paper for a band based in Mansfield called the

Atomites. They were looking for a guitar player, I played 'Shazam' (the Chet Atkins number) and they told me I had the job. **Pete Evans** was the drummer and **Leo Lyons** (born David William Lyons on November 30,1944 in Standbridge-Bedfordshire, England) was the bass player. Leo's just a month older than I am and he was keen on Bill Black and Scott La Faro. He is one of the few players who can make an electric bass sound like a slap stand up ! So I was Scotty Moore and he was Bill Black and we used to do 'That's all Right Moma' and stuff like that. We were also playing Shadows music to get gigs. I knew this singer from Nottingham who used to do well on the pub circuit, **Ivan Jay** was his name, so we roped him into it and changed the name to **Ivan Jay and the Jaymen** which later became **The Jaycats.**"

Leo Lyons: "I started out playing banjo, because my grandfather had one. As far as basses, I played bass on a guitar when I was in a garage band. Eventually I managed to buy a Hofner bass; it was similar to what was called the violin bass (the model used by Paul McCartney), but it was blonde and had a single cutaway. I was playing with a local band called the **Phantoms,** and there was another band that was very, very popular called the Atomites; they were going to turn professional and they asked me to join. The week I joined, their guitar player left and we advertised for another guitar player; Alvin joined and the Atomites became the **Jaybirds**."

Alvin Lee: "We came to London, I would be about seventeen, for about six months and nearly starved to death. Leo was the manager, he used to call himself Mr. Lyons. It was very funny, because he would ring up the pub owners the next day and say - how were they, were they great ? - and all this spiel. He was pretty good, but in London we hardly got any work at all. We came down to get work, but the only work we ever got was up North. We did a few American air force bases, but we were getting 15 quid a gig in Nottingham and they would only offer us 8 quid down there. Anyway, we didn't do very well so we went back to Nottingham and the singer, Ivan Jay, stayed in London. He didn't do anything and that was the last we heard from him. We got another singer called **Farren Christie** when we went back to Nottingham. We worked with him for awhile and were doing all right. We went over to Hamburg, Germany as the **Jaybirds** with a rhythm guitarist we got from Rugby and a new drummer, **Dave Quickmire**. Hamburg was very interesting, I learned a lot there. **Cliff Bennet** was in Hamburg with **Nicky Hopkins** on piano and **Strawberry Watson** on guitar. **Tony Sheridan** was there - a lot of good musicians were kicking around on

*the scene. **Albert Lee** was playing down the road in a club on the Reeperbahn called the Top Ten. A lot of Liverpool people were there and everybody was talking about the **Beatles** but they hadn't done anything yet. We saw photographs in windows of them in all the leather gear, and there were a lot of stories about **John Lennon**. Hamburg made us a lot more professional because we were playing to an attentive audience, which was more than we were doing before."* *The first time Alvin began to sing came at a gig in Hamburg at the famous **Star Club**: "It was at a club where the Beatles played regularly and we were going on for five weeks when our singer backed out at the last minute, so I was left with the singing chores. All I knew was Elvis Presley and Chuck Berry tunes, and they got reasonable reactions over there - which was the encouragement to keep that on line.*

When we got back to England we really pulled it together, like the band got into its own stuff, doing an R&B thing. We tried

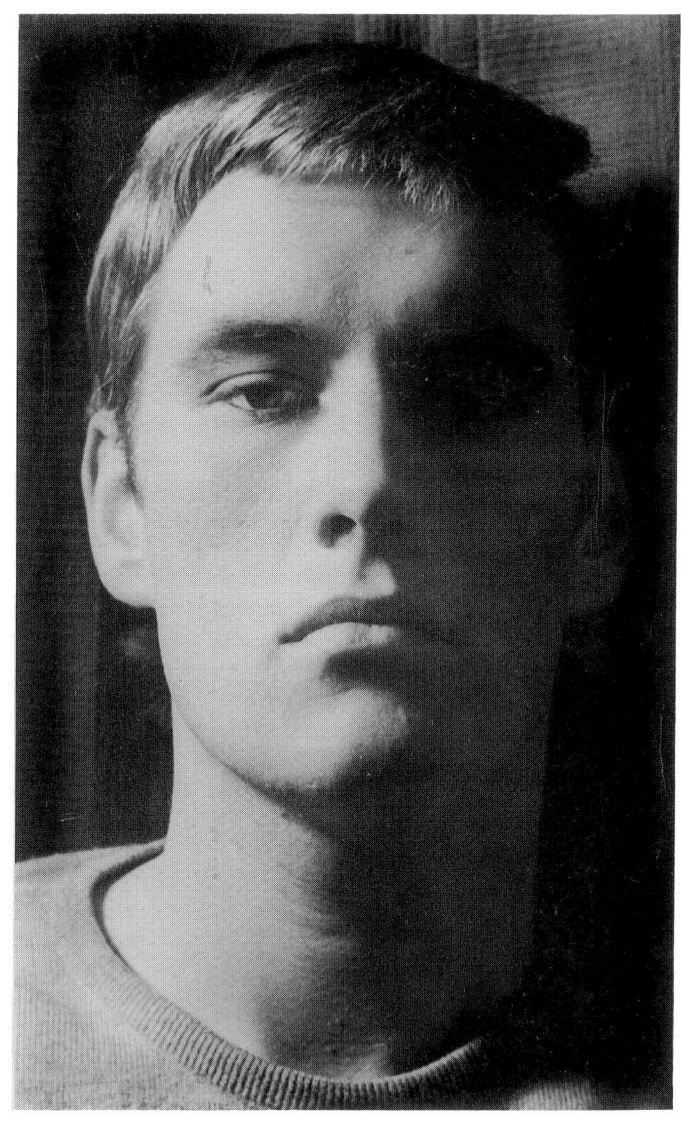

London again, moving to a slightly better part of Finsbury Park, but failed a second time with the result that we went back to Nottingham where we began to do pretty well. We were getting 40 quid on a Saturday night and doing Co-op halls and all that. Anyway, the drummer with us left. ***Ric Lee*** *(born Richard Lee on October 20, 1945 in Cannock-Staffordshire, England) was playing in a group called the* ***Mansfields*** *(who were previously called* ***Ricky Storm and the Storm Cats****) and doing Everly Brothers type things and Buddy Holly numbers.*
He was about the only drummer we had ever heard who could do that bass drum beat. He was reluctant to join at first, but somehow we talked him into it. We were still doing Chuck Berry stuff then and he was never into it as much as the other drummer."

As a boy, Ric wanted to be a drummer because his big brother also wanted to play drums, and if big brother could do it, so could Ric. But what started out as just another family "me-to" wound up an obsession and Ric soon centered his life around music. In school he studied flute, learning to read music and developed a good ear. Hearing Billy Cotten's Band on the BBC and then in person turned Ric completely around. He became very much influenced by the records of Joe Morello and Buddy Rich. So, beginning in ***August 1965****, the new* ***Jaybirds*** *line-up of* ***Alvin Lee, Leo Lyons and Ric Lee*** *was formed. They began performing all over the East Midlands and North of England, billed as "the biggest sounding trio in the country" and playing hard, guitar-based rhythm and blues.*

*In **1966** the band went to London for a third time:"Then, of all things, we auditioned for 'Saturday Night and Sunday Morning' at the Prince of Wales theater. They were interested in a Nottingham band - a bit more authenticity, as it were - to play in the wings and do a pub scene. We got the job and that was quite good, it meant regular money and enabled us to set up in London, but the play only lasted for five weeks." However the Jaybirds found more work at Southern Music, a Denmark Street song publisher, that needed musicians to record demos. So the band provided the backing required for dozens of potential hits. Through their contract with Southern Music, the Jaybirds hooked up with the vocal group **Ivy League** (formerly **Carter Lewis and the Southerners**) and for a while toured with them as their backing musicians while they performed their hit 'Funny How Love Can Be'. Although they needed the money, the Jaybirds soon grew tired of their role backing a pop group!*

*Convinced of their potential, in the Spring of **1967** the Jaybirds decided to contact **Chris Wright** who was becoming well known as an agent and manager in the North of England. **Alvin Lee:** "We were getting a free meal and 24 quid a week, which was pretty good, but the only gigs we were getting were in Wales and they were terrible. Although we could still get the backing jobs and do the odd session, everybody was very downhearted indeed. But during this period we were really together and the epitome of everything that was not commercial. There was a band around called Cock A-Hoop who were getting 20 quid a night, which was cool, and we decided that people did make money out of jazz and blues. The manager for Cock A-Hoop was Chris Wright and we told him that we could blow them off musically any day. So we did an audition for him in Manchester for ten quid - I think we made about four shillings each by the time we had taken out the petrol money and split it at the end."*

Ten Years After

***Chris Wright:** "Leo Lyons, bass player and organizer for a London-based blues band called the Jaybirds called and asked for a weekend of work in the North. They were really good and asked me to manage them straight away. I wanted to, but I thought it would be tough getting work over the summer. They still had the odd gig backing people like the Ivy League and the Flowerpot Men, but I managed to start getting them dates in their own right. The band went down well wherever it played and dates at some of London's famous clubs were coming our way." After Chris Wright signed on the Jaybirds, they added keyboard player **Chick Churchill** (born Michael George Churchill on January 2, 1949 in Flintshire-Wales) to broaden their sound.*

***Leo Lyons**: "Chick Churchill had joined us as a roadie; he was a keyboard player, but at the time he didn't have a keyboard." Chick had started playing piano at age five and he was a fan of Jimmie Smith, Jimmie McCriff and Brother Jack MacDuff. Chick's jazz influenced blues-rock playing added a strong rhythmic and harmonic foundation to the band.*

With their new four piece line-up the Jaybirds first changed their name to the Jaybird, "We dropped the S off to be a bit more trendy, and we were **The Jaybird**. Then we changed to the **Blues Trip**, and then **Bluesyard**."

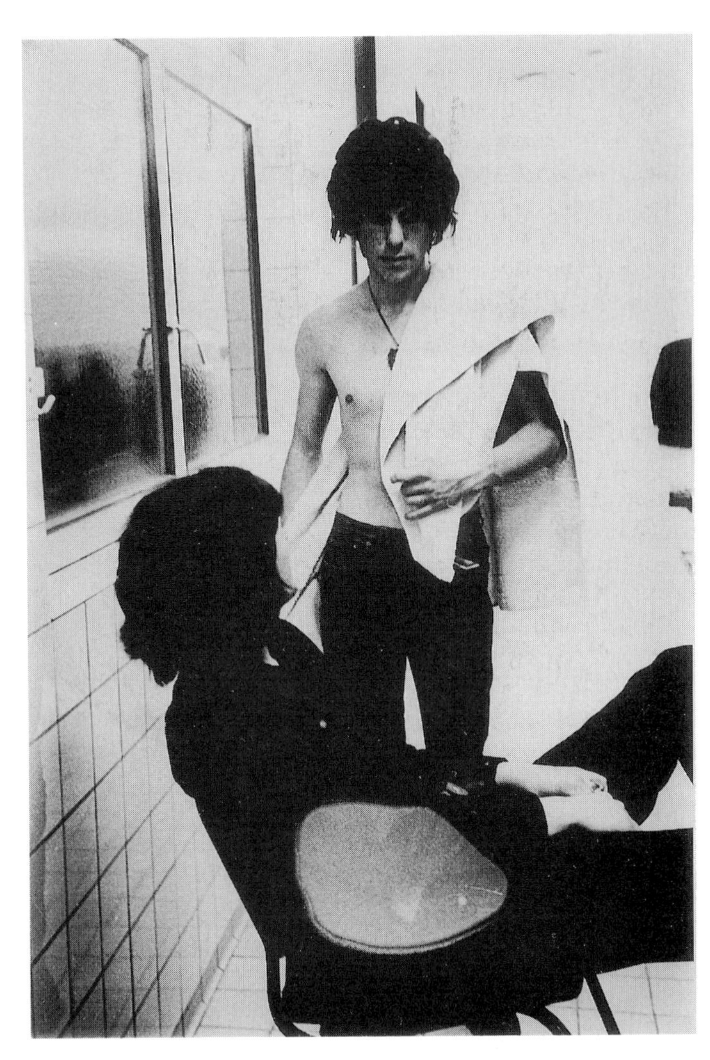

Leo Lyons got them an audition and their first gig at London's legendary **Marquee Club** supporting the **Bonzo Dog Band**. **Alvin Lee:** "Of all the clubs in London in those days, the Marquee was the most important. I remember that Leo got us an audition there, and we were all very scared of (owner) John Gee. But we knew John Gee was a jazz fan, so we did a quickly improvised version of 'Woodchopper's Ball' and got the gig. A lot of bands used to say to him that they were big fans of Frank Sinatra to get in. Our first gig there was an interval spot for the Bonzo Dog Band. The stage was literally smothered in blue smoke from their explosions - and we had to go and play! But we managed to build a small following among the blues freaks and got a residency. I was quite in awe of that place, I remember going to see groups there before we started - people like **Peter Green** with **John Mayall**."

Following their Marquee Club debut the band decided their current name placed a limitation on their music so, after that one gig as Bluesyard, they selected the new name **Ten Years After**. "Leo picked it out of about 100 names, which we narrowed down to 20 we liked." **Leo Lyons:** "I was looking through a newspaper, and I saw an article about the end of the draft, which is called National Service in England, referring to a radio program about 'ten years after' National Service. I showed it to the rest of the band and the manager, and we decided to go with that name. It had other connotations. Our music was sort of a cross between Muddy Waters, Chuck Berry & Elvis Presley."

Alvin Lee: *"We got Ten Years After out of the Radio Times. We liked the name because it did not pin us down musically - It didn't mean anything, it was very abstract. But we were nearly called 'Life Without Mother', that was the second one!"*

In late 1966-1967, the emerging ***Blues Boom*** *in England was the break that Ten Years After needed to gain attention to their music. Up until that point, the band had often been denied gigs because the club owners complained the clientele could not dance to the music. "The door really opened for us when* ***John Mayall*** *broke open the blues scene. Suddenly blues was the thing to be doing and I had this great repertoire of songs I could put in the set. It was like a breath of freedom, to suddenly say the blues was hip whereas before it wasn't. So I think we have John Mayall to thank for that."*

In ***August 1967*** *Ten Years After appeared at the Marquee's National Jazz and Blues Festival at Windsor and took it by storm. Chris Wright's relations with his agency became strained when he insisted on booking Ten Years After and their blues-based act into pop-oriented venues to keep them at work and a move to London became inevitable.* ***Alvin Lee:*** *"We got the gig at the Jazz Festival in Windsor and we went down well there. Then we got the residency at the Marquee, which did quite well - we grew from strength to strength as they say."*

At the same time, Chris Wright and rival agent ***Terry Ellis*** *met in London and decided they could generate enough business together to form a partnership and they set up an office in Terry's two bedroom apartment at 19 Blyth Road in Shepherds Bush.* ***Chris Wright:*** *"We put together a brochure, called ourselves the Ellis-Wright Agency, and sent it out to every possible client in the country that summer. I didn't have anywhere to live so I slept on the floor of Terry's apartment. I bought a sprawling mahogany table for $12 at a junk shop while Terry was in Morocco on vacation and it took up the entire sitting room. And we could just about fit the table,*

Terry, our booker and our secretary Dawn Ralston into that office.

Terry Ellis: *"We were booking all the time during the day and at night we were typing contracts." Ten Years After went into the studio to record an LP for Decca with Chris Wright negotiating his first record deal - a $720 advance and a royalty rate of three percent of retail (half of that overseas).*
Alvin Lee: *"We were getting a good name on the club circuit in London and we got approached by Decca Records. We actually did an audition and failed it, and then they called us up a few months later and said we want to make an album with you. We just got hooked up with the wrong A&R man when we did the audition. I think we were one of the first bands to actually make an album first, because in those days you used to make a single and if it did any good then they would let you make an album. The first album was, in fact, basically our live set. We didn't have to think much or write anything and the album was recorded in two days."*
The first, self-titled ***"Ten Years After"*** *album was released on Decca's new progressive* ***Deram*** *label on October 27, 1967 but Decca only pressed 1,000 copies of the LP and sent them all to the label's Manchester branch making it unavailable in the rest of England for weeks. Chris Wright felt that Decca's miscalculation cost him and Ten Years After a lot of ground, as well as a spot on the charts: "That taught us, we had our fingers much closer to the pulse of the British record market than the big record companies. At the age of 23, I realized that the giant record companies were not as big and giant as we thought." But London Records, Decca's American company had released Ten Years After's LP in the U.S. where it was gathering quick reaction from newly burgeoning underground FM stations, particularly in San Francisco. A letter from* ***Bill Graham*** *arrived on Chris Wright's desk inviting the group to play at his San Francisco* ***Fillmore Auditorium****. A U.S. tour was organized with the help of Lenny Poncher and International Management Company in return for a small percentage of the gross. When Ten Years After played the Bay City the "reception was magnificent". Graham had booked the group for two consecutive weekends in San Francisco, closing the old Fillmore Auditorium on the first, and opening the new one at the Carousel Ballroom on the second.*

Chris Wright: *"The group took both places by storm, playing numbers like 'Help Me Baby', 'I Can't Keep From Crying' and 'Woodchopper's Ball'. Both myself and the group developed a very good relationship with Bill Graham who was most helpful in breaking Ten Years After in America. He offered us a date at his newly opened*

*New York operation, the **Fillmore East**, on our way back to England. Ten Years After opened the show for **Janis Joplin** with Big Brother and the Holding Company, and the **Staple Singers**. The reaction in New York was every bit as good as it had been in San Francisco, and when I left New York in the middle of August to return home after a nine week trip, I knew that it was only a matter of time before Ten Years After would be one of the biggest groups on the American circuit."*

***Alvin Lee:** "We put the first album out, which did O.K., and then we heard it had done well in a place called America - which we had never even thought about. So we got a telegram from Bill Graham saying, if we ever got over there he would back us. So we got an American tour together and the whole thing went zoom!!"*

In June 1968, Ten Years After began a 7 week U.S. Tour - which was also the start of seven years on the road, with very few breaks in between.

***Ten Years After** would go on to make nine more classic albums and become a focal point of every major rock event (Woodstock, Atlanta Pop Festival, Isle of Wight, etc.) well into the next decade.*

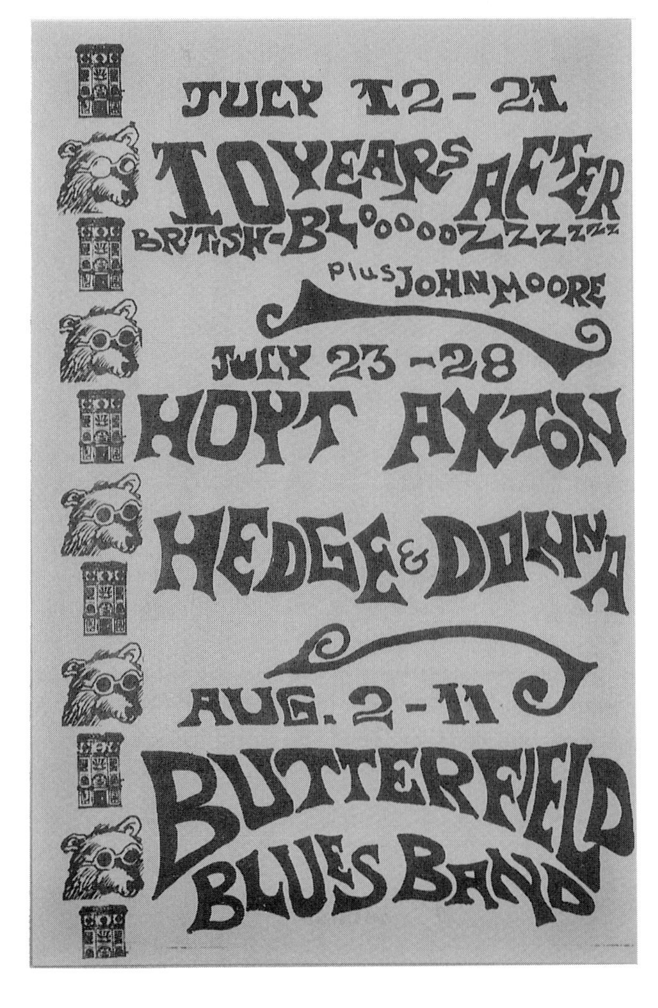

__Alvin Lee__ is widely considered as being in the elite hierarchy of legendary guitar players. He is a true innovator that took rock guitar to new levels of excitement. The legacy of Ten Years After continues to this day with frequent performances by Alvin Lee and original band members __Leo Lyons, Ric Lee__ and __Chick Churchill.__

The following pages offer a chronology of the innumerable club, auditorium, festival & stadium appearances made by Alvin Lee and Ten Years After during a career in music that spans more than thirty five years! Although by no means complete, this concert diary reveals why Ten Years After is considered a band of legendary status who have earned a respected place in Rock & Roll history.

PART TWO

"Fillmores, Festivals & Full Arenas"
Ten Years After - Concert Chronology

June 20, 1967
Marquee Club
London, England

Ten Years After open for John Lee Hooker.

June 29, 1967
Flamingo
Darlington, England

With Cock A Hoop.

June 30, 1967
Quay Club
Newcastle, England

July 1, 1967
St. Helens Grammar School, England

July 2, 1967
Jazz Club
Peterlee, England

July 4, 1967
Didsbury College
Manchester, England

July 5, 1967
University
Reading, England

July 6, 1967
University
Southampton, England

July 10, 1967
Marquee Club
London, England

July 22, 1967
Marquee Club
London, England

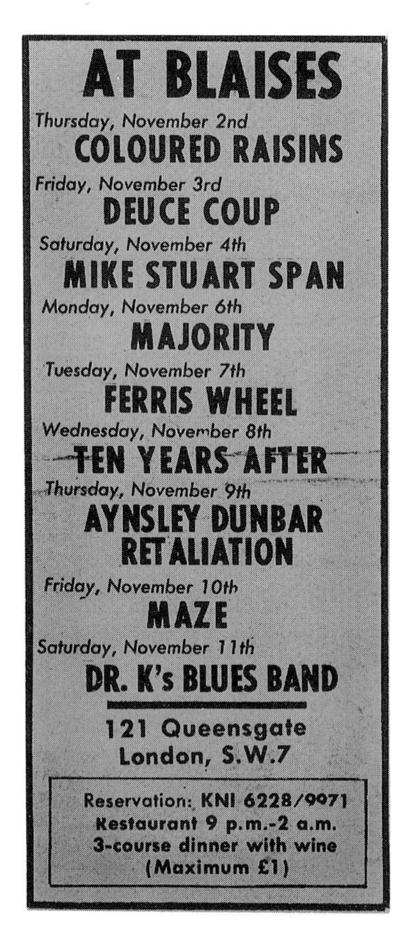

THE BLUE HORIZON
TEN YEARS AFTER
Plus Slaven and Vernon
"Nag's Head," 205 York Road, Battersea, S.W.11. Buses 44 and 170.

August 12, 1967
Balloon Meadow
Windsor, England

Ten Years After perform before an audience of 20,000 people at the 7th National Jazz & Blues Festival and receive a standing ovation.

August 18, 1967
Marquee Club
London, England

August 28, 1967
Marquee Club
London, England

September 4, 1967
Marquee Club
London, England

September 22, 1967
Marquee Club
London, England

October 6, 1967
Marquee Club
London, England

Ten Years After are filmed for a BBC-TV documentary about teenagers titled, "The Butterflies".

October 16, 1967
The Blue Horizon
London, England

October 20, 1967
Marquee Club
London, England

October 27, 1967
Release of first LP:
"Ten Years After"
(Deram DES 18009)

Side One tracks:
I Want To Know (McLeod 2:06), *I Can't Keep From Crying Sometimes* (Al Kooper 5:23), *Adventures Of A Young Organ* (Alvin Lee & Chick Churchill 2:29), *Spoonful* (Willie Dixon 5:49) *and Losing The Dogs* (Alvin Lee/Gus

Dudgeon 3:07).
Side Two tracks:
Feel It For Me (Alvin Lee 2:38), *Love Until I Die* (Alvin Lee 2:03), *Don't Want You Woman* (Alvin Lee 2:34) *and Help Me* (Williamson/Bass 9:45).

November 3, 1967
Marquee Club
London, England

November 8, 1967
Blaises
London, England

November 10, 1967
Marquee Club
London, England

November 11, 1967
Sussex University
Brighton, England

Ten Years After support the Jimi Hendrix Experience.

November 12, 1967
Saville Theater
London, England

November 17, 1967
Marquee Club
London, England

December 1, 1967
Manor House
London, England

December 8, 1967
Marquee Club
London, England

December 22, 1967
Marquee Club
London, England

January 5, 1968
Marquee Club
London, England

January 12, 1968
Manor House
London, England

January 13, 1968
School of Economics
London, England

January 19, 1968
Marquee Club
London, England

January 23, 1968
Klook's Kleek
London, England

January 30, 1968
"Fishmongers Arms"
Wood Green
London, England

February 1968
Single release:
"Portable People"
& "The Sounds"

February 1968
Kulttuuritalo
Helsinki, Finland

February 2, 1968
Lorensberg Circus
Gothenburg, Sweden

February 6, 1968
Marquee Club
London, England

February 9, 1968
"Bluesville 68"
Hornsey Wood Tavern - Manor House
London, England

February 1968
Gladsaxe Teen Club
Denmark

February 10, 1968
Pop Club
Brondby, Denmark

Day Of Phoenix is the opening act for Ten Years After and the Young Flowers.

February 11, 1968
Klub Bongo
Malmo, Sweden

Rock Your Mama, Spoonful, I May Be Wrong But I Won't Be Wrong Always, Summertime, I Can't Keep From Crying Sometimes (introduced by Alvin as "a new number off our LP, which I hope you will buy"), Spider In My Web, Help Me.

February 16, 1968
"Flower Pop - Holeby Bio"
Lolland, Denmark

Parts of this show are subsequently broadcast on the Danish DR-TV "Top Pop" show on February 24, 1968. Three numbers were included, the first was I May Be Wrong But I Won't Be Wrong Always. Alvin then says, "thank you very much...we will do another number for you...this is off our LP...it's called Love Until I Die". Following this number Alvin says, "thank you...we are going to finish the show...thank you for watching...this is a lovely number called Spoonful."

February 25, 1968
Marquee Club
London, England

With the Spirit of John Morgan.

February 26, 1968
Zodiac Club
Eden Park Hotel
Beckenham, England

February 27, 1968
Klook's Kleek
Railway Hotel
West Hampstead
London, England

March 1, 1968
City of Westminster College
London, England

March 8, 1968
Marquee Club
London, England

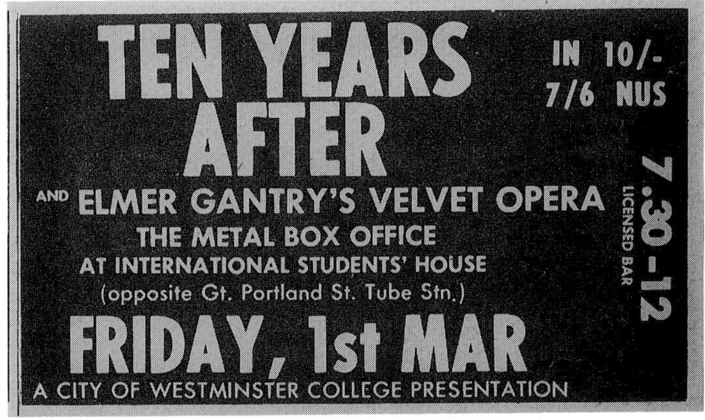

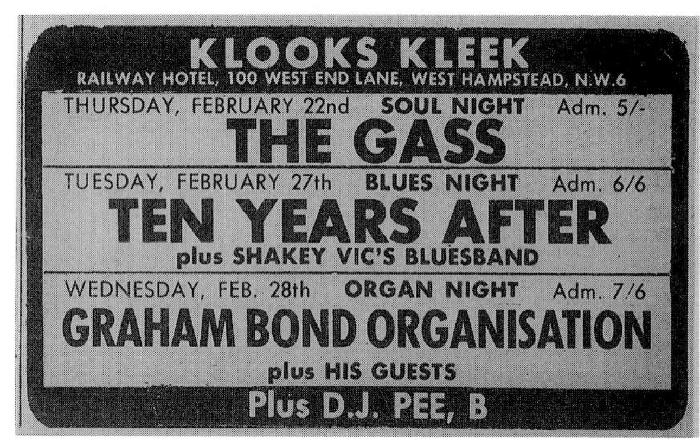

marquee
90 Wardour Street London W.1
Thursday, March 7th (7.30-11.0)
★ THE NITE PEOPLE
★ GRANNY'S INTENTIONS
Friday, March 8th (7.30-11.0)
★ BLUES NIGHT
★ TEN YEARS AFTER
★ THE SPIRIT OF JOHN MORGAN
Saturday, March 9th, (8.0-11.30)
★ STILL LIFE
★ THE OPEN MIND
Sunday, March 10th (7.30-10.30)
★ WHOLE LOTTA SOUL
with RADIO ONE D.J. STUART HENRY and BLUE RIVERS and the MAROONS
Monday, March 11th (7.30-11.0)
★ THE NICE
★ THE ATTACK
Tuesday, March 12th (7.30-11.0)
★ PROCOL HARUM
★ SPOOKY TOOTH
Wednesday, March 13th (7.30-11.0)
★ STUDENTS ONLY NIGHT
★ BRAVE NEW WORLD
★ LEE HAWKINS GROUP
marquee studios • 4 Track • Stereo • Mono • Recordings
10 Richmond Mews, W.1. 01-437 6731

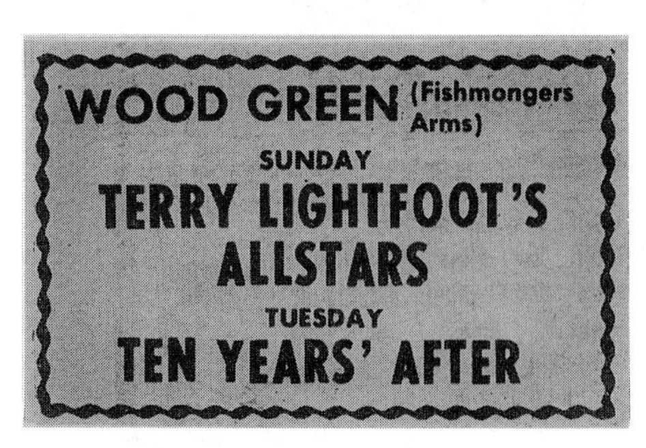

<u>March 15, 1968</u>
"Bluesville 68"
Hornsey Wood Tavern -
Manor House
London, England

<u>March 18, 1968</u>
The Cromwellian
London, England

<u>March 22, 1968</u>
Marquee Club
London, England

<u>March 23, 1968</u>
Corn Exchange
Chelmsford, England

<u>March 28, 1968</u>
Zodiac Club
Beckenham, England

<u>April 5, 1968</u>
Marquee Club
London, England

<u>April 1968</u>
Gladsaxe Teen Club
Denmark

<u>April 20, 1968</u>
Pop Club
Brondby, Denmark

With the Baronets, Tages and the ***Jeff Beck Group****.*

<u>May 2, 1968</u>
Metro
Birmingham, England

<u>May 4, 1968</u>
University
Norwich, England

<u>May 5, 1968</u>
Palezzo dello Sport
Rome, Italy

Ten Years After perform at the "1st International European Pop Festival".

<u>May 7, 1968</u>
Falconer Theater
Copenhagen, Denmark

Rock Your Mama (Alvin introduces the song by saying "this number is being recorded and released next week"), Spoonful, I May Be Wrong But I Won't Be Wrong Always, Summertime, Help Me, I'm Going Home.

Fleetwood Mac *and the Fugs also perform.*

<u>May 9, 1968</u>
Gothenburg, Sweden

<u>May 10, 1968</u>
Stockholm, Sweden

May 12, 1968
Cat Balou Club
Grantham, England

May 14, 1968
Klook's Kleek
Railway Hotel
West Hampstead
London, England

The show is recorded and later released as the "Undead" LP.

July 1968 BEAT INSTRUMENTAL Article by Rick Sanders:

Ten Years After have made records, certainly a very successful LP and a single, "Portable People". But they won their spurs with their volcanic live performances.
So, when they wanted an album to take with them on their American tour in June, a live recording seemed like a good move indeed.
And the obvious place for it was Dick Jordan's Klook's Kleek Club in West Hampstead, the home of many triumphs with an audience who have grown to look on the group as their own personal property. So it was arranged. Mike Vernon was to produce the record, while Roy Baker was to engineer and one Tuesday evening in May, I went along to witness the birth of an album.

Roy took me over to see the remarkable recording equipment for the evening. "We've carted a classical machine out of the studio, fitted it with limiters, echo, and so on, doctored the wiring and set the whole thing up in the Decca studio's canteen, which is linked up to the club just down the road."

He went on: "The acoustics in Klook's set a lot of recording problems, and to make matters even more difficult we could only put up one screen to separate the mikes. Otherwise the audience wouldn't be able to see a thing. We've got mikes in the chandeliers to catch the audience reaction, wires going everywhere and back, equipment filling every square inch. But it's going to be a great

session all the same." As the group waited to go on stage, I had a few words with drummer Ric Lee. He said: "We all know that live recordings can turn out pretty horrible. But we've got to have an LP to take to the States, and the one we're working on at the moment won't be finished in time. It's a complex, progressive album and we don't want to complete it in a panic - so we had to settle for the lesser of two evils, a live record or nothing at all. And it might turn out to be a fantastic record. You can't tell."

All the group were somewhat nervous. The LP had to be perfect the first time, a second go being out of the question, as the friendly gentlemen in blue were waiting to swoop the minute past the deadline of 11 o'clock.

At quarter to nine it started. Suddenly Alvin's guitar screamed into "Rock Your Mama", with the others in hot pursuit. The sound was almost frightening as Leo lashed into his battered Fender bass, wringing out a wild shuddering roar, with Ric working like mad at the drums and a cool unruffled Chick hidden in one corner of the stage and working miracles with the organ. Then straight into "Spoonful", pumping new blood into a song beaten to death by every no-talent group in the country, and on into more numbers, each one going down a bomb with the reverent congregation until the first set came to a searing end with "I'm Going Home."

Backstage I was greeted with a jet of water from manager Chris Wright's water pistol and loud cheers from all except Alvin (talking very seriously with a remarkably lovely girl in Indian gear) and Leo, who looked on the point of death by exhaustion. When he had dried himself out, I asked Leo what he thought of the first half. "Pretty happy, actually, though my bass was playing me up a bit. I like to get more of a string-bass sound. But it'll be OK on the tape - I hope."

Changing the subject, I asked about the USA tour. "We'll be away for five to seven weeks, depending on how it goes. We're

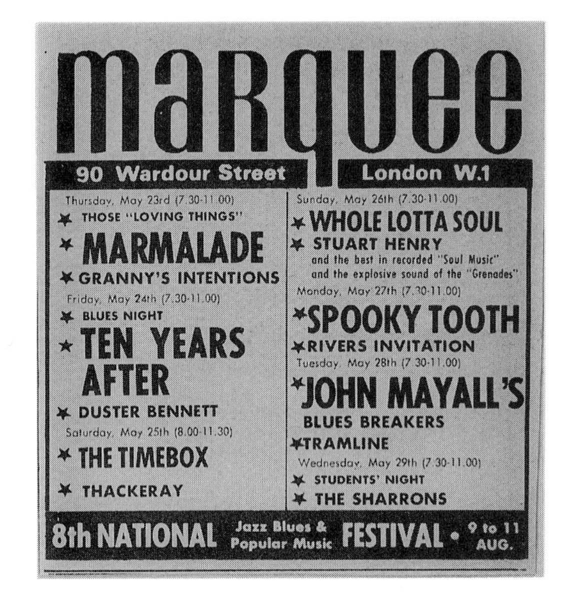

playing all over the place, including the Fillmores in San Francisco and New York. We're all very excited about what might happen."

At this point, Svengali Wright interrupted: "You know that over in Scandinavia they reckon Leo is the best bassist of all time. We've got a massive heap of cuttings and letters from Denmark, Norway and Sweden all raving about him."
How was Scandinavia? "We played a lot over there, and it was marvelous. They seem to have some sort of fixation about British groups and we couldn't put a foot wrong. I hope America goes as well!", said Leo.

Then the second set got under way. And it turned out to be even better than the first. The sweat poured off us as Ten Years After, in brilliant form, put a spell on the sardined audience.

Roars of appreciation for every number, with a special ovation for "Woodchopper's Ball", which had Alvin breaking sound barriers and speed records on his talking guitar, until Dick Jordan braved a fate considerably worse than death by calling a halt.

Just as we were leaving, a wildly enthusiastic Mike Vernon came bounding backstage. "Marvelous! Brilliant! Fantastic! Come and listen to the tapes!"

As it happened, we could only hear one of the songs, but it was enough to let us know. Next morning I phoned up Chris Wright. He was happy. "It's just too good!

Wait till America hears this - it's going to knock them sideways!"

There's an interesting conclusion to this story. A week after the Klook's Kleek session came the news that Decca were so excited about the LP that despite original plans to release it only in America, they are now going to put it on the British market. So it's a bonanza for Ten Years After fans - two great albums itching for release at the same time !

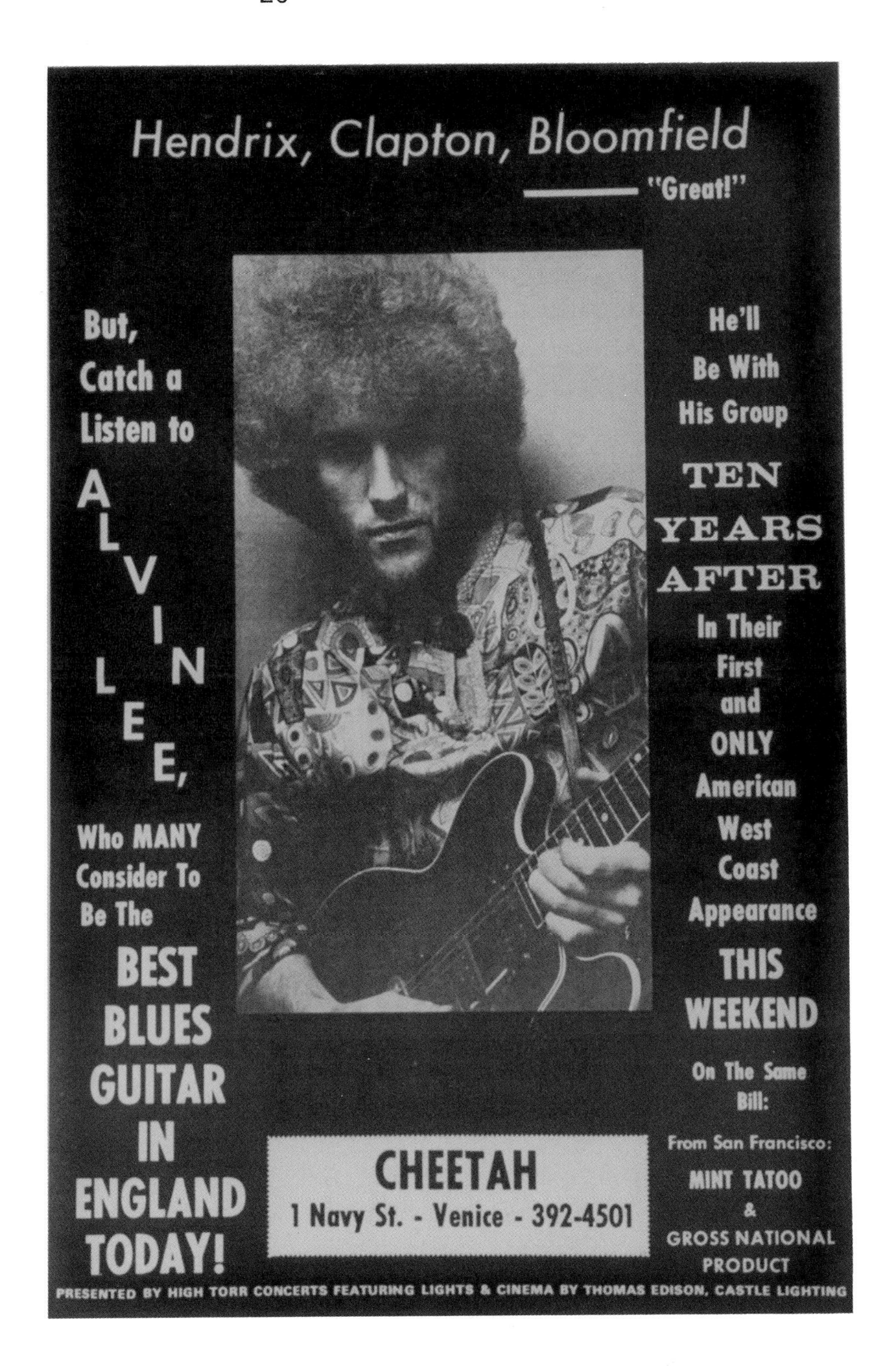

<u>**May 22, 1968**</u>
Wigan Technical College

<u>**May 23, 1968**</u>
St. Michael's Hall Oxford, England

<u>**May 24, 1968**</u>
Marquee Club London, England

<u>**May 25, 1968**</u>
Redditch College Worcestshire

<u>**May 26, 1968**</u>
Wooden Bridge Guildford, England

<u>**June 3, 1968**</u>
Ten Years After visit Ireland to play at a festival.

<u>**June 7, 1968**</u>
Marquee Club London, England

<u>**June 13, 1968**</u>
Ten Years After arrive in America to begin a seven week tour.

<u>**June 14 - 16, 1968**</u>
Cheetah Club Venice, California

<u>**June 24, 1968**</u>
Whiskey A Go Go Hollywood, CA

<u>**June 28 - 30, 1968**</u>
Fillmore Auditorium San Francisco, California

June 28 - First Set: Help Me, Rock Your Mama, Spoonful, I May Be Wrong But I Won't Be Wrong Always, No Title (introduced by Alvin as "a number called No Title Blues") Summertime/ Shangtung Cabbage (introduced as "a number featuring Ric Lee called Summertime Cabbage"), I Woke Up This Morning (Alvin introduces the song by saying, "this is the last number of the set, a ditty by Muddy Waters").

June 28 -Second Set: I Want To Know, Spider In My Web, Crossroads, Woodchopper's Ball. (The other artists on the bill were Canned Heat and Dan Hicks & His Hot Licks. Alvin, obviously impressed by Canned Heat, later paid tribute on the Alvin Lee & Co. LP track "Boogie On").

Alvin Lee: *"When I first came to America, I thought everybody would know Big Bill Broonzy and Lonnie Johnson, and I was very surprised that most Americans didn't have any idea who they were. I was taking American music, putting a little English energy into it, and bringing it back to America. It amazed me that so few Americans were aware of their musical heritage."*

July 5, 6 & 7, 1968
Fillmore West
San Francisco, California

Ten Years After are among the first bands to perform at the new Fillmore West. The other acts include the Paul Butterfield Blues Band and Truth.

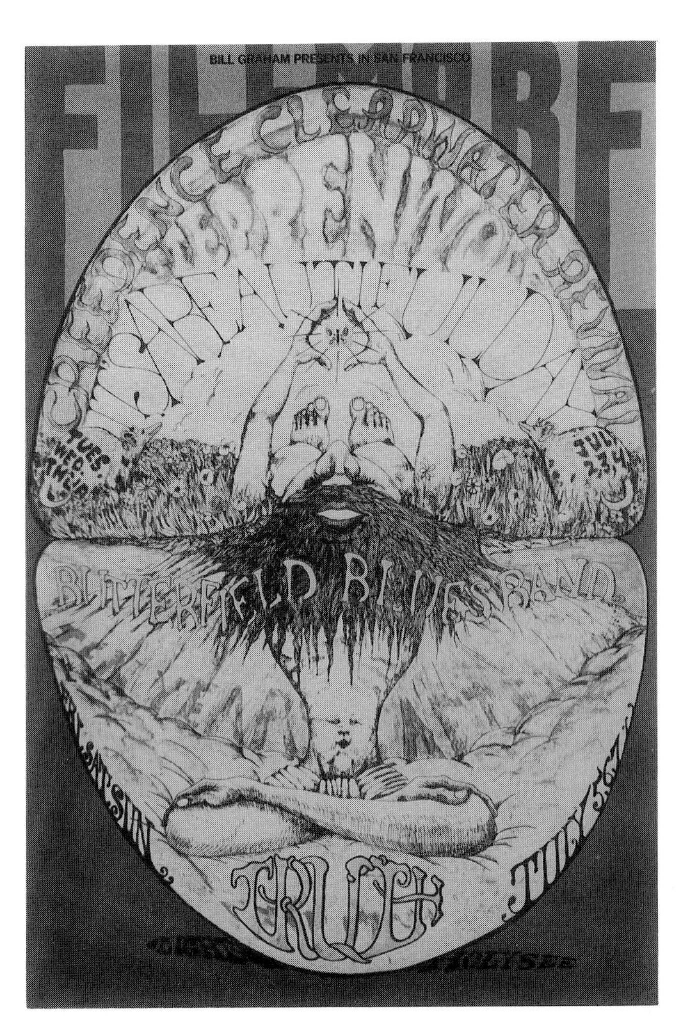

Bill Graham: *"The closing show at the Fillmore Auditorium was Creedence Clearwater Revival, Steppenwolf and It's A Beautiful Day. The next night we opened at the Carousel, now renamed the Fillmore West, with the Butterfield Blues Band and Ten Years After. Like Cream and Pink Floyd, Ten Years After was one of the English bands who exemplified something much different than what was going on in the American scene. I liked Ten Years After very much."*

<u>July 10, 1968</u>
Ten Years After perform "I Want To Know" on the Groovy Show in Los Angeles.

<u>July 12-21, 1968</u>
The Golden Bear
Huntington Beach, California

<u>July 26-28, 1968</u>
Cheetah Club
Los Angeles, CA

With Jose Feliciano.

<u>August 2 & 3, 1968</u>
Fillmore East
New York City, NY

With Big Brother & The Holding Company and The Staple Singers.

<u>August 4-6, 1968</u>
Steve Paul's
Scene Club, NY

Ten Years After spend the day in the studio on August 5th backing ***Guitar Crusher*** *(vocal) and* ***Jimmy Spruill*** *(lead guitar) on "Hambone Blues", and backing* ***Garfield Love*** *(vocal) and Jimmy Spruill on "Part Time Love". In the evening, TYA are joined onstage at The Scene Club by* ***Jimi Hendrix,*** *Mitch Mitchell and Larry Coryell for a jam!*
Alvin Lee: *"I met Hendrix a couple of times. He got up and jammed with me at Steve Paul's Scene club in New York. Because he is left handed he couldn't play the guitar, so he took the bass, turned it upside down and played an amazing solo on the bass. We just stopped and let him float off."*

<u>August 9-11, 1968</u>
Kempton Park
Sunbury
Middlesex, England

<u>August 12, 1968</u>
Cooks Ferry Inn
London, England

<u>August 16, 1968</u>
Marquee Club
London, England

<u>August 17, 1968</u>
Klook's Kleek
West Hampstead
London, England

<u>August 23, 1968</u>
California Ballroom
Dunstable, Scotland

<u>August 24, 1968</u>
Free Concert
Hyde Park, London

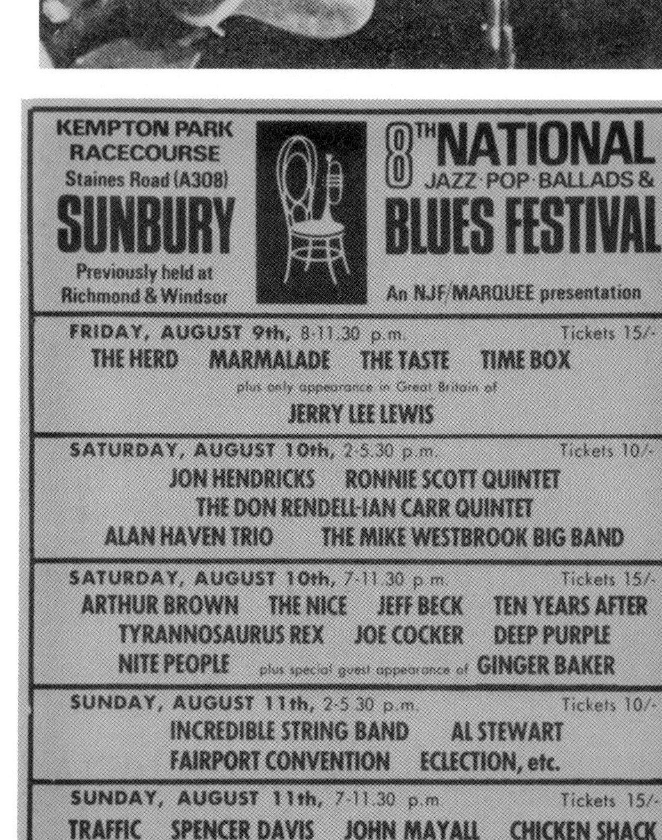

THE ELLIS-WRIGHT AGENCY LTD

Carrington House
130 Regent Street
London W1
Tel 01 734 9233
Cables Chrysalis London

26th July, 1968.

Dear Sir,

With reference to the engagement of

TEN YEARS AFTER

at Marquee

on Friday 16th and 30th August, 1968.

for a fee of: ~~£50~~ (Fifty)

we confirm that the 10 per cent booking commission will be equally divisible between our two agencies.

Yours sincerely,

Marquee Artists

for ELLIS-WRIGHT AGENCY LTD.

August 27, 1968
Klook's Kleek
West Hampstead
London, England

August 30, 1968
Marquee Club
London, England

August 31, 1968
Middle Earth at
The Roundhouse
London, England

Sept 3-12, 1968
The "Stonedhenge" tracks are recorded at West Hampstead Studios in London

September 13, 1968
Bluesville '68
Manor House
London, England

September 14, 1968
Tofts
Folkestone, England

September 15, 1968
Black Prince Hotel
Bexley, England

September 18, 1968
Toby Jug
Tolworth, England

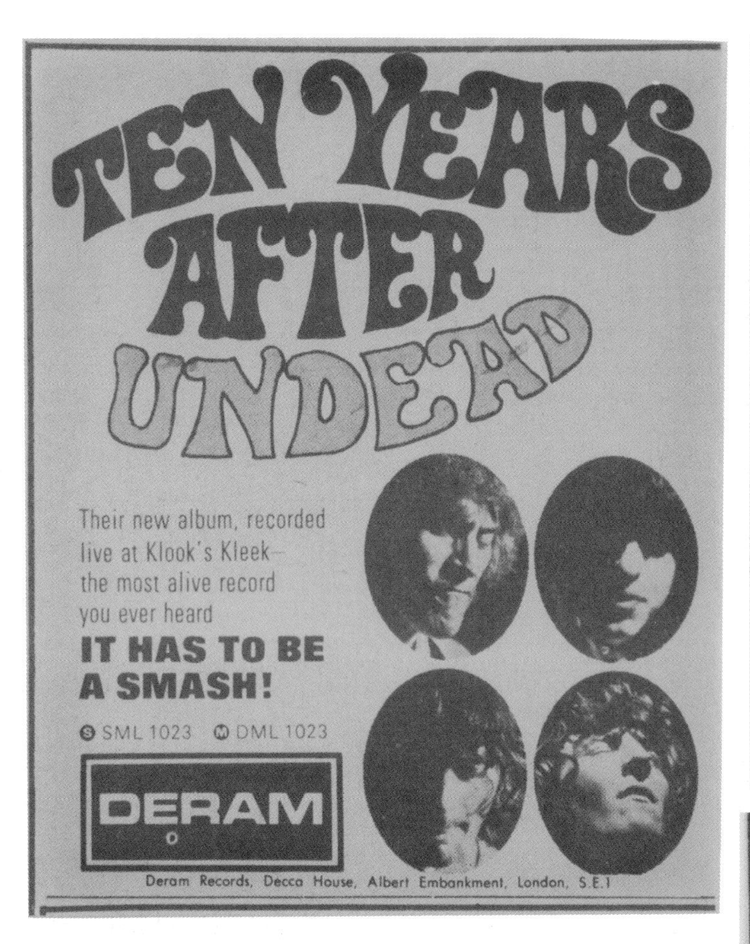

<u>September 19, 1968</u>
Le Metro
Birmingham,
England

<u>September 21, 1968</u>
Alex Discotheque
Salisbury, England

Release of the second Ten Years After LP: "Undead" (Deram DES 18016)

Recorded at Klook's Kleek on May 14th.
Side One tracks:
I May Be Wrong But I Won't Be Wrong Always (Alvin Lee 9:50), *Woodchopper's Ball* (Woody Herman/ Bishop 7:40).
Side Two: Spider In My Web (Alvin Lee 7:50), *Summertime/ Shangtung Cabbage* (George Gershwin/ Ric Lee 6:00) & *I'm Going Home* (Alvin Lee 6:30).

Leo Lyons: *"After the first album came out, we got the letter from Bill Graham saying he would be glad to book us if we would like to come over. So, we put together the American tour and we didn't have time to do a studio album, so we did the live album."*

Alvin Lee: *"When it came out, I was delighted. I heard it in Los Angeles when we were on the second American tour and I thought, well that's it.*

Thurs. Sept. 26 thru Sun. Sept. 29
BUDDY GUY
Back for a third fabulous engagement

Monday (23rd) thru Sunday (29th)
1ST & ONLY N. Y. APPEARANCE
DIRECT FROM L. A.
Performing "LIVE" their great hit "Back In The Street Again"
SUNSHINE COMPANY

September 30 thru October 3
TEN YEARS AFTER

Oct. 1st thru Oct. 7th
LYNN COUNTY BLUES BAND

October 15 thru 27
ALBERT KING
November 5, 6, 7
TRAFFIC

Uninhibited Dancing Available
ADMISSION Only $2.50.
Steve Paul's SCENE 301 West 46th St. JU 2-5760

What can we do? That's everything. That's probably as best as I'll ever play! I thought it really captured the band at its best. And I kind of had an inkling that there were going to be problems recording in the future because, in those two albums, that encompassed just about everything the band could do."

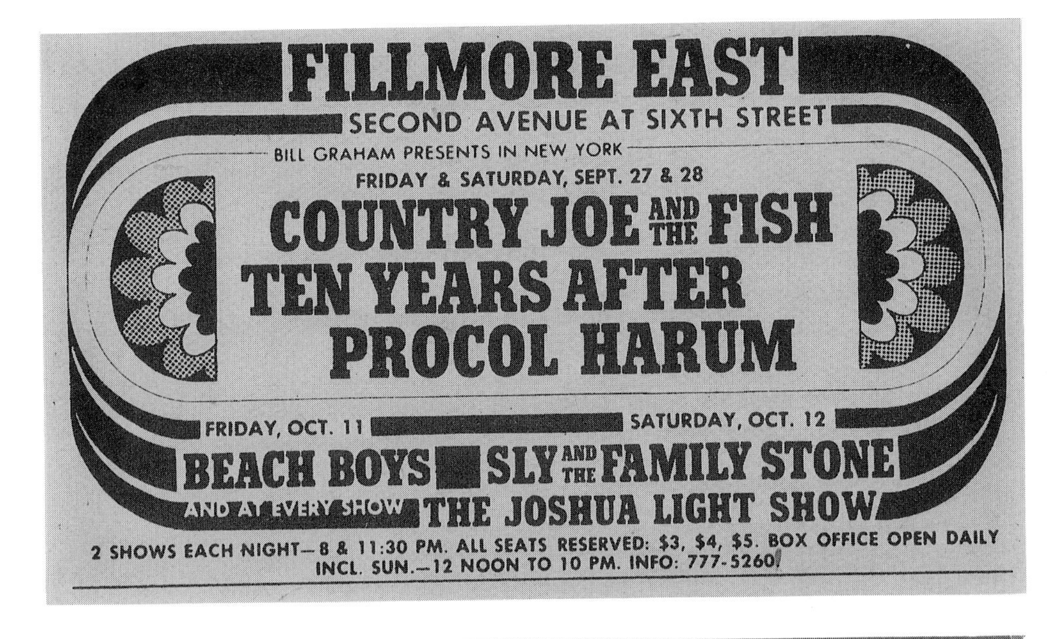

<u>September 22, 1968</u>
Boat Club
Nottingham, England

<u>Sept 27 & 28, 1968</u>
Fillmore East
New York City, NY

<u>Sept 30 - October 3</u>
Steve Paul's Scene Club, New York City

<u>October 4-6, 1968</u>
Grande Ballroom
Detroit, Michigan

The other acts on the bill are the Rationals and Orange Fuzz.

November 1968
Release of the single: "Hear Me Calling"/ "I'm Going Home"

November 7, 1968
Freeborn Hall
University of California
Davis, California

Ten Years After opens for Harpers Bizarre, who are on tour to promote their top 40 '59th St. Bridge Song' (Feeling Groovy). This is perhaps the most "bizarre" pairing of bands since the Jimi Hendrix Experience had been booked as opening act on the Monkees tour!

Nov 8 & 9, 1968
The Bank
Torrance, California

Nov 14-17, 1968
Fillmore West
San Francisco, California

The other acts on the bill were Country Weather and Sun Ra.

Nov 22 & 23, 1968
The Mill
Sacramento, California

10 YEARS AFTER BACK TO STATES

Ten Years After, who completed a smash-U.S. trip on December 8th, return to the States for the third time on February 8th following a Concert tour of Scandinavia. January sees the release in Britain of their new album "Stonedhenge" and their new single "Hear Me Calling" c/w "I'm Going Home".

Their recent U.S. tour has firmly established the group as one of the biggest English attractions and disc jockeys almost unanimously acclaimed them as "the group to take over from The Cream."

Nov 29 & 30, 1968
Shrine Auditorium
Los Angeles, California

With Jeff Beck, Moody Blues and Mint Tattoo.

December 22, 1968
Mothers, Erdington
Birmingham, England

December 26, 1968
Marquee Club
London, England

Ten Years After returns for a "Christmas Party" show at the club where it held a residency in 1967.

Chris Wright:
*"Christmas of 1968 was a difficult time, Ten Years After on their second tour of America in the autumn had grossed $32,000 but, with a much heavier touring schedule, had lost somewhere in the region of $5,000. Bills had to be paid and the Christmas of 1968 was bleak. On New Year's Eve of 1968, Terry and I had a discussion in Dee Anthony's room at the Mayfair Hotel. Following our conversation, Terry called Mo Ostin at Warner Bros. in Burbank and the next morning tickets were sent to London for Terry to fly to Los Angeles. He returned a week later with a check for around $30,000 to $40,000 having signed **Jethro Tull** to Warner for North America, and the company's cash problems were at an end."*

January 3, 1969
Van Dike Club
Plymouth, England

January 4, 1969
Town Hall
Glastonberry, England

January 12, 1969
Country Club
Haverstock Hill
London, England

January 17, 1969
Royal Albert Hall
London, England

Ten Years After perform at the Brunel University Students Carnival.

January 23, 1969
Bulls Head
Birmingham, England

January 24, 1969
Marquee Club
London, England

Ten Years After are supported by Woody Kearn

January 25, 1969
MELODY MAKER - TYA is first British group invited to the world's top Newport Jazz Festival:

*"Ten Years After will appear at the Newport Festival on July 4th and 5th. They are also to play two American concerts with the Woody Herman Orchestra during their fourth stateside trip in July. The concerts, arranged by Fillmore promoter **Bill Graham** will be in New York and San Francisco and the New York show will probably be at the famed Carnegie Hall. If these concerts are successful Graham will promote Herman and Ten Years After on college dates."*

February 1969
Gothenburg, Sweden

Article by Richard Green, from the March 8, 1969 edition of the NEW MUSICAL EXPRESS:

Ten minutes after Ten Years After had gone off stage, a thousand strong crowd of Swedish fans were on their feet stamping, clapping and yelling for more. This was my first introduction to the group that looks like developing into a major force this year and already has its first album in the LP charts.

Braving the bitter cold of a Gothenburg night, I left the warmth of Ten Years After's hotel to see them in action before a full concert hall. What I was to see dispersed for all time my slight feeling of cynicism about all the eulogies I had heard directed towards them. They over-ran by about twenty minutes or so on each forty-five minute set and came off stage wringing wet and exhausted - especially drummer Ric Lee who had delivered a fantastic 20-minute solo of "Summertime." I was pleasantly surprised to learn that there is more to the group than seeing how fast Alvin Lee can play his lead guitar.

Back in London, I invited Ric to come along for a drink and talk about the group's new album "Stonedhenge," which entered the chart last week. "It's a complete trip on its own" he began. "It's an album of numbers that we put on a record as opposed to numbers we do on stage. Each track is individual and people have said they like it because each track is so different." Thus, "Stonedhenge" is not typical of what Ten Years After do on stage and people like myself who had previously only witnessed a "live" performance are surprised when hearing the album. "Keeping the two things separate helps you to show your paces and widen your audience," Ric explained. "The first album was a display to get over to people, and the second was done in a rush and 'live.' This one was taken more slowly." "It's Alvin's inner self and we've come into it. We all worked on the arrangements and contributed bits. We started recording it before we went to the states in July and finished it sometime in August."

Ric pointed out that Ten Years After are trying to lose their blues tag and to this end have rehearsed a new act for their American tour which began last friday. "There's a lot of stuff on the album we can't do on stage," he went on. "I hope we haven't gone over people's heads. A lot of our numbers start, then develop into a jam session and people throw in ideas. For example, 'I Can't Keep From Crying Sometimes' once started off as a five minute thing and ended up as a twenty minute set. We always end up playing longer than we're due to." In the two years of its formation, the group has, according to Ric, become less mild in its musical attitudes. "There's a lot of freedom now but a lot more affinity with one another. Alvin's only got to drop the hint of a riff and we're off!" As one of the fast-rising groups, Ten Years After have noticed a change in the way bands are playing. "The majority of up and coming groups are more concerned with something to say," Ric commented. "People didn't use to think like that. They used to put this bit and that bit on a record and get a hit with the formula. It's sad that some groups used to do that, get a hit and disappear from the face of the earth."

How about a hit single for Ten Years After who are, essentially, an album group ? "A hit would be nice," Ric agreed. "It wouldn't make much difference to us money-wise but would establish us as a national name rather than an underground group." Then he left to rehearse the new act in preparation for two long American tours within the space of a few months. Ric is quite pleased about the visits, but

***Pete Townshend**, who was sitting with us, just shook his head and muttered: "Oh, my God!"*

<u>February 4, 1969</u>
Falkoner Theater
Copenhagen, Denmark

<u>February 8, 1969</u>
Pop Club
Brondby, Denmark

<u>February 16, 1969</u>
Golden Torch
Tunstall, England

<u>February 18, 1969</u>
Students Union
Manchester, England

<u>February 19, 1969</u>
Toby Jug
Tolworth, England

<u>February 20, 1969</u>
Swindon Locarno
London, England

<u>February 22, 1969</u>
Starlight Room
Boston, England

Release of the third Ten Years After LP: "Stonedhenge" Deram DES 18021

Tracks on Side One are: Going To Try (Alvin Lee 4:50), *I Can't Live Without Lydia* (Chick Churchill 1:20), *Woman Trouble*

(Alvin Lee 4:36), *Skoobly-Oobly-Doobob* (Alvin Lee 1:41), *Hear Me Calling* (Alvin Lee 5:43). *Side Two tracks include: A Sad Song* (Alvin Lee 3:24), *Three Blind Mice* (Trad.; Arr. Ric Lee 0:55), *No Title* (Alvin Lee 8:12), *Faro* (Leo Lyons 1:09) and *Speed Kills* (Alvin Lee/Mike Vernon 3:32). *The LP charts at #6 in the UK.*

Alvin Lee:
"Stonedhenge was the first experimental album and also the influence of the West Coast, the San Francisco thing. The Jefferson Airplane and the Grateful Dead, were already creeping in there, with the strange sound effects and oddities going on."

Ric Lee: *"That was also the album on which we all did a separate track."*

<u>February 25, 1969</u>
Marquee Club
London, England

<u>Feb 28 & March 1</u>
Fillmore East
New York City, NY

<u>March 2, 1969</u>
Electric Circus
Toronto, Canada

<u>March 6-9, 1969</u>
Fillmore West
San Francisco, California

Set List - March 7th: "Since My Baby Walked Out On Me" (traditional blues), Adventures Of A Young Organ (jam), No Title, Good Morning Little School Girl, (the song has not yet evolved into the familiar arrangement with the classic Lee/Lyons guitar and bass interplay), Spoonful, Hobbit, I Can't Keep From Crying Sometimes, Help Me (introduced by Alvin as "a golden oldie"), I'm Going Home.
The other bands on the bill were Spirit and Country Weather.

March 14-15, 1969
The Fillmore
Los Angeles, CA

March 16, 1969
Sound Factory
Sacramento,
California

March 21, 1969
The Gardens
Vancouver,
British Columbia

March 22, 1969
Eagles Auditorium
Seattle, Washington

Set List: Spoonful, I'm Going Up High (rare and unreleased tune that lived up to it's title - Alvin soars on this song with a mesmerizing solo!), Spider In My Web, Good Morning Little School Girl, Hobbit, I Can't Keep From Crying Sometimes, Help Me, I'm Going Home.

March 28 & 29, 1969
Rose Palace
Pasadena, California

Dance concert with Ten Years After, Savoy Brown Blues Band, Cold Blood and Aum.

March 30, 1969
Labor Temple
S.E. Minneapolis,
Minnesota

April 3, 1969
Westchester County
Center/White Plains,
New York

April 4, 5 & 6, 1969
Electric Factory
Philadelphia, PA

April 9 & 10, 1969
Fillmore East
New York City, NY

***Jimi Hendrix** comes to watch the April 10th show.*

The other acts on the bill were The Nice and Family.

April 11 & 12, 1969
Kinetic Playground
Chicago, Illinois

April 15, 16 & 17
The Tea Party
Boston,
Massachusetts

April 18, 1969
Island Gardens
West Hempstead, NY

April 19, 1969
State University
of New York
Stony Brook, NY

April 25 & 26, 1969
The Image
Miami, Florida

April 27, 1969
Civic Arena
Baltimore, Maryland

May 2, 1969
College for Women
New London, CT

May 3, 1969
Clark University
Worcester,
Massachusetts

May 6, 1969
Free Trade Hall
Manchester, England

May 8, 1969
Royal Albert Hall
London, England

With Jethro Tull and Clouds.

NEW MUSICAL EXPRESS concert review by Richard Green:

I realize that Alvin Lee, of the Ten Years After group, doesn't like the tag "The Fastest Guitar In The West," but at times at the Albert Hall on Thursday his high-pitched speed almost broke the sound barrier ! On "Help Me Baby," he played with the aid of a drumstick and blew thousands of minds. He and Leo Lyons, the bassist, often stood so close together and played so furiously, there was hardly a plectrum's width between them. Most of Ten Years After's music is free-form, Alvin starting a riff and the rest following on. He lowers his head, shuts his eyes and plays with expertise. Ric Lee's drumming is at times frantic (almost Keith Moon-ish), but generally sympathetic to Alvin's guitar - he played a five minute solo which earned a standing ovation. With Alvin lurching about the stage, Leo bending over his bass guitar, Chick Churchill standing and shaking his hair and Ric getting strange sounds from his drum set, fury was created. An out and out rock number which included bits of "Whole Lotta Shakin Goin' On", "Mean Woman Blues" and "Maybelline" gave the voices a chance to pierce the atmosphere and caused thousands of fans to rise to their feet stamping, clapping and whistling. A triumphant return for the group.

The Logical Progression towards Perfection

AUDIENCE

Sole Rep. RONDO PROMOTIONS
7 Kensington Church Court, London, W.8
Ring Tony Hodges at 01-937-3793

BATH FESTIVAL OF BLUES
RECREATION GROUND

THIS SATURDAY
JUNE 28th

FEATURING:

FLEETWOOD MAC
JOHN MAYALL • TEN YEARS AFTER
LED ZEPPELIN • NICE

CHICKEN SHACK • JON HISEMAN'S COLOSSEUM
MICK ABRAHAMS' BLODWYN PIG • KEEF HARTLEY
GROUP THERAPY • LIVERPOOL SCENE • TASTE
SAVOY BROWN'S BLUES BAND • CHAMPION JACK DUPREE
CLOUDS • BABYLON • PRINCIPAL EDWARD'S
MAGIC THEATRE • DEEP BLUES BAND • JUST BEFORE DAWN

D.J. **JOHN PEEL**

REFRESHMENTS & HOT SNACKS WILL BE AVAILABLE ALL DAY	In case of bad weather there will be a substantial amount of undercover accommodation	IN ADVANCE All day 18/6. Eve. only 14/6 ON DAY All day 22/6 Eve. only 16/6

TICKETS OBTAINABLE FROM BATH FESTIVAL BOX OFFICE, ABBEY CHAMBERS, ABBEY CHURCHYARD, BATH, SOMERSET

GEORGE WEIN Presents the 16th Annual

NEWPORT JAZZ FESTIVAL

July 3 thru July 6, 1969
At Festival Field • Newport, Rhode Island

Four Evening Concerts — *Thursday: For the Jazz Aficionado* — Willie Bobo, Kenny Burrell, Bill Evans/Jeremy Steig, Young-Holt Unlimited, Freddie Hubbard, Sonny Murray, Anita O'Day, Sun Ra, and others. *Friday: An Evening of Jazz-Rock* — Jeff Beck, Blood, Sweat and Tears, Roland Kirk, Steve Marcus, Ten Years After, Jethro Tull; and others. *Saturday*: Dave Brubeck/Gerry Mulligan, Woody Herman, Sly and the Family Stone, O. C. Smith, World's Greatest Jazz Band, and others. *Sunday: Schlitz Mixed Bag* — Herbie Hancock, B. B. King, Buddy Rich Orch., Buddy Tate Band, Joe Turner, Winter, Led Zeppelin, and others.

Three Afternoon Concerts — *Friday*: Giant Jam Session with Jimmy Smith and Friends. *Saturday*: Art Blakey, Gary Burton, Miles Davis, Mothers of Invention, Newport All-Stars, Red Norvo, Tal Farlow, Ruby Braff, and others.
Sunday: An Afternoon with James Brown.

Evening and Sunday Afternoon Tickets:
$3.50, 4.50, 5.50, 6.50 — Box Seats $10.00
Friday and Saturday Afternoon — General Admission $4.00

THE NEWPORT FOLK FOUNDATION Presents the
NEWPORT FOLK FESTIVAL
July 16 thru July 20

May 9, 1969
Colston Hall
Bristol, England

With Jethro Tull.

May 12, 1969
Kings Hall
Romford, England

May 13, 1969
Guildhall
Portsmouth, England

With Jethro Tull.

May 14, 1969
City Hall
Newcastle, England

May 15, 1969
Town Hall
Birmingham, England

June 21, 1969
Starlight Room
Boston, England

June 24, 1969
Queens College
Oxford, England

With Pink Floyd.

June 28, 1969
Festival of Blues
Recreation Grounds
Bath, England

Fleetwood Mac, Ten Years After and John Mayall headline over Led Zeppelin, The Nice, Chicken Shack, Savoy Brown, Colosseum, Taste, Bloodwyn Pig, Keef Hartley, Clouds and others.

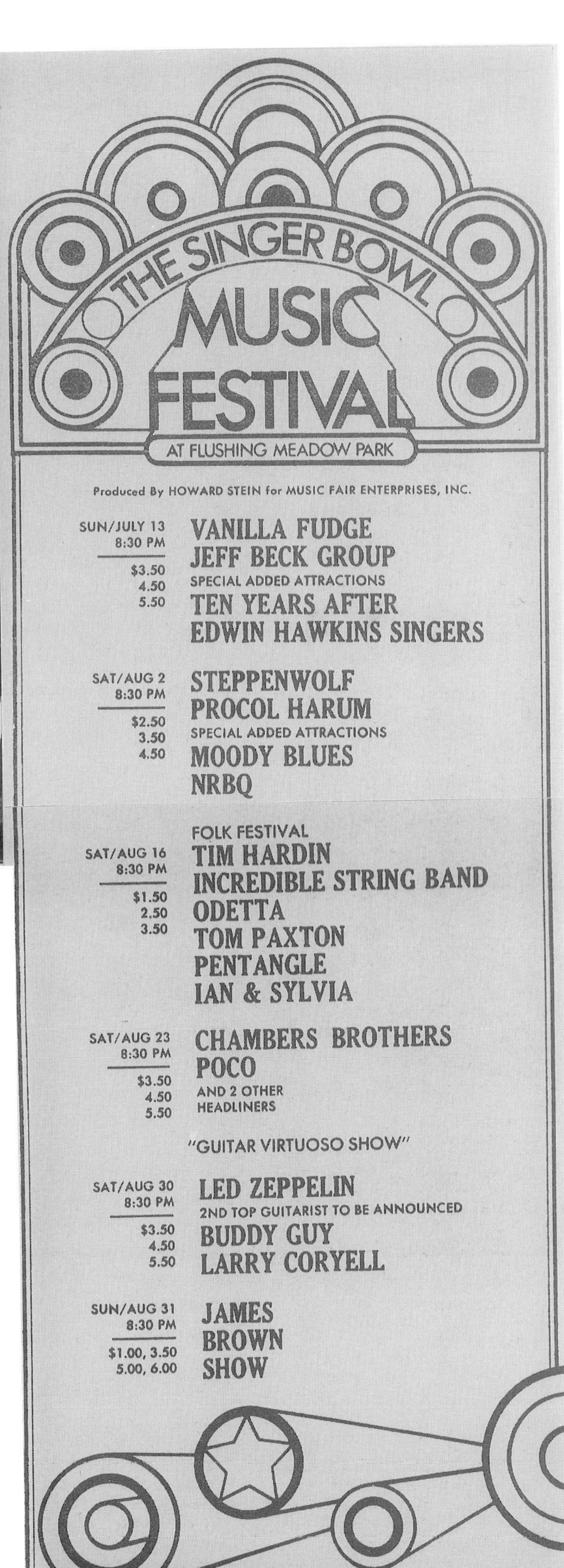

<u>July 4, 1969</u>
Newport Jazz Festival, Rhode Island

Ten Years After perform "I May Be Wrong But I Won't Be Wrong Always", "Good Morning Little School Girl" and "Help Me". They appear on the same night as Jeff Beck, Jethro Tull, Roland Kirk, Steve Marcus and Blood, Sweat & Tears. It is the only time that rock bands are invited to play at this event.

Alvin Lee:
"We started the tour at Newport, which didn't really work out - to say the least. Shall we say sometimes you get those days when you shouldn't have got up, and that was one of them. We could not find the dressing room, the amps broke down and the P.A. system was crummy. We did three numbers and the guy who was worried about the fences came on after the third number and he said there would now be a fifteen minute intermission. And we had only just warmed up....can't win them all !!"

July 12, 1969
Laurel, Maryland

Partial Set List: Spoonful, Help Me (a marathon length version with incredible guitar playing by Alvin), I'm Going Home.

July 13, 1969
Singer Bowl
New York City, NY

Ten Years After's set includes Spoonful, Good Morning Little Schoolgirl, Help Me and I'm Going Home. Also appearing were the Edwin Hawkins Singers, the Jeff Beck Group and Vanilla Fudge. The show ends with Jeff Beck, Glenn Cornick from Jethro Tull, Ric Lee, Jimmy Page & Robert Plant from Led Zeppelin, and Rod Stewart in a jam session performing "Jailhouse Rock".

July 16, 1969
Schaefer Music Festival Wollman Skating Rink Central Park, NYC

Two shows are performed at 7:00 PM and 9 PM. The Spencer Davis Group opens for Ten Years After. Their set includes: I May Be Wrong But I Won't Be Wrong Always, Hobbit, Good Morning Little Schoolgirl, Help Me and I'm Going Home.

July 22-24, 1969
Fillmore West
San Francisco, California

With the Ike & Tina Turner Review and The Flock.

July 25, 1969
Houston, Texas

With Procol Harum.

July 25-27, 1969
First Seattle Pop Festival
Gold Creek Park
Woodinville, Washington

Ten Years After performs on the 26th. Other acts that performed during this three day festival included: Chuck Berry, Tim Buckley, The Byrds, Chicago Transit Authority, Albert Collins, Alice Cooper, Bo Diddley, The Doors, The Flock, Flying Burrito Brothers, Guess Who, It's A Beautiful Day, Led Zeppelin, Santana, Spirit, Ike & Tina Turner Review, Vanilla Fudge and The Youngbloods.

July 27, 1969
Balboa Stadium
San Diego, California

Also performing were: Jefferson Airplane, Sons Of Champlin and Congress Of Wonders.

<u>August 1969</u>
Release of the fourth TYA album "Ssssh" Deram DES 18029

Alvin takes over as the producer on this album and it is destined to become one of the top "underground" rock LP's of the period ! The Side One tracks include: Bad Scene (Alvin Lee 3:20), *Two Time Mama* (Alvin Lee 2:05), *Stoned Woman* (Alvin Lee 3:25), *Good Morning Little School Girl* (J. L. Williamson 6:34). *The tracks on Side Two are: If You Should Love Me* (Alvin Lee 5:25), *I Don't Know That You Don't Know My Name* (Alvin Lee 1:56), *The Stomp* (Alvin Lee 4:34) *and I Woke Up This Morning* (Alvin Lee 5:25).

The album reaches #4 in the U.K. charts and #20 in the U.S.

Leo Lyons:
"When we got a production deal with Chrysalis between us and Decca, we were allowed to record whenever we wanted to, with a budget.

Prior to that, we were told when to record, how long we were recording, and more or less we had to record at Decca studios. So we moved over to an independent recording studio called Morgan Studios, and that was an eight-track. So the Ssssh album was the first one that was done on the eight-track and for us was a turning point."

August 2, 1969
Tea Party
Boston, Massachusetts

Partial Set List: Spoonful, Good Morning Little School Girl, I'm Going Home.

August 16, 1969
St. Louis, Missouri

Ten Years After perform on the same bill with Nina Simone, leaving at 5:00 AM the next morning for their appearance at the Woodstock Festival.

August 17, 1969
Woodstock Music & Arts Festival
Bethel, New York

Partial Set List: Good Morning Little School Girl, Help Me, I Can't Keep From Crying Sometimes and I'm Going Home.

Excerpt from the Woodstock chronicle: BAREFOOT IN BABYLON, by Robert Spitz:

"Sunday's format was shaping up to be

W O O D S T O C K 1 9 6 9

groups who were hard rockers and mostly English. There was room on the bill for three more acts and they had to be killers. John Morris called ***Frank Barselona*** *who was the head of* ***Premier Talent****, the most influential hard rock booking agency in the United States. Barselona quickly sold him the Jeff Beck Group (who never made it to the festival) and Ten Years After for a combined price of $18,000. Ten Years After was an up and coming progressive blues band with a dazzling lead guitarist named Alvin Lee. Some critics invested Lee with the title of Clapton's logical heir, which aroused national interest in the group. Lee, the Woodstock people were informed, had a bad back and was canceling unimportant dates to recuperate, but his manager,* ***Dee Anthony****, guaranteed he would be at Woodstock ready to play if he personally had to bring Alvin in on a stretcher. And play he did !! Lee stepped into the spotlight with his cherry red guitar and exhibited the technique that earned him his reputation as fastest fingers in the west. His hands effortlessly performed formidable lead riffs like a well oiled machine. If Lee's back was aggravating him, it certainly was not affecting his playing. Ten Years After tore through a two hour set of gut wrenching progressive blues, icing the cake with a nine minute rendition of Going Home."*

The following quotes from film director Michael Wadleigh are from the October 1970 issue of AMERICAN CINEMATOGRAPHER

"During the three and a half days of filming, I was constantly on stage with four other camera men shooting the musical numbers in sync-sound. On-stage, together with the camera men and their assistants, were our two Assistant Directors and Supervising Editors, ***Martin Scorsese*** *and Thelma Schoonmaker. Initially, we had planned on shooting very neatly according to the order in which the performers were scheduled to appear but that schedule soon went right out the window.*

The performers could not drive into the area, because nobody could drive anywhere. They had to be flown in by helicopter and they went on whenever they arrived. There was no way of finding out who

went on next, let alone the order of songs they were going to perform. As a general rule, we would shoot each group's first number as well as their last or encore. The rain did some terrible things to us. In the first place, it shorted some of our electrical connections and, secondly, all that rain and humidity caused the film emulsion to swell and we had constant jamming problems. Our equipment failures, however were not the worst of it. The real horror was experienced by the five cameramen shooting on stage in sopping wet clothing while the rain poured down. All of a sudden there would be a short circuit to one of the cameras and you would see a camera man just sort of go crazy for awhile, as 110 volts of electricity went jolting through his body. Later, we were able to see zig-zag patterns on the film caused by the electric discharge coming right through the camera."

Alvin Lee: *"Had it not been for the rain storm, we would have probably flown in by helicopter, played, and gone out again within two hours. But we were about to go on and the rain storm broke. There was no way anybody could play with the sparks flying up on the stage. The rain storm was actually the highlight of Woodstock for me. I thought it was better than all the bands. There's no way half a million people can run for shelter, so they just sat there and started singing, and I took a walk around the lake and kind of joined in with the audience and experienced it first-hand, which was good. When we finally did go on there was a lot of brouhaha, because nobody wanted to go on first 'cause of the risk of shock. I think we eventually took the plunge and said, Oh, what the hell, If we get electrocuted, we will get good publicity ! And we went out and actually had to stop playing during 'Good Morning Little School Girl' and retune because of the atmospherics. The storm had done so many changes in the atmosphere, the guitars went way out of tune. I actually had to say, Scuse us, but*

we've got to stop and retune - but the audience didn't seem to mind, they were just having fun anyway."
Leo Lyons: *"We had played in St. Louis the night before with Nina Simone. We left about five in the morning, flew to New York and then flew to Woodstock by helicopter. We hadn't had anything to eat, but when we got to the site,* ***Pete Townsend*** *came up to us and said 'Don't eat or drink anything, it's all spiked with acid!' And then, of course, it started raining and we were in the back of a truck for about seven or eight hours. By the time we hit the stage, it was pretty flooded."*
Michael Wadleigh: *"In terms of sheer footage, the bulk of the film we ended up with, about 80% I'd say, was shot by the five on-stage camera crews and was devoted to the musical numbers. But the other 20% - the footage shot by our five documentary crews, is what gives the picture its substance and heart. In the end, there was 120 hours of film (315,000 feet !) and 81 hours of sound recording (including 53 hours of music). We had filmed 36 different groups of entertainers and, during the editing, we eventually whittled that down to a total of 14. The choice was made on the basis of two criteria: what the music had to say, and how good they were as performers. Our first cut ran seven and a half hours in length, including finished opticals for the multiple images. We chipped away at it, dropping certain groups entirely and complete musical numbers, until we got it down to four hours. The hardest part was to get that last hour out of it, in order to end up with the three-hour version now playing in the theaters."*

The following excerpt is from the MAKING FILMS IN NEW YORK magazine October 1970 issue story: "Woodstock The Longest Optical"

"Ten Years After offered us a simple optical solution. We filmed only one number of this group, that everlasting encore, 'Goin' Home'. We began filming with three cameras. Mid-way, one of the cameras ran out of film. When we saw the rushes together with the sound, we realized right away we had to show Alvin Lee, the lead performer in triple image. So at the point at which the third camera ran out of film, we simply took the continuing image from the right side, flipped it, and let it run on the left side to continue the triple image optical throughout. It is also a sequence that has very few cuts. When filmed, the sequence ran eleven minutes; in the final edited version, it runs nine."
Alvin Lee: *"I'm Going Home is part of the group, but we never wanted it to be a whole part. The movie was natural enough, we were just doing our thing. But it wasn't too helpful - it put too much concentration on that one number, whereas that number was played at the end of an hour and a half set and was the climax. We were also getting into a lot of more or less structured things. I thought at the time it might have been better for us had they put in a number like 'Can't Keep From Crying' where we extend the instrumental side more, or the boogie time, but it happened the way it did.*
The film crossed us over to the masses rather than a cult thing. It was the end of the underground.
A lot of people say the Woodstock movie made Ten Years After, but it only catapulted us into that mass market and in a way it was the beginning of the end. Going into ice hockey arenas, where you can't hear much, the sound's terrible and you can't see the audience wasn't that much fun and it was a decline of enjoying touring as much as we had done previously. Also, the sad thing about Woodstock, it seemed it was the peace generation

coming together and then they all went home, and never got together again. It dissipated afterwards."

August 24, 1969
Rose Palace
Los Angeles, California

Partial Set List: Spoonful, Good Morning Little School Girl, Hobbit, Bad Scene, I Can't Keep From Crying Sometimes, Help Me.

August 26-28, 1969
Fillmore West
San Francisco, California

The other acts were Terry Reid and The Barkays. The Ten Years After and Terry Reid concert footage seen in the ***"Groupies"*** *film documentary was most likely shot during these shows. It was made over a nine month period in 1969 at locations across the U.S., including: the Fillmore West, Fillmore East, Boston Tea Party, the Scene Club in Miami, etc. The ninety two minute color film explores the lives of young fans of rock stars, particularly the girl groupies. It includes backstage and concert footage of Ten Years After, Terry Reid, Spooky Tooth and Joe Cocker & The Grease Band. The Ten Years After footage (about 10 minutes total) consists of comments from Alvin Lee and live clips of Help Me and Good Morning Little Schoolgirl.*

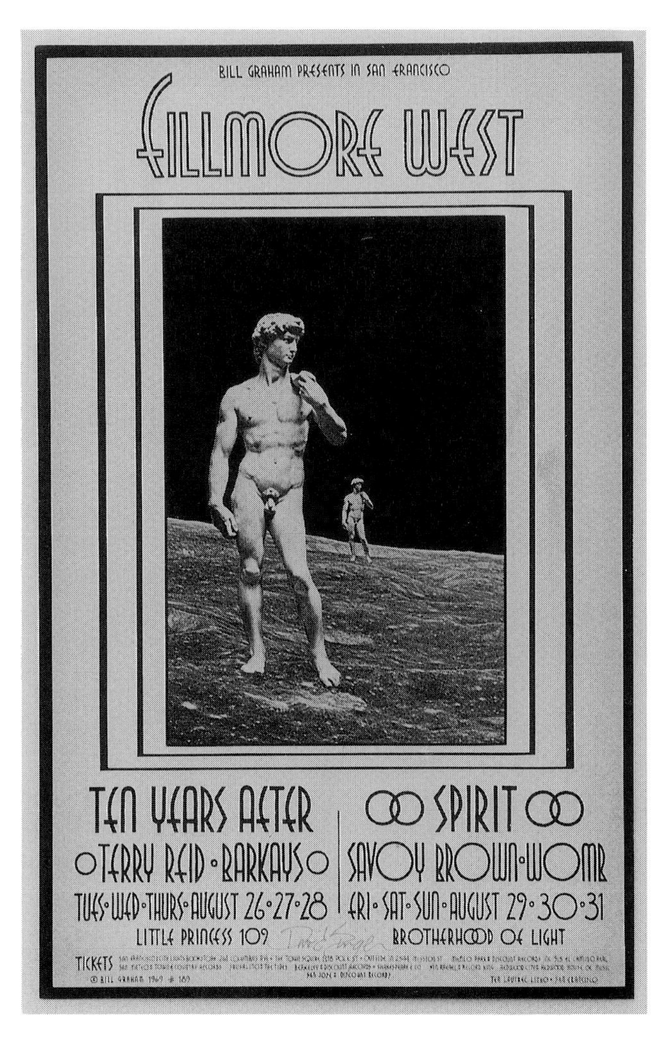

September 1, 1969
Texas International Pop Festival
Dallas, Texas

Good Morning Little School Girl, I Can't Keep From Crying Sometimes, Hobbit, Spoonful, I'm Going Home.

This 3 day event was filmed in 16mm color and in 1992 a work print of some footage saw limited release as a home video titled: "Got No Shoes/Got No Blues". Several of the artists that performed are shown in the video, including: Grand Funk Railroad, Tony Joe White, James Cotten Blues Band, Chicago Transit Authority, Sweetwater, Led Zepellin, Ten Years After and Janis Joplin.

The TYA Segment included in the video is "Spoonful", although it is only a rough edit. To date, the complete Texas Pop film has never been released.

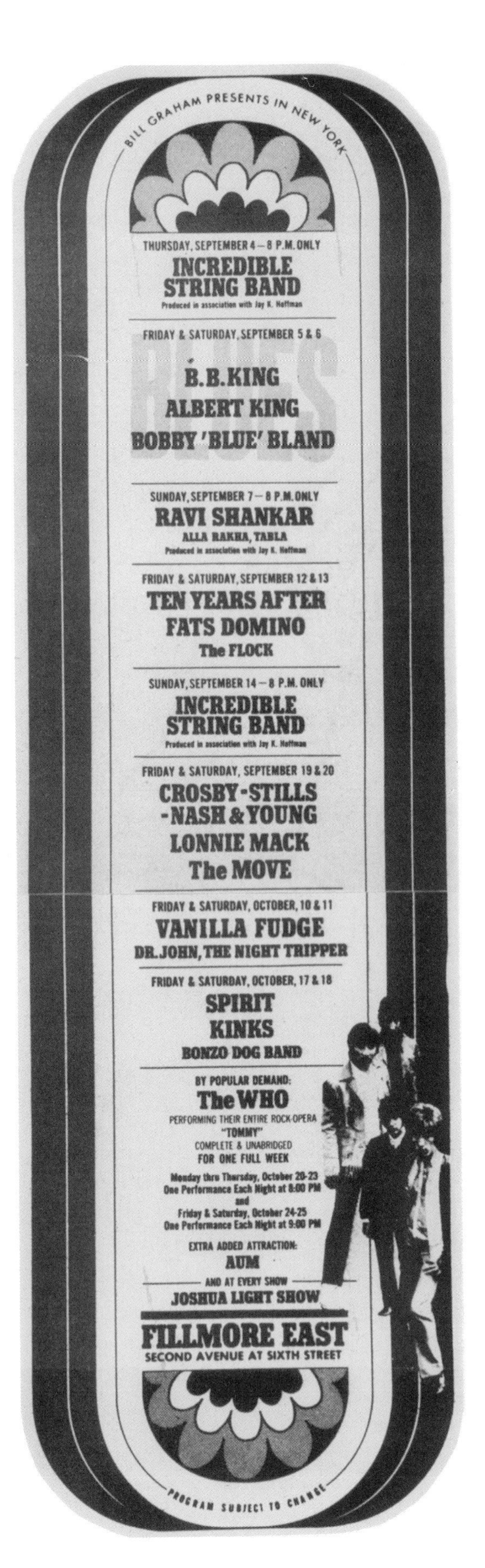

<u>Sept 12-13, 1969</u>
Fillmore East
New York City, NY

Other acts on the bill were The Flock, Mother Earth and Fats Domino.

<u>October 11, 1969</u>
The Polytechnic Large Hall, Little Titchfield Street London, England

<u>October 18, 1969</u>
First Music Festival
Paris, France

<u>October 24, 1969</u>
Actuel Festival
Amougies, Belgium

<u>October 27, 1969</u>
Ten Years After play "Bad Scene" on the US TV show "Music Scene"

Also appearing on the show were: Jerry Lee Lewis, Smith, Richie Havens, Janis Joplin, Michael Cole and Isaac Hayes.

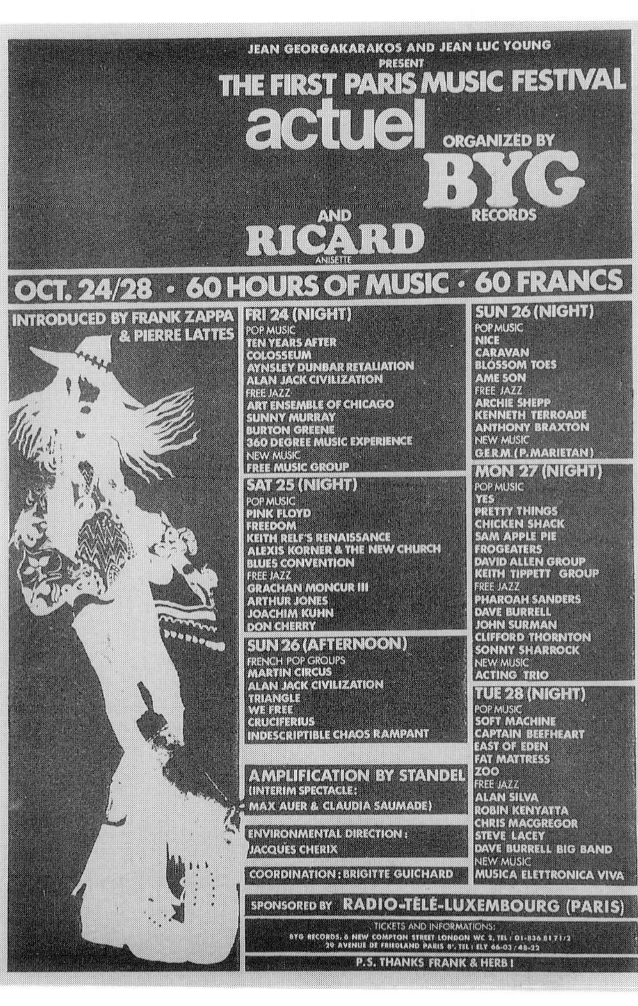

November 1969
Que Club
Gothenburg, Sweden

November 7-9, 1969
Jazz Festival
Berlin, Germany

November 17, 1969
Jahrhunderthalle
Frankfurt, Germany

I May Be Wrong But I Won't Be Wrong Always (introduced as "a song by Count Basie"), Spider In My Web, Good Morning Little School Girl, I Can't Keep From Crying Sometimes, I'm Going Home.

November 21, 1969
Stadthalle
Vienna, Austria

December 3, 1969
Kulttuuritalo
Helsinki, Finland

Spoonful, I May Be Wrong, Hobbit, School Girl, No Title, Scat Thing, I Can't Keep From Crying.

December 6, 1969
"Beat 69"/K. B. Hallen Copenhagen, Denmark

Parts of this show are broadcast on Danish DR-TV in two parts on December 13, 1969 and May 16, 1970. The songs included in the TV broadcasts were: I May Be Wrong But I Won't Be Wrong Always, Good Morning Little School Girl, Scat Thing and I Can't Keep From Crying Sometimes.

December 9, 1969
City Hall
Newcastle, England

Supporting TYA on this tour of England were Bloodwyn Pig and Stone The Crowes.

December 10, 1969
Town Hall
Birmingham

December 11, 1969
Guildhall
Southampton

December 12, 1969
Albert Hall
Nottingham, England

December 13, 1969
Colston Hall
Bristol, England

December 15, 1969
Royal Albert Hall
London, England

December 17, 1969
Usher Hall
Edinburgh, Scotland

December 19, 1969
Free Trade Hall
Manchester, England

February 8, 1970
Lyceum Strand
London, England

February 1970
University Of Hartford, Connecticut

Love Like A Man, Good Morning Little School Girl, Working On The Road, Hobbit, Spider

In My Web, Scat Thing, I Can't Keep From Crying Sometimes, I'm Going Home.

February 26, 1970
Fillmore East
New York City, NY

The other acts on the bill were John Hammond and Zephyr with Tommy Bolin.

Feb 27 & 28, 1970
Fillmore East
New York City, NY

The other acts on the bill were Doug Kershaw and Zephyr. Ten Years After's set list for the February 28th show was: Love Like A Man, Good Morning Little Schoolgirl, Working On The Road, Hobbit, Help Me, I'm Going Home, Sweet Little Sixteen and Roll Over Beethoven.

March 12-15, 1970
Fillmore West
San Francisco, California

The supporting acts were Buddy Rich, Sea Train and Kimberly.

Excerpt from the book "Bill Graham Presents":

*I liked Ten Years After very much as a band but one aspect of their show personified a lot of my difficulty with rock and roll. The drum solo. The endless, seemingly nonmusical drum solo. Not that theirs was worse than any other. It was not even really bad drumming. It was just like eating dry Cheerios without milk and fruit. I wanted to set an example for all the bands as to what **real** drumming was all about. So I flew to Las Vegas. Through a friend, I was introduced to Buddy Rich and we went to have dinner. He was playing there with Frank Sinatra at the time. I told him I ran a place called the Fillmore in San Francisco and that on this certain show, I had a headliner from England, a group that was very good but they always did a drum solo I didn't care for. I told Buddy I wanted*

them all to see what a drummer really did. What a real drummer was all about. He said, "Fuck rock and roll! Those fuckin' kids. Fuck them. These fuckin' asshole drummers can't hold one stick or my dick." He just went on and on. "Those fucking pieces of shit make all these fucking millions of dollars....". Buddy didn't like rock and roll too much. The regular price for the middle act at the time was thirty-five hundred a night. I said, "I'd like to offer you five thousand a night because you're Buddy Rich and it would be an honor to have you in our room. But I want to let you know that the act before you and the act after you will be rock and roll. So it may be tough on you." He said, "What do you mean? The audience? Fuck 'em. You just pay me. We'll play."

The night of the show, Sea Train opened. We set up for Buddy Rich. Little old fashioned band stands to hold up the song books, which the kids had never seen before. We set up this little midget drum kit for Buddy. One bass, one little snare, bang bang, that was it. I went into the dressing room to say hello to him and his band was all in

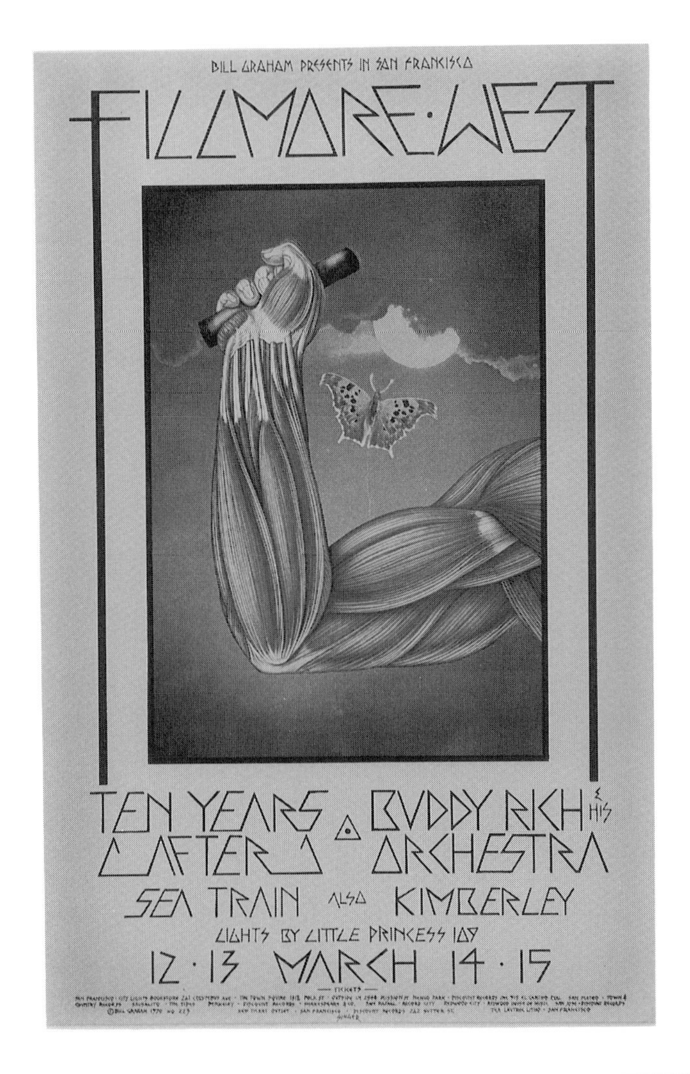

cardigan jackets with Hawaiian shirts with big flowers on them. Buddy was wearing a turtleneck. The kids outside were already yelling, "TEN YEARS AFTER! ALVIN! WE WANT ALVIN!" He heard this and he said, "The fuck are they yelling out there? Assholes!" On and on. I said, "Buddy, you know, I grew up in New York and I used to sneak into the Metropole to see you play so don't take this wrong. But would you let me see your song titles?" "What? Are you out of your fucking mind?" I said, "I'm not

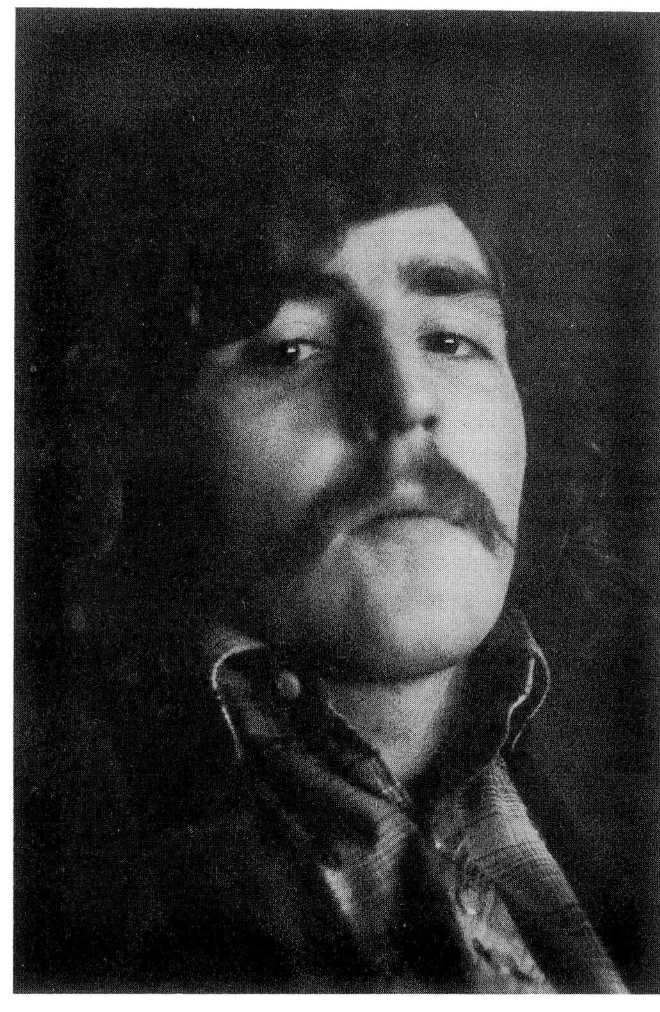

going to tell you what to do. But if you would consider playing something familiar to them, it would help." "They don't know shit out there." I said, "Buddy, can I see your book?" "Here!" I went through the book and he had "Norwegian Wood" in there, the Beatles' song. I said, "Would you consider the possibility of opening with Norwegian Wood? They know the song and it would just hit them right off." "All right," he said. "All right."

The band came out and Buddy was standing on the side, waiting to be introduced. I said, "Check this out. Would you welcome please, the very best there is...Buddy Rich and his Orchestra." Buddy sat down at the drums. As I was making the introduction, people were screaming, "ALVIN! TEN YEARS AFTER! ROCK AND ROLL!" The brass section stood up and played that opening riff from "Norwegian Wood". Then Buddy took off. Bam bam bam bam boom boom boom whanga whanga whanga boom! The entire room swerved. All the kids going to get something to eat turned around and looked at the stage. Buddy fucking wailed! Dadah! Bababah! Lahaladam! Mopah! The room was mesmerized. They were eating something they had never eaten before and they could not believe how good it was. They were just ***glued*** *to the stage. He held that room for an hour. And he was great. He went off and the kids went wild. "MORE! MORE! BUDDY!" I went into the dressing room. I said, "Buddy, they really.." "Fuck 'em!" Now some of his musicians had really loved it. They'd had the time of their lives. Because they were in "Weed Land". It was home. After Vegas, they never thought they'd see anything like this again. I said, "Listen, you got to go back out. Buddy, come on." He said, "Nah nah nah." But his other musicians were gesturing that I should keep after him. They*

wanted to go back out. I said, "Buddy, I'm going to take you out there." "No, you're not." I picked him up and carried him out and put him down right next to the drum kit and they went crazy !

Now, I had prepared myself for what came next. I had rehearsed it eight thousand times. We were now in the break, setting up for Ten Years After. I walked into their dressing room and said hello to Alvin Lee and Leo Lyons, their bass player, and Chick Churchill, their keyboard guy. Ric Lee, their drummer, was sitting at his drum pad going brrrrr, brrrrr with his sticks. Warming up at that black rubber pad. He said, "Hey Bill. How you doin'?" I shook his hand and put my other hand on his shoulder. I said, "Ric, how are you? Hey man. Can't wait for your solo tonight, baby!" He didn't do one. They walked out and played a harsh set of rock and roll and if Ric took three seconds to go off by himself, that was it. It was great.

<u>March 21, 1970</u>
Olympic Auditorium
Los Angeles, California

Love Like A Man (introduced as "A new thing called..."), Good Morning Little School Girl, Working On The Road (introduced as "another one off our new album which is just escaping, it's a short one called Working On The Road"), Spider In My Web (introduced by Alvin as "Jack Nasty Blues"), Hobbit, 50000 Miles Beneath My Brain (Alvin says "this is another new one"), I'm Going Home.

<u>March 27-29, 1970</u>
Winter's End Festival
Miami, Florida

<u>April 3 & 4, 1970</u>
Capitol Theater
Portchester, New York

Stone The Crows open for Ten Years After. The TYA set list for both shows is: Love Like A Man, Good Morning Little Schoolgirl, Working On The Road, Hobbit, 50,000 Miles Beneath

My Brain, Scat Thing, I Can't Keep From Crying Sometimes, I'm Going Home and Sweet Little Sixteen.

April 1970
Ten Years After conclude their fifth tour of America and begin a tour of Germany.

April 1970
Release of the fifth Ten Years After LP: "Cricklewood Green" Deram DES 18038

Despite a frantic touring schedule, Alvin Lee's songwriting continues to grow and improve. The tracks on Side One are: Sugar The Road (Alvin Lee 3:46), *Working On The Road* (Alvin Lee 4:15), *50,000 Miles Beneath My Brain* (Alvin Lee 7:37) and *Year 3000 Blues* (Alvin Lee 2:17). *Side Two: Me And My Baby* (Alvin Lee 4:12), *Love Like A Man* (Alvin Lee 7:13), *Circles* (Alvin Lee 3:55) and *As The Sun Still Burns Away* (Alvin Lee 4:42). *The album makes #4 in the U.K. and stays in the charts for 27 weeks. It reaches #14 in the U.S.*

Alvin Lee: *"On Cricklewood Green, at one point, during 'Working On The Road' which is still one of my favorite songs, the tape actually slurs - it slows. Somebody leaned on the tape machine when we were recording it, and nobody even noticed at the time ! So that gives you a clue as to what state we were in. Producers, engineers and band, no one noticed it."*

May 1970
Release of the TYA single: "Love Like A Man"

This single release of "Love A Man" has the studio version on Side A and Side B contains a live version recorded in February at the Fillmore East - it reaches the top ten in the U.K.

May 8, 1970
Lyceum Ballroom London, England

Ten Years After start a British tour. The supporting acts are Matthew's Southern Comfort and Writing On The Wall.

NEW MUSICAL EXPRESS concert review by Richard Green:

Rock and Roll is a much maligned phrase these days, being used - particularly by Americans who should know better - to describe almost any group or band that plays anything but straight teenybop music. What it should be used in connection with is the sort of concert given by Ten Years After at the London Lyceum on

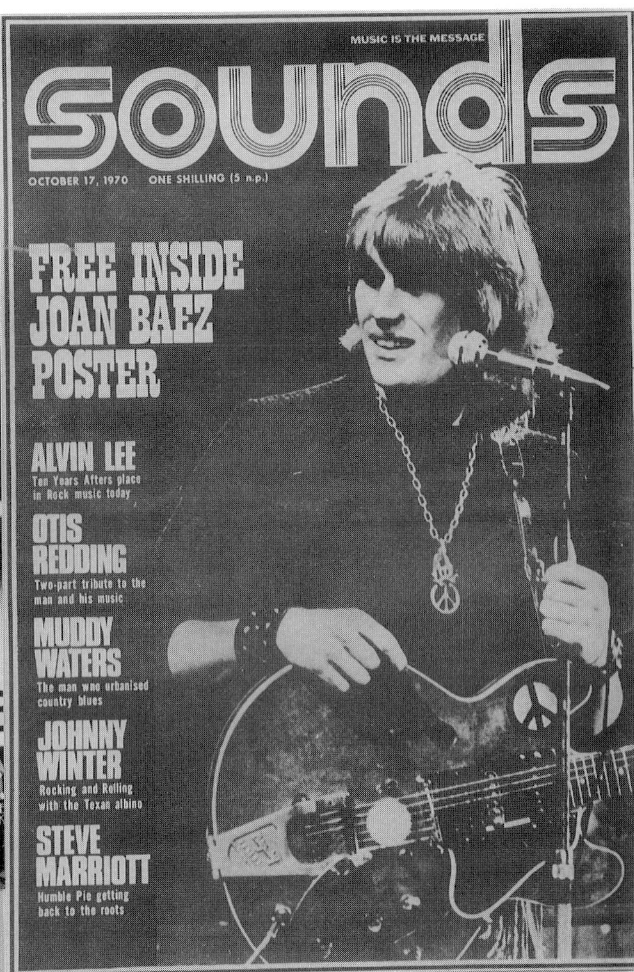

IMPROVISING BLUES GUITAR

An Instruction Manual Based On Recorded Solos By:

BB KING · T-BONE WALKER · LOWELL FULSON · ALVIN LEE · JERRY GARCIA · MIKE BLOOMFIELD · JIMI HENDRIX · ALBERT KING · ERIC CLAPTON

Friday night to a wildly enthusiastic audience. As the start to a brief tour, the concert gave all the signs of much goodness to come on subsequent dates. Whether lengthy and frequent American tours have helped or not is a moot point but the group has certainly improved since the last time I saw them at the Albert Hall last year. Alvin still dominates the stage and his wizardry with the guitar becomes more interesting with every appearance. He is unquestionably one of the fastest guitarists around but this does not mean, as is the case with so many others, that skill is sacrificed for speed. His closeness with the other members of the group - Leo Lyons (bass guitar), Chick Churchill (organ) and Ric Lee (drums) has, if anything, become even tighter than before.

Ten Years After's audiences tend to be vociferous and the yells of encouragement at the Lyceum were good to hear. The roar of appreciation that went up at the end of each number and following each solo was long and noisy. Ric Lee's drum solo was particularly good, being quiet and intricate.

Typical Alvin Lee licks were produced during "Good Morning Little Schoolgirl", which is fast becoming a Ten Years After standard. It has been banned in parts of America because of one line which didn't even cause a raised eyebrow this side of the Atlantic. As a total contrast to that number's brashness, "Me And My Baby" from the new album was light and jazzy and a real joy. Also from "Cricklewood Green" was "50,000 Miles Beneath My Brain," another of Alvin's compositions which included a bit of "Cat's Squirrel" towards the end.

The evening was going really well when Ten Years After went into "I'm Going Home" and the atmosphere became electric. This is another of the group's most famous numbers and is pure out and out rock. Dancing broke out as strains of "Whole Lotta Shakin' Goin' On" came through and Alvin and Leo started a fine piece of interplay between them with the lead guitarist bent almost double over his instrument, which seems to be a member of his body at times. Shouts of "Sweet Little Sixteen" resulted in the Chuck Berry song being performed to wild delight and it was almost like the days of the old Teddy Boy concerts once more.

A deserved triumph for Ten Years After who have come a step nearer to the "world's most exciting group" tag.

May 9, 1970
Guildhall
Southampton, England

May 11, 1970
Town Hall
Birmingham, England

May 13, 1970
City Hall
Newcastle, England

May 1970
Hautes Etudes Commerciales
Jouy En Josas, France

Partial Set List: Good Morning Little School Girl; 50,000 Miles Beneath My Brain, Help Me, I Can't Keep From Crying Sometimes, I'm Going Home.

BILL GRAHAM PRESENTS IN NEW YORK
FILLMORE EAST
BYRD
© 1970 by Fillmore East Corporation.

Leo Lyons
Ric Lee
TEN YEARS AFTER
Alvin Lee (lead guitar) and Leo Lyons (bass) began playing together as teenagers in Nottingham, England. After adding Ric Lee (drums) and Chick Churchill (organ), Ten Years After took shape. The group became a top attraction in London clubs, and, after appearing at the Windsor Jazz and Blues Festival, gained national recognition in England. They've toured the US extensively since then; this is their sixth engagement at Fillmore East. Their latest album is Cricklewood Green.

AN AFTERMATH-PURE CANE PRODUCTIONS PRESENTATION
COSMIC CARNIVAL
Traffic (with Stevie Winwood) & Ten Years After & Mothers of Invention (with Frank Zappa) & Ike & Tina Turner & Love & Sweetwater & A Beautiful Day & Allman Brothers & Albert King & Mountain & Majester Ludi & Sun Country & Third Rail & Shelly Isaacs & Baby & Fat Jessie & Sabudi
4 huge closed circuit color video screens
JUNE 13 ALL SEATS RESERVED CONTINUOUS MUSIC
ATLANTA BRAVES STADIUM, ATLANTA, GA.
10:00 A.M. to 12 MIDNITE $3.00 $5.00 $6.00 $7.00
Master of ceremonies Murray Roman
Sound provided by Hanley
MAIL ORDERS Aftermath-Pure Cane Productions P.O. Box 4062 Atlanta, Ga.
NEW YORK
(N.Y.C.) All Together - 793 Lexington Ave.
GEORGIA
(AUGUSTA) Home Folks - 227 8th St.
(COLUMBUS) Twaddle and Balderdash - 3302 Victory Drive
(SAVANNAH) Norwood Records - 18 West State St.
TENNESSEE
(CHATTANOOGA) Jack's Music Shop - 608 Market St.
(NASHVILLE) Sgt. Pepper's - 1715 21st Ave.
(MEMPHIS) Grand Central Station - 521 South Highland

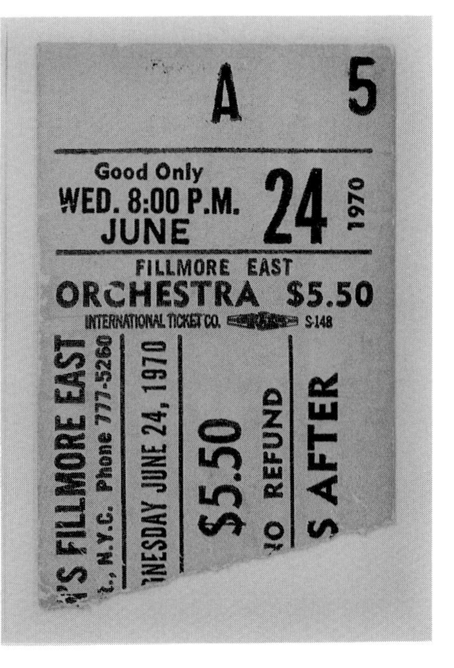
A 5
Good Only
WED. 8:00 P.M.
JUNE
24
1970
FILLMORE EAST
ORCHESTRA $5.50
INTERNATIONAL TICKET CO.
S-148
FILLMORE EAST
N.Y.C. Phone 777-5260
JUNE 24, 1970
$5.50
REFUND
S AFTER

May 21, 1970
Music Hall
Aberdeen, Scotland

The supporting act is T-Rex.

May 22, 1970
Greens Playhouse
Glasgow, Scotland

With Wilde Horse (location changed from Kelvin Hall).

May 24, 1970
Caird Hall
Dundee, Scotland

With T-Rex.

May 25, 1970
Free Trade Hall
Manchester, England

May 26, 1970
Usher Hall
Edinburgh, Scotland

June 13, 1970
Cosmic Festival
Braves Stadium
Atlanta, Georgia

June 14, 1970
Cincinnati Pop Festival
Crosley Field
Cincinnati, Ohio

In addition to Ten Years After, other acts who appeared were: Traffic, Grand Funk Railroad, Mountain, Mott The Hoople, Iggy Pop & The Stooges, Bob Seger System, Alice Cooper, Bloodrock, Zephyr, Savage Grace, Sky, Mighty Quick, Damnation of Adam's Blessing, Third Power, Brownsville Station, Cradle and the Mike Quatro Jam Band.

June 15 - 17, 1970
Tea Party
Boston, Massachusetts

Mott the Hoople is the opening act.

June 24 & 25, 1970
Fillmore East
New York City, NY

The other acts are Illinois Speed Press and Catfish.

June 26, 1970
Aragon Ballroom
Chicago, Illinois

Ten Years After is the featured act. Other artists on the bill are B.B. King, Brownsville Station and Mott The Hoople.

June 27 & 28, 1970
Canadian National Expo Grandstand
Toronto, Canada

These two concert dates are part of the Trans Continental Pop Festival (a.k.a. the Trans-Canada tour or "Festival Express" since the mode of transportation was by train). The other tour stops included Montreal, Winnipeg and Calgary.
In addition to Ten Years After, the other bands on this tour included: The Band, Janis Joplin, Traffic, Grateful Dead, Delaney & Bonnie, Buddy Guy, Mountain, Tom Rush, Sea Train and Melanie. Color film footage of several of the groups,

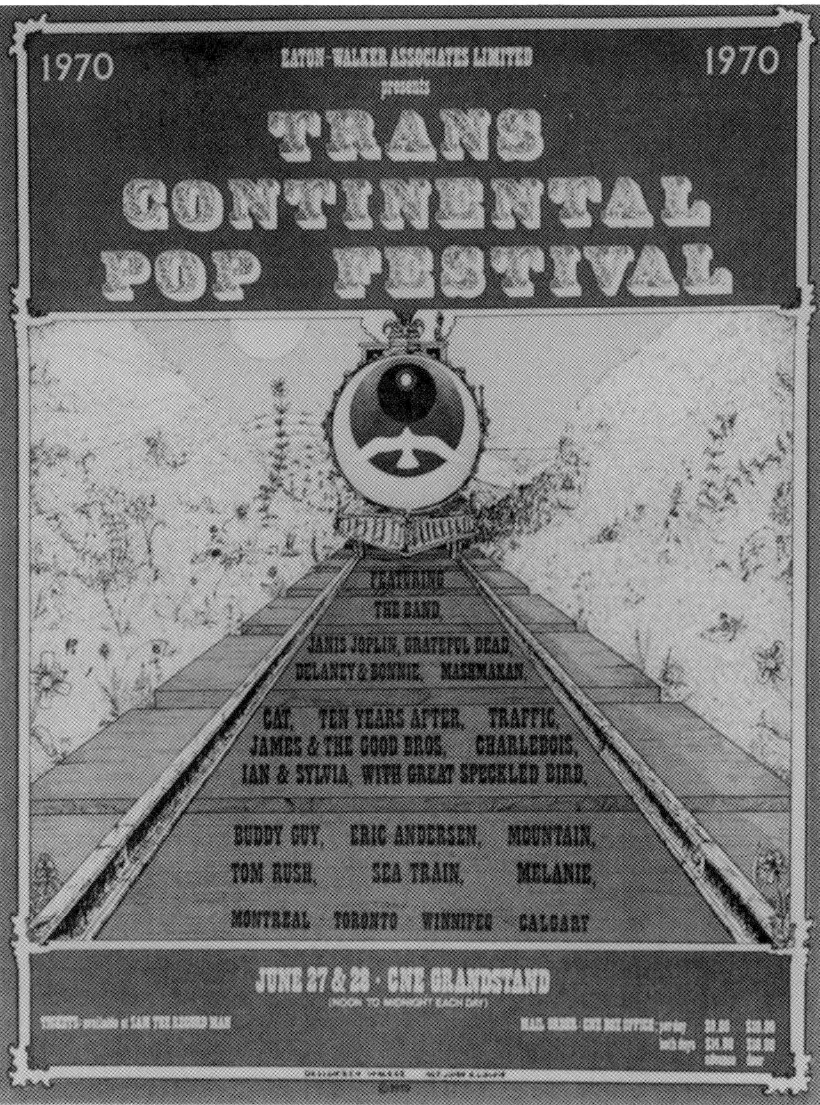

including Ten Years After, The Band, Janis Joplin, Traffic and the Grateful Dead was shot at various stops during this tour of Canada. Ten Years After was filmed performing I Can't Keep From Crying Sometimes and Love Like A Man, however the footage remains unreleased.

The only "Festival Express" footage used to date is of the Band and Janis Joplin. The Band's footage appears in: "The Band Authorized Video Biography" released in 1995 by ABC Video. Janis Joplin "Festival Express" concert footage appears in the biography film "Janis" and, more recently, in the VH-1 TV "Legends" profile.

July 1, 1970
Harvard Stadium
Boston, Massachusetts

Ten Years After is supported by Mott The Hoople. The concert is one of several held at the Harvard University football stadium as part of the 1970 Schaefer Music Festival in Boston. Some of the other concerts included: The Band on June 22; B.B. King, Paul Butterfield & James Cotten on June 29; Miles Davis, Buddy Miles & Seatrain on July 8, Ike & Tina Turner on July 15; and, on August 12, the final live concert appearance of Janis Joplin before her untimely death.

July 5, 1970
2nd Atlanta International Pop Festival
Gainesville, Georgia

Ten Years After perform on Sunday, the third day of the festival - which also featured: The Bob Seger System, Spirit, Terry Reid, Johnny Winter, Grand Funk Railroad, Richie Havens and the Allman Brothers Band (their second performance at the three day festival). The festival ends at

dawn on Monday with the Memphis State University cast of Hair leading the crowd in a sing-a-long of "Aquarius/Let The Sunshine In". A film crew apparently shot many of the musical performances but, due to lawsuits and legal entanglements that followed, the negative is rumored to still be sitting in a lawyer's vault in Nashville. The only footage seen to date is of Jimi Hendrix on the "Atlanta Pop" home video release.

Ric Lee comments from DISC AND MUSIC ECHO:

"Our recent three-week American stint was not too enjoyable.

Alvin Lee (Ten Years A

We played to 300,000 at a festival in Atlanta and there were really bad vibrations. About a third of the crowd paid and the other two-thirds just broke in. They think that things like that should be free. Free concerts are great at the right time and place but the trouble in America is the kids don't have any respect for the slightest bit of authority. There's a real revolutionary feeling over there. We played at a sport stadium at Harvard and it was really violent with people crashing the barriers and that sort of thing."

July 17, 1970
The Spectrum
Philadelphia, PA

July 18, 1970
New York Pop Festival at Downing Stadium Randall's Island, New York

Ten Years After perform: Love Like A Man, Good Morning Little School Girl, No Title, Hobbit, Scat Thing, I Can't Keep From Crying Sometimes, I'm Going Home, Sweet Little Sixteen.

Also scheduled on the same day were: Delaney & Bonnie and Friends, Richie Havens, Ravi Shankar, Tony Williams Lifetime, John McLaughlin & Larry Young jamming with Jack Bruce, Eric Clapton and special guest Miles Davis. The sound is provided by Hanley and the performances are projected by closed circuit to a giant TV screen in the stadium.

July 1970
San Bernardino, California

July 22, 1970
The Forum
Los Angeles, California

Love Like A Man, Good Morning Little School Girl, No Title, Hobbit, Scat Thing, I Can't Keep From Crying Sometimes, I'm Going Home, Sweet Little Sixteen.

July 23, 1970
Tarrant County Convention Center
Dallas, Texas

July 24, 1970
Public Auditorium
Cleveland, Ohio

With Joe Cocker.

July 28-30, 1970
Fillmore West
San Francisco, California

Special mid-week shows. The other acts on the bill with Ten Years After are Cactus and Toe Fat.

August 5, 1970
West Palm Beach, Florida

August 6, 1970
Curtis Hixon Hall
Tampa, Florida

August 7, 1970
Goose Lake Park
Farmington, Michigan

Unreleased film exists that includes Ten Years After's encore "Sweet Little Sixteen" - after which Alvin Lee hurls his famous '59 Gibson ES-335 over his head and boots it clear across the stage.

August 8, 1970
Allen Theater
Cleveland, Ohio

August 9, 1970
Strawberry Fields Festival - Mosport Race Track
Toronto, Canada

Concert review from RPM Weekly by Jim Thompson of CKBB:

The setting was just perfect at Canada's biggest rock filled gathering with 50,000 youths in attendence, the majority being American, bringing with them botherhood and freedom as a theme to the 500 acre Mosport Park. Supergroup Ten Years After, led by Alvin Lee's turned-on guitar and vocals, were called back for two encores by the frenzied youths who stood up and danced during the entire performance. The medley, "I'm Going Home" was the highlight of the entire festival.

August 1970
Capitol Theater
Portchester, NY

PHOTOS by: BEKEN of COWES, I.O.W.

<u>August 30, 1970</u>
Isle Of Wight Festival
Afton Down
I.O.W., England

Love Like A Man, Good Morning Little School Girl, No Title, Hobbit, Classical Thing, Scat Thing, I Can't Keep From Crying Sometimes, I'm Going Home, Sweet Little 16.

The 1970 Isle of Wight Festival in England was the third and largest pop festival held on the island. In fact, it was the largest event of its kind, attracting over 600,000 people. It has often been referred to as "the last of the great festivals".

*The **first** Isle of Wight festival in 1968 got started as a fund raising event for the Isle of Wight Indoor Swimming Pool Association and it was ultimately called the "Great South Coast Bank Holiday Pop Festival". It was held on August 31, 1968 at a barley field on Ford's Farm near Godshill. The event was attended by 10,000 people and began at 8:00PM, concluding at 8:30AM the following morning. The performers included: Tyrannosaurus Rex, Ansley Dunbar Retaliation, Plastic Penny, Smile, The Move, Pretty Things, Jefferson Airplane,*

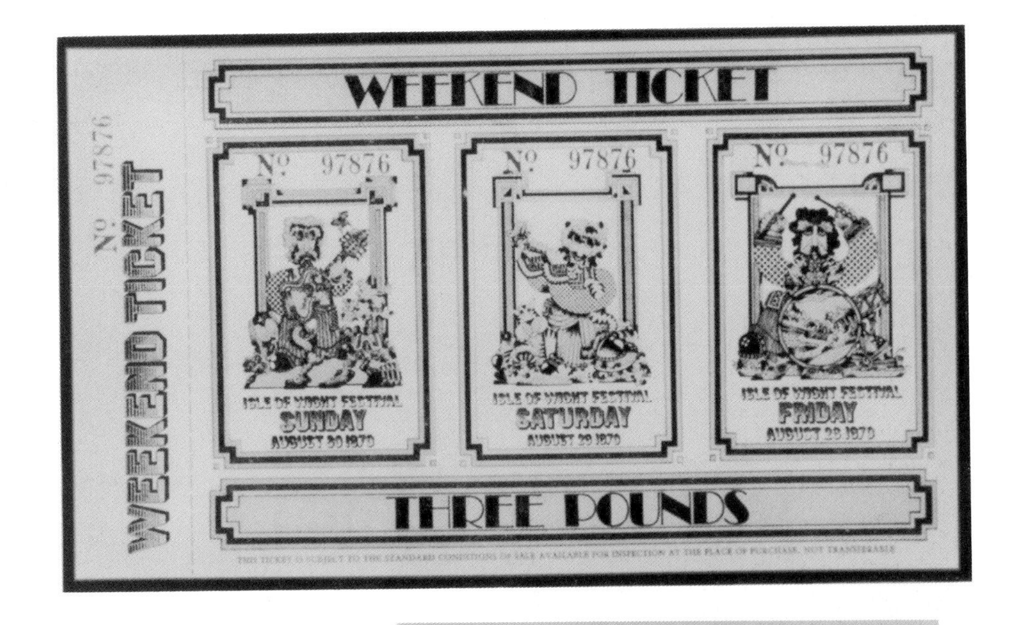

The Crazy World of Arthur Brown, Fairport Convention and The Cherokees.

The ***second*** *Isle of Wight pop festival was again organized by the three Foulk brothers - Ray, Ron & Bill and rock promoter Rikki Farr, who collectively set up Fiery Creations. The second festival would be held at Woodside Bay at Wootton Creek near Ryde. It was to headline Bob Dylan and would also feature The Band. The other performers who appeared during this three day festival in 1969 were - Friday 8/29: Marsupilami, Election, Bonzo Dog Doo-Dah Band and The Nice. Saturday 8/30: Gypsey, Blodwyn Pig, Edgar Broughton Band, Ansley Dunbar Retaliation, Marsha Hunt, Pretty Things, Family, The Who, Fat Mattress, Joe Cocker & The Grease Band and The Moody Blues. Sunday 8/31: Liverpool Scene, Third Ear Band, Indo-Jazz Fusions, Gary Farr, Tom Paxton, Pentangle, Julie Felix, Richie Havens, The Band and Bob Dylan. The audience had grown to nearly 200,000 people by the time Bob Dylan concluded the festival.*

The ***third*** *Isle of Wight Festival in 1970 was to be huge in every way. It was to run a full five days from Wednesday, August 27th through Sunday, August 31st. It took 3-4 weeks to build the 38 acre site at East Afton Down. The event was to include a total of 45 performers, who appeared as follows- Wednesday 8/27: Judas Jump, Rosalie Sorrels, Kathy Smith, Kris Kristofferson & Mighty Baby. Thursday 8/28: Supertramp, Gilberto Gil & Caentano Veloso, Black Widow, Groundhogs & Terry Reid. Friday 8/29: Fairfield Parlour, Hawkwind, Arrival, Lighthouse, Taste, Tony Joe White, Chicago, Family, Procol Harum, Voices of East Harlem & Cactus. Saturday 8/30: John Sebastian, Shawn Philips, Lighthouse, Joni Mitchell, Tiny Tim, Miles Davis,* ***Ten Years After****, Emerson, Lake & Palmer,*

PHOTOS by: BEKEN of COWES, I.O.W.

The Doors, The Who, Melanie and Sly & The Family Stone. Sunday 8/31: Good News, Kris Kristofferson, Ralph McTell, Heaven, Free, Donovan, Pentangle, Moody Blues, Jethro Tull, Jimi Hendrix, Joan Baez, Leonard Cohen and Richie Havens.

The 1970 Isle of Wight Festival included many Woodstock veterans and promised to be everything that Woodstock was, but bigger. Sizewise, the 1970 Isle of Wight Festival was indeed bigger than Woodstock, however it ultimately showed that the Woodstock dream ended in August 1969. The 1970 Isle of Wight Festival had many more problems than Woodstock. Abbie Hoffman was the only protester at Woodstock and Pete Townsend promptly ended that by putting the imprint of a Gibson SG on his head. But, at the 1970 Isle of Wight festival, protesters came in abundance.

The Woodstock festival turned into a free concert primarily because there was no real fence to stop people from coming in, and they entered in an almost innocent way. At the I.O.W. festival adequate barriers had been put in place, but certain people were determined to make it a free concert and violent attempts were made to break down the fences. Reference to the 1970 Isle of Wight Festival as the "last event of its kind" is appropriate. What occurred peacefully at Woodstock turned sinister at the 1970 Isle of Wight festival.

Regardless of how historians will recall the 1970 I.O.W. festival, the music lived up to its billing. It has been said that ***Jimi Hendrix*** *had an off night, but most agree that his performance still had the expected moments of brilliance.* ***The Who*** *put on a particularly great show, which fortunately has been released in its entirety on home video. One account written shortly after the event states that, "Ten Years After were certainly one of the most popular and successful bands of the festival, and were greeted like prophets of the rock age". The Murray Lerner "Message To Love" film released in 1995 offers a fine documentary of the event. It shows that*

Ten Years After were at their peak, as seen in a 5 minute edit of their epic rendition of Al Kooper's, "I Can't Keep From Crying Sometimes".

September 4, 1970
Deutschlandhalle
Berlin, Germany

This event was billed as the "Super Concert '70" and, in addition to Ten Years After, the bill included Jimi Hendrix, Procol Harum, Canned Heat, Cat Mother and Murphy Blend.

September 5, 1970
Hamburg, Germany

September 6, 1970
Love and Peace Festival/Isle of Fehmarn, Germany

Also appearing were: Canned Heat, Emerson Lake & Palmer, Ginger Baker's Airforce, Jimi Hendrix, Procol Harum, Rod Stewart & The Faces, Taste and others. Sadly, the Isle Of Fehmarn Festival was to be the final concert performance by Jimi Hendrix.

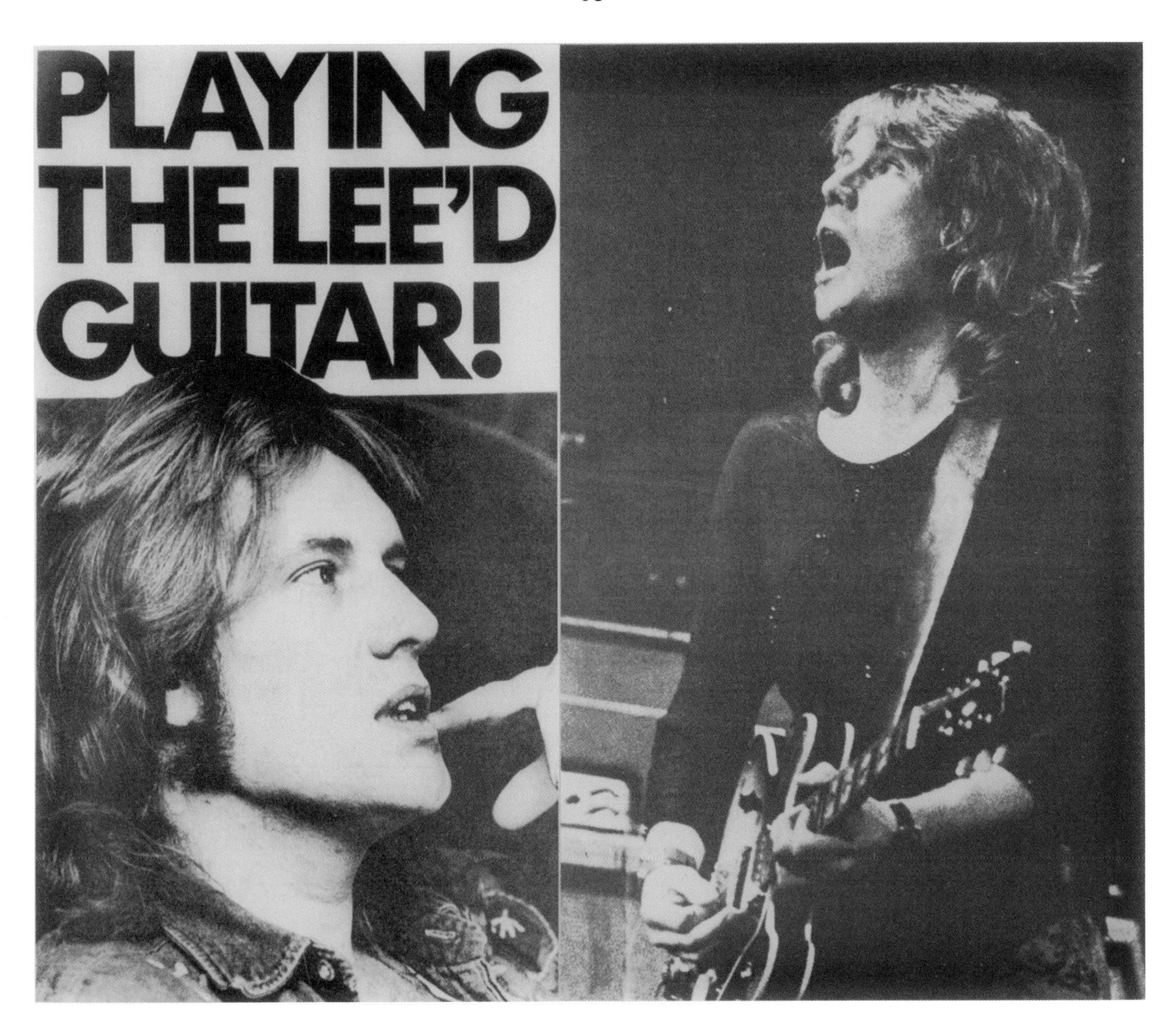

October 17, 1970
MELODY MAKER reports a Ten Years After tour of Britain:

Ten Years After will do special concert dates in Britain at the end of the month. TYA have chosen specific ballrooms to appear in and requested that admission prices should be kept as low as possible.

Dates so far fixed include Bournemouth Pavilion, Dunstable Civic Hall, Weston Super-Mare Winter Gardens Pavilion, and Liverpool St. Georges Hall. The group is currently completing work on a new album at London's Olympic Studios and leave for a three week tour of America, opening at Madison Square Garden in New York on November 13th.

They will do more British dates on their return and are planning to use a specially designed PA system during all their appearances.

October 27, 1970
Olympia
Paris, France

Chicken Shack is the opening act.

The concert is broadcast in France on Europe 1 radio. The songs performed included: Love Like A Man, Good Morning Little School Girl, I Say Yeah, Hobbit, She Lies In The Morning, Spider In My Web, I'm Going Home.

November 1, 1970
Pavillion
Bournemouth,
England

November 2, 1970
Civic Hall
Dunstable,
England

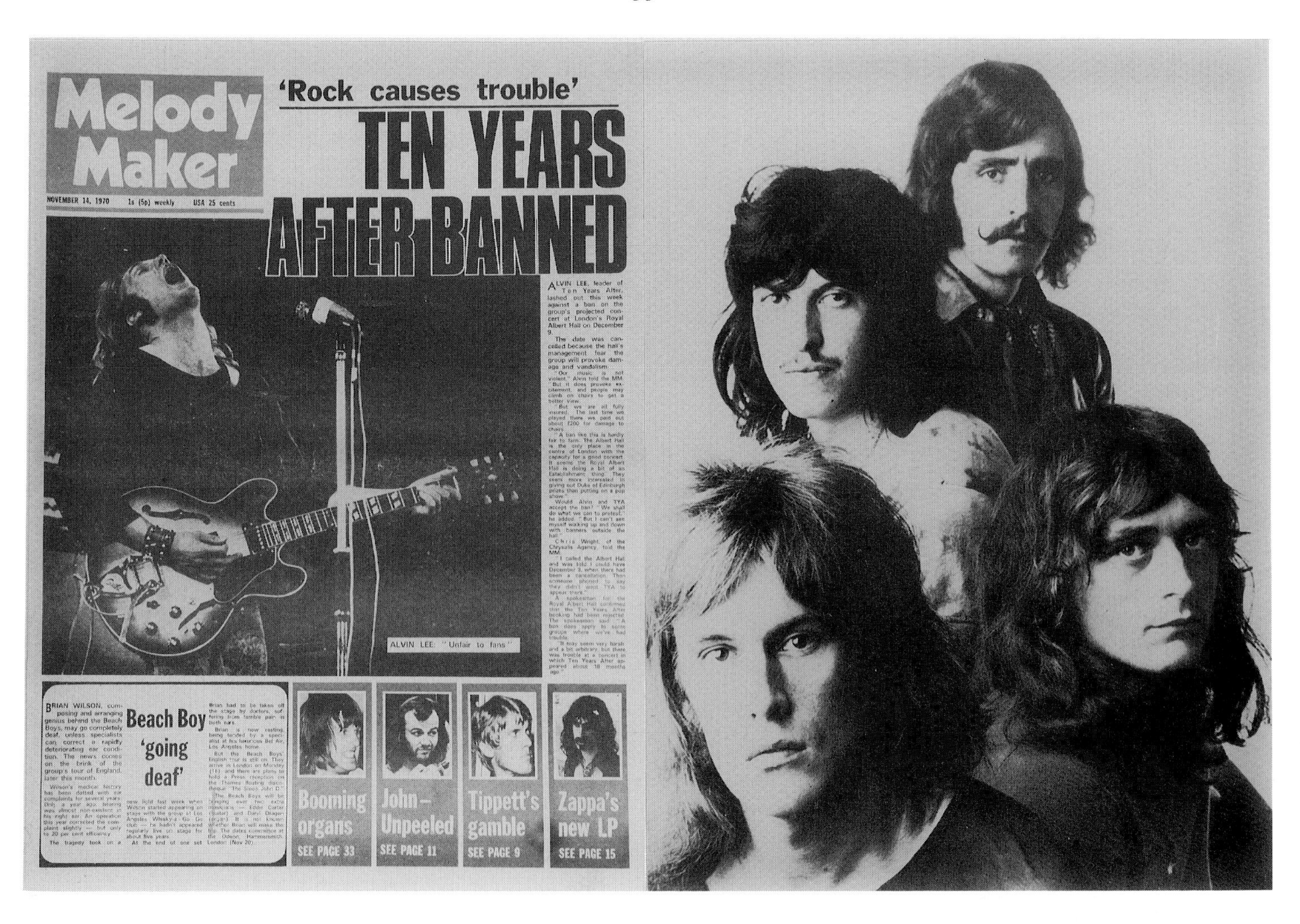

Melody Maker

NOVEMBER 14, 1970 1s (5p) weekly USA 25 cents

'Rock causes trouble'

TEN YEARS AFTER BANNED

ALVIN LEE, leader of Ten Years After, lashed out this week against a ban on the group's projected concert at London's Royal Albert Hall on December 9.

The date was cancelled because the hall's management fear the group will provoke damage and vandalism.

ALVIN LEE: "Unfair to fans"

Beach Boy 'going deaf'

Booming organs SEE PAGE 33

John – Unpeeled SEE PAGE 11

Tippett's gamble SEE PAGE 9

Zappa's new LP SEE PAGE 15

Nov 11 & 12, 1970
Eastown Theater
Detroit, Michigan

November 13, 1970
Madison Garden
New York, New York

Ten Years After perform for the first time at MSG before a sell out crowd.

November 14, 1970
The Spectrum
Philadelphia, PA

MELODY MAKER reports Dec. 9 TYA Concert at London's Albert Hall canceled

A spokesman for the Royal Albert Hall confirmed that the Ten Years After booking had been rejected, saying "A ban does apply to some groups where we've had trouble. It may seem very harsh and a bit arbitrary, but there was trouble at a concert in which Ten Years After appeared about 18 months ago."

Alvin Lee's response: "Our music is not violent, but it does provoke excitement and people may climb on chairs to get a better view. But we are fully insured. The last time we played there we paid out about 200 pounds for damage to chairs."

November 16, 1970
Memorial Auditorium
Dallas, Texas

Love Like A Man, I'm Coming On, Slow Blues (not "Slow Blues in C"), "Since My Baby Left Me" (traditional blues tune, actual title unknown - very similar to the song performed at the 3/7/69 Fillmore West concert), Good Morning Little School Girl, Hobbit, She Lies In The Morning, I'm Going Home, Sweet Little Sixteen.

November 17, 1970
Municipal Auditorium
San Antonio, Texas

November 18, 1970
Sam Houston Coliseum
Houston, Texas

November 19, 1970
Jailai Fonton
Miami, Florida

November 20, 1970
The Syndrome
Chicago, Illinois

November 21, 1970
Community Center
Berkeley, California

Love Like A Man, I'm Coming On, Slow

Blues, Good Morning Little School Girl, Hobbit, She Lies In The Morning, Going Home, Sweet Little Sixteen.

November 22, 1970
Hic Arena
Honolulu, Hawaii

November 25, 1970
Center Arena
Seattle, Washington

November 26, 1970
Freedom Palace
Kansas City, MO

November 27, 1970
The Warehouse
New Orleans, LA

November 28, 1970
San Jose, California

November 29, 1970
Sports Arena
San Diego, California

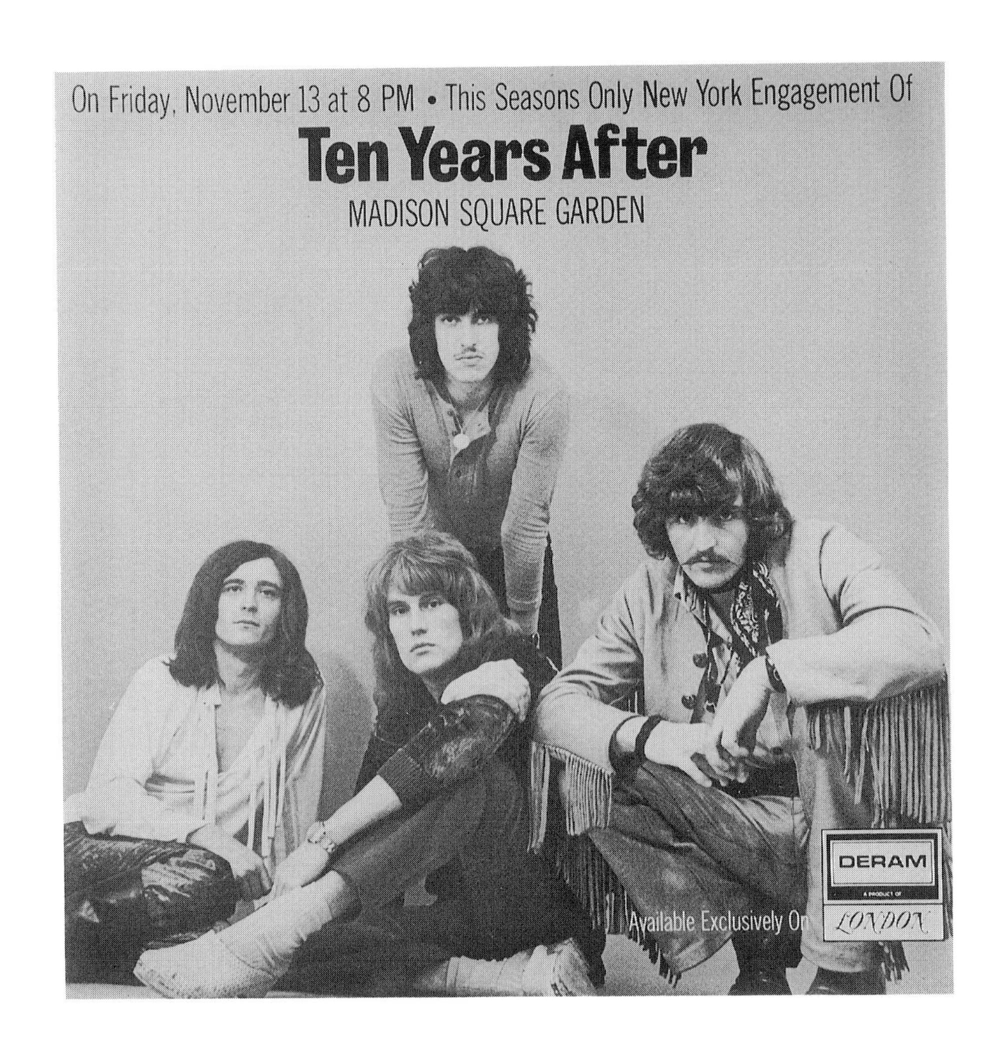

December 1, 1970
Municipal Auditorium
Atlanta, Georgia

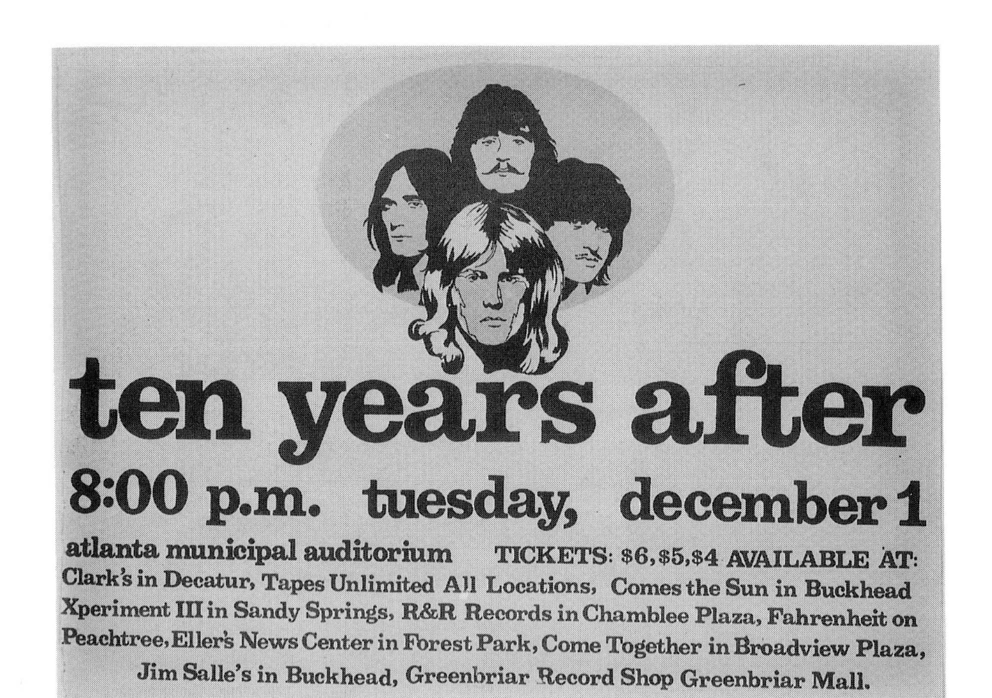

December 26, 1970
Release of the sixth Ten Years After LP: "Watt" Deram DES 18050

The studio tracks are recorded at Olympic Studios. Side One includes: I'm Coming On (Alvin Lee 3:45), *My Baby Left Me* (Alvin Lee 5:20), *Think About The Times* (Alvin Lee 4:41), *I Say Yeah* (Alvin Lee 5:15). Side Two: *The Band With No Name* (Alvin Lee 1:35), *Gonna Run* (Alvin Lee 6:00), *She Lies In The Morning* (Alvin Lee 7:21) *and, recorded live at the Isle Of Wight Festival, Sweet Little Sixteen* (Chuck Berry 4:08). *This album gets to #5 in the U.K. and to #21 in the U.S.*

Alvin Lee: *"I was campaigning for a break, because in those days, we would do like a 10-week tour of America, come back to England for three days, do a five-week tour of Germany, another three days off, Scandinavia and Italy, and then somebody would say, 'You're in the studio next week for the next album'. And I was writing songs in the taxi on the way to the studio, and not really having any time. Watt was*

definitely suffering from no time to write. In fact, even the title - it should have been titled 'What', and it came out as Watt."

<u>January 1971</u>
Circus Krone
Munich, Germany

Love Like A Man, No Title, Once There Was A Time, Slow Blues In C (the song and lyrics have not yet evolved into the familiar version that was later included on the Recorded Live LP), Hobbit, One Of These Days, She Lies In The Morning, I'm Going Home, Sweet Little Sixteen.

<u>January 14, 1971</u>
Deutschlandhalle
Berlin, Germany

Love Like A Man, No Title, Once There Was A Time (Alvin says,"this is a new number that's never been recorded -

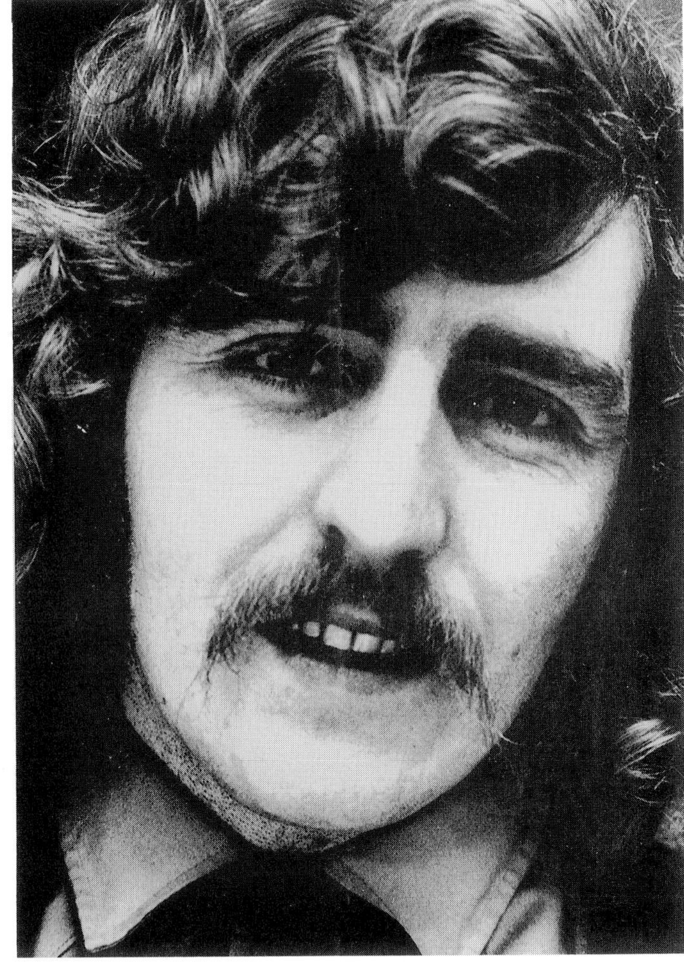

anyone making a bootleg recording, suggest you copyright the song as well"), Slow Blues In C (different lyrics), Hobbit, One Of These Days, "You're Walking Around With Your Head In The Sky" (actual title unknown, a rare number never released on an LP - the song evolves into an extended jam with a pulsating counter-rhythm by Ric Lee and a long organ solo by Chick Churchill before Alvin takes over on guitar), I'm Going Home.

February 26, 1971
Concert Hall
Gothenburg, Sweden

February 27, 1971
K. B. Hallen
Copenhagen, Denmark

Love Like A Man, No Title, Once There Was A Time, Hobbit, One Of These Days, "You're Walking Around With Your Head In The Sky" (introduced as "another new one"), She Lies In The Morning (great extended solo by Alvin), I'm Going Home.

February 28, 1971
Music Hall
Hamburg, Germany

March 7, 1971
Munich, Germany

March 8, 1971
Dusseldorf, Germany

March 9, 1971
Munster, Germany

March 10, 1971
Hall 16 du Wacken
Strasbourg, France

The Mick Abraham's Band opens for Ten Years After. Partial set list: Love Like A Man, No Title, Slow Blues In C, She Lies In The Morning, I'm Going Home, Sweet Little Sixteen.

March 13, 1971
Casino
Montreux, Switzerland

Ten Years After perform afternoon and evening shows supported by the Mick Abrams Band.

March 17, 1971
PalaEuropa
Rome, Italy

Love Like A Man, No Title, Once There Was A Time, Slow Blues In C, Hobbit, One Of These Days, I'm Going Home.

<u>March 25, 1971</u>
Brussels, Belgium

Supertramp opens. Ten Years After perform without Chick Churchill who was ill.

<u>April 8, 1971</u>
Cobo Hall
Detroit, Michigan

<u>April 14, 1971</u>
Coliseum
Indianapolis, Indiana

<u>April 16, 1971</u>
Boston Garden
Boston, Massachusetts

Supporting acts were Cactus and Humble Pie.

<u>April 18, 1971</u>
State Fair Coliseum
Syracuse, New York

<u>April 20, 1971</u>
Fillmore East
New York City, NY

Love Like A Man, No Title, Silly Thing, Once There Was A Time (introduced by Alvin as "a new song you've never heard before"), Slow Blues In C, Hobbit, One Of These Days (Alvin says "we're going to do another new number, this is in the spiritual key of E"). A note of interest is that Alvin incorporates the low E tuning key riff into this song, which was later to

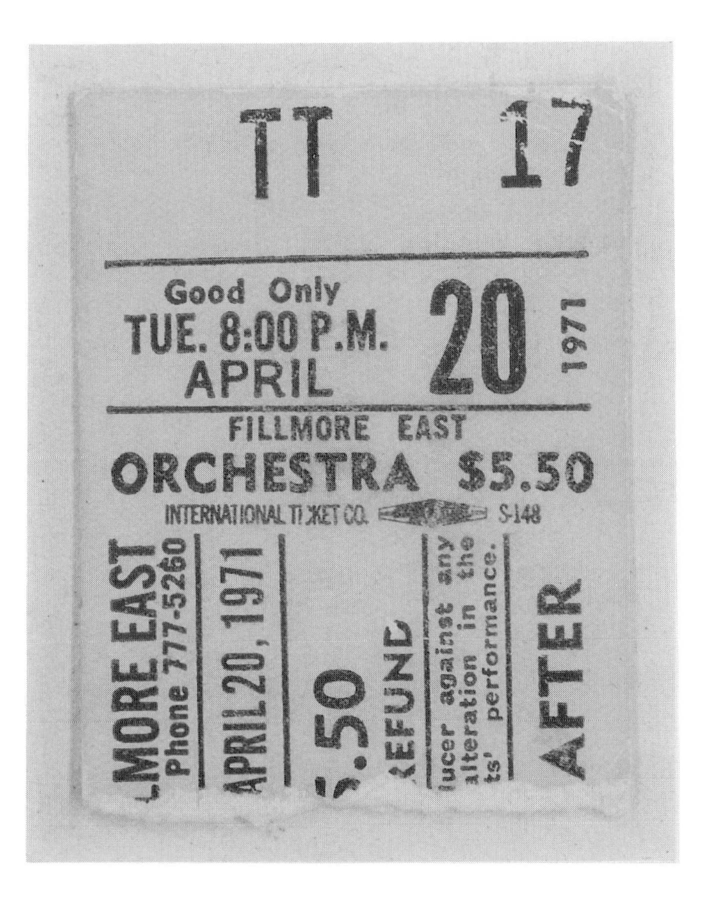

TEN YEARS AFTER

Ten Years After was formed in 1967, bringing together the collective talents of Alvin Lee (lead guitar and vocals), Leo Lyons (bass) Chick Churchill (organ) and Ric Lee (drums). Their latest album, on London Records, is entitled *Watt*.

J. GEILS BAND

The J. Geils Band is a Boston-based blues group that has been together in various forms for the past six years. Their present lineup includes J. Geils (lead guitar), Seth Justman (keyboards), Danny Klein (bass), Magic Dick (harp) and Stephen Bladd (drums). The band now records for Atlantic, and this is their second appearance at Fillmore East.

become a regular part of the "I Can't Keep From Crying Sometimes" guitar crescendo, She Lies In The Morning, I'm Going Home, Sweet Little Sixteen, Good Morning Little School Girl. (The opening act was the J. Geils Band).

April 29, 1971
Memorial Coliseum
Portland, Oregon

Concert review from "THE OREGONIAN":

Several thousand young people, most of them long hairs looking for heavy sounds of acid rock, got what they bargained for in headliner group Ten Years After at the Memorial Coliseum Thursday night in the most together concert heard there in some time. Ten Years After came on after an intermission marred when a young man jumped out of a coliseum window and was removed to a hospital. Alvin Lee's band can mock other groups music with much tongue-in-cheek but, when it chooses to play, the music flows and there's very little adrenalin left in the system after it's over. It is a physical, emotional group to hear and the casual listener just does not exist. You must become involved in Ten Years After's music. Lee is a guitar master and proved he can do just about anything with his electric six-stringer. He's obviously studied his instrument but he's also obviously a genius in picking and arranging the band's music. Besides Alvin, there is Ric Lee on drums, Chick Churchill on keyboards and Leo Lyons, the speed-fingered bassist.

April 30, 1971
Winterland
San Francisco, CA

May 2, 1971
Arena
Long Beach, CA

The support act was Humble Pie. The show is sold out and 400 disappointed fans who can't get in are cleared out with tear gas after engaging in a bottle throwing spree.

May 1971
The Forum
Los Angeles, CA

Love Like A Man, No Title, Once There Was A Time, Slow Blues In C, One Of These Days, Hobbit, She Lies In The Morning, I'm Going Home, Sweet Little Sixteen.

<u>August 1, 1971</u>
Merriweather Post Pavilion
Columbia, Maryland

The opening act is Mylon LeFevre & Holy Smoke. This was an afternoon show and a minor riot occurred when fans without tickets tore down the fences and set fire to the security shed.

August 6, 1971
Manhattan College
Gaelic Park, Bronx
New York City

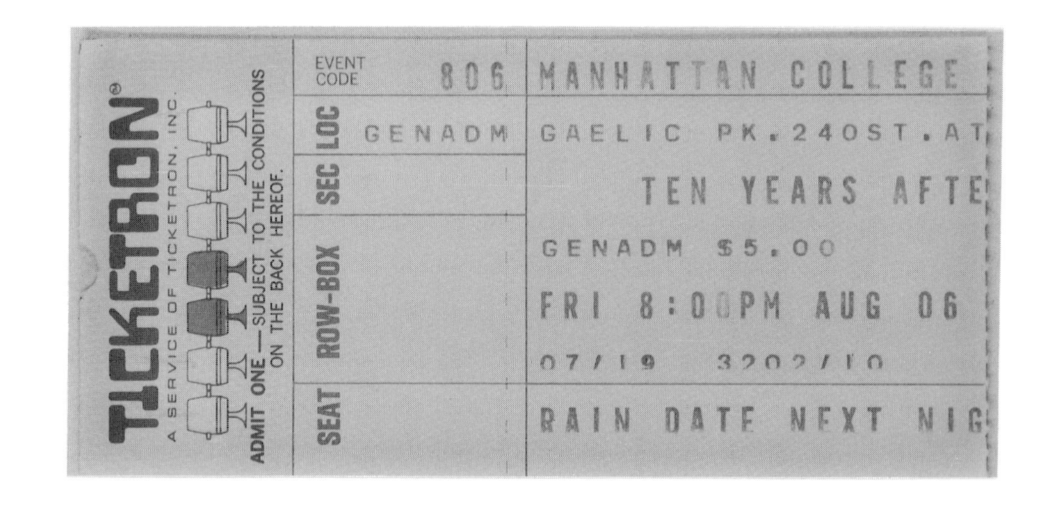

The opening act is the Edgar Winter Band.

Concert review from THE SOUNDS by Chuck Pullin:

The audience had come to see Ten Years After without question. Many simply arrived minutes before Ten Years After took the stage, missing the balance of Edgar Winter's fine set. Over 8,000 tickets were sold up to the day of the concert, while another 3-4,000 lined up the afternoon of the show for tickets. Despite a rash of violence that has plagued many outdoor concerts this summer, the audience was well behaved and respectful of Alvin, Chick, Ric and Leo. Without question, the concert was exciting. Many bands lose whatever magic they contain after working together for some period of time. However, that is not the case with TYA. Even though they had not played for a few months, they were as tight and as creative as ever. Leo Lyons' bass runs were visual to the eye and splendid to the ear as ever. Ric Lee still has that great drum style that puts him high above the other drummers that are working in rock music today. I can't recall Chick Churchill's

organ playing sounding better. And finally, Alvin Lee...Most of the yells between songs were aimed at Alvin, who has the image that most audiences want of rock guitarists. However, Alvin is one of the hardest working, creative guitarists in music today and a fine musician. His style and drive are beyond compare, and he thrilled the audience by using his harmonica and microphone stand on the neck of his guitar much in the same way guitarists use a slide technique. Alvin's style and skill have grown over the last few years, and he still sings quite well. Many of the selections played were from the band's new album "A Space In Time". "Hard Monkeys" and "Baby Won't You Let Me Rock 'n Roll You" were songs that went down well, followed by an encore of "I'm Going Home". The 12,000-plus fans that came out to see Ten Years After reaffirmed the popularity and fine music the band is able to effortlessly create. It's good to see them work and remain untouched from the changes other bands go through. For some that question the popularity of the band, I can safely say it was not owing to a mass advertising effort, rather the simple fact that they are a fine band and discriminating audiences as in the past have the good taste to see them at work.

Aug 20 & 21, 1971
Paramount Northwest
Seattle, Washington

Concert review from THE SEATTLE TIMES by Carole Beers:

Ten Years After, the English quartet that for seven years has been doing instant replays of funky fifties rock 'n roll, played a fantastic concert before a capacity audience in the first of two sold out shows last night at the Paramount Northwest. They have seven albums to their credit, but their lasting appeal is obviously due to a keen sense of showmanship. They play what their fans like and want to hear; the tumultuous shouting, stomping and boogying of the audience after and sometimes during their numbers was proof of that. What they played was a little blues, played in a B.B. King style, a little country, a little jazz and a lot of hard driving rock. The pace never slowed, and melodies and rhythms were varied enough to keep interest and excitement high.

Ten Years After works well as a group, but a lot of credit must go to two especially fine musicians: Alvin Lee, who plays lead guitar and is described in the biography as "sex symbol for the outside", and Leo Lyons, described as the "fastest bass in the West". Besides playing great lead guitar, with intricate fingering and the use of the microphone pole to bar chords, Lee hollers a song pretty well and now and then blows blues harmonica.

Lyons matches Lee's energetic playing with fine bass work. He plays the bass guitar almost as if it were the lead, with arpeggios and runs that show marked jazz influence. During solo numbers and duets with Lee, his fast and excellent fingering earned the standing ovations they received.

The drummer, Ric Lee, is above average and played a fine solo. The audience shook the building with their demands for an encore. After what seemed like five minutes of yelling and clapping, the audience got their frequently requested favorite, "I'm Going Home". It was Ten Years After's big song in the film Woodstock, and it was no less a success last night. Concerts West and Paramount Northwest deserve credit for bringing such a great show.

July 24, 1971
Memorial Auditorium
Dallas, Texas

August 28, 1971
Kiel Auditorium
St. Louis, Missouri

The J. Geils Band opens. Towards the end of the show, Alvin Lee tells the crowd to move closer. The fans storm the stage, the riot police are called in and Ten Years After are unable to complete the last song.

September 1971
Release of the single: "I'd Love To Change The World"/"Let The Sky Fall"

By December "I'd Love To Change The World" becomes a top 40 hit, and it still receives frequent airplay!

Alvin Lee:
"I was embarrassed about that song because I don't like preaching in music. I like music to be apolitical and I thought I was maybe pushing my luck. To start off, I was criticizing freaks and hairies in the first line, and I thought, I'm gonna upset a lot of people with this song, and I nearly didn't even put the song forward. But it was a good song although I don't think it's a typical Ten Years After song. In fact, we never have played it live. The record company would come to the gig and say, 'When are you doing your hit?' and I would say, 'We don't play it - What's the point? It's a hit already'. But, you know, it was evident that people didn't come to the concerts to hear us play the records, they came for the whole emersion in the live concert thing."

September 14, 1971
Bristol, England

Ten Years After open a British tour, all eleven dates are sold out.

September 15, 1971
Philharmonic Hall/Liverpool, England

September 16, 1971
City Hall
Newcastle, England

Sept. 18 & 19, 1971
Coliseum Theater
London, England

On Saturday, Ten Years After are the first band to play a midnight show at London's famous Coliseum Theater. It is followed by an evening show on Sunday.

DISC AND MUSIC ECHO concert review by Gavin Petrie:

"I wonder how much of the applause and adulation that forced Ten Years After to come back for a third encore at London's Coliseum this week should have gone to the greats of rock-n-roll like Carl Perkins, Chuck Berry, etc., whose songs it was that finally got the audience to their feet."

"And that's no put down of TYA. They are a good, strong colorful band - but seem a bit aimless until they get to the rock-n-roll encores. Their blues base shows right from the beginning, but then it wanders off to some raunchy R-n-B, to country guitar pickin', flamenco, jazzy runs, acid rock, then back to rock."

"It's a joy to see and hear four such excellent musicians work together and individually without interest flagging. Leo Lyons' all-action bass playing was a knockout. Ric Lee's drum solo was just the right length, and was vibrant and exciting. Alvin Lee, of course, is still the strength, although I am disappointed that such a talented guitarist is not a bit more creative. Echoes of other styles from other times still creep through. If TYA wanted to they could be the best rock-n-roll band in the world, but just now they are an exciting band without a style. For all that I'd go see them again just to grab some of that excitement !"

September 20, 1971
Guildhall
Southampton, England

September 22, 1971
De Montford Hall
Leicester, England

September 26, 1971
Free Trade Hall
Manchester, England

September 27, 1971
St. George's Hall
Bradford, England

September 28, 1971
City Hall
Sheffield, England

October 1971
Release of
the seventh
Ten Years After LP:
"A Space In Time"
Columbia KC 30801

This is the first Ten Years After release on the Columbia & Chrysalis record label. When the Ten Years After deal expired with Decca and London, Chris Wright and Terry Ellis began marketing the act with the American record labels, one of which was Columbia - headed by Clive Davis. Davis saw Ten Years After perform in New York and in his own biography about the music business states that the $1 million he paid the band was the first million dollar contract he ever made.

Side One includes: One Of These Days (Alvin Lee 5:55), *Here They Come* (Alvin Lee 4:38), *I'd Love To Change The World* (Alvin Lee 3:43), *Over The Hill* (Alvin Lee 2:27) and *Baby Won't You Let Me Rock & Roll You* (Alvin Lee 2:15). *Side Two contains: Once There Was A Time* (Alvin Lee 3:20), *Let The Sky Fall* (Alvin Lee 4:18), *Hard Monkeys* (Alvin Lee 3:10), *I've Been There Too* (Alvin Lee 5:43) and *Uncle Jam* (Alvin Lee, Ric Lee, Chick Churchill & Leo Lyons 1:57). *The album went gold for half a million sales and reached #17 in the U.S. charts, and #36 in the U.K. It stayed in the charts for over six months.*

Alvin Lee:
"I eventually dug my heels in and said, 'I have just got to have some time and I wanted six months off, which was ludicrous. I think it ended up about three months off. It gave me time to sit with the acoustic guitar and write some good songs, and I think Space In Time was the culmination of that. A bit of time and there was space to write - Space In Time. I think it is still my favorite Ten Years After album, because we had time to work on it."

<u>October 4, 1971</u>
Town Hall
Birmingham, England

<u>October 15, 1971</u>
"Space In Time" is released in the U.K.

<u>November 1, 1971</u>
Boston Garden
Boston, Massachusetts

Ten Years After start their 12th tour of America. The set list for this concert is: One Of These Days, No Title, Once There Was A Time, Good Morning Little School Girl, Hobbit, Slow Blues In C, Jam, Classical Thing, Scat Thing, I Can't Keep From Crying Sometimes, I'm Going Home, Baby Won't You Let Me Rock & Roll You. She Lies In The Morning has been replaced in the set with an extended jam. Near riotous conditions prevail at this show and the performance had to be stopped several times due to fans rushing the stage.

<u>November 10, 1971</u>
Sports Arena
San Diego, CA

<u>November 11, 1971</u>
The Forum
Los Angeles, California

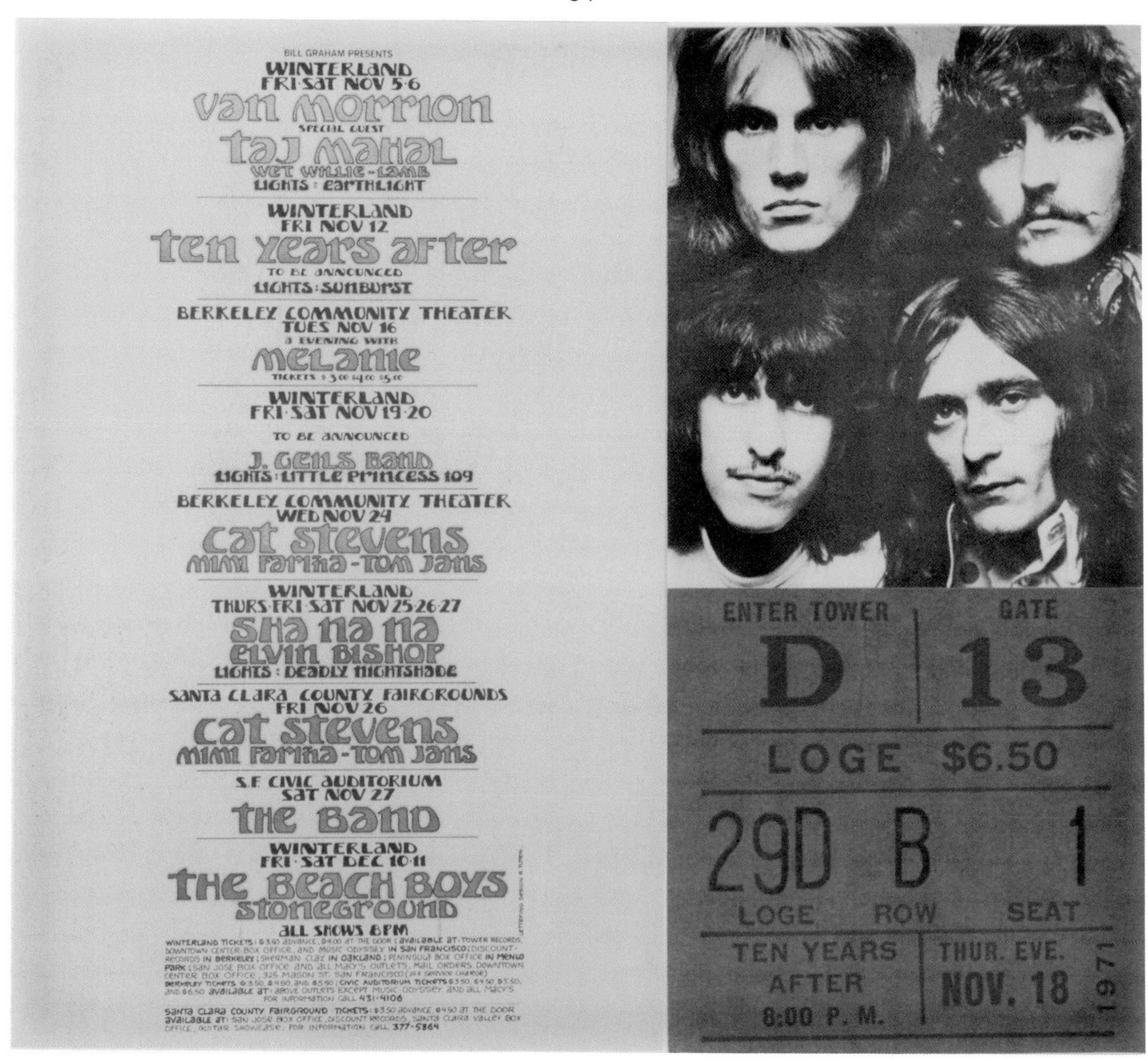

One Of These Days, No Title, Once There Was A Time, Good Morning Little Schoolgirl, Hobbit, Slow Blues In C, Jam (Alvin says, "we've been doing a jam every night, this is another in a series"), Classical Thing, Scat Thing, I Can't Keep From Crying Some-times, Going Home, Baby Won't You Let Me Rock & Roll You.

<u>November 12, 1971</u>
Winterland
San Francisco, CA

<u>November 13, 1971</u>
Hic Arena
Honolulu, Hawaii

<u>November 16, 1971</u>
Coliseum
Denver, Colorado

<u>November 18, 1971</u>
Madison Square Garden
New York City, NY

<u>November 19, 1971</u>
William & Mary College
Williamsburg, VA

<u>November 20, 1971</u>
Duke University
Durham, NC

<u>November 21, 1971</u>
Cobo Hall
Detroit, Michigan

<u>November 22, 1971</u>
Dane County College
Madison, Wisconsin

<u>November 24, 1971</u>
Homer Hesterly Armory
Tampa, Florida

<u>Nov 25, 1971</u>
Fiesta del Sol,
Puerto Rico

In addition to Ten Years After, the following other artists were scheduled: the Allman Brothers, the Beach Boys, the Chambers Brothers,

Ike & Tina Turner, John Mayall, Jose Feliciano, Lamb, Mountain, Poco, Procol Harum, Richie Havens and Stevie Wonder.

December 1971
R.A.I.
Amsterdam, Holland

One Of These Days, No Title, Once There Was A Time, Good Morning Little School Girl, Hobbit, Classical Thing, Scat Thing, I Can't Keep From Crying Sometimes, Silly Thing, I'm Going Home, Sweet Little Sixteen. (The show is bootlegged as a double LP "Live In Amsterdam").

January 1972
Release of the single: "Baby Won't You Let Me Rock & Roll You"/"Once There Was A Time"

January 8, 1972
University
Reading, England

Ten Years After start a tour of British universities, which will include visits to campuses at: Birmingham, Sheffield, Lancaster, Cardiff, Liverpool, Leeds, Brighton, Nottingham, Salford and Leicester. Supporting Ten Years After at selected gigs is Jude, a group formed by ex-Procol Harum guitarist ***Robin Trower*** *and ex-Jethro Tull drummer Clive Bunker. Jude was the first band that Chris Wright and Terry Ellis signed for their new* ***"Chrysalis"*** *record company.*

Chris Wright:
"That project was an

HURRY 50 FREE ALBUMS MUST BE WON SEE INSIDE

MUSIC IS THE MESSAGE

sounds

August 28, 1971 6p

HAVENS' STORMY FOREST Page 9

FLINT IN THE FUTURE Page 11

TEN YEARS AFTER exclusive LP review inside

BRITISH DATES FOR TRAFFIC

Concerts with Seatrain

TRAFFIC WILL do four special British concert dates this September—two of them with US band Seatrain who are making their first appearance in Britain.

Both bands appear at the Royal Albert Hall on September 23—the first time Traffic have appeared there—and at Liverpool Stadium on the 25th.

Traffic's solo concerts are at Plymouth Guild Hall 19, and at Leicester De Montfort Hall 20.

Seatrain play a solo concert at Birmingham's Kinetic Circus on September 24.

Traffic's live album "Welcome To The Canteen", recorded at Fairfield Hall, Croydon, and the Oz benefit concert, is released on September 3. They are currently in the studios recording new material for an album to be released at the end of October. The band leave for a four-week tour of the States on September 30 and go on from there for concerts in Japan.

DEAD DUE IN SPRING

GRATEFUL DEAD make their first British concert appearances in early spring. Venues and dates are being set for the band around late March following dates in Europe.

Dead's live double album will be released in early October and the Jerry Garcia solo album will be out early in the new year.

BROUGHTON TALK-IN CENTRE PAGES

BRUCE, FREE HYDE PARK CONCERT P.2

ANOTHER YES MAN PAGE 7

BO DIDDLEY R&B's Muhammad Ali

New Musical Express EVERY FRIDAY 5p

No 1286 Week ending September 18, 1971

RETURN OF THE EVERLYS

Curved Air

James Taylor scare

WHEN ROD STEWART WAS SACKED

TEN YEARS TOUR SELL OUT

Extra dates added New album set

TEN YEARS AFTER, who opened their first British tour for 18 months to a standing room only audience at Bristol on Tuesday have virtually sold out all of the 11 dates so far fixed and plans are now in hand to extend the tour, adding at least two dates in Scotland.

This weekend the group become the first ever to play a midnight concert at London's famous Coliseum Theatre. They do a midnight show on Saturday followed by an evening performance on Sunday.

The group's new album "A Space In Time" has now been set for release here on October 16 on the Chrysalis label but there are no plans to issue their current American hit single "I'd Love To Change The World," a track from the album.

TYA and their manager Chris Wright are known to be reluctant ...

Nice album suppressed

TEN YEARS AFTER: Alvin Lee

HAZLEWOOD TALKS ABOUT FRANK AND NANCY

INSIDE: PAUL SIMON, SEEKERS, CLIFF, BASSEY

New Musical Express EVERY FRIDAY 5p

No 1299 Week ending December 25, 1971

NMExclusive.. NMExclusive.. NMExclusive.. NMExclusive..

TEN YEARS AFTER BRITISH TOUR SET

ALVIN LEE Ten Years After

TEN YEARS AFTER — who returned from the United States last week with their first Gold Disc, awarded for one million dollars' sales of "A Space In Time"— open the New Year with a tour of selected British universities. It will be the first time the outfit has played the university circuit since 1969.

The tour opens at READING on January 8, then visits universities at BIRMINGHAM (13), SHEFFIELD (14), LANCASTER (15), CARDIFF (19), LIVERPOOL (21), LEEDS (22), BRIGHTON (25), NOTTINGHAM (27), SALFORD (28) and LEICESTER (29).

Supporting Ten Years After at Birmingham, Cardiff, Brighton and Nottingham will be Jude — the group formed by ex-Procol Harum guitarist Robin Trower and ex-Jethro Tull drummer Clive Bunker. Supertramp is the second act at Sheffield, Salford and Leicester. Supporting acts for the other four venues are still being finalised.

"This tour is something we've wanted to do for a while now," Alvin Lee explained. "It was the University audiences, along with the London clubs like the Marquee, who picked up on us in the first place and we want to keep our communication with this audience."

T. Rex Jan concert

Bolan solo on benefit album

September 8, 1973 U.S./Canada 50c 7p

NEW MUSICAL EXPRESS

WORLD'S LARGEST SELLING WEEKLY MUSIC PAPER

Three ex-Byrds and a Burrito here this month – country package dates

The ultimate STONES low-down

TEN YEARS AFTER TOUR

And Alvin goes gospel

On the eve of the nationwide tour, a complete fact-packed discography, analysis of every record they ever made

A QUIET WHIFF

TEN YEARS AFTER hit the road for a special British tour — aimed at giving the lie to a split within the band — which kicks off at Plymouth Guildhall on Saturday week (15). Exclusive dates are listed on p.4 of this week's NME.

In the same article Alvin Lee describes the tour as "experimental".

Also revealed: details of his upcoming solo gospel album.

*unmitigated disaster, I saw them on their first engagement and it was terrible. A few months later I saw them on their last, although, at the time, the group didn't know it. Robin went away and came back with another band featuring a new drummer and Jimmy Dwar, the bass player, on vocals. It was their first appearance at Keil, Germany where a rapturous audience of over 5000, there to see Ten Years After, gave the group three encores. Not long afterwards came **'Bridge of Sighs'**, which was the first Chrysalis platinum album."*

Alvin Lee remarks from the NEW MUSICAL EXPRESS:

"This tour is something we've wanted to do for a while now, it was the University audiences, along with the London clubs like the Marquee, who picked up on us in the first place and we want to keep our communication with this audience."

<u>January 13, 1972</u>
University
Birmingham, England

Supported by Jude with Robin Trower and Clive Bunker.

<u>January 14, 1972</u>
University
Sheffield, England

Supported by Supertramp.

<u>January 15, 1972</u>
University
Lancaster, England

<u>January 19, 1972</u>
University
Cardiff, England

<u>January 21, 1972</u>
University
Liverpool, England

<u>January 22, 1972</u>
University
Leeds, England

<u>January 25, 1972</u>
University
Brighton, England

Supported by Jude.

<u>January 27, 1972</u>
University
Nottingham, England

Supported by Jude.

<u>January 28, 1972</u>
University
Salford, England

Supported by Supertramp.

<u>January 29, 1972</u>
University
Leicester, England

Supported by Supertramp.

<u>February 1972</u>
K.B. Hallen
Copenhagen, Denmark

<u>February 21, 1972</u>
Concert Hall
Gothenburg, Sweden

<u>March 1972</u>
Release of the eighth Ten Years After LP: "Alvin Lee & Company" Deram DES 18064

The album consists of previously unreleased tracks recorded for Deram, including the two tracks that had appeared on the first Ten Years After single in February 1968.

Side One: The Sounds (Alvin Lee 4:04), *Rock Your Mama* (Alvin Lee 2:53), *Hold Me Tight* (Alvin Lee 2:16) *and Standing At The Crossroads* (E. Johnson/E. Campbell/P. James 3:46). *Side Two: Portable People* (Alvin Lee 2:12) and *Boogie On* (Alvin Lee 14:44). *This LP reaches #55 in the U.S. charts.*

<u>March 3, 1972</u>
Deutschlandhalle
Berlin, Germany

One Of These Days, Once There Was A

Time, Standing At The Station, Good Morning Little School Girl, Slow Blues In C, Jam, Sweet Little Sixteen, Baby Won't You Let Me Rock & Roll You.

March 8, 1972
Ebertshalle
Ludwigshafen, Germany

March 25, 1972
Brussels, Belgium

March 28, 1972
Bolzano, Italy

March 29, 1972
Reggio, Italy

March 30, 1972
Rome, Italy

April 1, 1972
Festhalle
Frankfurt, Germany

April 2, 1972
Karlsruhe, Germany

April 3, 1972
Festhalle
Bern, Switzerland

The set list includes You Give Me Loving which is introduced by Alvin as "a new number".

April 13, 1972
Ten Years After begin another North American Tour.

April 16, 1972
Memorial Auditorium
Buffalo, New York

Procol Harum opens for Ten Years After.

April 28, 1972
Coliseum
Vancouver, BC

May 4, 1972
Nippon Budokan
Tokyo, Japan

Ten Years After with Procol Harum. The TYA set list is: One Of These Days, Once There Was A Time, Good Morning Little School Girl, Hobbit, Slow Blues In C, Scat Thing, I Can't Keep From Crying Sometimes, I'm Going Home/Blue Suede Shoes, Sweet Little Sixteen.

May 6, 1972
Koseinenkin Hall
Osaka, Japan

May 7, 1972
Festival Hall
Osaka, Japan

May 27, 1972
Community Center
Tucson, Arizona

With Procol Harum.

June 1972
Ten Years After record the tracks for "Rock & Roll Music To The World"

August 13, 1972
Berkshire - Reading, England

Ten Years After headlines on the third

FREE ELP and JETHRO in JAPAN

NEW MUSICAL EXPRESS

SLY STONE: Now you see him now you don't ...

DAVID GEFFEN: Taking care of Neil and Joni...

BOWIE: Will the Dorchester ever be the same again?

JULY 29, 1972 U.S./Canada 50c 6p

TYA FESTIVAL TOP

Reading bill toppers, new album in September

TEN YEARS AFTER make their first British appearance since January when they top the bill on the third and last night of the Reading Jazz, Blues and Rock Festival on Sunday, August 13.

It will be the first festival TYA have played in this country since the Isle of Wight in 1970, and something of a nostalgic gig. It was the 1967 Jazz and Blues Festival that first brought the band widespread popular acclaim.

This week, TYA finished recording a new album to be released here by Chrysalis on September 15. Titled "Rock And Roll Music To The World", the album was recorded at Olympic Studios in London and on the Rolling Stones' mobile van in the South of France.

Alvin Lee told the NME on Monday: "This album is leaning more towards rock'n'roll music — but rock in its American sense, and not the English interpretation, which means Chuck Berry.

"What we wanted to do with this LP was to find a natural music for TYA, and that's why two of the tracks were recorded in France on the Stones' mobile.

"The tracks cut at Olympic have a natural feel too — we recorded most of them in one take so they have a lot more atmosphere and punch, rather than being as structured as 'A Space In Time'."

● *The FACES top the bill on the second night of the Reading Festival (12). Full running order for the event is on page 3.*

and last day of the ***11th National Jazz, Blues, Folk and Rock Festival****. This was the first year this event was held in Reading, and on future occasions it would be advertised simply as the* ***Reading Rock Festival****. On the bill with Ten Years After were: Quintessence, Status Quo, Roy Wood's Wizard, Stray, Matching Mole, Vinegar Joe, Gillian McPherson, Stachridge, Sutherland Brothers, Mahatma Kane Jeeves and String Driven Thing.*

Reading Festival Concert Review from THE SOUNDS by Ray Telford:

Billtoppers Ten Years After played late on Sunday evening. It was their first appearance in Britain since January and their first British festival since the Isle of Wight in 1970. However, for all the time TYA have been out of earshot, their audience seemed less enthusiastic about the group's return than you might have expected. It could be that they stayed away just that bit too long, at least long enough for the fickle public to latch on to heroes other than Alvin Lee.

As a stage spectacle Ten Years After are quite impressive and whatever your opinion of Alvin Lee, musician, you have to admit that he is one of the precious few good rock and roll showmen ever to have come out of this country. Musically, TYA don't wander far from the kind of riffy raunch which earned them their first fans some years back and in this respect they could possibly afford to open up a little, maybe by more use of Chick Churchill's fine organ playing, to add more light and shade into the act. Anyway, few left feeling that depressed or feeling they had wasted time and money. A good festival and without doubt the best this year so far.

September 23, 1972
"Ten Years After in Germany" - report from THE SOUNDS by Billy Walker:

*Leo Lyons is sitting in the dressing room of the **Stadthalle** in **Bremen**, back resting on the metal lockers that run along two of the four walls, applying methylated spirit to the tips of his fingers from a tiny plastic bottle that accompanies him on every gig. Ten Years After are on the first of a week of gigs through Germany and Austria - and bassist Leo wiles away the boredom before their set by running through a sound check with Alvin Lee, toughening up the fingers of his right hand and sampling the odd bottle from a crate of Coca Cola and beer resting on the bare dressing room table. Like most "artist's" rooms, whether you are headlining or just a bottom bill support band this one's empty (apart from tubular chairs and a couple of tables), without character and nestles under the banking of the cycle track which is housed in the Stadhalle.*

This tour promises to be an important one for TYA, important as it's followed closely by two tours of America (making their US tours total around seventeen), and the first time they've played since the Reading Festival where they enjoyed three encores and a barrage of bad press. Strangely, Ten Years After are one British band that have never really enjoyed good press since their start around six years ago. They've almost always sent the fans home smiling but have had to scimp around for whatever rave reviews were going. Reading was a prime example and as a result TYA were hurt by what the music Press had to say. But their problem is almost certainly a question of image. It's an image that was basically built up in America, where image is all important and ability secondary in most of their Press. The idea of Alvin Lee "fastest" or "greatest" guitarist alive, are both ridiculous observations about any musician and is certainly an image that Alvin himself has never tried to foster.

And their "Woodstock" appearance, which reached millions via cinema screening, has meant that they are almost duty bound to play "Goin' Home" on every gig since, thus having one foot planted too firmly in the past. Therefore, every time Alvin sets foot on stage some of the Press are inevitably saying "OK, let's see what the greatest guitarist around can do," and of course if he doesn't shape up the reviews reflect badly.

And while TYA aren't naive enough to believe that what the Press say is taken as gospel, how about the people who weren't at Reading ? They had no way of gauging the band's performance other than what they read and TYA are certain it wasn't a fair representation of what their gig was like. But Reading's over, and Leo, Chick Churchill, Alvin and Ric Lee file out from the dressing room on the long walk to the stage. In the stadium itself the crash barriers are pressed tight against the stage as more press their way to the front. The wooden banked walls stretch up steeply with rows of seats around their edge. Stray, who are accompanying TYA, have left the stage heavy with smoke from their exploding odds and ends and the audience in a good mood for moving around a bit. Without the slightest sign of fuss Ten Years After are on and Alvin announces "One Of These Days", which drives really hard for an opening number, guitar and tough harp from Alvin who confesses after "You Give Me Loving", the next number, "three wrong notes there."

GIANT WALLCHART EXTRA

NEW MUSICAL EXPRESS

Jagger

'KLEIN IS A PERSON TO BE AVOIDED'

LENNON

BOWIE

BOLAN

October 7, 1972 U.S./Canada 50c 6p.

TEN YEARS AFTER TOUR DATES

DATES FOR TEN YEARS AFTER's first British tour since the beginning of 1972 were announced this week and are published on page 3.
The band will interrupt its 16th series of American dates for the tour, which will also include a London concert not yet finalised.

HENDRIX

TWO YEARS TO the month after his death some of the world's biggest-name virtuosos of the guitar join NME today in nominating JIMI HENDRIX World's No. 1 Guitarist.
This extraordinary tribute to Hendrix's brilliance is revealed in part two of the NEW MUSICAL EXPRESS Annual Musicians' Poll. The chart is found by turning to the centre of the What's On supplement and opening out.

PAGE INDEX

"Loving" has Chick Churchill playing stabbing, authoritative organ which conjure up shades of Santana with a close jazz/rock feel that was TYA's trademark in their early years.

"Here's another one you might remember," announces Alvin before launching into "Good Morning Little Schoolgirl", rubbing his guitar across the microphone stand which brings a roar from the crowds who clap along in time while Alvin and the remarkable Leo rustle up a rocking little jam in the middle of the stage, backed by the barest of percussive rhythm from Ric. During the next number the stage monitors blow and Alvin attempts to explain to the audience that: "We're going to jam until the system comes on." During this jam TYA really work up a sweat, playing hard for a four-piece with Leo's bass making it tough for everyone else to compete - even Alvin's nice laid back guitar breaks.

"Standing At The Station" shows a slower less rock-based opening and this slightly subdued angle lends itself well to Chick's organ solo, but the audience seem to be willing the band for more speed and

during the next number are chanting for "Going Home". From the side of the stage the sound doesn't seem too good, only snatches of Alvin's vocals filter across and the organ seems to be on top of Leo's bass for much of the set. But a change of position only reverses the dominance of the hall's acoustics-banked wooden halls and a very hollow sounding stage doesn't seem to be helping too much. "I Can't Keep From Crying Sometimes" seems to have the right sort of rhythms to compliment TYA's skills to the fullest. The many changes in texture is a nice relief from the frantic, non-stop raving of the faster numbers and it grows to encompass almost every sort of music the band can play. It's a refreshing fifteen minutes in the set.

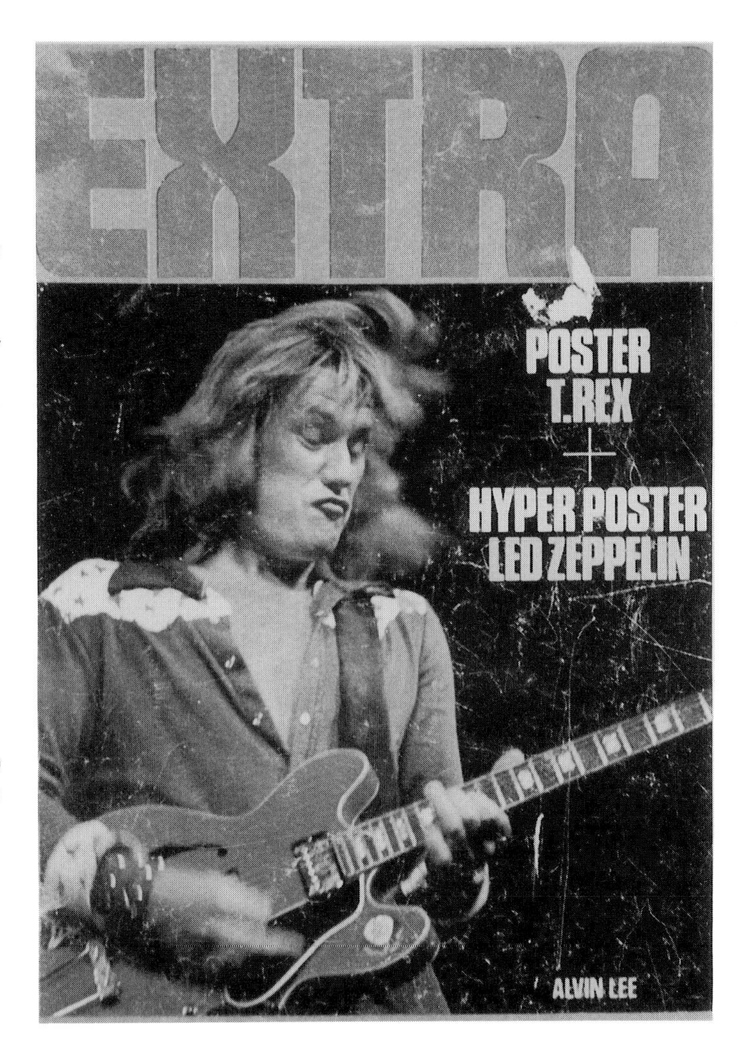

The numbers run on and on and things are really roasting by the end, "Goin' Home" follows as everyone knows it must with Leo Lyons, his head shaking about like a rag doll, plugging in those thick bass lines while Chick leaves the keyboards to play congos on the edge of the stage. Two encores follow - Chuck Berry's "Sweet Little Sixteen", and "Baby Won't You Let Me Rock And Roll You" - and the over zealous actions of the lighting man leave TYA in mid-exit as the house lights go up and for a minute they are all frozen in slight embarrassment while the audience waits for something to follow.

Back in the dressing room they sit round one of the tables discussing the set. Dis-satisfied with the sound on stage Alvin believes it wasn't a very good gig at all. Ric Lee asks what everyone else thought and the whole band are genuinely interested in outside opinions or criticisms. But they're not too despondent, even Chick who admits that his fingers were too stiff after such a long layoff. They must get better is the general opinion but the real test will be when they listen critically to the tapes of the gig. Every TYA gig is taped and everyone's eager to see who did what wrong where.

Overall the show was a good one. TYA aren't into any real stage showmanship like Bowie, Bolan or Slade, and this is something which audiences, both at home and abroad are aware of. The Bremen gig appeared to go from frenzied number to the next and the definite lack of light and shade in the overall act left a void. Ten Years After have been together, without personnel change, for an awful long time now and this, plus the upsurge of theatrics around them, might cause the non-TYA fan to view the band in a rather dull light, but from this gig (and the following day at Essen) it's obvious that they are still one of leading rock and roll bands in the world, warts and all. The "trial by tape" that evening - or was it early next morning - proved to be a release for TYA. The sound was a vast improvement from the expected and everything looked rosier for the next gig at the 8,000 capacity Grugahalle in Essen.

"On the Road with Ten Years After in Germany" DISC magazine report by Caroline Boucher:

Dusseldorf - Day two of Ten Years After's German tour: Having flown in from Bremen, driven from airport to hotel; hotel to backstage, the long wait continues to get onstage, and actually fulfill the purpose of the whole exercise. Until you go on tour the word 'wait' doesn't really mean too much, but on the road it takes on a whole new significance. You wait in airport lounges, outside airports for the coach, in hotel lobbies, in draughty backstage corridors or backstage in a world of wires and harassed roadies. Then after the gig you wait and wait until the crowds clear and the band can escape safely.

The arrival at the Essen gig from Dusseldorf was nothing short of spectacular when the bus bearing us all swished in to the stage door, all the lights blazing so that every kid outside the building swarmed round leaving you to swim for your life through a sea of people. But Ten Years After are seasoned tourers and nothing seems to worry them; after 15 tours of America and still sane they obviously can't allow anything to. We arrive at the Essen Grugahalle as the band Stray reach the end of a good set (they're on the tour with TYA).

The band's five tons of equipment has mostly been set up by their small army of roadies who dance by the side of the stage at their more ecstatic moments. The band is fairly wary of Essen - last time they played there, a crowd of 3,000 outside the building broke in through the windows to see the gig for free and TYA had to foot the glass bill. Already one of the crowd outside has broken a window, but rumor has it he was apprehended shortly after.

Part one of the long dressing room vigil begins, sitting around in a monastic cell of a room on hard plastic chairs drinking beer and coke. Down below the window, a rousing sing song is in progress by those who refuse to pay to get in. The German audiences are currently on a big free gig kick, and although the promoter lowered his original ten marks a head to ten marks per couple to entice the final few in, they remained adamantly singing in perverse two part harmony down below, handing out showers of Jesus Freaks literature.

Back in the dressing room, Ric Lee is reminiscing about the two gigs the band did a great many years back when Ric tied sparklers to his drumsticks and Alvin played his guitar when all the lights were down. Although it was very effective in practice, they couldn't get them lit on the night and were left to play in total darkness.

Alvin is expecting Steve Ellis and American singer, Mylon to join the tour tomorrow. He, Leo and Ian Wallace have all been doing sessions with Mylon at **Roger Daltry's** home studio and hope to release the results in an album sometime.

Ten Years After's next album is just out called "Rock and Roll Music to the World". It is their first in almost a year and some tracks are from their experimenting in the South of France with the Rolling Stones' mobile unit in February. "We hired a house just to see if it would be different from going to the studios every day in London. This new album is more of a rock album than any of the others, and we've tried to get a much more live sound. It's worried us in the past that the albums have been very different from the stage act and it's taken us a long time to work out why. We used to use the stage equipment in the studio but we found it was so loud we had to turn it down so that it wasn't making any distinction - it was too clean and clinical. The secret is to have *much smaller equipment turned up full. The last album was more songs and melodies. That was because before then it was the Woodstock aftermath that featured "Going Home" and we thought we'd get away from that for a while just to show we could play other stuff, because a lot of people just picked up on Woodstock. So we did a structured album to show there was another side of us and now we thought we'd go back to rock again."*

Recently, TYA came round to thinking they might do a single, because the singles market seemed so less "poppy" than it used to. But when their record company told them it had to be two minutes long, Alvin told them to forget it. Another reason they had steered clear of singles was that they were frightened of a flash in the pan, non-lasting success. "The only time concerts are threatened is when you get a hit record or are in a film or you become the darling of the 'Daily Mirror'. I think Marc Bolan and David Bowie will realize it sooner or later."

The band do their 16th tour of America shortly. They are still a dazzling success out there and don't seem to diminish at all. Even to the extent that Alvin was offered 3,000 pounds to do a toothpaste ad the last time he was there. The offer he said was tempting, but the thought of getting off the plane to be confronted by a giant image wasn't.
The whole group has also been offered a variety of awful film roles. One of the themes was of an English rock band going to America in search of Robert Johnson, getting busted and sent to jail. Alvin is freed by a beautiful girl in a white Cadillac, and when they turned down the script, the guy rewrote it and returned it nine months later. We'd do it if something good turned up, but I'm still involved with making my own movies and want to do one about my own environment. Meanwhile back in the dressing room the roadies have finally finished setting up and it is time to go on.

Stray had a bit of electrical trouble with their set, and when Ten Years After get on Alvin's mike fails

LENNON 'SUPERALBUM' REVIEWED INSIDE

DISC AND MUSIC ECHO 6p USA 30c

OCTOBER 2, 1971

Fairweather man joins the Strawbs

JACK BRUCE BAND ON TOUR DATES

ALVIN LEE (PICTURED) on TYA and the cool assassins See page 3

Jethro—present and past

JETHRO TULL and Ten Years After are both set for their concert debuts at New York's Madison Square Gardens soon.

Jethro, number 13 in the chart with "Life Is A Long Song," appear October 18 on their return to the States, where their "Aqualung" album has qualified for a platinum disc (sales of one million units).

Meanwhile, a double LP, "Living In The Past," containing past hit singles, previously unreleased tracks and a special book of the group's history, plus 10 full colour pictures, is out next month.

Ten Years After's first appearance at Madison Square Gardens is a month after Jethro — on November 18.

FRAMPTON The vegetarian who was sick with Pie — Page 20

MANFRED 'NOW I CAN LIVE AGAIN' SEE PAGE 10

within seconds. The audience, still annoyed from waiting an hour between groups, starts whistling and shouting. More trouble as the lights fuse the mikes and the circuit is clearly under pressure. They do a quick "jam" to drown some of the noise. Finally after shouting at the lights people, the show got underway. The band played a mixture of old things, stuff from the new album, an Al Kooper number and ended with Rock-n-Roll encores.

As a band they're playing well together these days - better than when I last saw them. The empathy between Alvin, Rick and Leo nowadays seems to be amazing - especially with Alvin and Leo. Unfortunately the organ doesn't feature dominantly enough in most of the numbers and seems rather superfluous. When Chick does do a more featured solo such as "Standing At The Station," he's really good. Rick Lee's drum solo was a little too prolonged, especially with the audience in it's edgy mood. But honors have to go to Alvin and Leo for their lovely inter-twined guitar work. Alvin's crystal clear style is still good although he does tend to shape each number rather the same - soft start, crescendo, climax, end. A heavy number alternated with a lighter thing would perhaps be a better substitute. Leo is getting better and better as an inventive bass player.

By the end of the show the audience is frenzied and scaling the enormous crash barrier - there are about three or four thousand in the hall. Someone about three rows back has an arm in plaster but nonetheless waves it ceaselessly. There are two encores. Then another endless wait in the dressing-cell for crowds to disperse so we can escape to the hotel. Then another wait at the hotel for food at 3:00 AM and the thought that the whole process is repeated tomorrow and the next day and the next day and the next day . . .

September 1972
Concert Hall
Vienna, Austria

September 26, 1972
Maple Leaf Gardens
Toronto, Canada

With Frampton's Camel and the Edgar Winter Group.

October 1972
Release of the ninth TYA LP: "Rock & Roll Music To The World" Columbia KC 31779

The tracks on Side One are: You Give Me Loving (Alvin Lee 6:31), *Convention Prevention* (Alvin Lee 4:25), *Turned Off T.V. Blues* (Alvin Lee 5:12) *and Standing At The Station* (Alvin Lee 7:07). *Side Two includes: You Can't Win Them All* (Alvin Lee 4:05), *Religion* (Alvin Lee 5:44), *Choo Choo Mama* (Alvin Lee 4:00), *Tomorrow I'll Be Out Of Town* (Alvin Lee 4:26) and *Rock & Roll Music To The World* (Alvin Lee 3:40). *This album reaches #43 in the U.S. and #27 in the U.K.*

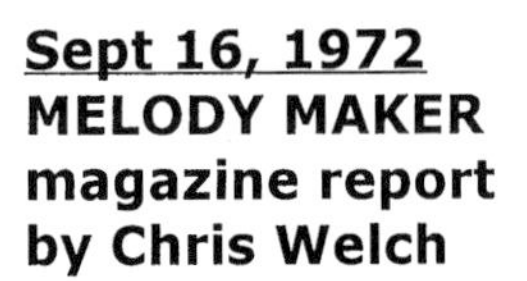

Sept 16, 1972
MELODY MAKER magazine report by Chris Welch

The new Ten Years After album is called "Rock And Roll Music To The World," and is certainly their best effort since "Undead." Although not a "live" album, it was cut on the Stone's mobile unit in France and gives TYA a spontaneity and brilliance that has been lacking on previous albums.

***Alvin Lee**:*
The music is an amalgamation of all four of us. On this LP we strived to make it natural music from the band, with nothing different, just for the sake of it. It's more of a rock album. After Woodstock we wanted to contrast what that and 'Going Home' had done for us, and we didn't just want to be a rock and roll band. We tried to do something different and progressive on the albums. We always like to end our sets with some rock but wanted to try and do something else as well, so people could hear a bit of everything."

"We recorded the new album in a chateau in France. We did five days rehearsal then spent five days with the Stone's mobile. At the time we thought the results hadn't been that good, and the experiment hadn't worked. But when we got the tapes together it sounded really good. It's captured an atmosphere on record that we have never got before. Like, the drums were just set up in a room lined with marble, and the drums got a bright sound you couldn't repeat in studio conditions. We kept it all very basic, but there are some really good solos from Chick. On "Standing At The Station" it took nearly six hours to mix the Moog synthesizer and organ tracks together. The first two albums we did were representative of how we played at the time. 'Stonedhenge,' the third one was influenced by flower power, and the others were aimed to be progressive. This album is just how we are now."

October 1972
Academy of Music New York City, NY

One Of These Days, You Give Me Loving, Good Morning Little School Girl, Jam in "G", Rock & Roll Music To The World, Hobbit

(introduced as "Rambling Rose"), Standing At The Station, Turned Off TV Blues, brief Jam (introduced by Alvin as a "Fox Trot"), Classical Thing, Scat Thing, I Can't Keep From Crying Sometimes, I'm Going Home, Sweet Little Sixteen, Choo Choo Mama, Baby Won't You Let Me Rock & Roll You (instrumental only, an exhausted Alvin mis-cues on the vocal), Roll Over Beethoven/ I Hear You Knockin' But You Can't Come In/Johnny B. Goode (medley).

Comment: *The New York Academy of Music show was about as close as you can come to the quintessential TYA concert! The whole band was in top form and played flawlessly, it would have made a fantastic live LP.*

<u>October 5, 1972</u>
Music Hall
Boston, Massachusetts

One Of These Days, You Give Me Loving, Good Morning Little School Girl, Jam (introduced by Alvin as a "Jazz Jam"), Rock & Roll Music To The World, Hobbit, Standing At The Station, Turned Off TV Blues, Classical Thing, Scat Thing, I Can't Keep From Crying Sometimes, I'm Going Home, Sweet Little Sixteen, Choo Choo Mama, Baby Won't You Let Me Rock & Roll You.

<u>October 26, 1972</u>
Hard Rock
Manchester, England

MELODY MAKER concert review by Penny Bosworth:

A little while ago, TYA would have been greeted with hysteria before a chord had been struck. Perhaps they tried to get away from this after Woodstock, but, starting their tour at Manchester's Hard Rock on Thursday they proved their stickability and rated the best reaction from the fans since the place opened. It is easy to generate excitement with good old rock 'n roll. Alvin Lee knew it years ago - and he knows it still. So "Blue Suede Shoes" and other worn-out buddies mixed with "Goin' Home To See My Baby" sent everyone home happy. But what came before? An object lesson on how to move on while still playing the same chords, some rattling good bass by Leo Lyons, and a bit of scorching guitar-picking which made one wonder why Lee didn't set sparks flying from his fingertips! Leo Lyons worked at the bass like he'd kill it before he let go and (disregarding an awful boom on the PA) he made it sing. Sad though, that organist and electric pianist Chick Churchill didn't get much chance to sparkle. The title "Standing At The Station" was too stationary to describe Alvin's work on this new LP track. He did everything but play guitar with his toes, using drum-sticks and mike stands to fret forth torrents of sound from the top of the neck to body at twice the speed of light!

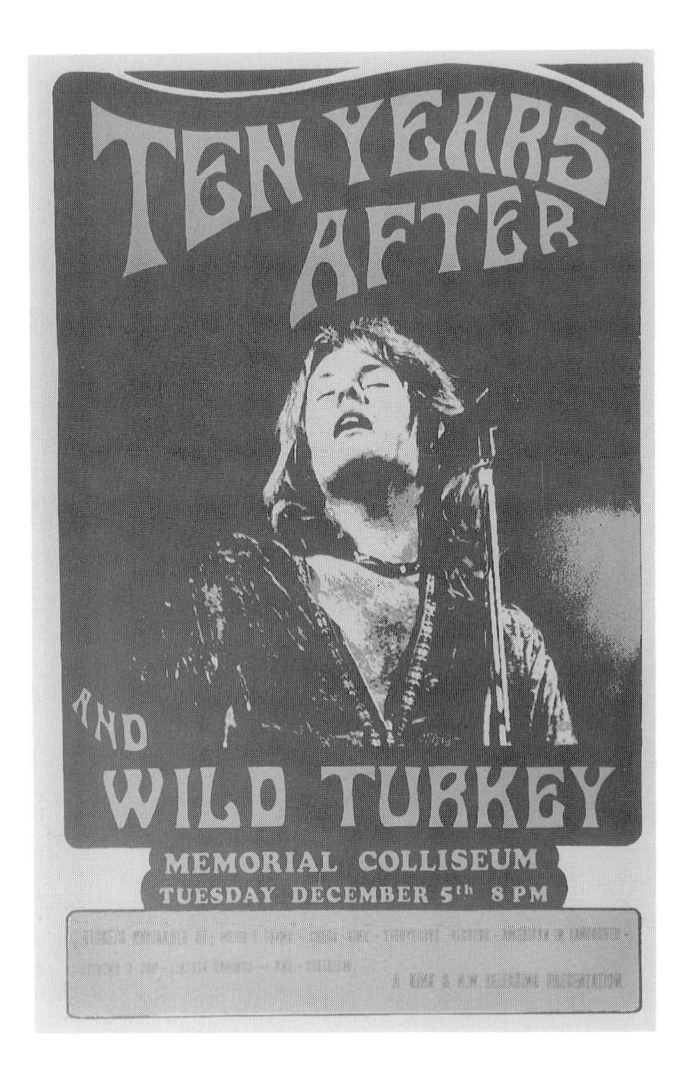

The opening act was Brinsley Schwartz, traveling incognito as backers for new singer Frankie Miller.

October 28, 1972
Town Hall
Birmingham, England

October 29, 1972
City Hall
Newcastle, England

Ten Years After is supported by Frankie Miller's Full House.

October 30, 1972
Caley Cinema
Edinburgh, Scotland

Nov 2 & 3, 1972
Rainbow
London, England

Frankie Miller opens. The TYA set list includes: You Give Me Loving, Good Morning Little School Girl, Rock & Roll Music To The World, Rainbow Express (drum solo), Standing At The Station, Turned Off TV Blues, I Can't Keep From Crying, I'm Going Home, Choo Choo Mama.

November 4, 1972
Stadium
Liverpool, England

November 6, 1972
DeMontfort Hall
Leicester, England

November 7, 1972
St. George's Hall
Bradford, England

November 8, 1972
Victoria Hall
Stoke On Trent
Hanley, England

One Of These Days, You Give Me Loving, Good Morning Little School Girl, Jam, Rock & Roll Music To The World, Turned Off TV Blues, Classical Thing, Scat Thing, I Can't Keep From Crying Sometimes, I'm Going Home, Choo Choo Mama.

November 21, 1972
Century II
Convention Hall
Wichita, Kansas

The opening band supporting Ten Years After is ***ZZ Top****.*

November 29, 1972
Coliseum
Denver, Colorado

Dec 1 & 2, 1972
Winterland
San Francisco, California

December 1972
Center Arena
Seattle, Washington

One Of These Days, Silly Thing, You Give Me Loving, Good Morning Little School Girl, Rock & Roll Music To The World, Hobbit, Standing At The Station, Turned Off TV Blues, Crossroads (Alvin says, "Here's an old one called Crossroads !"), Classical Thing, Scat Thing, I Can't Keep From Crying Sometimes, I'm Going Home, Choo Choo Mama, Sweet Little Sixteen.

SEATTLE TIMES concert review by Patrick MacDonald:

The rock group Ten Years After has been around a long time - since 1967 when they began playing black American blues in small town British dance halls.
They were from the beginning somewhat of a popular band, but it wasn't until the film Woodstock in 1970 that they became one of the top international groups. Their eleven minute song "Goin' Home" was one of the show-stoppers at Woodstock. Drawing music and lyrics from the whole history of rock, the tune seemed to epitomize the essence of the event. Last night at the arena, the band stopped the show again with "Goin' Home", and although he must be tired of playing it after all these years, lead guitarist Alvin Lee played the amazingly fast, complicated riffs with exactness and electrifying energy.

There is nothing quite so exhilarating as a rock guitarist who knows what he's doing. The electric guitar is an instrument capable of an astonishingly wide range of expression and Alvin Lee understands it like few ever have. His playing for the full house audience last night was virtuoso from the first notes of the opening song to the last of the second encore. And the rest of the band - Chick Churchill on organ and electric piano, Leo Lyons on bass and Ric Lee on drums - was with him all the way. It's no wonder that they play together so well. The same four members have been working together all these years and they have established a kind of communication that makes them sound as one. They have achieved a unity that is rare in rock bands. But it also must be said that in playing one-night stands year after year they have allowed a few things in their act to lapse into routinization--like drummer Ric Lee's solo, which lasted only about eight minutes but seemed twenty, and the mumbling, unintelligible introduction to the songs. Overall, however, the band is certainly one of the best. And they showed why in their fine concert of blues and rock last night.

<u>December 5, 1972</u>
Memorial Coliseum
Portland, Oregon

With Wild Turkey

<u>December 7, 1972</u>
The Forum
Los Angeles, CA

With Wild Turkey and Malo.

<u>December 8, 1972</u>
Sports Arena
San Diego, CA

<u>December 13, 1972</u>
Palladium
Hollywood, CA

Spoonful (Alvin introduces the song by saying "you might remember this !"), You Give Me Loving, Good Morning Little School Girl, Rock & Roll Music To The World, Jam in the key of E, Hobbit (introduced as "Hollywood Express"), Standing At The Station, I May Be Wrong But I Won't Be Wrong Always (Alvin says "we would like to do something a bit different for old time's sake, this is something we used to do"), Classical Thing, Scat Thing, I Can't Keep From Crying Sometimes, I'm Going Home, Choo Choo Mama.

<u>January 26, 1973</u>
Concertgebouw
Amsterdam, Holland

<u>January 27, 1973</u>
De Doelen
Rotterdam, Holland

<u>January 29, 1973</u>
L' Olympia
Paris, France

Wild Turkey opens for Ten Years After. The set list is: One Of These Days, Spoonful, You Give Me Loving, Good Morning Little School Girl, Rock & Roll Music To The World, Hobbit, Standing At The Station, Turned Off T.V. Blues, I Can't Keep From Crying Sometimes, Help Me, I'm Going Home, Choo Choo Mama, Sweet Little Sixteen.

February 2, 1973
Frankfurt, Germany

February 12, 1973
Ostseehalle
Kiel, Germany

The opening act is Robin Trower.

February 14, 1973
Deutschlandhalle
Berlin, Germany

Partial Set List: You Give Me Loving, Good Morning Little School Girl, Rock & Roll Music To The World, Hobbit, Silly Thing, Standing At The Station, Turned Off TV Blues, Help Me, Choo Choo Mama.

Comment: *The version of Help Me performed at this show rivals the one heard on the Recorded Live LP! Limited disc space was probably a factor at the time, but it is unfortunate Standing At The Station, Turned Off T.V. Blues, or even one of the great jams often performed during this period were not included on the 'Recorded Live' album.*

February 16, 1973
Oberrheinhalle
Offenburg, Germany

Robin Trower opens for Ten Years After.

March 21, 1973
Scandinavium
Gothenburg, Sweden

March 22, 1973
Kungliga Hallen
Stockholm, Sweden

April 5, 1973
Civic Hall
Dunstable, England

April 6, 1973
City Hall
Sheffield, England

April 8, 1973
Fairfield Hall
Croydon, England

One Of These Days, You Give Me Loving, Good Morning Little School Girl, Endoplasm (drum solo), Rock & Roll Music To The World, Standing At The Station, Jam (approximately 20 minutes), Slow Blues In C, Help Me, short jam while Alvin replaces a string, I'm Going Home, Sweet Little Sixteen, Choo Choo Mama.

April 14, 1973
University
Reading, England

April 15, 1973
Civic Hall
Guildford, England

April 26, 1973
Concertgebouw
Amsterdam, Holland

April 30, 1973
Met Center
Minneapolis, Minnesota

Foghat opens for Ten Years After.

May 6, 1973
Auditorium
Memphis, Tennessee

Concert Review from THE COMMERCIAL APPEAL by Richard Kofoed:

"Ten Years After Brings Rock Crowd Out of Seats" - The cavernous North Hall of the Auditorium throbbed for three hours last night as a youthful crowd of 2,481 heard the beat of two British rock groups, The vibrant sounds came from a group called Ten Years After, who were a hit at the Woodstock rockfest a few summers ago, and a five member bunch called the Strawbs - formerly known as Strawberry. Strawbs set the mood but it wasn't until after intermission, when a pink frisbee was sailed numerous times throughout the crowd, that the standing ovations began when Ten Years After stood center stage. The name of the group itself jarred memories and made one realize how much the top 40 charts in this country have changed during the past decade when the Beatles left their indelible English mark on pop music. Alvin Lee, the front-man lead guitarist captured most of the spotlight which cut through the London-fog-like haze caused by those who chose to ignore the "No Smoking" decree issued before the concert (it wasn't cigarette smoke).

A drum solo by Ric Lee and an offering called "Rock and Roll Music To The World" were well received (I caught one of his flying drumsticks, was that close). Songs from the Strawbs new album, such as "The River" and "Down By The Sea" helped the flow of the rock concert but didn't make any big waves.

May 8, 1973
Sports Stadium
Orlando, Florida

Partial Set List: Rock & Roll Music To The World, Spoonful, Turned Off T.V. Blues, I'm Going Home, Sweet Little Sixteen. These songs are

HIT PARADER MAGAZINE

A CHARLTON PUBLICATION

TEN YEARS AFTER look back MICK JAGGER'S MOVIES JANUARY TYME

WORDS TO ALL YOUR HIT SONGS

BRIDGE OVER TROUBLED WATER
HOUSE OF THE RISING SUN
CALL ME
DO THE FUNKY CHICKEN
NEVER HAD A DREAM COME TRUE
MA BELLE AMIE
THE RAPPER
KENTUCKY RAIN
THE THRILL IS GONE
TRAVELIN' BAND
WHO'LL STOP THE RAIN
JUST SEVENTEEN
THE DECLARATION OF INDEPENDENCE
RAG MAMA RAG
STIR IT UP & SERVE IT
EVERYBODY'S OUT OF TOWN
IT'S A NEW DAY PT 1
GOT TO HOLD ON TO THIS FEELING
EASY COME, EASY GO
THE BELLS
MESSAGE FROM A BLACKMAN

CONVERSATION with AL KOOPER NEW YORK ROCK and ROLL ENSEMBLE

THE IKE and TINA TURNER INTERVIEW SHA NA NA

MAY 1970/50¢

CIRCUS

Country Folk Boom: SEBASTIAN, RONSTADT, TAYLOR

BREAKIN' THE BLUES WITH TEN YEARS AFTER
JOHN MAYALL, JOE COCKER

record mirror

MAY 16, 1970. Vol. 17 No. 19.

told RM: "The two British concerts will be presented in conjunction with a major London promoter on the 24th 25th September. Together with CBS Records we are planning a giant reception for the group."

Highlights of the concerts will be broadcast over Radio Luxembourg's

Rolling Stones Into Cassettes

SEVEN ROLLING STONES cassettes head Decca's entry into the tape market this autumn. More and more disc companies are going into the tape market and Decca is planning its entry in a big way with nine Tom Jones titles and four from Engelbert.

And there will be material from the Moody Blues, two cassettes from Ike and Tina Turner, a collection of Decca hits plus John Mayall, Mantovani and the Bing Crosby album, "Hey Jude, Hey Bing."

Decca now follow EMI, Philips, Polydor, Pye, CBS Warner-Reprise and Ember who have already made inroads into the tape market. All this material will be issued on cassette and retail price is still to be finalised. The tapes will be introduced in the autumn – probably in August or September – with an initial release of 60 titles.

SAME SONG– DIFFERENT SPEED

TEN YEARS AFTER are home again. And back from America with them comes their latest single – an eight and an half minute live version of 'Love Like A Man', recorded at New York's Fillmore East.

What makes the record so different is that it plays at 33 1/3 r.p.m. – and on the other side is the same song at 45 r.p.m. The studio version of course.

The group's fifth tour of America ended in April – since then they've been in Germany – and the single was recorded at New York's famous rock centre at the end of February – and now it's going up the charts in America like a rocket.

On Friday the band started their current British tour at London's Lyceum Ballroom. They will be visiting Southampton, Birmingham, Manchester and Scotland before their next tour of the States due in June.

And then there's their album, 'Cricklewood Green' which is currently in the top five album charts.

This makes three in a row for TYA – their two previous albums "Stonedhenge" and "Sssh" have both made the top five.

Which, as someone must have said before, can't be bad.

BEST/46
la meilleure actualité de l'évolution musicale
année/numéro 46/mai 1972/mensuel/3,50 francs/Belgique 40 FB
T.REX
jethro tull
couleur

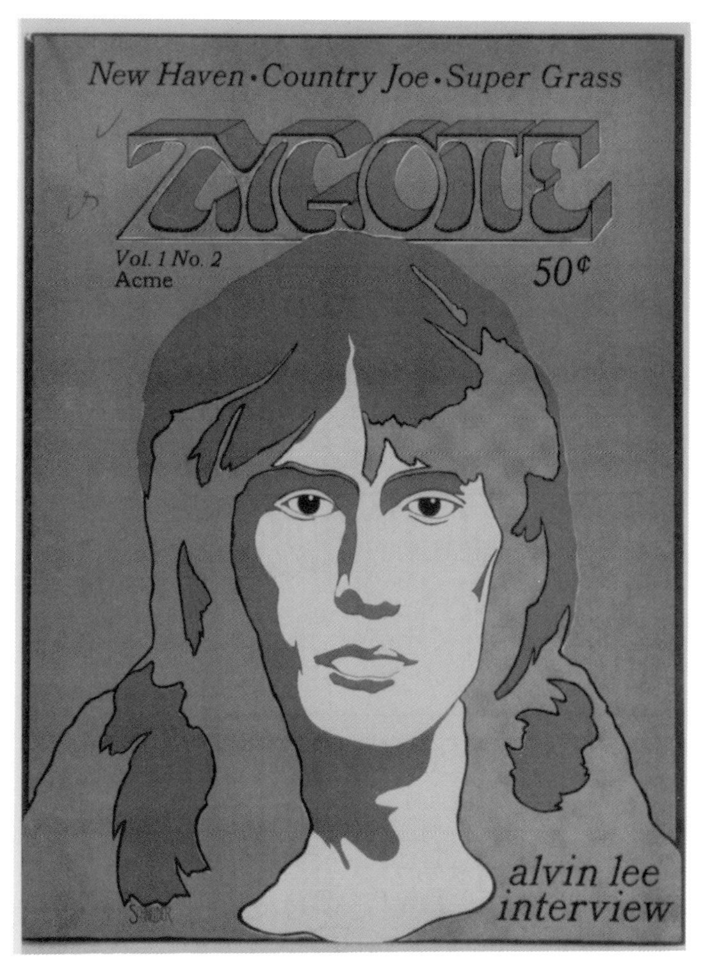
New Haven · Country Joe · Super Grass
ZYGOTE
Vol. 1 No. 2
Acme
50¢
alvin lee
interview

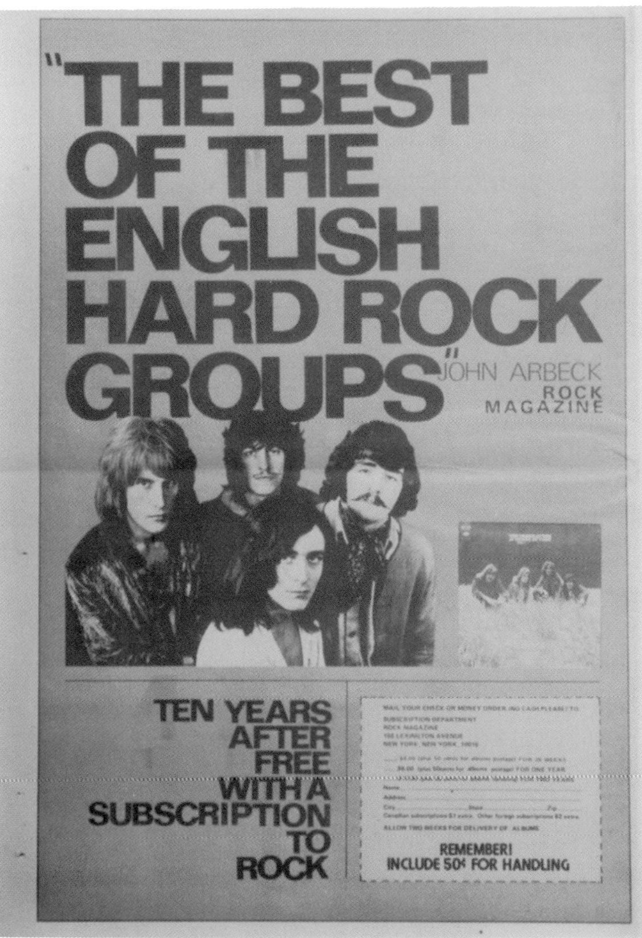
"THE BEST OF THE ENGLISH HARD ROCK GROUPS"
JOHN ARBECK
ROCK MAGAZINE
TEN YEARS AFTER FREE WITH A SUBSCRIPTION TO ROCK
REMEMBER!
INCLUDE 50¢ FOR HANDLING

ROCK
CCC
35¢
sept. 27, 1970
ZAP! Can it be Alvin Lee, Jim Morrison, Leon Russell, Dave Mason, the Juke Box ripoff & even Dick Clark all in this issue?
Meanwhile......

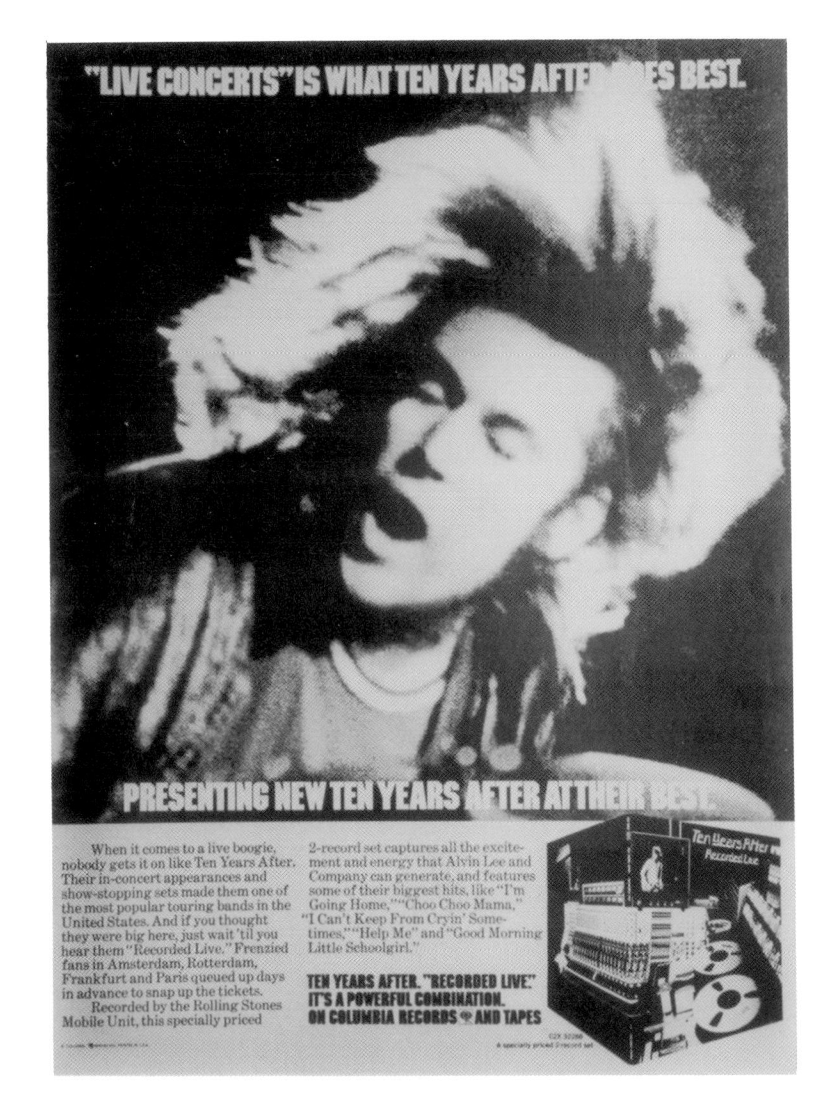

subsequently broadcast on the King Biscuit Flower Hour Radio Show.

<u>May 18, 1973</u>
Nagoya Kokaido
Nagoya, Japan

Albert Hammond is the opening act for Ten Years After on this tour of Japan.

<u>May 19, 1973</u>
Kyoto Kaikan
Kyoto, Japan

<u>May 21 & 22, 1973</u>
Koseinenkin Hall
Osaka, Japan

<u>May 23, 1973</u>
Nippon Budokan
Tokyo, Japan

One Of These Days, You Give Me Loving, Good Morning Little School Girl, Rock & Roll Music To The World, Hobbit, Standing At The Station, Slow Blues In C, Silly Thing, Help Me (introduced by Alvin as "an old blues tune by Sonny Boy Williamson called Help Me Baby"), Get Back (yes - that Beatles song !), I'm Going Home, Sweet Little Sixteen, Choo Choo Mama.

<u>June 1973</u>
Release of the tenth Ten Years After LP: "Recorded Live" Columbia C2X 32288

This double album consists of live material recorded with the Rolling Stones' mobile recording truck at Ten Years After concerts performed in Amsterdam, Rotterdam, Frankfurt and Paris during January 1973.
Side One: One Of These Days (Alvin Lee Frankfurt 5:36), *You Give Me Loving* (Alvin Lee - Frankfurt 5:25) and *Good Morning Little School Girl* (Sonny Boy Williamson Frankfurt 7:15).
Side Two: Hobbit (Ric Lee - Frankfurt 7:15) and *Help Me* (Williamson & Bass - Amsterdam 10:44).
Side Three: Classical Thing (Alvin Lee - Paris

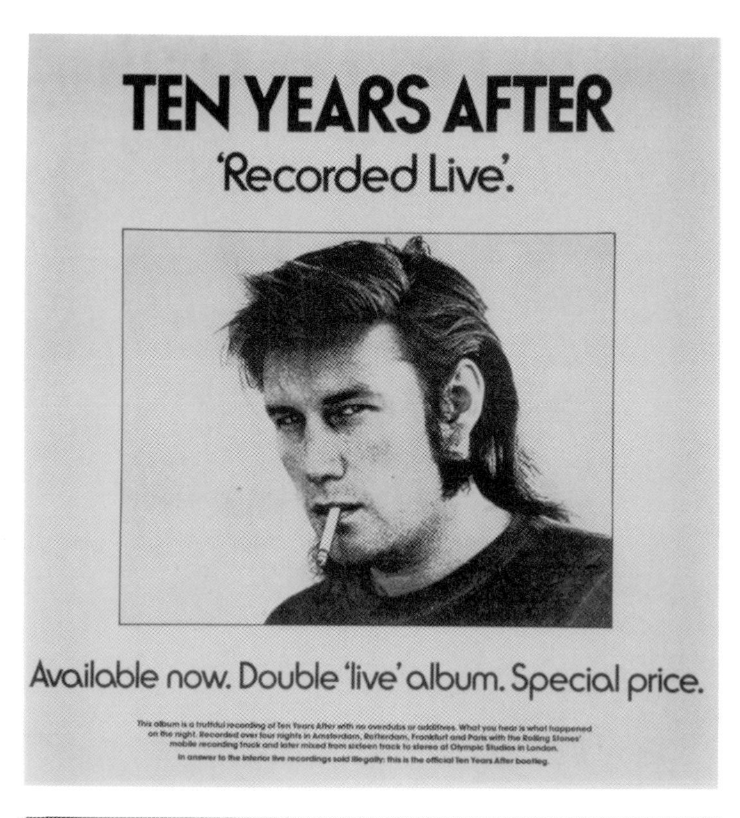

0:55), *Scat Thing* (Alvin Lee - Paris 0:54), *I Can't Keep From Crying Sometimes - Part 1* (Kooper - Paris 1:57), *Extension On One Chord* (Alvin Lee, Leo Lyons, Chick Churchill & Ric Lee - Paris 10:46) and *I Can't Keep From Crying Sometimes - Part 2* (Kooper - Paris 3:19). *Side Four: Silly Thing* (Alvin Lee - Frankfurt 0:26), *Slow Blues in "C"* (Alvin Lee - Frankfurt 7:24), *I'm Going Home* (Alvin Lee - Frankfurt 9:30) and *Choo Choo Mama* (Alvin Lee - Frankfurt 2:56). *This release reaches #39 in the U.S. and #36 in the U.K.*

July 1973
Release of the single: "I'm Going Home"/"You Give Me Loving"

August 3, 1973
Alexandra Palace London, England

This performance by Ten Years After is part of the London Music Festival series. Other acts preceding TYA were Ruby, Glenn Cornick's Wild Turkey, Fumble and Barclay James Harvest.

MELODY MAKER concert review by David Lewis:

It takes a lot to make a cavernous grotto like the Pally overheat and drip sweat, but Alvin Lee and Ten Years After did exactly that, and saved what could otherwise have been a rather mundane evening. When Ten Years After thankfully shook the place into action with a much needed shot of rhythm 'n' blues, it was like a breath of fresh air after the turgid staleness of the previous few hours.

Alvin Lee looked and sounded in fine fettle, pouting his lips, blowing out his cheeks and contorting his face into a different grimace for every chord he played. He's no slouch on guitar, but whether he's overrated or not is immaterial - the fact is he feels the blues and it's for that reason he can drag a drowsy audience up onto its feet and turn it into a clapping, stomping rabble. Earbashers like "Rock 'n' Roll Music To The World" and "Standing At The Station" were mesmeric and by the time the band lurched into their signature tune "Goin' Home," the back of the hall looked like a battlefield, with exhausted bodies slumped among the piles of rubbish and the walking wounded still boogying away to themselves, oblivious of everything bar the music. Perhaps the acoustics in Alexandra Palace are not all that good, and it may get a bit uncomfortable at

times - but after all it was supposed to be an indoor festival, not a plush concert affair. And if it meant another opportunity to hear good live music in London, it surely was a good idea.

August 14, 1973
St. Louis, Missouri

September 15, 1973
Guildhall
Plymouth, England

Article from the September 8, 1973 NEW MUSICAL EXPRESS:

Ten Years After are to make their first British tour in almost a year. The news of the 14 day tour was announced by Chrysalis this week and effectively puts an end to recent rumors that the group were about to split up. The tour, which opens at Plymouth Guildhall on September 15, is the first from the group this year and is their first British appearance since they headlined at the Alexandra Palace Music Festival a month ago. Rumors concerning the breakup of the group began circulating at the time of the release of "Recorded Live", the group's current album. TYA stopped touring at that time as both Alvin Lee and organist Chick Churchill had begun work on solo projects. It was rumored that Alvin Lee was to leave the group and form a new band with various musicians - namely ex-King Crimson members Mel Collins and Boz, who he had recently been playing with at the recently completed studio at his home.

During the past two months, Lee has been working constantly on an album, recorded at his studio with American gospel singer Mylon LeFevre. The album consists entirely of new songs written by Lee and Mylon with additional material from star musicians who also guested on the album. "I'm looking forward to going on the road with Ten Years After again," Lee said. "It's going to be a tour on which we can experiment - especially during the later part of the tour when we've got back into playing England again. Since we've been off the road during the last few months I've been working with Mylon - who's a gospel singer from Georgia - and we've just about finished an album together. It's not my

solo album, it's the two of us with some good people who came down to help. A solo LP is another project I have in mind for the future."

Also at the mixing stage is a solo album from TYA's organist Chick Churchill. Both the Alvin Lee/Mylon Le Fevre album and the Chick Churchill album will be released later this year.

September 16, 1973
Town Hall
Torquay, England

September 17, 1973
Top Rank
Swansea, Wales

September 20, 1973
Colston Hall
Bristol, England

September 22, 1973
Pier Pavillion
Hastings, England

September 30, 1973
New Theatre
Oxford, England

October 3, 1973
Free Trade Hall
Manchester, England

October 4, 1973
University
Leeds, England

October 5, 1973
Mayfair Ballroom
Newcastle, England

October 6, 1973
Heriot Watt University
Edinburgh, Scotland

October 12, 1973
University
Lancaster, England

October 13, 1973
University
York, England

October 15, 1973
Civic Hall
Wolverhampton, England

October 19, 1973
Apollo
Glasgow, Scotland

October 20, 1973
Edward Herbert Building
Loughborough University, England

The support band is Stray Dog.

October 1973
Release of the Chick Churchill single: "Broken Engagements"/ "Dream of Our Maker Man"

November 2, 1973
Alvin Lee & Mylon LeFevre LP "On The Road To Freedom" is released

The album is recorded at Alvin Lee's Space Studios. Guest artists include **Jim Capaldi, Mick Fleetwood, George Harrison, Rebop, Steve Winwood** *and* **Ron Wood.** *Tracks on Side One include: On The Road To Freedom* (Alvin Lee 4:15), *The World Is Changing* (Mylon LeFevre 2:44), *So Sad/No Love Of His Own* (George Harrison 4:37), *Fallen Angel* (Alvin Lee 3:20), *Funny* (Alvin Lee 2:50) and *We Will Shine* (Mylon LeFevre 2:33). *Side Two includes: Carry My Load* (Alvin Lee 2:59), *Lay Me Back* (Mylon LeFevre 2:59), *Let 'Em Say What They Will* (Ron Wood 2:53), *I Can't Take It* (Mylon LeFevre 2:54), *Riffin'* (Alvin Lee/Mylon LeFevre 3:36) and *Rockin' Til The Sun Goes Down* (Alvin Lee/Mylon LeFevre 3:15). *This LP reaches U.S. #138 in early 1974.*

Felix Pappalardi *discovered Mylon Le Fevre singing backup and introduced him to New Orleans producer* ***Allen Toussaint****. They helped Mylon form the band Holy Smoke. Several artists have recorded Mylon's songs, including: Elvis Presley, Johnny Cash, Merle Haggard and Mahalia Jackson. Alvin met Mylon when Holy Smoke opened for Ten Years After during four of their American tours. The "On The Road To Freedom" album first began*

when Alvin was helping Mylon and his guitarist, Steve Sanders, record several tracks at ***Roger Daltry's*** *home studios in Sussex. The album was completed when Alvin finished putting together his own* ***Space Studios*** *in Buckinghamshire.*

November 1973
Release of the single: "So Sad"/"Riffin"

November 30, 1973
Alvin Lee & Mylon LeFevre perform on the Midnight Special TV show.

This was episode #44 of the Midnight Special TV series and, according to NBC, was broadcast to an audience of thirty three million viewers. It was hosted by Procol Harum and also featured Humble Pie, Alvin Lee & Mylon LeFevre, and Steeleye Span. Alvin Lee and Mylon performed "Rockin' Til The Sun Goes Down", "Carry My Load", and "The World Is Changing". The Alvin & Mylon segment was taped at the Rainbow Room on the top floor of Biba's London department store at Kensington High Street. Backing Alvin and Mylon were ***Steve Winwood, Jim Capaldi, Mike Patto, Boz Burrell, Ian Wallace*** *and* ***Tim Hinkley.*** *Among the audience were* ***George Harrison, Rich Grech*** *and **Leggs Larry Smith.** Alvin had been gigging with Ten Years After right up to the Saturday night before the program was due to be filmed. The show was put on with about two days notice. Two mixes were done for the program, one in mono for TV and the other in stereo for FM radio.*

__January 1974__
Release of the single: "The World Is Changing"/ "Riffin"

__February 1974__
Release of the Chick Churchill LP: "You and Me" Chrysalis 1051

Also performing on the album are: Gary Pickford-Hopkins (vocals), Martin Barre (guitar), Leo Lyons (bass), Cozy Powell (drums), Bill Jackman (baritone sax), Ric Lee (drums), Rodger Hodson (guitar & bass), Rick Davies (drums), Bernie Marsden (guitar) and Vicki Brown, Margo Newman & Barry St. John (backing vocals). Songs on Side One: "Come and Join Me", "Broken Engagements", You and Me" and "Reality In Arrears". Side Two: "Dream of Our Maker Man", "Ode To An Angel", "You're Not Listening", "Chiswick Flower", "The Youth I Dreamt In Slipped Away" and "Falling Down An Endless Day" (All songs written by Chick Churchill).

__February 1974__
Ten Years After record the tracks for the "Positive Vibrations" album at Space Studios

__March 3-21, 1974__
Alvin Lee & Company rehearse at Space Studios

Report from SOUNDS magazine:

*Alvin Lee's concert on Friday, March 22nd, at the Rainbow will be recorded for an album which will be released in two or three months. The album may also feature some studio tracks and the backing musicians will be **Neil Hubbard, Alan Spenner, Tim Hinkley, Mel Collins** and **Ian Wallace**. Since announcement of the solo concert, there has been a spate of TYA 'split' rumours. A spokesman for Alvin Lee told SOUNDS that "this is regarded purely as a one off project, the same thing as his album with Mylon LeFevre. As far as we know he has no intentions of leaving Ten Years After." The concert will be filmed by an independent production company and will be screened in America and Europe. There will also be plans for transmission here.*

March 22, 1974
Rainbow Theater
London, England

Alvin Lee performs with Mel Collins (Sax & Flute), Ian Wallace (Drums), Tim Hinkley (Keyboards), Alan Spenner (Bass), Neil Hubbard (Guitar) and Dyan Birch, Frank Collins & Paddie McHugh (Backing Vocals). The concert is recorded and will later be released as the Alvin Lee & Company "In Flight" double LP. This concert was also filmed and two of the songs "Don't Be Cruel" and "Money Honey" were subsequently broadcast on the U.K. TV "Old Grey Whistle Test" show a few weeks later, but the film has otherwise remained unreleased.

Article from NEW MUSIC EXPRESS:

Alvin wanted to do a couple of nights at the Rainbow, but soon discovered that the only available date was March 22nd, which left him exactly four short weeks to prepare himself for such a trial by ordeal. ***Alvin Lee:*** *"I only finalized the actual personnel of the band 10 days before the gig." With just one week to go, Lee then assembled everyone together at his newly constructed 16 track Space Productions recording studio.*
"I had a whole bunch of songs which had been the overlap from the last three years of recording - songs that weren't really suited to Ten Years After's high energy approach."
The musicians were in the studio where they were to remain for the next 50 hours, during which time they rehearsed and arranged almost two thirds of the 23 numbers Lee had tentatively scheduled. After that, rehearsals were taken at a far more leisurely pace.
As it transpires, the gig came pretty close to backfiring on the participants. Seeing as the event was being recorded for an album, plans had been carefully drawn up for the band to spend the entire day of the concert doing a complete 'dress' rehearsal and sound check at the theatre. With this in mind, the band assembled in time to catch the milkman making his early morning delivery but, as they were about to dump their cases into the hired coach, the vehicle suddenly sprang into life and tore off down the desolate country lane at alarming speed and vanished clear out of sight. Thirty minutes later a phone call revealed that the driver had suddenly been stricken with acute appendicitis and had driven himself to the nearest hospital for emergency treatment.
Alvin: "In the end, we had to drive up to town in a convoy of vans, jeeps and rattletraps. By the time we reached the Rainbow we only had time to run through five numbers."

April 1974
Release of the 11th Ten Years After LP: "Positive Vibrations" Columbia PC 32851

Side One tracks are: *Nowhere To Run* (Alvin Lee 4:22), *Positive Vibrations* (Alvin Lee 2:23), *Stone Me* (Alvin Lee 4:14), *Without You* (Alvin Lee 6:18) *and Going Back To Birmingham* (R. Penniman 3:33).
Side Two includes: It's Getting Harder (Alvin Lee 3:58), *You're Driving Me Crazy* (Alvin Lee 4:14), *Look Into My Life* (Alvin Lee 4:53), *Look Me Straight Into The Eyes* (Alvin Lee 3:57) and *I Wanted To Boogie* (Alvin Lee 2:36).
The album reaches #81 in the U.S. charts.

Album review from MELODY MAKER:

No Messing about, straight into the funky riff and blues-stained vocals on "Nowhere To Run". You might say "I've heard all this before," but that is a definition of popular art. It's very familiarity is part of the reason for the survival of a brand of music that some thought exhausted by 1969. But, here they are, one of the oldest bands in captivity still going strong. And after a few bars, your head starts to nod and feet do wiggle in a kind of Pavlov's dog reaction. And tunes like "Positive Vibrations" are quite pleasant, with Alvin singing very nicely and playing unusually laid back guitar for a TYA gig. Chick Churchill's piano rings merrily and Chick elsewhere adds electric piano, clavinet and a spot of Moog. And as we progress further, "Stone Me" has an extremely effective boogie beat with a trace of harmonica from Alvin that takes us back to the steamy blues clubs of yesteryear. Rick Lee swings on the drums and it's a lot of fun. TYA vocals in general seem to have taken a turn for the better, with less of the old anguished yelling, and more tuneful harmonizing, as on "Without You." But just in case old TYA fans are impatient with all this trend toward sweet nothings, "Going Back To Birmingham" has Alvin cutting a rug and slashing the carpets. "It's Getting Harder," has Chick Churchill getting a big band sound from his keyboards, and lot's of wah-wah chuckling away. Note the excellent production here, is maintained throughout, and helps make this one of the best, if least publicized

of their albums. The rest of the material continues through some sprightly rock 'n' roll. "You're Driving Me Crazy", a neatly arranged "Look Into My Life," and "Look Me Straight Into The Eyes," and a cheerful farewell "I Wanted To Boogie."

April 1974
Release of the single: "I Wanted To Boogie"/ "It's Getting Harder"

April 18, 1974
City Hall
Sheffield, England

April 19, 1974
Birmingham, England

SOUNDS magazine review by Phil Holt:

Ten Years After have not been in the public eye much of late, and so it was interesting to note at Birmingham Town Hall on Friday night that their followers still rate them as highly as ever. The stage was surrounded before a note was played and the group kept them there with a performance of solid, tight rock music. On closer examination though, the act really fell into two halves. For a long time the group's playing was very routine. Everything was in its right place but TYA gave the impression of having been through it countless times before. Obviously they have, but if the time arrives when you're no longer into your own music, then perhaps the time

has arrived to call it a day. However the last third of their set showed that there's life in them old bones yet. Leo Lyons, who had been working hard all night to try and ignite Mssrs. Lee, Lee and Churchill, eventually succeeded. Alvin Lee leant heavily into his guitar and made a mockery of the CND badge that it supported. Chick Churchill lost that air of amused indifference and Ric Lee who had been soundly thrashing his drums all evening, found the extra energy to give them an even more thorough going over. Still, all's well that ends well, and it was nice to see TYA eventually doing justice to themselves because their moody music has always needed the stimulous of a live appearance to really come over, and it would have been a pity if on one of their rare appearances they had failed to do so.

April 20, 1974
Rainbow Theater
London, England

April 21, 1974
City Hall
Newcastle, England

April 22, 1974
Free Trade Hall
Manchester, England

TYA performs their final U.K. concert.

April 25, 1974
Arena Hall
Deurne, Belgium

The supporting band is the Italian progressive rock group: Premiata Forneria Marconi.

April 28, 1974
Holstebrohallen
Holstebro, Denmark

May 3, 1974
Eberthalle
Ludwigshafen, Germany

Rock & Roll Music To The World, Nowhere To Run, Good Morning Little School Girl, It's Getting Harder, Hobbit, Love Like A Man, Slow Blues In C, Look Me Straight Into The Eyes, Classical Thing, Scat Thing, I Can't Keep From Crying Sometimes, I'm Going Home, Sweet Little Sixteen, Choo Choo Mama

May 7, 1974
Palais des Sports
Paris, France

Partial set list: Rock & Roll Music To The World, Good Morning Little School Girl, It's Getting Harder, Love Like A Man, Slow Blues In C, I Can't Keep From Crying Sometimes, I'm Going Home, Sweet Little Sixteen, Two Time Mama.

May 13, 1974
Madison Square Garden
New York City, NY

Start of the U.S.A. "Positive Vibrations" Tour.

Concert Review from RECORD WORLD:

*"The overall theme of this evening might have been 'boogie till your brains fall out' because that is what happened on this Monday evening at New York's cavernous sport's palace as Ten Years After led by the incredible Alvin Lee rocked on for a full house of totally receptive fans. **ZZ Top** opened the show with a strong set of Texas boogie rock and was successful except for the fact that they were far too loud to really be appreciated in performing material from their albums, especially their latest 'Tres Hombres'. The three man band had the crowd on their feet almost throughout their set. The group, however, does need to*

examine their decibel level. Sitting in the orchestra was, at times, a painful experience. Following a twenty five minute intermission, Alvin Lee and Ten Years After took to the stage to the roaring approval of 18,000 gathered for the event. Opening with 'Rock & Roll Music To The World', they stayed right on target for well over an hour and gave the crowd everything they wanted from their new LP Positive Vibrations, as well as previous outings over the span of the group's ten years as recording artists.

Alvin Lee, one of the premier guitarists in rock (if not **the** best around today) was in unusually rare form, even when things were not going right all the time. Early tuning and string problems brought about his comment, 'I'll probably break me leg next'. After those kinks were ironed out, the music flowed fast and furious. In rapid succession, the crowd was presented with 'Good Morning Little School Girl', 'Love Like A Man', the group's classic 'I'm Going Home' and encores of 'Sweet Little Sixteen', 'Roll Over Beethoven' and others that continually had the fans up and dancing. Also, the course of the set offered Chick Churchill with a strong keyboard solo and an unusually entertaining drum solo by Ric Lee. It's hard to believe that Ten Years After has been one complete unit now for ten years with no personnel change, but listening to their set here at the Garden proved that of every other English rock blues boogie band in existence today, this is one organization that is talented on every level. Here's hoping that Ten Years After will still be rocking on for yet another ten."

<u>May 15 & 16, 1974</u>
Music Hall
Boston,
Massachusetts

Set List - May 15th: Rock & Roll Music To The World, Nowhere To Run, Good Morning Little School Girl, It's Getting Harder, Hobbit, Love Like A Man, Slow Blues In C, Look Me Straight Into The Eyes, Classical Thing, Scat Thing, I Can't Keep From Crying Sometimes, I'm Going Home. Encores: Sweet Little Sixteen, Choo Choo Mama, Roll Over Beethoven.

The set list for the May 16th Boston set was the same, but with only two encores.

May 17, 1974
The Spectrum
Philadelphia, PA

May 18, 1974
Arena
Hershey, PA

May 19, 1974
Civic Center
Baltimore, Maryland

May 21, 1974
Cincinnati, Ohio

May 22, 1974
The Omni
Atlanta, Georgia

May 23, 1974
St. Petersburg, Florida

May 24, 1974
Miami, Florida

May 25, 1974
Veteran's Memorial Coliseum
Jacksonville, Florida

May 26, 1974
Municipal Auditorium
Birmingham, AL

May 28, 1974
Cobo Hall
Detroit, Michigan

May 29, 1974
Ohio State Fairgrounds
Columbus, Ohio

May 30, 1974
Amphitheater
Chicago, Illinois

May 31, 1974
St. Paul, Minnesota

June 1, 1974
Memorial Auditorium
Kansas City, Missouri

June 4, 1974
Municipal Auditorium
San Antonio, Texas

June 5, 1974
Sam Houston Coliseum
Houston, Texas

June 6, 1974
Tarrant County Convention Center
Ft. Worth, Texas

June 7, 1974
Oklahoma City, Oklahoma

June 8, 1974
Civic Center
El Paso, Texas

June 9, 1974
Phoenix, Arizona

<u>June 11, 1974</u>
Bakersfield, California

<u>June 12 & 13, 1974</u>
Cow Palace San Francisco, California

<u>June 14 & 15, 1974</u>
Shrine Auditorium Los Angeles, California

<u>June 16, 1974</u>
Fresno, California

ALVIN LEE & COMPANY

<u>Oct 2 - Nov 13</u>
Alvin Lee & Co. rehearse at Space Studios for their upcoming tour

<u>November 1974</u>
Release of the Alvin Lee & Company double LP: "In Flight" Columbia PG 33187

Songs included on this album recorded live at the Rainbow Theater on March 22 are: Side One - Got To Keep Moving, Going Through The Door, Don't Be Cruel, Money Honey and I'm Writing You A Letter. Side Two - You Need Love Love Love, Freedom For The Stallion, Every Blues You've Ever Heard and All Life's Trials. Side Three - Intro, Let's Get Back, Ride My Train, There's A Feeling and Running Round.

Side Four - Mystery Train, Slow Down, Keep A Knocking, How Many Times, I've Got Eyes For You Baby, I'm Writing You A Letter (encore). After the release of the album, which reaches #65 in the U.S. charts, Alvin Lee goes on tour with Mel Collins, Ian Wallace, Steve Thompson and Ronnie Leahy.

November 21, 1974
Tivolis Concertsal Copenhagen, Denmark

Got To Keep Moving, Let's Get Back, Running Round, Freedom For The Stallion, Somebody's Calling Me, All Life's Trials (Alvin says, "this is an acoustic guitar....this is a song called All Life's Trials"), Time In Space, How Does It Feel, There's A Feeling, Let The Sea Burn Down, Every Blues You've Ever Heard, Percy's Blues (Alvin says, "this is a kind of jazz thing that Mel wrote, it's called Percy's Blues"), Money Honey, Going Through The Door, I'm Writing You A Letter, Ride My Train (the last two numbers feature super guitar solos by Alvin).

November 25, 1974
Concert Hall Gothenburg, Sweden

December 7, 1974
Heidelberg, Germany

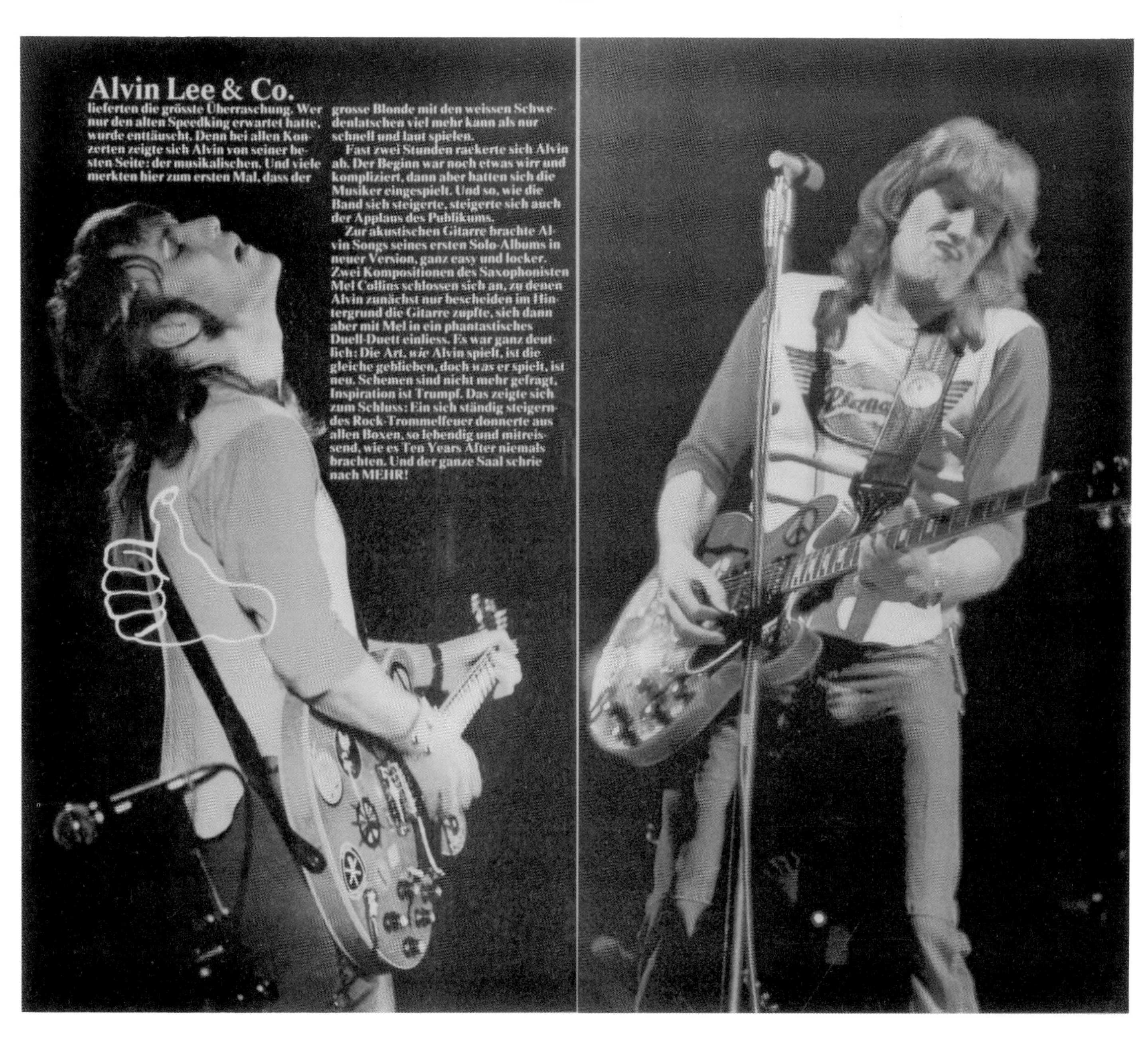

Alvin Lee & Co.

lieferten die grösste Überraschung. Wer nur den alten Speedking erwartet hatte, wurde enttäuscht. Denn bei allen Konzerten zeigte sich Alvin von seiner besten Seite: der musikalischen. Und viele merkten hier zum ersten Mal, dass der grosse Blonde mit den weissen Schwedenlatschen viel mehr kann als nur schnell und laut spielen.

Fast zwei Stunden rackerte sich Alvin ab. Der Beginn war noch etwas wirr und kompliziert, dann aber hatten sich die Musiker eingespielt. Und so, wie die Band sich steigerte, steigerte sich auch der Applaus des Publikums.

Zur akustischen Gitarre brachte Alvin Songs seines ersten Solo-Albums in neuer Version, ganz easy und locker. Zwei Kompositionen des Saxophonisten Mel Collins schlossen sich an, zu denen Alvin zunächst nur bescheiden im Hintergrund die Gitarre zupfte, sich dann aber mit Mel in ein phantastisches Duell-Duett einliess. Es war ganz deutlich: Die Art, *wie* Alvin spielt, ist die gleiche geblieben, doch *was* er spielt, ist neu. Schemen sind nicht mehr gefragt. Inspiration ist Trumpf. Das zeigte sich zum Schluss: Ein sich ständig steigerndes Rock-Trommelfeuer donnerte aus allen Boxen, so lebendig und mitreissend, wie es Ten Years After niemals brachten. Und der ganze Saal schrie nach MEHR!

December 14, 1974
Kilburn Gaumont State
London, England

January 10, 1975
Orpheum Theater
Boston, Massachusetts

Got To Keep Moving, Let's Get Back, Somebody's Calling, Somebody Waltz, Freedom For The Stallion, All Life's Trials, Time In Space, There's A Feeling, Every Blues You've Ever Heard, Percy's Blues, Money Honey, Jam (while Alvin replaces a broken string), Going Through The Door, I'm Writing You A Letter, Ride My Train & Slow Down.

January 12, 1975
Music Hall
West Hartford, Connecticut

January 18, 1975
Academy of Music
New York City, NY

Partial Set List as broadcast on the King Biscuit Flower Hour: Somebody's Calling, Somebody Waltz, Going Through The Door, Money Honey, and 'Ride My Train' (which contains one of Alvin Lee's best recorded guitar solos!)

Concert review from CASHBOX:

"It turns out, surprisingly, that the Alvin Lee of Alvin Lee & Company is ***not*** *the Alvin Lee of Ten Years After. After seven years which saw him develop into the Woodstock generation's prototypical flash guitarist, Lee has*

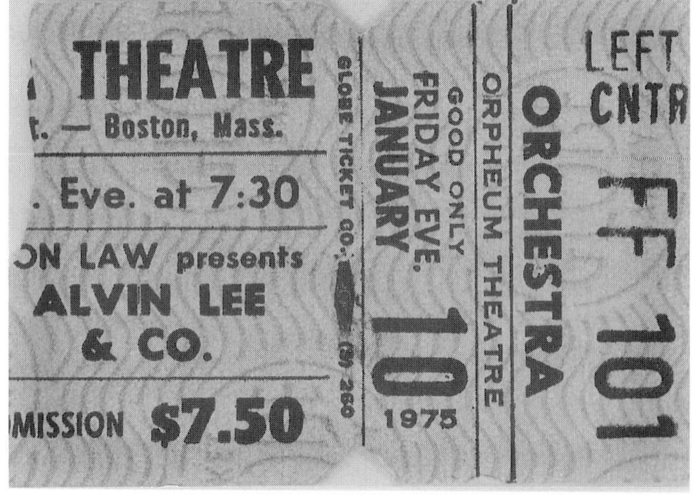

finally begun to free himself from his long stagnant image to again develop as a creative performer. With Ten Years After perhaps in permanent retirement Alvin has assembled an excellent crew of musicians, which includes ex-King Crimsonites Mel Collins (reeds, woodwinds) and Ian Wallace (drums); Ronnie Leahy (keyboards) and Steve Thompson (bass) were once with Stone The Crows. The group is rounded out with a percussionist and several back-up vocalists."

*"The new Lee material is successfully eclectic jazz/blues/rock in which the Columbia artist is more the conductor of the band than **the** band. His incredible technique is tempered these days with taste, demonstrating the famed speed only at the peaks of his rare solos, and leaving a lot of room for the other musicians to stretch out. Particularly impressive were a beautiful instrumental written by Mel Collins which featured his fine sax playing, a Collins-Ian Wallace jazz tune which highlighted Wallace's great percussive abilities, plus the Lee tunes - the funky 'Let's Get Back' and 'There's a Feeling' and Allen Toussaint's mellow 'Freedom For The Stallion'.*

Alvin Lee can still 'boogie with the beat' but he is an artist who has matured as both arranger and soloist and is now

a premiere rock performer well beyond the bounds of pubescent acid-blues."

January 19, 1975
Lisner Auditorium
Washington D. C.

January 22, 1975
Kleinhans Music Hall
Buffalo, New York

Gentle Giant opens for Alvin Lee & Company.

January 24, 1975
Masonic Auditorium
Detroit, Michigan

February 7, 1975
Long Beach Arena, California

Partial Set List: Every Blues You've Ever Heard, Percy's Blues (Alvin says, "On the alto sax Mel Collins will now perform one of his own compositions entitled Percy's Blues"), Money Honey, Going Through The Door, I'm Writing You A Letter.

February 11, 1975
Memorial Coliseum Portland, Oregon

The other performers on the bill were the James Cotten Blues Band and Johnny Winter.

Concert review from the OREGONIAN JOURNAL:

As leader of the popular British rock band Ten Years After, Alvin Lee was never a practitioner of subtlety. But Lee's reputation as "fastest guitar in the west" perpetrates an image he would just as soon forget. "I was getting to be known as an overplayer" said Lee in explaining why he decided last year to put TYA on the shelf indefinitely and concentrate on a new direction with his music. "People were coming to the concerts looking for a celluloid hero, something I'm not," he added. So now, in place of the mortar barrage that characterized much of TYA's music, we have Alvin Lee & Co., a toned down and much more diversified group of musicians than TYA ever was. Tuesday evening at Memorial Coliseum, Alvin Lee & Co. succeeded in carrying off its share of applause and an encore from the audience of around 6,500. There's not much room for comparison between TYA and Alvin's new band. In the case of Ten Years After, Lee was more or less locked into a pattern of random soloing, while the band concentrated on decibel assault. The new band's format seeks a more compatible balance between Lee and the five other musicians. (The group also includes two female vocalists who add some nice touches). Lee is in the spotlight most of the time but

not always for the purpose of dishing out speedy riffs, though there were enough of them to satisfy old TYA fans. He shares much of the work with Mel Collins on tenor sax, who moves the band towards a jazz flavor.

<u>**March 14, 1975**</u>
Brunel University
Uxbridge, England

Alvin Lee, Mel Collins, Ian Wallace, Ronald Leahy and Steve Thompson perform at the Social Club.

<u>**March 15, 1975**</u>
University
Loughborough,
England

BRUNEL UNIVERSITY S.U. SOCIAL CLUB
KINGSTON LANE, UXBRIDGE

FRI., 14th March

ALVIN LEE & CO

(featuring Alvin Lee, Mel Collins, Ian Wallace, Ronald Leahy & Steve Thompson)

+ SUPPORT

Tickets £1.20 (inc. VAT)

DISCO, BAR, LIGHTS & FOOD

WED., 19th MARCH

BE-BOP DELUX

+ DISCO

Admission 50p

Tube — Uxbridge Buses 203, 204, 227

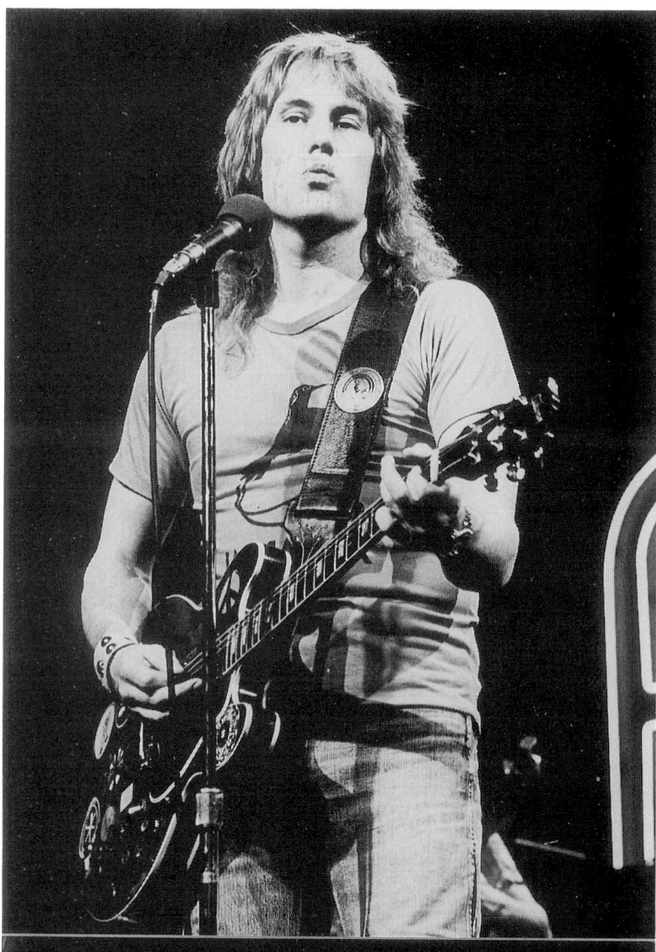

March 21, 1975
Alvin Lee & Co. appear on the Midnight Special TV show

This was episode #117 of the Midnight Special TV show and it was hosted by Black Oak Arkansas. The guest performers included Alvin Lee & Company, Montrose and Grey Ghost. Alvin Lee & Company performed "Somebody's Calling Me", "Time and Space", "Going Through The Door" and "Ride My Train".

March 22, 1975
Roundhouse
Dagenham
Essex, England

March 23, 1975
Pavilion
Hemel Hempstead, England

Concert Review from MELODY MAKER:

"Alvin Lee is a hunk of raw power and dynamism, as he incredibly demonstrated at Hemel Hempstead on Sunday. The rhythms were fast, driving and pulsating. From the word go Lee was in total command of the situation. There wasn't a second to reflect on whether his talents were more suitably utilized in Ten Years After. The individuality of his new act was cemented by some fluid jazzy saxophone played by the delightful Mel Collins. Add congas, bass, keyboards and drums, all with their own riveting style - and you couldn't get much further removed from TYA. Numbers like 'Freedom For The Stallion', and 'Money Honey' showed that the word company aptly described this outfit. Without one the others would be helpless. And in order to keep ravers drooling until the last moment, the definitive Lee solo was suppressed for the encore, then he really let rip."

March 27, 1975
Mayfair
Newcastle, England

March 29, 1975
Pavilion
Leescliffe, England

TEN YEARS AFTER

July - August 1975
Final American Tour

After the breakup of the band was announced in 1974, Ten Years After agreed to perform a final tour of the U.S. The song set for this big 40 date "farewell tour" was as listed for the August 21st Boston concert below. The 1975 Ten Years After U.S. tour has been described as "huge" and profit-wise it was their biggest ever, but after 8 years of "working on the road", the band felt it was time to quit.

Chris Wright:

"In the summer of 1974 the eventual breakup became a reality. While I had been expecting it, seeing tensions growing over a period of time, it was nonetheless a very upsetting affair. I had been closely and emotionally associated with the group since 1967 and many of my most pleasurable experiences in the music business involved this group and its development. A lot of hard work on the part of everyone went into building a

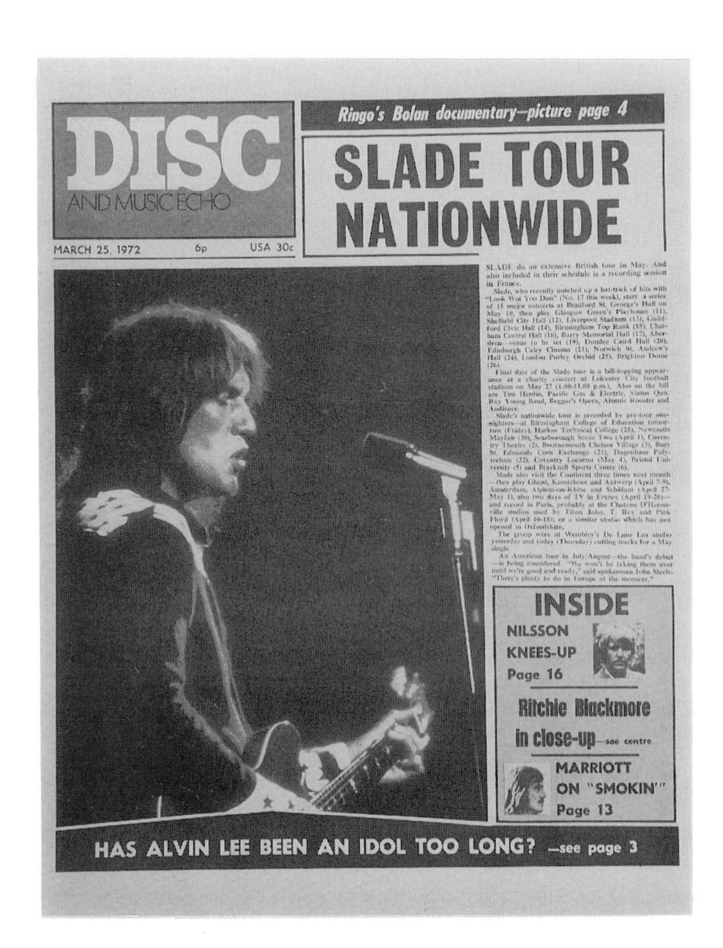

DISC
AND MUSIC ECHO

MARCH 25, 1972 6p USA 30c

Ringo's Bolan documentary—picture page 4

SLADE TOUR NATIONWIDE

SLADE do an extensive British tour in May. And also included in their schedule is a recording session in France.

Slade, who recently notched up a hat-trick of hits with "Look Wot You Dun" (No. 17 this week), start a series of 15 major concerts at Bradford St. George's Hall on May 10, then play Glasgow Green's Playhouse (11), Sheffield City Hall (12), Liverpool Stadium (13), Guildford Civic Hall (14), Birmingham Top Rank (15), Chatham Central Hall (16), Barry Memorial Hall (17), Aberdeen venue to be set (19), Dundee Caird Hall (20), Edinburgh Caley Cinema (21), Norwich St. Andrew's Hall (24), London Purley Orchid (25), Brighton Dome (26).

Final date of the Slade tour is a bill-topping appearance at a charity concert at Leicester City football stadium on May 27 (1.00-11.00 p.m.). Also on the bill are Tim Hardin, Pacific Gas & Electric, Status Quo, Roy Young Band, Beggar's Opera, Atomic Rooster and Audience.

Slade's nationwide tour is preceded by pre-tour one-nighters—at Birmingham College of Education tomorrow (Friday), Harlow Technical College (25), Newcastle Mayfair (30), Scarborough Scene Two (April 1), Coventry Theatre (2), Bournemouth Chelsea Village (3), Bury St. Edmunds Corn Exchange (21), Dagenham Polytechnic (22), Coventry Locarno (May 4), Bristol University (5) and Bracknell Sports Centre (6).

Slade also visit the Continent three times next month—they play Ghent, Kamtehout and Antwerp (April 7-9), Amsterdam, Alphen-on-Rhine and Schidam (April 27-May 1), also two days of TV in France (April 19-20)—and record in Paris, probably at the Chateau D'Herouville studios used by Elton John, T. Rex and Pink Floyd (April 10-18); or a similar studio which has just opened in Oxfordshire.

The group were at Wembley's De Lane Lea studio yesterday and today (Thursday) cutting tracks for a May single.

An American tour in July/August—the band's debut—is being considered. "We won't be taking them over until we're good and ready," said spokesman John Steele. "There's plenty to do in Europe at the moment."

INSIDE

NILSSON KNEES-UP Page 16

Ritchie Blackmore in close-up—see centre

MARRIOTT ON "SMOKIN'" Page 13

HAS ALVIN LEE BEEN AN IDOL TOO LONG? —see page 3

DISC
and MUSIC ECHO 1s

SEPTEMBER 5, 1970 EVERY THURSDAY USA 25c

I. o. W. 'Never again'
see this page

Jethro: big UK tour

JETHRO TULL top a nationwide British tour next month. It will be the group's first appearance here—apart from last weekend's Isle of Wight spot — for nearly 18 months.

Full tour dates—which include a closing concert at London's Royal Albert Hall on Tuesday, October 13 — are as follows:

SHEFFIELD City Hall, September 23
NOTTINGHAM ALBERT HALL (24)
BIRMINGHAM TOWN HALL (25)
NEWCASTLE CITY HALL (27)
LEICESTER De Montfort Hall (28)
ABERDEEN Music Hall (30)
DUNDEE Caird Hall (October 1)
GLASGOW Green's Playhouse (2)
MANCHESTER Free Trade Hall (3)
BRISTOL Colston Hall (4)
SOUTHAMPTON Guildhall (9)
LONDON Albert Hall (13)

Inside Britain's best-selling colour pop weekly

ELP GO OUT ON THE ROAD

Keith Emerson

EMERSON, Lake and Palmer follow up last weekend's Isle of Wight concert debut with a full British tour.

It opens at Wolverhampton on September 21, and so far TWO London venues are included. Further dates are to be added.

Full tour is: WOLVERHAMPTON Civic Hall (September 21), HULL City Hall (25), LONDON Royal Festival Hall (26), LEICESTER De Montfort Hall (27), PORTSMOUTH Guildhall (28), LEEDS City Hall (October 1), NEWCASTLE City Hall (4), BRIGHTON Dome (7), GLASGOW Playhouse (9), DUNDEE Caird Hall (11), BRISTOL Colston Hall (19), BOURNEMOUTH Winter Gardens (20), BIRMINGHAM Town Hall (21), CROYDON Fairfield Hall (25), and SHEFFIELD City Hall (27).

Hendrix concert—free show? see page 4

Alvin says 'no' to movies.
Feature on page 3

Supreme Mary Wilson —exclusive p. 11

I. O. W. THE DISILLUSIONED ORGANISERS SPEAK

THE Third Isle Of Wight Festival of Music, billed as "the last great event," has lived up to its name—there will never be another.

As nearly half the estimated 600,000 people at East Afton Farm pitched camp on "Devastation Hill," overlooking the site, the festival's pressman said: "We will never organise another Isle Of Wight pop festival — or another festival anywhere. We are all very disillusioned."

At presstime it was estimated that Fiery Creations, promoters of the festival were £92,000 in debt, with over £20,000 lost in damage to property on Sunday alone.

Says Ron Foulk: "I suppose the shout for free music was inevitable. But the spirit which created this festival—a defiance of convention—has now destroyed it."

And many of those backstage at the weekend confirmed that not only was this the last Isle Of Wight festival, but the last big pop festival in Britain.

Now turn to page 5 for complete beginning-to-end coverage.

Billboard Publication

record mirror

March 27, 1971 8p

BEATLES BREAK-UP SINGLE BY RINGO

BY RM NEWS TEAM

RINGO Starr's new single, 'Don't Come Easy', will probably be released in three weeks — and Apple spokesmen say it is easily the best thing he has ever written. He penned both words and music.

Only doubt is which of three versions will be used. Klaus Voorman and George Harrison are featured on one and Eric Clapton makes a 'guest' appearance on another.

But the main interest could be on the 'B' side, described as a 'fairly satirical' comment on what is happening to the Beatles right now. In fact, it was written last August but is still relevant to today's Beatle break-up — and subsequent spate of solo singles.

The 'A' side was written a year ago. Sample lyrics: "If you wanna sing the blues, you gotta pay your dues and you know it don't come easy." It was recorded at the EMI studios in Abbey Road and at Trident Studios.

Ringo is currently working on a new album in his studio at home and is learning to play guitar.

NEW KINKS MAXI DISC

THE first ever maxi-single from the Kinks is released on Pye this Friday. And two LPs, one by Ray Davies and one by the Kinks, are also lined up.

The four tracks on the maxi-single are all taken from the film 'Percy' and titles are 'God's Children', 'The Way Love Used To Be', 'Moments' and an instrumental version of 'Lola'. The record runs for 13 minutes and is the first maxi to be released on Pye.

Meanwhile, the Kinks are planning to record tracks for their next album, 'Kinks Part II', while on their U.S. tour.

The Ray Davies album is titled 'Songs I Did For Auntie' and is made up of compositions he wrote for two BBC TV series, 'Where Was Spring?' and 'At The Eleventh Hour'.

Nottingham's most famous pop son

YOUR TOWN

Once again RM breaks new ground and turns the spotlight on pop in the provinces

This week: NOTTINGHAM, the home of TYA... INSIDE

COMING SOON: NEWCASTLE

Plus, this week, in your plus pop paper

DEEP PURPLE • JAMES BROWN
CHAIRMEN • JETHRO TULL

For Arrival now read survival

ARRIVAL: CAROL, who has left, is on far right

ARRIVAL, missing from the public eye for the last nine months after their "I Will Survive" hit single, have a new start.

The group have changed personnel, broken with discoverer and manager Tony Hall, and switched record companies.

A single, the Jim Webb composition "Let My Life (Let It Be A Love Story)", is being released on CBS this Friday, and Arrival will also begin work in the early part of April on an album.

The band has signed a four-year worldwide deal with CBS for an undisclosed five-figure sum.

Referring to their split with Tony Hall, who has guided their career from the start, they said: "The group thank Tony Hall for his assistance in developing our career and acknowledge our indebtedness professionally to Tony's companies and Decca Records."

Arrival is currently a four-piece outfit, featuring vocalists Dyan Birch, Paddy McHugh and Frank Collins, and organist Tony O'Malley. Other members, drummer Lloyd Courtney, bassist Don Hume and vocalist Carol Carter, left the group recently after a disagreement about musical policy.

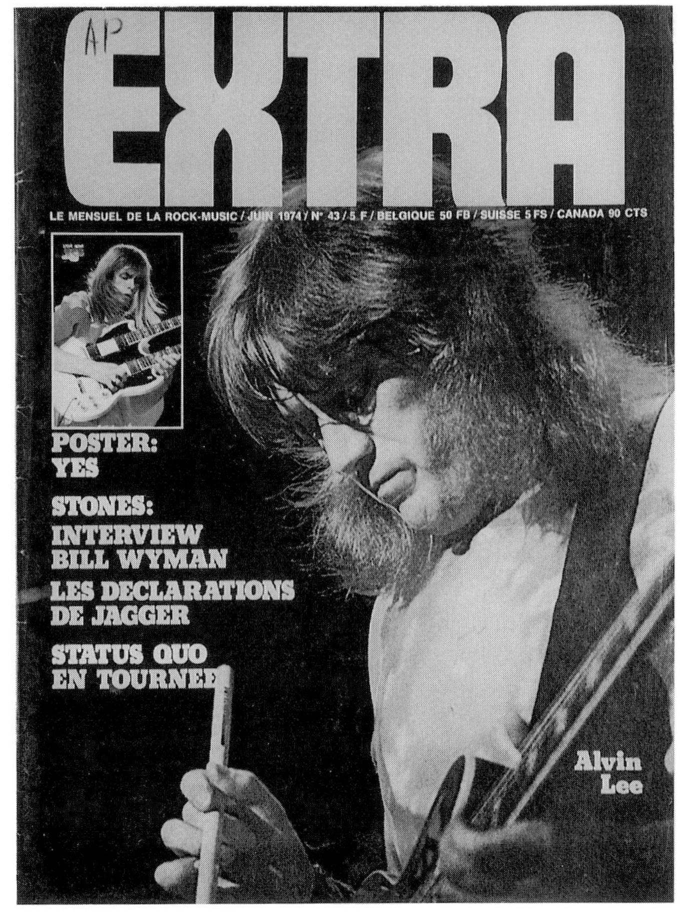

EXTRA

LE MENSUEL DE LA ROCK-MUSIC / JUIN 1974 / N° 43 / 5 F / BELGIQUE 50 FB / SUISSE 5 FS / CANADA 90 CTS

POSTER: YES

STONES: INTERVIEW BILL WYMAN

LES DECLARATIONS DE JAGGER

STATUS QUO EN TOURNEE

Alvin Lee

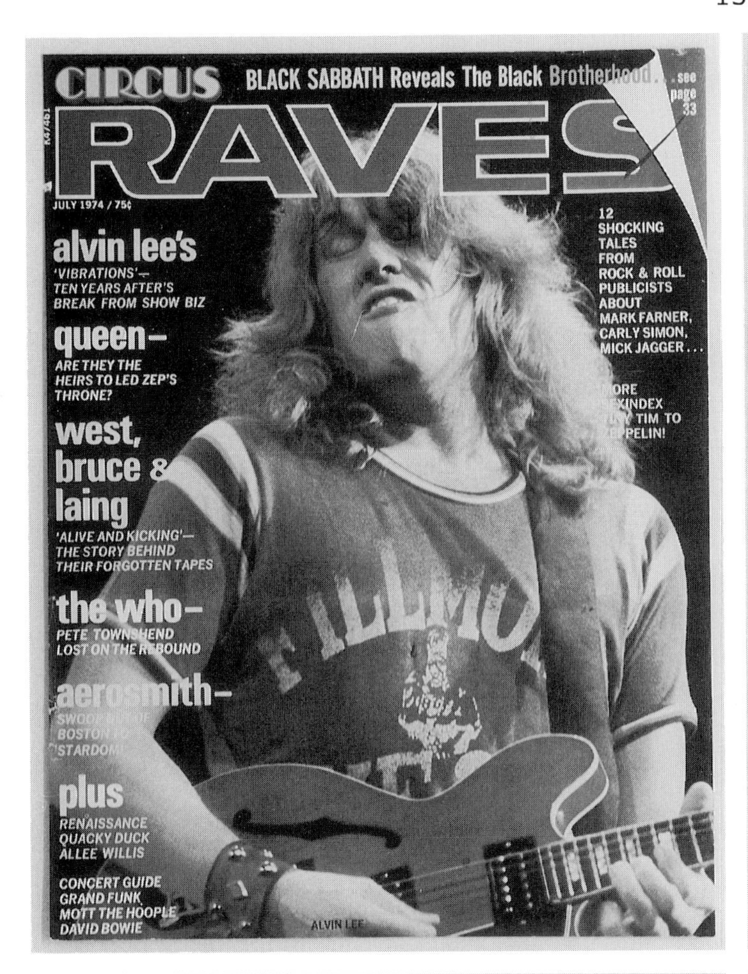
CIRCUS
BLACK SABBATH Reveals The Black Brotherhood . . . see page 33
RAVES
JULY 1974 / 75¢
alvin lee's
'VIBRATIONS'— TEN YEARS AFTER'S BREAK FROM SHOW BIZ
queen–
ARE THEY THE HEIRS TO LED ZEP'S THRONE?
west, bruce & laing
'ALIVE AND KICKING'— THE STORY BEHIND THEIR FORGOTTEN TAPES
the who–
aerosmith–
plus
RENAISSANCE
QUACKY DUCK
ALLEE WILLIS
CONCERT GUIDE
GRAND FUNK
MOTT THE HOOPLE
DAVID BOWIE
12 SHOCKING TALES FROM ROCK & ROLL PUBLICISTS ABOUT MARK FARNER, CARLY SIMON, MICK JAGGER . . .
ALVIN LEE

MusicWorld &
DEC '74 25p
BEAT
& INTERNATIONAL RECORDING STUDIO
INSTRUMENTAL
PRICES OF OVER 3000 NEW GUITARS, AMPS, SPEAKERS, KEYBOARDS & DRUMS
THE NEW ALVIN LEE
NEIL YOUNG'S FUTURE
RON WOOD RECORDING AT HOME
SONGWRITERS: THE LAW'S ON YOUR SIDE
DRUM SURVEY

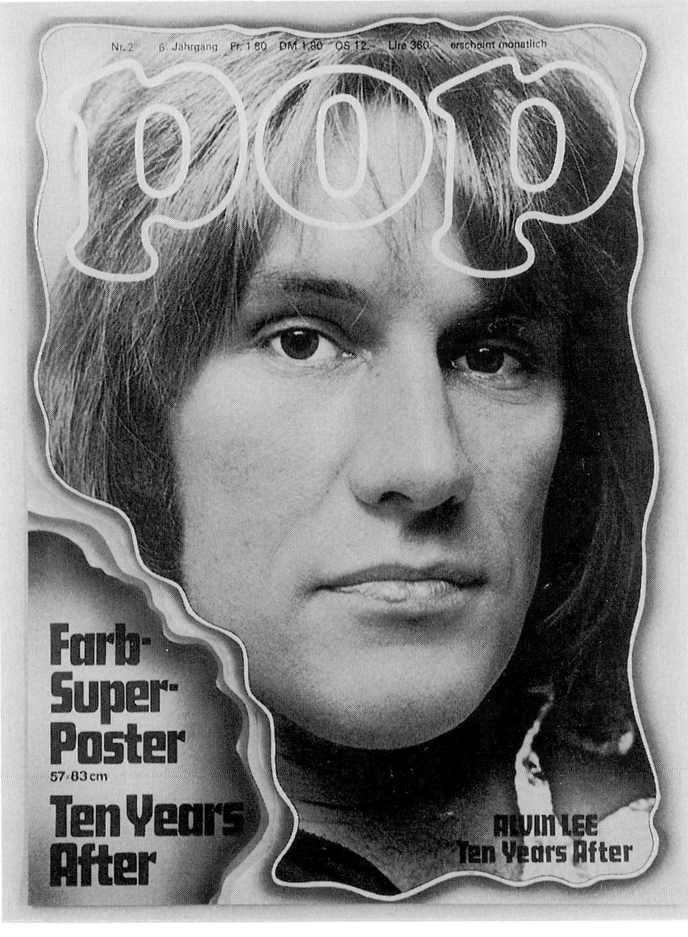
pop
Farb-Super-Poster
57×83 cm
Ten Years After
ALVIN LEE
Ten Years After

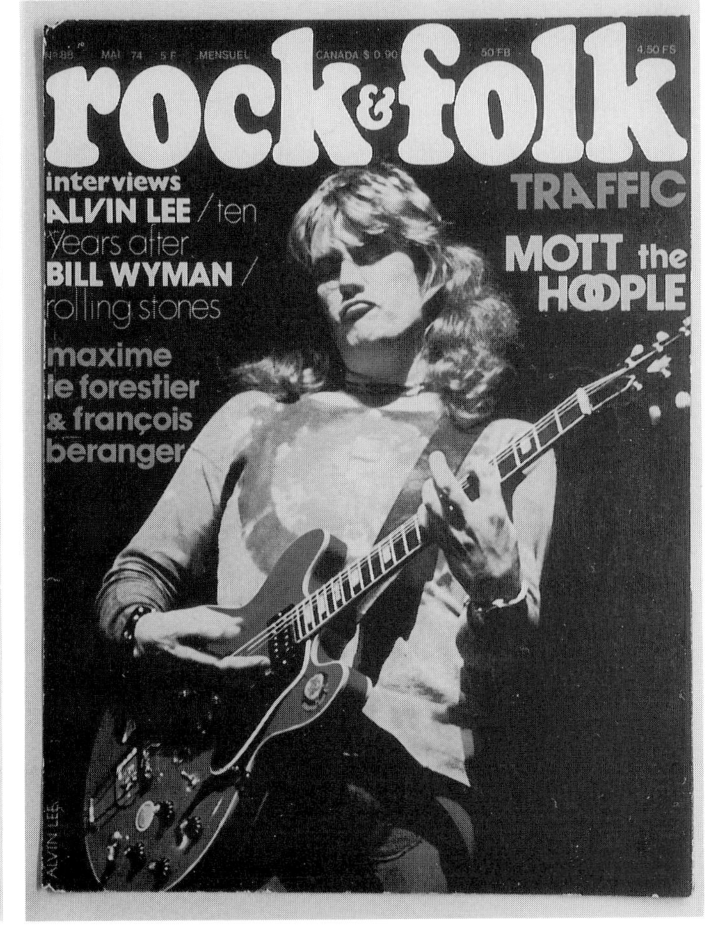
rock&folk
interviews
ALVIN LEE / ten Years after
BILL WYMAN / rolling stones
maxime le forestier & françois beranger
TRAFFIC
MOTT the HOOPLE
ALVIN LEE

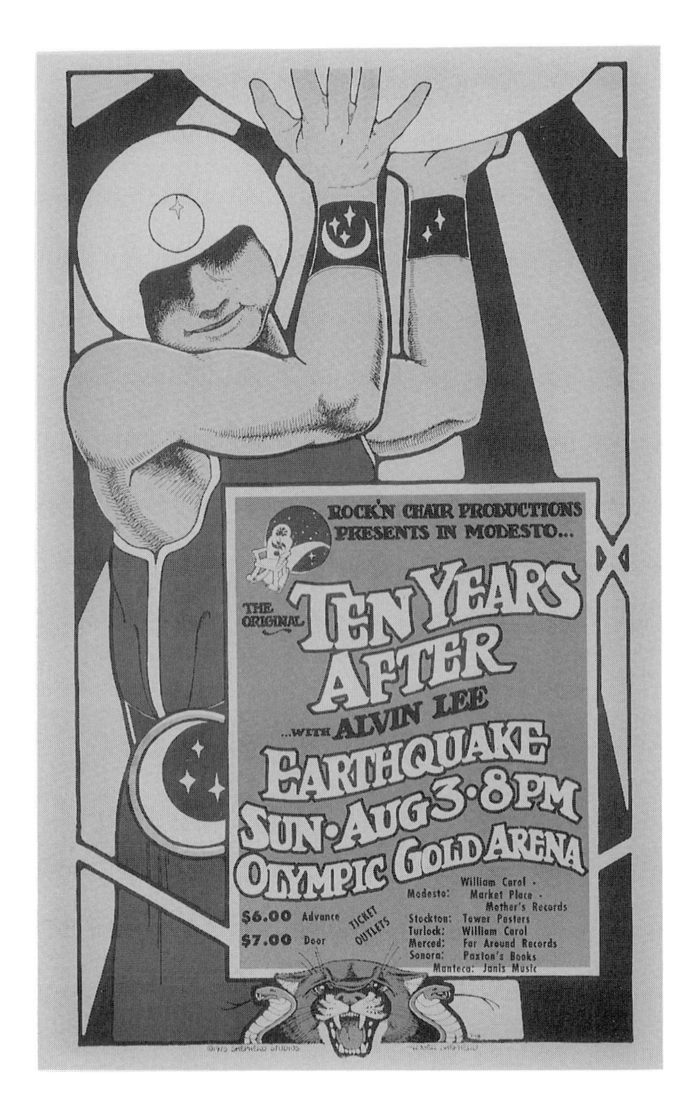

solid and long term career which, as the personalities grew apart, it became more difficult to keep coordinated. In the summer of 1975 I managed to persuade the group to reform for another highly successful tour in the U.S. but by the end of the tour the final writing was on the wall.

Alvin Lee: *"We were going through the 'Country House Syndrome', we all had nice houses in the country and were starting families and things like that. There wasn't really that much will to go out and sit in the Holiday Inn for six months. Also, the other syndrome of a band breaking up was we were all building our own home studios, and nobody wanted to go and play out, we all wanted to stay in and make our own music. I think it's a natural thing to happen. I think we just weren't communicating. We had just spent all those years working together and, I think, quite naturally just drifted apart a bit, started to find other interests beside the band. I think, in a way, it was quite fitting we finished then, because we were always very honest. It was a very honest band, there was no bullshit, no hyping, and really, the honesty was going out of it, and we got disenchanted with that. We were going out and playing automatically."*

"Our music had turned into such a steady format that it was really getting a bit boring. Playing rock 'n' roll every night for five or six years can get a bit dull. It's like being a traveling jukebox - plug in and away you go. Next night, same thing. It took a break to get us out of that."

The first gig of the 1975 tour was in Birmingham, Alabama. "We hardly saw each other for fourteen months after having seen each other every day for eight years. We got there the day before and went to bed. The next day we went to the gig, rehearsed for half an

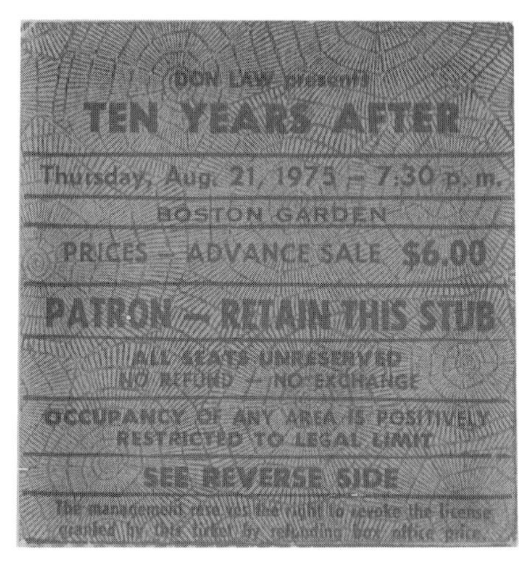

hour in a Winnebago, went out and did an incredible set. It all came back just like that after fourteen months!"

<u>**August 3, 1975**</u>
Olympic Golden Arena
Modesto, California

Opening for Ten Years After is a band called Earthquake.

<u>**August 4, 1975**</u>
Winterland
San Francisco, California

<u>**August 10, 1975**</u>
St. Benard Civic Center
New Orleans, LA

The Outlaws open for Ten Years After and play their second professional gig !

<u>**August 21, 1975**</u>
Boston Garden
Massachusetts

Lynyrd Skynyrd opens for Ten Years After. The TYA set list is: Rock & Roll Music To The World, Love Like A Man, Good Morning Little School Girl, Slow Blues In C, "We're In Boston" (brief Shuffle), Hobbit, One Of These Days, Classical Thing, Scat Thing, I Can't Keep From Crying Sometimes, I'm Going Home, Sweet Little Sixteen, Choo Choo Mama.

<u>**August 22, 1975**</u>
Roosevelt Field, New Jersey

This show was billed as "The Battle Of The Bands".

Concert review from CIRCUS MAGAZINE:

Determined to prove he was born to rock and roll, Alvin Lee has reformed Ten Years After and is fighting hard to avoid becoming an anachronism. They are still playing the same old songs but with more conviction than they've mustered in years. So far their most impressive victory on the comeback road was a Battle of the Bands at Jersey City's Roosevelt Stadium with Lynyrd Skynyrd and Rod Stewart & The Faces, which Ten Years After won hands down!

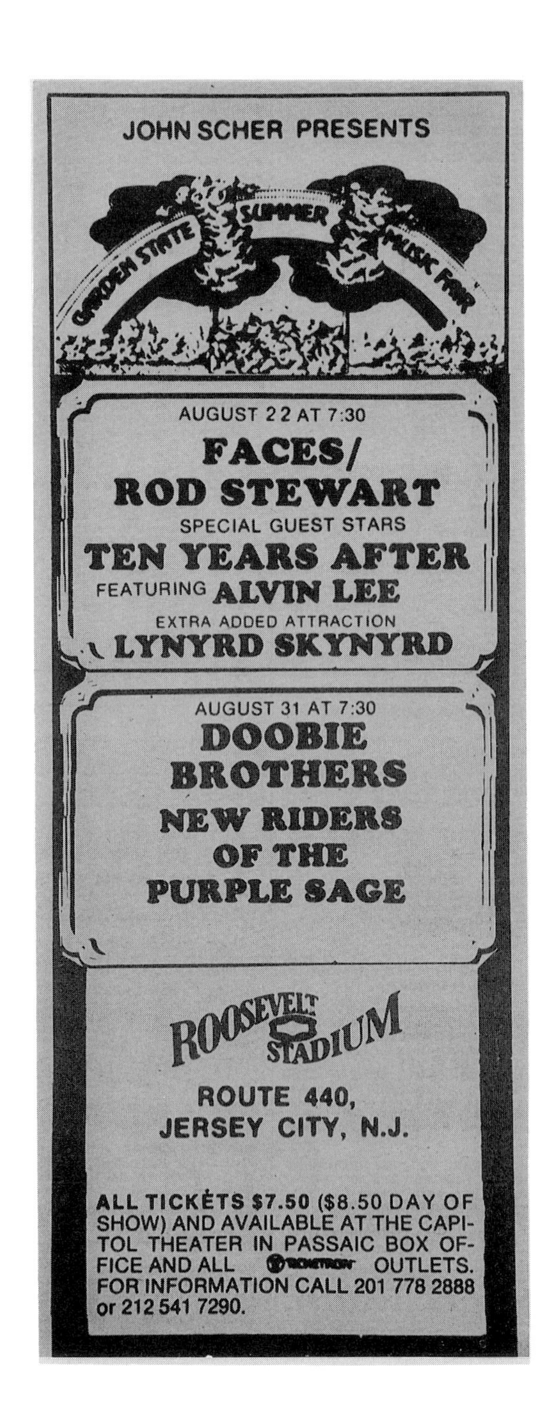

<u>August 24, 1975</u>
Commack Arena
Long Island, New York

The bill also includes Peter Frampton and Sassafras. Part of the "Frampton Comes Alive" LP is from this concert.

<u>August 1975</u>
The Spectrum
Philadelphia, PA

Ten Years After is supported by Peter Frampton.

DAILY PLANET concert review by Jim Bugno:

Showing much of the same drive that characterized their earlier efforts, Ten Years After featuring Alvin Lee returned to headline a Spectrum concert. They turned in a fine set near the end of a reunion tour. The set was comprised of solid favorites; "R&R Music To The World", "I Can't Keep From Crying Sometimes", "Good Morning Little Schoolgirl", "Love Like A Man" and, of course, "I'm Going Home" among others. Just how good were they ? Good enough to remind me of the way they were introduced at the old ***Electric Factory*** *the first time they headlined there: "Ladies & Gentlemen" the announcer proudly and sincerely stated, "One of the greatest - Ten Years After!"*

<u>September 1975</u>
Release of the LP:
"Pump Iron"
Columbia PC 33796

Alvin wanted to name this album ***"As The Sea Burns Down"*** *but the record company issued it as Pump Iron. Other artists who perform on the album include:* ***Tim Hinkley*** *(keyboards),* ***Bryson Graham*** *(drums),* ***Ian Wallace*** *(drums),* ***Boz Burrell*** *(bass),* ***Mel Collins*** *(soprano sax),* ***Ronnie Leahy*** *(organ),* ***Steve Thompson*** *(bass) and* ***Andy Pyle*** *(bass). The songs on Side One are: One More Chance* (Alvin Lee 3:52), *Try To Be Righteous* (Alvin Lee 4:04), *You Told Me* (Alvin Lee 3:40), *Have Mercy* (Alvin Lee 2:50) and *Julian Rice* (Alvin Lee 4:59). *Side Two: Time And Space* (Alvin Lee 2:44), *Burnt Fungas* (K. Armstrong 3:13), *The Darkest Night* (Alvin Lee 2:26), *It's All Right Now* (Alvin Lee 2:37), *Truckin' Down The Other Way* (Alvin Lee 2:31) *and Let The Sea Burn Down* (Alvin Lee 6:46).

<u>April 24, 1976</u>
University
Cardiff, England

The opening band was FBI. This was the first date of the "Saguitar Tour", named after Alvin's astrological sign Sagitarius. An LP of the same name was scheduled for release on May 28th, and it was preceded by a single: "Sea Of Heartbreak" (a former hit by country artist Don Gibson) with "It's A Gaz" on the B-Side. But the ***"Saguitar"*** *album was with-held, reportedly due to contract disputes, and unfortunately it never got released.*

<u>April 30, 1976</u>
University
Bradford, England

<u>May 1, 1976</u>
Birmingham,
England

<u>May 7, 1976</u>
University
Bristol, England

<u>May 8, 1976</u>
Ipswich - Gaumont,
England

<u>May 15, 1976</u>
University
York, England

<u>May 19, 1976</u>
Queensway Hall
Dunstable, England

<u>May 22, 1976</u>
Polytechnic
Leicester, England

<u>May 23, 1976</u>
Roundhouse
Chalk Farm
London, England

With ***Jeff Beck****, Kraan and the George Hatcher Band.*

<u>May 31, 1976</u>
Roots Hall Stadium
Essex, England

The "Southend Sounds 76" open air concert at the Southend United football grounds.

<u>**Oct 76 - Jan 77**</u>
Alvin Lee Band jams and records at Space Studios

Some of the tracks are released later by Chrysalis on the LP "Let It Rock" in 1978.

TEN YEARS AFTER

<u>**April 18 - May 13**</u>
Alvin Lee, Leo Lyons, Chick Churchill and David Potts record at Space Studios

The songs recorded were: "Who's Winning The Human Race", "Ain't Nuthin Shakin", "The Devil's Screaming" (jams), "Can't Sleep At Night", "I'm A Tail Dragger", "You Can't Always Get What You Want" and "It's A Gas", but the project was scrubbed.

CIRCUS MAGAZINE inaccurately reports:

"Ten Years After have reformed in secrecy and have virtually completed a comeback album for release by early summer. A major tour is being lined up in America from July onward, with British dates set for later in the year. The personnel includes three original members: ***Alvin Lee****, guitar and vocals,* ***Leo Lyons*** *on bass,* ***Chick Churchill*** *on keyboards, and* ***David Potts*** *replacing* ***Rick Lee*** *on drums. Lee is too involved in his production company to participate."*

TEN YEARS LATER

Alvin forms a power trio with Tom Compton on drums and Mick Hawksworth on bass.

<u>**April 1978**</u>
Release of the Ten Years Later LP: "Rocket Fuel" RSO RS13033

All titles are written by Alvin Lee. The album is recorded and mixed at Space Studios.

Side One contains: Rocket Fuel (3:17), *Gonna Turn You On* (4:58), *Friday The 13th* (4:56), *Somebody Callin' Me* (2:46) *and Somebody's Waltz* (3:09). *Side Two includes: Ain't Nuthin' Shakin'* (5:02), *Alvin's Blue Thing* (0:27), *Baby Don't You Cry* (3:15), *The Devil's Screaming - Pt. 1* (1:31), *(The Battle) and The Devil's Screaming - Pt. 2* (8:14). *The album climbs to #15 in the U.S.*

<u>**April 8, 1978**</u>
Gustav-Siegle Haus Stuttgart, Germany

The concert is broadcast live on WLIR-FM radio: Gonna Turn You On, Good Morning Little School Girl (Alvin says, "this is a song some of you might remember, it's called Mario Andretti"), Help Me, It's a Gaz (Alvin says, "we're gonna boogie on the bass"), Ain't Nuthin' Shakin' (includes a 25 minute drum solo by Tom Compton), Scat Thing, Hey Joe, I'm Going Home, Choo Choo Mama, Rip It Up.

August 26, 1978
Donaupark
Ulm, Germany

Other acts on the bill included: Genesis, Frank Zappa, Joan Baez, John McLaughlin & The One Truth Band, Scorpions and Brand X.

September 1, 1978
Radrennbahn - Mungersdorf
Cologne, Germany

September 3, 1978
Ludwigsparkstadion
Saarbrucken, Germany

September 8, 1978
Hammersmith Odeon
London, England

Gonna Turn You On, Good Morning Little School Girl, Help Me, It's a Gaz (Alvin says, "the chaps in the Rolling Stones mobile truck are physically changing over the tapes, they are actually recording this

April 15, 1978
Stadthalle
Offenbach, Germany

April 26, 1978
Pavilion de Paris
Porte de Panpin
Paris, France

The show is taped and part of it is later broadcast on the BBC "Old Grey Whistle Test" TV show.

May 19, 1978
Winterland
San Francisco, California

Partial Set List: I'm Gonna Turn You On, Good Morning Little School Girl, Help Me, Ain't Nuthin' Shakin', Scat Thing, Hey Joe, I'm Going Home.

May 31, 1978
Armadillo World Headquarters
Austin, Texas

July 1978
Stage West
Hartford, Connecticut

July 23, 1978
Calderone Concert Hall - Long Island
Hempstead, NY

live"), Scat Thing (brief version), Ain't Nuthin' Shakin' (Alvin says, "this is a new one off Rocket Fuel"), Scat Thing, Hey Joe, I'm Going Home, Choo Choo Mama, Rip It Up, Sweet Little Sixteen, Roll Over Beethoven.

<u>September 13, 1978</u>
Grugahalle
Essen, Germany

Gonna Turn You On, Help Me, Ain't Nuthin' Shakin', It's a Gaz, Hey Joe, Scat Thing, I'm Going Home, Choo Choo Mama, Rip It Up, Sweet Little Sixteen and Roll Over Beethoven. This concert is taped and several songs are broadcast on the "Rockpalast" TV program: Gonna Turn You On, Help Me, Ain't Nuthin' Shakin', I'm Going Home and Roll Over Beethoven. The rest of the concert and a pre-show interview with Ten Years Later were also shot on video, however the 42 minute TV broadcast was limited to the five songs listed above.

<u>September 29, 1978</u>
Deutschlandhalle
Berlin, Germany

Partial Set List: Got To Keep Moving, Gonna Turn You On (Alvin says, "brand new number from a brand new record called Rocket Fuel....it's called I'm Gonna Turn You On"), Friday The 13th, Good Morning Little School Girl, Help Me, Ain't Nuthin' Shakin' (Alvin says, "We've got a new number for you.... it's called Ain't Nuthin' Shakin' But The Leaves On The Trees"), Scat Thing (an extended version), I'm Writing You A Letter, Hey Joe.

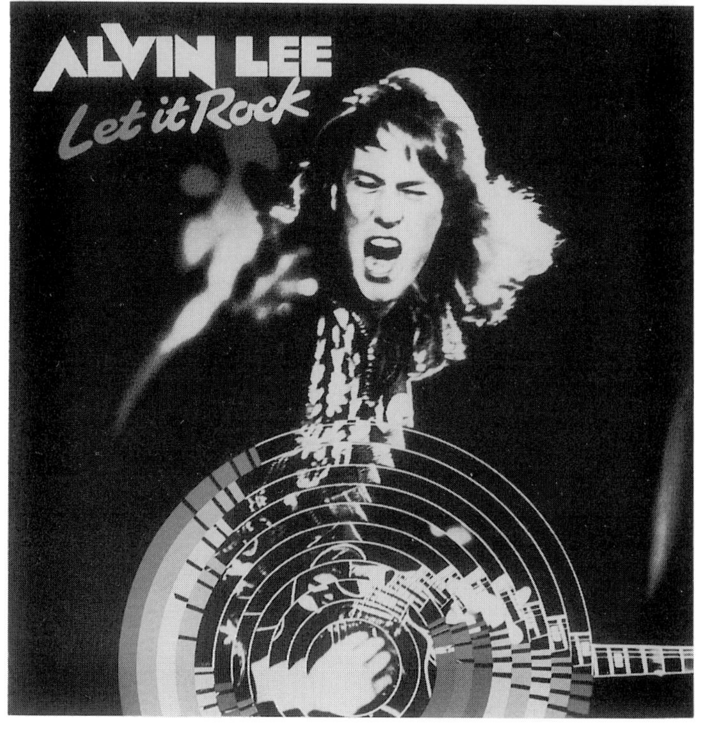

<u>December 1978</u>
Release of the Alvin Lee LP: "Let It Rock"
Chrysalis CHR 1190

This LP consists of tracks that the Alvin Lee Band had recorded at Space Studios between November 1976 and January 1977. The record company's decision to release it probably had a lot to do with Alvin's renewed popularity with Ten Years Later! Side One includes: Chemicals, Chemistry, Mystery and More (3:47), *Love The Way You Rock Me* (3:17), *Ain't Nobody* (5:05), *Images Shifting* (4:41) *and Little Boy* (4:43). *Side Two contains: Downhill Lady Racer* (3:40), *World Is Spinning Faster* (5:27), *Through With Your Lovin'* (5:00), *Time To Meditate* (3:55) and *Let It Rock* (2:59). *It has been stated that the "Let It Rock" LP is the missing* ***"Saguitar"*** *album that had been scheduled for release in May 1976, however that was a separate project and the music remains unreleased.*

May 15, 1979
Flint, Michigan

May 16, 1979
Saginaw, Michigan

May 17, 1979
Cobo Hall
Detroit, Michigan

May 18, 1979
Chicago, Illinois

May 19, 1979
Hammond, Indiana

May 22, 1979
Atlanta, Georgia

May 23, 1979
Dothan, Alabama

May 24, 1979
Columbus, Georgia

May 25, 1979
Jacksonville, Florida

May 26, 1979
Miami, Florida

May 27, 1979
Ft. Myers, Florida

May 31, 1979
The Warehouse
New Orleans, Louisiana

Black Oak Arkansas is the opening act.

June 1, 1979
Huntsville, Alabama

June 2, 1979
Mobile, Alabama

June 9, 1979
Stanley Theater
Pittsburgh, PA

June 15, 1979
Calderone Hall
Hempstead, NY

June 26, 1979
Portland, Oregon

June 27, 1979
Seattle, Washington

June 28, 1979
Auditorium
Oakland, California

June 29, 1979
Long Beach, CA

August 26, 1979
Ulm, Germany

September 1979
Release of the LP: "Ride On"
RSO RS13049

Side One is recorded at Space Studios and contains the following Alvin Lee titles: Too Much (3:49), *It's A Gaz* (4:01), *Ride On Cowboy* (3:12), *Sittin'*

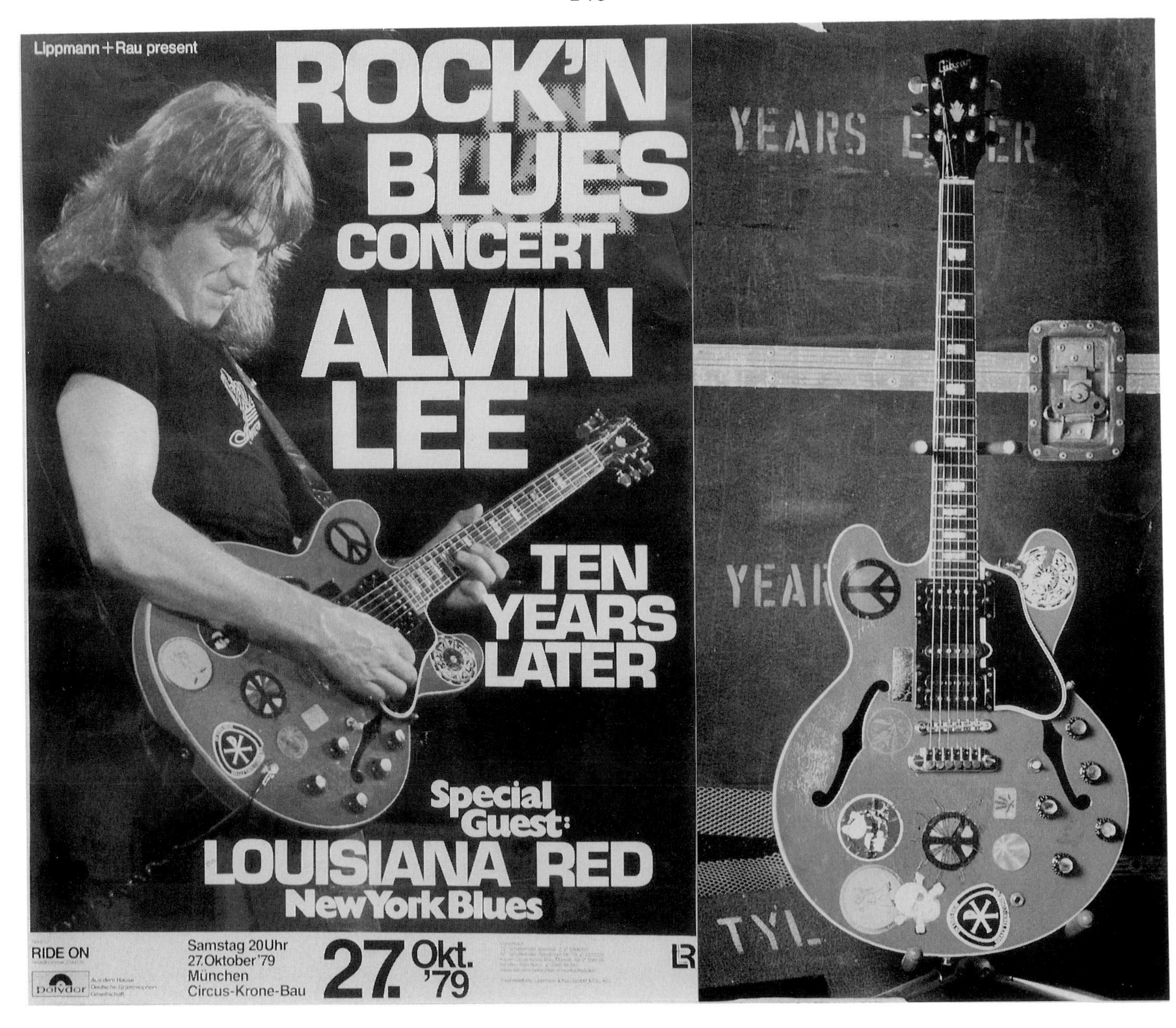

Here (3:58) *and Can't Sleep At Night* (2:31). *Side Two contains the following live concert recordings from the September 1978 Hammersmith Odeon show in London: Ain't Nuthin' Shakin'* (5:08), *Scat Encounter* (0:57), *Hey Joe* (5:41) *and Going Home* (8:15). *The album reaches #158 in the U.S.*

The following singles from the LP are also released in September: "Ride On Cowboy"/ "Sittin' Here" and "Ride On Cowboy"/"Can't Sleep At Night".

September 3, 1979
Saarbrucken, Germany

October 27, 1979
Circus Krone
Munich, Germany

November 20, 1979
BBC-TV "Old Grey Whistle Test" show

TYL perform "Hey Joe".

November 26, 1979
Odeon
Birmingham, England

November 27, 1979
DeMontfort Hall
Leicester, England

November 28, 1979
Hammersmith Odeon
London, England

November 29, 1979
City Hall
Newcastle, England

November 30, 1979
Colston Hall
Bristol, England

December 19, 1979
Cow Palace
San Francisco, California

Ten Years Later open for Kansas.

January 6, 1980
Civic Auditorium
San Jose, California

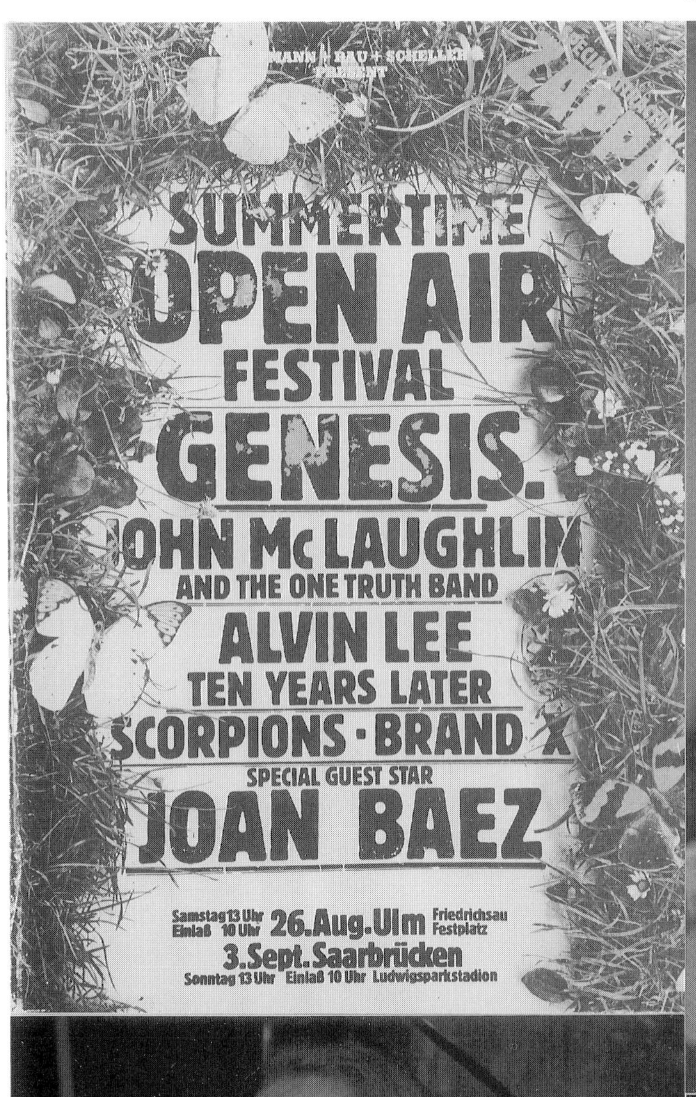
SUMMERTIME
OPEN AIR
FESTIVAL
GENESIS.
JOHN McLAUGHLIN
AND THE ONE TRUTH BAND
ALVIN LEE
TEN YEARS LATER
SCORPIONS · BRAND X
SPECIAL GUEST STAR
JOAN BAEZ
Samstag 13 Uhr
Einlaß 10 Uhr
26. Aug. Ulm
Friedrichsau
Festplatz
3. Sept. Saarbrücken
Sonntag 13 Uhr Einlaß 10 Uhr Ludwigsparkstadion

Ludwig
Ludwig

May 1980
Ric Lee joins a reformed version of Chicken Shack with Stan Webb (guitar & vocals), and Andy Pyle (bass).

The outfit lasts two years until May 1982. During this period they record two LPs, "Chicken Shack" (Gull Records) and "Roadie's Concerto" (RCA).

ALVIN LEE BAND

Alvin Lee (lead guitar & vocals), Steve Gould (guitar & vocals), Mickey Feat (bass & vocals) and Tom Compton (drums).

September 30, 1980
Pavillion
Bath, England

October 1980
Release of the Alvin Lee Band LP: "Free Fall"
Atlantic SD 19287

The album tracks are recorded at Space Studios and remixed at Marcus Musik in London. Side One includes: I Don't Wanna Stop (Gould & Feat 4:11), *Take The Money And Run* (Rafferty 4:28), *One Lonely Hour* (Lee & Gould 4:28), *Heartache* (Lee & Gould 3:15) *and Stealin'* (Gould 3:28). *Side Two: Ridin' Truckin'* (Lee 3:34), *No More Lonely Nights* (Gould & Lee 4:27), *City Lights* (Lee 4:05), *Sooner Or Later* (Arnell 3:32) and *Dustbin City* (Christmas 2:38).

October 1, 1980
Top Rank
Birmingham, England

October 2, 1980
King George's Hall
Blackburn, England

October 3, 1980
City Hall
Hull, England

October 4, 1980
Market Hall
Carlisle, England

October 5, 1980
Tiffany's
Glasgow, Scotland

October 6, 1980
Town Hall
Middlesbrough, England

October 8, 1980
Top Rank
Sheffield, England

October 9, 1980
Palais
Nottingham, England

October 10, 1980
University
Cardiff, Wales

October 11, 1980
Liesure Center
Maidenhead, England

October 14, 1980
University
Liecester, England

October 15, 1980
Sussex University
Brighton, England

October 16, 1980
Art Center
Poole, England

October 17, 1980
Surrey University
Guildford, England

October 21, 1980
Strand Lyceum
London, England

With Chevy and the Ronnie Lane Band.

November 1980
Release of the single: "I Don't Wanna Stop"/ "Heartache"

December 5, 1980
Park West
Chicago, Illinois

Are You Ready (To Rock & Roll), Good Morning Little School Girl, Heartache, No More Lonely Nights, Ridin' Truckin', Help Me (Alvin says, "we would like to do a little blues... Chicago is the home of the blues !"), Slow Down, Scat Thing, Stealin', I'm Going Home, Choo Choo Mama, Rip It Up, Sweet Little Sixteen, Roll Over Beethoven.

December 16, 1980
Las Vegas, Nevada

The Alvin Lee Band opens for Kansas.

December 19, 1980
Cow Palace
San Francisco, CA

December 26, 1980
Calderone Concert Hall - Long Island
Hempstead, NY

The following songs are broadcast during the BBC Rock Hour Show on WLIR-FM: Are You Ready, Good Morning Little School Girl, No More Lonely Nights, Ridin' Truckin', Stealin', I'm Going Home, Choo Choo Mama, Rip It Up.

December 27, 1980
Loew's Center for the Performing Arts
Worcester, Massachusetts

December 30, 1980
Capitol Center
Largo, Maryland

December 31, 1980
Cobo Hall
Detroit, Michigan

This show is broadcast on WABX-FM radio: Are You Ready, Good Morning Little School Girl, No More Lonely Nights, Ridin' Truckin', Help Me, Stealin' (with drum solo by Tom "Animal" Compton), Slow Down, Scat Thing, Hey Joe, "Going Down To Detroit" (brief improvisation by Alvin), I'm Going Home, Choo Choo Mama, Rip It Up, Sweet Little Sixteen.

January 7, 1981
Paramount Theater
Seattle, Washington

January 8, 1981
Portland, Oregon

March 1981
Release of the single: "Ridin' Truckin"

July 1981
Release of the single: "Take The Money"/"No More Lonely Nights"

ALVIN LEE BAND

Alvin Lee (guitar & vocals), ***Mick Taylor*** *(slide guitar), Fuzzy Samuels (bass) and Tom Compton (drums).*

October 1981
Release of the single: "Can't Stop"

October 26, 1981
Palasport
Turin, Italy

One Of These Days, Honey Pie, Good Morning Little School Girl, Slow Blues In C, Love Like A Man, Going Through The Door (Alvin says, "got a nice melody for you now, this is a song called Going Through The Door"), Can't Stop (Alvin says, "this is a new song from a new album, which I think has been escaped over here, it's called RX-5 if you buy it"), I'm Writing You A Letter (includes a drum solo by Tom Compton), Help Me, I'm Going Home, Choo Choo Mama.

October 27, 1981
Firenze, Italy

One Of These Days, Good Morning Little School Girl, Love Like A Man, Slow Blues In

C, Going Through The Door (Alvin says, "we're gonna do a tune as opposed to a blues, this is a song called Going Through The Door"), Slow Down, Can't Stop, I'm Writing You A Letter, Just Another Boogie (with solos by Fuzzy Samuels and Tom Compton), Help Me, I'm Going Home, Choo Choo Mama.

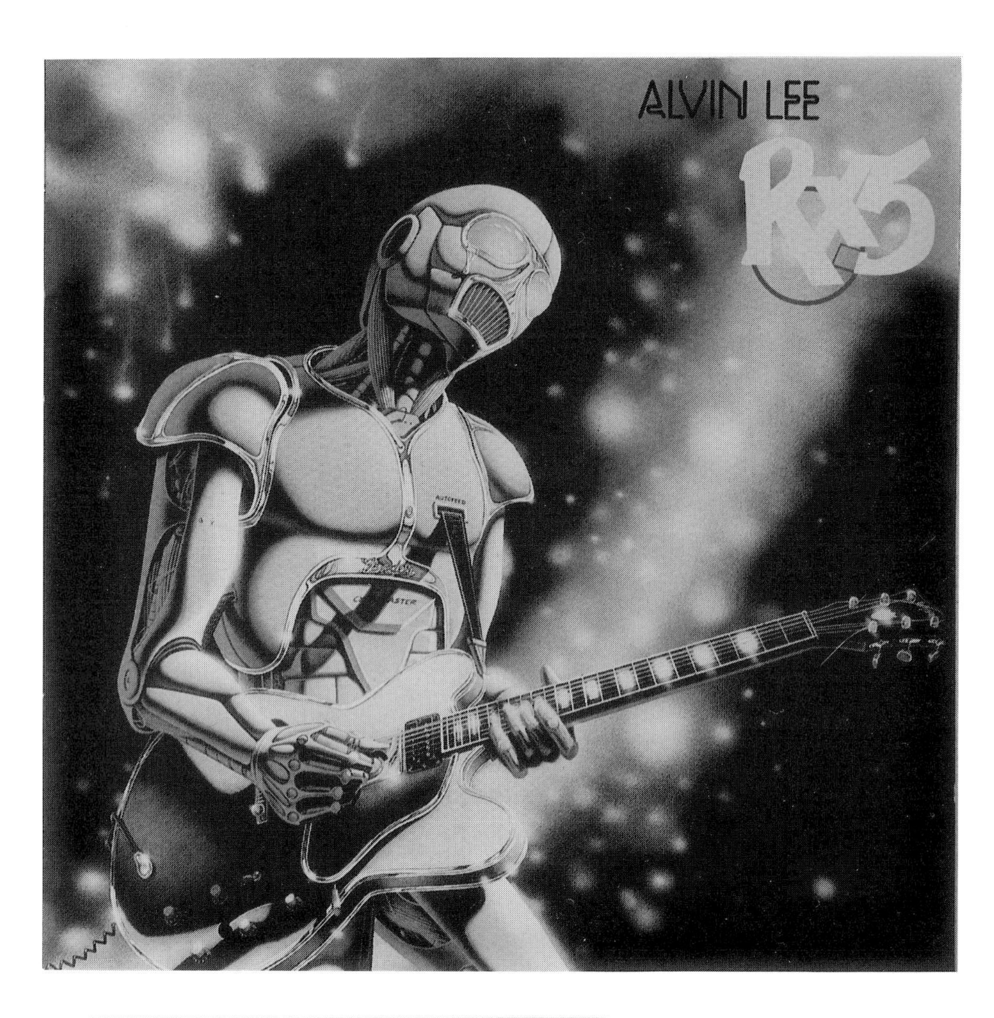

October 28, 1981
Milan, Italy

One Of These Days, Honey Pie, Good Morning Little School Girl, Slow Blues In C, Love Like A Man, Going Through The Door, Slow Down, Can't Stop, Scat Thing, I'm Writing You A Letter, Just Another Boogie (with bass and drum solos), Sweet Little Sixteen, Going Home.

October 29, 1981
Rome, Italy

One Of These Days, Honey Pie, Good Morning Little School Girl, Slow Blues In C, Love Like A Man, Going Through The Door, Slow Down, Can't Stop, I'm Writing You A Letter, Just Another Boogie, Help Me, I'm Going Home, Choo Choo Mama, Sweet Little Sixteen.

November 1981
Release of the Alvin Lee Band LP: "RX5" Atlantic SD 19306

The album is recorded at Space Studios and includes ***Alvin Lee, Steve Gould, Mickey Feat, Tom Compton*** *and* ***Chris Stainton****. Side One: Hang On* (Gould 3:46), *Lady Luck* (Gould 3:04), *Can't Stop* (Alvin Lee 5:09), *Wrong Side Of The Law* (Rootham/ Robson 3:10) *and Nutbush City Limits* (Ike Turner 3:50). *Side Two: Rock n' Roll Guitar Picker* (Alvin Lee 3:05), *Double Loser* (Alvin Lee 2:55), *Fool No More* (Feat/Gould 5:10), *Dangerous World* (Gould 3:40) *and High Times* (Gould 5:25).

November 12, 1981
Paris, France

One Of These Days, Honey Pie, Good Morning Little School Girl, Slow Blues In C, Love Like A Man, Going Through The Door, Can't Stop, Just Another Boogie, I'm Writing You A Letter, I'm Going Home, Choo Choo Mama, Sweet Little Sixteen, Slow Down.

November 14, 1981
Montpelliere, France

Good Morning Little School Girl, One Of These Days, Slow Blues In C, Love Like A Man, Can't Stop, Help Me, Slow Down, Just Another Boogie, Choo Choo Mama, Sweet Little Sixteen, Scat Thing, I'm Going Home.

November 17, 1981
Hammersmith Odeon
London, England

November 24, 1981
Bethlehem, Pennsylvania

One Of These Days, Good Morning Little School Girl, Slow Blues In C, Honey Pie, Can't Stop, Slow Down, Just Another Boogie, I'm Going Home, Choo Choo Mama.

November 28, 1981
My Father's Place
Roslyn, New York

Radio Broadcast - Partial Set List: One Of These Days, Honey Pie, Good Morning Little School Girl, Slow Blues In C, Love Like A Man.

December 1981
Release of the single: "Rock & Roll Guitar Picker"/ "Dangerous World"

December 3, 1981
Capitol Center
Largo, Maryland

One Of These Days, Good Morning Little School Girl, Slow Blues In C, Honey Pie, Can't Stop, Slow Down, Just Another Boogie, I'm Going Home, Choo Choo Mama.

December 4, 1981
Spectrum
Philadelphia, Pennsylvania

One Of These Days, Good Morning Little School Girl, Slow Blues In C, Honey Pie (introduced by Alvin as "Pecan Pie"), Can't Stop, Slow Down, Just Another Boogie, I'm Going Home, Choo Choo Mama.

December 5, 1981
Salisbury, Maryland

One Of These Days, Good Morning Little School Girl, Slow Blues In C, "Pecan Pie", Can't Stop, Slow Down, Going Home, Choo Choo Mama.

December 15, 1981
Stages
Granite City, Illinois

December 21, 1981
Chicago, Illinois

Partial Set List: Can't Stop, Slow Down, Just Another Boogie, I'm Going Home, Choo Choo Mama.

ALVIN LEE BAND

Fuzzy Samuels *(bass) and* ***Tom Compton*** *(drums).*

March 1982
Single release: "Nut Bush City Limits"/ High Times"

June 4, 1982
Pavilhao of Belenenses
Lisbon, Portugal

June 5, 1982
Pavilhao Infante de Sagres
Porto, Portugal

February 1983
The Chance
Poughkeepsie, NY

February 26 1983
Calderone Hall
Hempstead, NY

February 27, 1983
The Palladium
New York City, NY

One Of These Days, Rock & Roll Guitar Picker, Good Morning Little School Girl, Slow Blues In C, Love Like A Man, Ain't Nuthin' Shakin', Scat Thing, Hey Joe, Classical Thing, Ordinary Man (Alvin says, "Here's a brand new song"), Slow Down, Help Me, Going Home.

March 1, 1983
Owing's Mill, Maryland

March 4, 1983
E.M. Loewe's
West Hartford, CT

March 7, 1983
Toad's Place
New Haven, CT

March 12, 1983
Park West
Chicago, Illinois

March 13, 1983
Stan & Ollies
Kalamazoo, Michigan

March 14, 1983
Music Theater
Royal Oak, MI

March 17, 1983
Stages
Granite City, Illinois

March 18, 1983
Uptown Theater
Kansas City, Missouri

March 20, 1983
Richie's 3D Club
Kenner, Louisiana

April 8, 1983
Palo Alto, CA

May 2, 1983
Worcester, Massachusetts

May 11, 1983
Luxembourg, Belgium

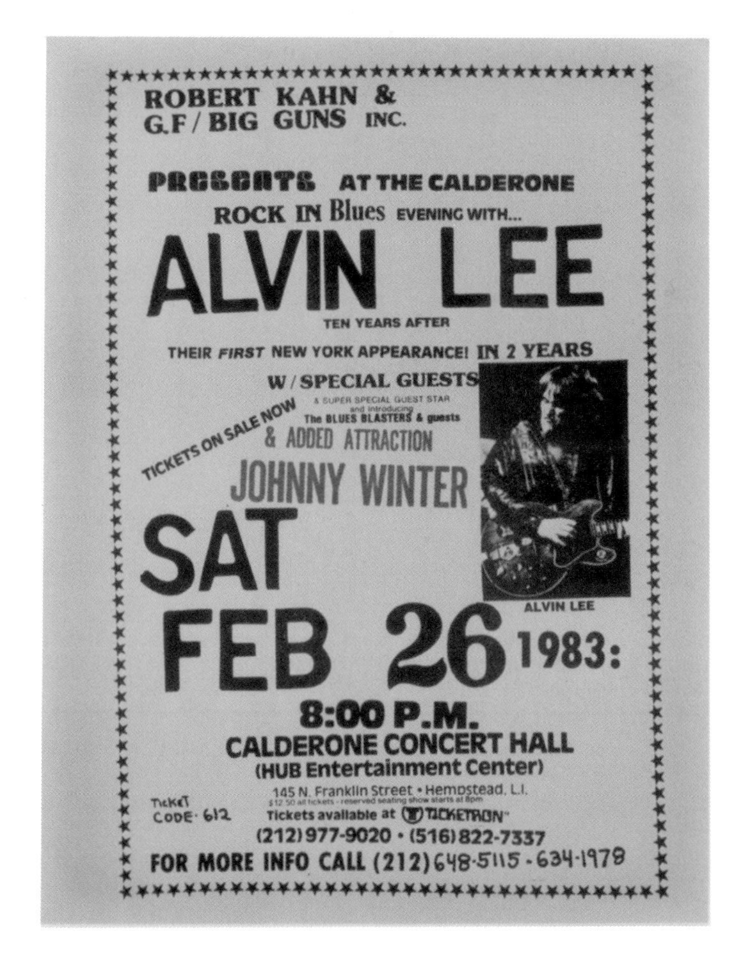

May 18, 1983
Berlin, Germany

May 23, 1983
Ludwigsburg, Germany

TYA-FIRST REUNION

Alvin Lee, Leo Lyons, Ric Lee and Chick Churchill join for three performances in 1983.

<u>July 2 & 3, 1983</u>
Marquee Club
London, England
(Silver Jubilee Celebration)

With Keith Christmas and Martin Ball.

Set List: Love Like A Man, I May Be Wrong But I Won't Be Wrong Always, Good Morning Little School Girl, Hobbit, Slow Blues In C, Woodchopper's Ball, Help Me, I Got My Mojo Working/Mystery Train (medley), Scat Thing, I Can't Keep From Crying Sometimes, I'm Going Home, Sweet Little Sixteen, Choo Choo Mama.

***Comment:** Ten Years After returns in great form! The concert is taped and released on home video.*

<u>August 28, 1983</u>
23rd National Jazz, Blues & Rock Festival
Reading, England

Love Like A Man, Good Morning Little School Girl, Suzie Q (Alvin says, "this is a new song for us, but it's about 500 years old"), Slow Blues In C, Hobbit, I May Be Wrong But I Won't Be Wrong Always, Help Me, Scat Thing, I Can't Keep From Crying Sometimes, I'm Going Home (.."this is a song we did at a little gathering called Woodstock"), Choo Choo Mama. The concert is broadcast on BBC radio and subsequently released on CD (Raw Fruit Records FRSCD003).

<u>September 3, 1983</u>
Fastnacht Festival
Basel, Switzerland

Love Like A Man, Good Morning Little School Girl, Suzie Q, Slow Blues In C, Woodchopper's Ball, Hobbit, I May Be Wrong But I Won't Be Wrong Always, Help Me, "We're Really Rockin In Basel" (short shuffle), Scat Thing, I Can't Keep From Crying Sometimes, I'm Going Home, Choo Choo Mama, Sweet Little Sixteen.

ALVIN LEE BAND

Alvin Lee, Tom Compton and Fuzzy Samuels.

September 13, 1983
London Victory Club
Tampa, Florida

Rock & Roll Guitar Picker, Good Morning Little School Girl, Slow Blues In C, I May Be Wrong But I Won't Be Wrong Always, Love Like A Man, Ain't Nuthin' Shakin', Scat Thing, Hey Joe, Help Me, Slow Down, I'm Going Home, Choo Choo Mama, Sweet Little Sixteen.

September 1983
Stanley Theater
Pittsburgh, Pennsylvania

One Of These Days, Rock & Roll Guitar Picker, Good Morning Little School Girl, Slow Blues In C, Love Like A Man, Ain't Nuthin' Shakin', Scat Thing, Hey Joe, Slow Down, I'm Going Home, Choo Choo Mama, Sweet Little Sixteen.

September 23, 1983
Owings Mill, Maryland

September 24, 1983
L'Amour West
Bay Ridge
Brooklyn, New York

One Of These Days, Rock & Roll Guitar Picker, Good Morning Little School Girl, Slow Blues In C, Love Like A Man, Ain't Nuthin' Shakin', Silly Thing, Hey Joe, Slow Down, Help Me, Going Home, Choo Choo Mama, Sweet Little Sixteen.

September 1983
North Brunswick, New Jersey

September 30, 1983
Agora Ballroom
West Hartford, Connecticut

October 5, 1983
The Skyway
Scotia, New York

One Of These Days, Rock & Roll Guitar Picker, Good Morning Little School Girl, Slow Blues In C, Love Like A Man, Ain't Nuthin' Shakin', Scat Thing, Hey Joe, Slow Down, Silly Thing, I'm Going Home, Choo Choo Mama.

October 6, 1983
The Channel
Boston, Massachusetts

Concert review by Steve Morse, the BOSTON GLOBE:

Endless rockers from the 60's have slipped into cynacism, but not Alvin Lee. The former leader of Ten Years After has spent the last decade in the Twilight Zone, but he's happier than he has been in a long while. "I'm just thrilled to be touring," he said after Thursday's incendiary comeback show. "It's great to be in the clubs where you can really see your fans, instead of being in those concrete monoliths in front of 20,000 people and having no idea why you're there. Back then, I often felt like a traveling jukebox."

In the 60's, along with Jimi Hendrix and Led Zeppelin, Ten Years After were the heaviest of the heavies. They blasted out molten-lava blues rock with such velocity that Alvin Lee was nicknamed ***Captain Speedfingers****. The band spearheaded the Woodstock festival in 1969, and that same summer I saw them blow away a delirious outdoor crowd in Bath, England, headling over Led Zeppelin, Fleetwood Mac and John Mayall.*

"Some people ***live*** *just to see this band," as* ***Boston Tea Party*** *emcee J.J. Jackson once said in praise. Alas, the 70's kayoed them. Burned out, Lee retreated to a country estate in England. The band broke-up in the*

mid-70's, after which Lee suffered through management problems, released five solo albums ("they're all terrible because I had to compromise") and ended up without a label. Which is just fine with him: "It's like I'm 16 again. There's no pressure now. I'm managing myself and no one's telling me what to do. It may take two years to get another album out, but I'm not going to compromise on it."

Following a solid hard-edged pop set from Johnny Barnes, Lee, who is still a major attraction in Europe, electrified the sellout 1500 at the Channel. Fronting a power trio that included old friend Tom Compton on drums and ex-Manassas member Fuzzy Samuel on bass, he bulled through a host of old Ten Years After classics (keyed by the bluesy "Good Morning Little Schoolgirl" and the knife-edged "Love Like A Man"), adding one new cut, the flashy "Rock & Roll Guitar Picker". Employing his old tricks of using the mike stand as a slide and a drumstick as a pick, he had the crowd jumping on tables and screaming for more. He whipped off a "Hey Joe" that rivaled Hendrix' hallucinogenic version. And he climaxed with his racehorse signature tune, "Goin' Home", which digressed into Carl Perkins' "Blue Suede Shoes," Jerry Lee's "Whole Lotta Shakin" and Elvis' "Hound Dog" before careening back for the final coda. An exraordinary show.

<u>October 7, 1983</u>
L'Amour East
Queens, New York

<u>October 14, 1983</u>
Rooftop Skyroom
Buffalo, New York

<u>October 15, 1983</u>
Music Theater
Royal Oak, Michigan

<u>October 21, 1983</u>
Park West
Chicago, Illinois

One Of These Days, Rock & Roll Guitar Picker, Good Morning Little School Girl, Slow Blues In C, Love Like A Man, Ain't Nuthin' Shakin', Scat Thing, Hey Joe, Slow Down, Help Me, Going Home, Choo Choo Mama, Sweet Little Sixteen.

<u>February 17, 1984</u>
Nurnberg, Germany

One Of These Days, Rock & Roll Guitar Picker, Good Morning Little School Girl, Slow Blues In C, Love Like A Man, Money Honey (Alvin says, "here's an old Elvis song"), Ain't Nuthin' Shakin', Scat Thing, Hey Joe, I'm Writing You A Letter (super performance of the song !), Slow Down, Help Me, I'm Going Home, Choo Choo Mama, Sweet Little Sixteen, Rip It Up.

<u>February 18, 1984</u>
Arena
Gmunden, Austria

<u>February 21, 1984</u>
Theater Fabrik
Munich, Germany

<u>February 23, 1984</u>
Copenhagen, Denmark

<u>February 24, 1984</u>
Aarhus, Denmark

<u>February 28, 1984</u>
Quartier Latin
Berlin, Germany

<u>March 1984</u>
Saint Avold, France

<u>March 8, 1984</u>
Rezzato, Italy

One Of These Days, Rock & Roll Guitar Picker, Good Morning Little School Girl, Slow Blues In C, Love Like A Man, Ain't Nuthin' Shakin', Scat Thing, Hey Joe, Slow Down,

Help Me, I'm Going Home, Choo Choo Mama, Sweet Little Sixteen.

March 24, 1984
Genoa, Italy

April 1, 1984
Vienna, Austria

August 27, 1984
Nostell Priory Fair
Wakefield, England

October 18, 1984
Paradise Rock Club
Boston, Massachusetts

One Of These Days, Rock & Roll Guitar Picker, Good Morning Little School Girl, Slow Blues In C, Love Like A Man, Ain't Nuthin' Shakin', Scat Thing, Hey Joe, Slow Down, Help Me, I'm Going Home, Choo Choo Mama, Sweet Little Sixteen.

Comment:
Alan Young has replaced Tom Compton on the drums.

October 27, 1984
Harpo's
Detroit, Michigan

October 28, 1984
Top Of The Rock
Grand Rapids, Michigan

October 31, 1984
Mississippi Nights
St. Louis, Missouri

November 6, 1984
Headliner's
Madison, Wisconsin

One Of These Days, Rock & Roll Guitar Picker, Good Morning Little School Girl, Slow Blues In C, Love Like A Man, Ain't Nuthin' Shakin', Scat Thing, Hey Joe, Moving Too Fast, Help Me, I'm Going Home, Choo Choo Mama, Sweet Little Sixteen.

November 8, 1984
Strand Theater
Marietta, Georgia

One Of These Days, Rock & Roll Guitar Picker, Good Morning Little School Girl, Slow Blues In C, Love Like A Man, Ain't Nuthin' Shakin', Scat Thing, Hey Joe, Moving Too Fast, Slow Down, Help Me, I'm Going Home, Choo Choo Mama, Sweet Little Sixteen.

November 29, 1984
Alexandra Rock Theater, Denmark

December 7, 1984
Alabamahalle
Munich, Germany

One Of These Days, Rock & Roll Guitar Picker, Good Morning Little School Girl, Slow Blues In C, Love Like A Man, Ain't Nuthin' Shakin', Scat Thing, Hey Joe, Nutbush City Limits, Slow Down, Help Me, I'm Going Home, Rip It Up.

December 8, 1984
Stuttgart, Germany

One Of These Days, Rock & Roll Guitar Picker, Good Morning Little School Girl, Slow Blues In C, Love Like A Man, Ain't Nuthin' Shakin', Scat Thing, Hey Joe, Nutbush City Limits, Slow Down, Help Me, I'm Going Home, Choo Choo Mama, Sweet Little Sixteen.

March 15, 1985
The Palms
Milwaukee, Wisconsin

One Of These Days, Rock & Roll Guitar Picker, Slow Blues In C, Good Morning Little School Girl, Love Like A Man, Hey Joe, Slow Down, I'm Going Home, Choo Choo Mama, Sweet Little Sixteen.

September 4, 1985
Nurnberg, Germany

Partial Set List: One Of These Days, Rock & Roll Guitar Picker, Good Morning Little School Girl, Slow Blues In C, Love Like A Man, Ain't Nuthin' Shakin', Scat Thing, Hey Joe, Nutbush City Limits, Slow Down, Help Me.

September 5, 1985
Theater Fabrik
Munich, Germany

One Of These Days, Rock & Roll Guitar Picker, Good Morning Little School Girl, Slow Blues In C, Love Like A Man, Ain't Nuthin' Shakin', Scat Thing (with a flamenco guitar intro by Alvin), Hey Joe, Moving Too Fast, Slow Down, Help Me, I'm Going Home, Choo Choo Mama, Sweet Little Sixteen.

ALVIN LEE BAND

Alvin Lee (guitar & vocals), Steve Gould (bass) and Alan Young (drums).

May 16, 1986
Jurahalle
Neumarkt, Germany

One Of These Days, Good Morning Little

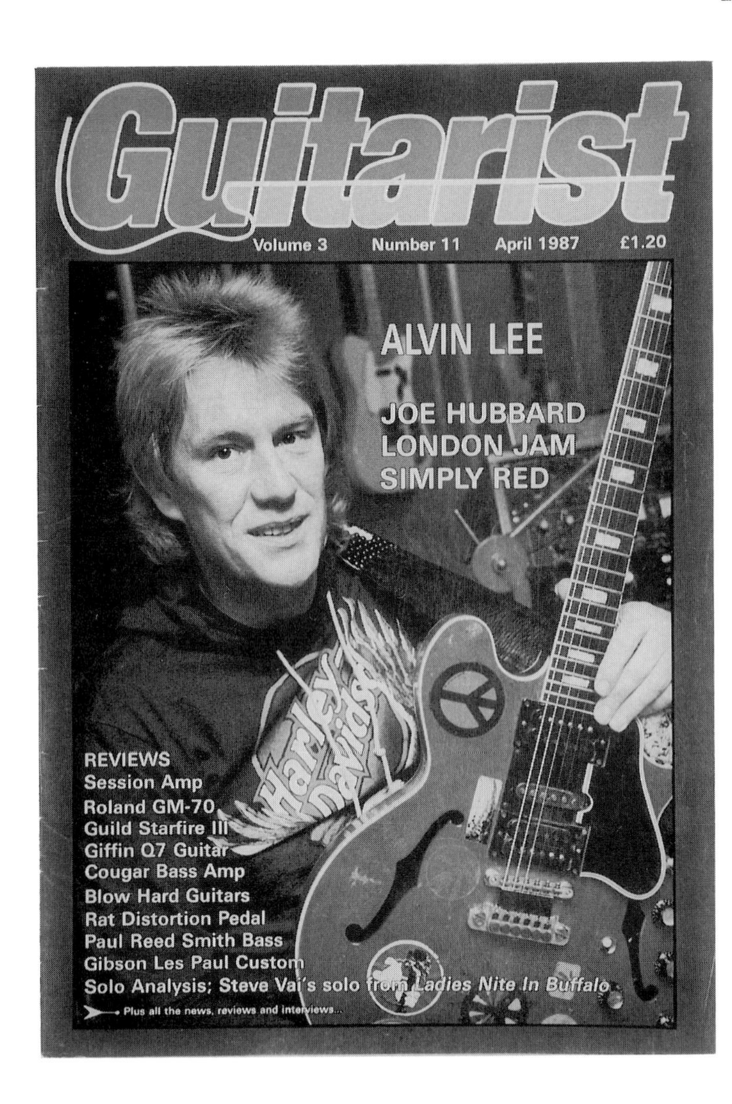

School Girl, Slow Blues In C, Detroit Diesel, Ain't Nuthin' Shakin', Shot In The Dark, Ordinary Man, Love Like A Man, Hey Joe, Slow Down, Help Me, I'm Going Home, Sweet Little Sixteen.

May 19, 1986
Zeche
Bochum, Germany

August 1986
Release of the Alvin Lee LP: "Detroit Diesel"
21 Records
7-90517-1

The tracks are recorded at Space Studios and mixed at Ridge Farm, Surrey and West Side Studios, London. In addition to Alvin Lee, the other artists appearing on this album are: ***Leo Lyons****, Alan Young, Tim Hinkley, Steve Gould, Mickey Feat, David Hubbard, Vicky Brown, Bryson Graham,* ***Jon Lord****,* ***Boz Burrell*** *and* ***George Harrison****. Side One includes: Detroit Diesel* (Lee/Gould 4:45), *Shot In The Dark* (Lee/Hubbard 4:02), *Too Late To Run For Cover* (Lee/Hinkley 3:48), *Talk Don't Bother Me* (Lee 3:38) *and Ordinary Man* (Lee 4:00). *Side Two contains: Heart Of Stone* (Lee/Gould 4:07), *She's So Cute* (Lee 3:18), *Back In My Arms Again* (Lee 3:46), *Don't Want To Fight* (Lee/Gould 4:25) *and Let's Go* (Lee/Gould 3:30).

August 1-3, 1986
Open Air Festival
Jubeck, Germany

Also on the bill are Status Quo, Ian Cussick and 22 other acts.

September 1986
Release of the single: "Detroit Diesel"/"Let's Go"

November 20, 1986
Marseille, France

One Of These Days, Detroit Diesel (Alvin says, "this is a new song on a new album, when it gets here, it's called Detroit Diesel"), Good Morning Little School Girl, Slow Blues In C, Rock & Roll Guitar Picker, Don't Want To Be A Soldier (Alvin says, "we would like to do a number featuring Alan on the drums, it's a John Lennon song"), Love Like A Man, She's So Cute (Alvin says, "Here's a new one off the Detroit Diesel album, it's called She's So Cute"), Scat Thing, Hey Joe, Ordinary Man, Slow Down, Help Me, I'm Going Home, Choo Choo Mama, Sweet Little Sixteen.

January 1987
Release of the single: "Detroit Diesel"/"She's So Cute"

January 27, 1987
Posthof
Linz, Austria

January 29, 1987
Metropol
Vienna, Austria

February 26, 1987
Bergerweeshuis
Deventer, Holland

One Of These Days, Detroit Diesel (Alvin says, "this is a song called Detroit Diesel, a new song"), Good Morning Little School Girl, Slow Blues In C, Rock & Roll Guitar Picker, Don't Want To Be A Soldier (with Alan Young drum solo - Alvin ends the song with the guitar riff from Peter Gunn), Love Like A Man, She's So Cute (Alvin says, "this is another new song you may have never heard, if not you are gonna hear it now"), Scat Thing, Hey Joe, Ordinary Man (Alvin says, "this is another new one we're gonna try"), Slow Down, Help Me, I'm Going Home.

February 27, 1987
Azotod
Utrecht, Holland

February 28, 1987
Paradiso
Amsterdam, Holland

March 1, 1987
T'Noorderlight
Tilburg, Holland

One Of These Days, Detroit Diesel, Good Morning Little School Girl, Slow Blues In C, Rock & Roll Guitar Picker, Don't Want To Be A Soldier, Love Like A Man, Silly Thing, She's So Cute, Scat Thing, Hey Joe, Slow Down, Help Me, I'm Going Home, Choo Choo Mama, Rip It Up.

March 5, 1987
Steinbruchtheater
Nieder Ramstadt, Germany

March 12, 1987
Paradise Rock Club
Boston, Massachusetts

One Of These Days, Good Morning Little School Girl, Slow Blues In C, Rock & Roll Guitar Picker, Don't Want To Be A Soldier, Love Like A Man, She's So Cute, Scat Thing, Hey Joe, Slow Down, Help Me, I'm Going Home, Choo Choo Mama, Rip It Up.

March 19, 1987
Hammerjack's
Baltimore, Maryland

March 20, 1987
L'Amour East
Queens, New York

March 21, 1987
Satellite Lounge
Cookstown, New Jersey

April 1, 1987
Alrosa Villa
Columbus, Ohio

April 9, 1987
Brat Stop
Kenosha, Wisconsin

April 10, 1987
Zivko Ballroom
Hartford, Wisconsin

One Of These Days, Detroit Diesel, Good Morning Little School Girl, Slow Blues In C, Rock & Roll Guitar Picker, Don't Want To Be A Soldier, Love Like A Man, She's So Cute, Scat Thing, Hey Joe, I'm Going Home, Choo Choo Mama, Sweet Little Sixteen.

April 18, 1987
Westport Playhouse
St. Louis, Missouri

May 2, 1987
Stadtfest
Vienna, Austria

May 5, 1987
Steinbruchtheater
Nieder Ramstadt, Germany

One Of These Days, Detroit Diesel, Good Morning Little School Girl, Slow Blues In C, Rock & Roll Guitar Picker, Don't Want To Be A Soldier, Love Like A Man, She's So Cute, Scat Thing, Hey Joe, Slow Down, Help Me, I'm Going Home, Choo Choo Mama, Sweet Little Sixteen.

May 7, 1987
Music & Action
Esslingen, Germany

One Of These Days, Detroit Diesel, Good Morning Little School Girl, Slow Blues In C, Rock & Roll Guitar Picker, Don't Want To Be A Soldier, Love Like A Man, She's So Cute, Scat Thing, Hey Joe, Slow Down, Help Me, I'm Going Home, Choo Choo Mama, Sweet Little Sixteen, Rip It Up, Nutbush City Limits.

May 29, 1987
Great Woods
Mansfield, Massachusetts

One Of These Days, Detroit Diesel, Good Morning Little School Girl, Slow Blues In C, Rock & Roll Guitar Picker, She's So Cute, Love Like A Man, Scat Thing, Hey Joe, I'm Going Home, Choo Choo Mama, Rip It Up.

May 30, 1987
Music Hall
West Hartford, Connecticut

June 12, 1987
Meriweather Post Pavillion
Columbia, Maryland

June 13, 1987
The Boathouse
Norfolk, Virginia

June 19, 1987
Syria Mosque Ballroom
Pittsburgh, PA

June 23, 1987
Massey Hall
Toronto, Canada

One Of These Days, Detroit Diesel, Good Morning Little School Girl, Slow Blues In C, Rock & Roll Guitar Picker, She's So Cute, Scat Thing, Hey Joe, I'm Going Home (Alvin says, "right now we got a trip for you, we would like to take you back to Woodstock... this is my Woodstock guitar Big Red, this is the song I'm gonna play... it's called I'm Going Home"), Choo Choo Mama, Rip It Up.

June 27, 1987
Symphony Hall
Springfield, MA

__June 28, 1987__
Music Theater
Warwick, RI

One Of These Days, Detroit Diesel, Good Morning Little School Girl, Slow Blues In C, Rock & Roll Guitar Picker, She's So Cute, Love Like A Man, Scat Thing, Hey Joe, I'm Going Home.

__August 9, 1987__
Paramount Theater
Seattle, Washington

__August 12, 1987__
Pavillion
Concord, California

One Of These Days, Detroit Diesel, Good Morning Little School Girl, Slow Blues In C, Rock & Roll Guitar Picker, She's So Cute, Love Like A Man, Scat Thing, Hey Joe, I'm Going Home, Choo Choo Mama, Rip It Up.

__August 13, 1987__
Cabaret
San Jose, California

__August 21, 1987__
Harpo's
Detroit, Michigan

__August 30, 1987__
Toad's Place
New Haven, Connecticut

One Of These Days, Detroit Diesel, Good Morning Little School Girl, Slow Blues In C, Rock & Roll Guitar Picker, She's So Cute, Love Like A Man, Scat Thing, Hey Joe, Slow Down, Help Me, I'm Going Home, Choo Choo Mama, Rip It Up.

__November 26, 1987__
Vienna, Austria

__June 9, 1988__
Palais de Sports
Clermont Ferrand, France

One Of These Days, Detroit Diesel, Good Morning Little School Girl, Slow Blues In C, Rock & Roll Guitar Picker, She's So Cute, Love Like A Man, Scat Thing, Hey Joe, Slow Down, Help Me, Johnny B. Goode, I'm Going Home, Choo Choo Mama, Rip It Up.

TYA - 2ND REUNION

In the summer of 1988, Ten Years After agree to play several festivals in Germany and Austria. This initiates the second reformation of the original band, an extensive run of great concerts and a new LP. As was the case in 1983, TYA have lost none of their chops and are playing better than ever.

July 8, 1988
Graz, Austria

Rock & Roll Music To The World, Hear Me Calling, Hey Joe, Good Morning Little School Girl, Slow Blues In C, Love Like A Man, Hobbit, I Woke Up This Morning, Scat Thing, I Can't Keep From Crying Sometimes, Slow Down, Baby Won't You Let Me Rock & Roll You, Help Me, I'm Going Home, Choo Choo Mama.

July 9, 1988
"Out On The Green"
Volkspark Dutzenteich
Nurnberg, Germany

Ten Years After perform for a crowd of 20,000 people: Rock & Roll Music To The World, Good Morning Little School Girl, Hear Me Calling, Slow Blues In C, Hobbit, Love Like A Man, Johnny B. Goode, Help Me, I'm Going Home, Choo Choo Mama.

July 13, 1988
Waldstadion
Giesen, Germany

August 27, 1988
Molson Park
Blues Festival
Barrie, Ontario

Rock & Roll Music To The World, Hear Me Calling, Good Morning Little School Girl, Slow Blues In C, Love Like A Man, Hobbit, Johnny B. Goode, Classical Thing, Scat Thing, I Can't Keep From Crying Sometimes, Slow Down, Baby Won't You Let Me Rock & Roll You, Help Me, I'm Going Home, Choo Choo Mama, Sweet Little Sixteen.

***Comment:** Ten Years After play for the first time in North America since 1975 and put on an incredible show!*

September 1988
Blues Festival
Telegen, Holland

This concert is broadcast on radio: Good Morning Little School Girl, I Woke Up This Morning (traditional Muddy Waters version), Love Like A Man, I Woke Up This Morning (the Sssh LP Version !), Scat Thing, I Can't Keep From Crying Sometimes, Help Me, I'm Going Home.

NIGHT OF THE GUITARS TOUR

***Alvin Lee** participates in a "Guitar Slingers" tour of England with: **Randy California** (Spirit), **Pete Haycock** (Climax Blues Band), **Steve Howe** (Yes), **Steve Hunter** (Lou Reed/ Alice Cooper), **Robbie Kreiger** (The Doors), **Andy Powell & Steve Turner** (Wishbone Ash) and **Leslie West** (Mountain).*

November 20, 1988
Colston Hall, Bristol

November 21, 1988
St. Georges Hall
Bradford, England

November 22, 1988
City Hall, Newcastle

November 23, 1988
Edinburgh, Scotland

November 24, 1988
Royal Court
Liverpool, England

November 25, 1988
Apollo, Manchester

November 26, 1988
Hammersmith
Odeon, London

TEN YEARS AFTER

<u>**December 1, 1988**</u>
Kurhalle
Vienna, Austria

Rock & Roll Music To The World, Hear Me Calling, Good Morning Little School Girl, Slow Blues In C, Love Like A Man, Hobbit, I Woke Up This Morning, Victim Of Circumstance, Scat Thing, I Can't Keep From Crying Sometimes, Johnny B. Goode, Slow Down, Baby Won't You Let Me Rock & Roll You, Moving Too Fast, Help Me, I'm Going Home, Choo Choo Mama, Sweet Little Sixteen.

<u>**December 2, 1988**</u>
Olympiahalle
Innsbruck, Austria

<u>**December 7, 1988**</u>
Idraetshal
Odense, Denmark

Ten Years After is supported by Mayday.

<u>**December 14, 1988**</u>
Rosengarten
Mannheim, Germany

Rock & Roll Music To The World, Hear Me Calling, Good Morning Little School Girl, Slow Blues In C, Victim Of Circumstance, Hobbit, I Woke Up This Morning, Love Like A Man, Johnny B. Goode, Scat Thing, I Can't Keep From Crying Sometimes, Blue Suede Shoes, Slow Down, Help Me, I'm Going Home, Choo Choo Mama, Sweet Little Sixteen.

<u>**December 16, 1988**</u>
Volkshaus
Zurich, Switzerland

<u>**December 18, 1988**</u>
Neumarkt, Germany

<u>**December 1988**</u>
Deutches Museum
Munich, Germany

Rock & Roll Music To The World, Hear Me Calling, Good Morning Little School Girl, Slow Blues In C, Victim Of Circumstance, Hobbit, I Woke Up This Morning, Scat Thing, Moving Too Fast, Slow Down, Help Me, I'm Going Home, Choo Choo Mama, Sweet Little Sixteen.

<u>**June 17, 1989**</u>
Open Air Festival
New Schoonebeek, Holland

<u>**June 18, 1989**</u>
t'Noorderligt
Tilburg, Holland

Rock & Roll Music To The World, Hear Me Calling, "That Will Be The Day" (great medley performed to a "Dust My Broom" beat), Good Morning Little School Girl, Slow Blues In C, Victim Of Circumstance (Alvin says,"we just recently recorded this number, it's available at your local pawn shops"), Hobbit, I Woke Up This Morning, Love Like A Man, Leo plays a bass solo after changing a broken string, Johnny

B. Goode, Scat Thing, I Can't Keep From Crying Sometimes, Let's Shake It Up, Slow Down, Help Me.

November 1989
Release of the twelfth LP by Ten Years After: "About Time" Chrysalis 210 180

The album is produced and engineered by Terry Manning. Side One includes: Highway Of Love (Lee/Gould 5:13), *Let's Shake It Up* (Lee/Gould 5:14), *I Get All Shook Up* (Lee 4:38), *Victim Of Circumstance* (Lee 4:29), *Going To Chicago* (Lee/Hinkley 4:22) *and Wild Is The River* (3:53 Lee/Gould). *Side Two contains: Saturday Night* (Lee/Gould 4:06), *Bad Blood* (Lyons/Crooks 7:09), *Working In A Parking Lot* (Lyons/Nye/Crooks 4:52), *Outside My Window* (Lee/Gould 5:47) and *Waiting For The Judgment Day* (Lee/Gould 4:30). *The single "Highway Of Love"/"Rock & Roll Music To The World" is also released in November.*

Leo Lyons:

"Unfortunately, the album came out at a time when I think the personnel at the record company were changing; the album wasn't a huge success sales-wise."

November 5, 1989
The Acadia
Dallas, Texas
(Start of 1989 U.S. Tour)

Rock & Roll Music To The World, Hear Me Calling, Good Morning Little School Girl, Slow Blues In C, Let's Shake It Up, Hobbit, Bad Blood, Saturday Night, Love Like A Man, Johnny B. Goode, I Can't Keep From Crying Sometimes, Victim Of Circumstance, I'm Going Home, Choo Choo Mama, Sweet Little Sixteen.

November 11, 1989
Hammerjack's
Baltimore, Maryland

Opening for Ten Years After is Flies On Fire.

November 12, 1989
Theater Of
The Living Arts
Philadelphia, PA

Rock & Roll Music To The World, Hear Me Calling, Good Morning Little School Girl, Slow Blues In C, Let's Shake It Up, Hobbit, Love Like A Man, Saturday Night, Bad Blood, Johnny B. Goode, Scat Thing, I Can't Keep From Crying Sometimes, Victim Of Circumstance, I'm Going Home (with a great extended guitar solo), Choo Choo Mama, Rip It Up.

November 13, 1989
New Haven,
Connecticut

November 14, 1989
Paradise Rock Club
Boston, Massachusetts

Rock & Roll Music To The World, Hear Me Calling, Good Morning Little School Girl, Slow Blues In C, Let's Shake It Up, Hobbit, Love Like A Man, Saturday Night, Bad Blood, Johnny B. Goode, Scat Thing, I Can't Keep From Crying Sometimes, Victim Of Circumstance, Going Home, Choo Choo Mama, Rip It Up.

BOSTON GLOBE concert review by Steve Morse:

If you were primed for a good old-fashioned, rowdy jam session, then Ten Years After was the ticket on Tuesday. There was nothing calculated or prepackaged about this nearly two-hour journey to delirium. "Most of the set was a big jam, really. It beats working for a living," bassist Leo Lyons joked dryly after the set. Ten Years After, who became superstars after their cataclysmic Woodstock Festival appearance in 1969, are back on the road after a 14-year absence. They're schlepping around like young upstarts - traveling by bus and playing in 14 states in the last 15 days - but they're playing with the savvy, free-wheeling looseness of old pros. Their Tuesday show, played before a sold-out crowd and aired live over WBCN, was like a rock revue of the past three decades. Not only did they play their Woodstock classics (the acid sped-blues of "Goin' Home" induced flashbacks) and new songs (their ZZ Top-like boogie of "Shake It Up" and "Victim of Circumstance"), but also touched base, even if just for a quick chorus or jamming guitar riff, with Cream's "Sunshine of Your Love," Jimi Hendrix' "Foxy Lady," Chuck Berry's "Johnny B. Goode," Carl Perkins' "Gone Gone Gone," Little Richard's "Rip It Up" and the Elvis Presley hit "Hound Dog".

The entire show was like a crazed but refreshing mosaic - fundamental rock 'n' roll played by a band that's rediscovered its chemistry and sense of humor. "Everybody take their acid now," singer/guitarist Alvin Lee said at one point. And addressing an imaginary groupie down front, he joked, "If you must take your clothes off, don't jump on stage." Lee, whose flashy soloing was to the 60's what Stevie Ray Vaughan is today, pulled out all the stops using the mike stand as a slide bar on his

guitar, and even grabbing drummer Ric Lee's sticks to get some otherworldly distortion on his strings. And he added some supersonic scatting that sounded like Bobby McFerrin at 78 rpms. Meanwhile, the rhythm section of Rick Lee and Leo Lyons blasted through the jam, and organist Chick Churchill (the first musician I ever saw jump on the speakers at the old Boston Tea Party in the 60's) added his signature brand of cross-rhythmic mayhem, plus some air guitar to incite the well-oiled crowd.
The old songs never sounded better.

"Choo Choo Mama" was a ripping encore, while the Blues Project's "I Can't Keep From Crying" was turned into a wildly explosive 10-minute trip to Jupiter.
The band stuck mostly to blues & blues-rock, ignoring its early '70s ventures into psychedelia, but they still played with an authority that defied the years. And this doesn't look like a one shot reunion: Ten Years After hopes to return to these parts around February for a show at the Orpheum.

November 16, 1989
The Ritz
New York City, NY

November 17, 1989
Penny Arcade
Rochester, New York

Rock & Roll Music To The World, Hear Me Calling, Good Morning Little School Girl, Slow Blues In C, Let's Shake It Up, Hobbit, Love Like A Man, Saturday Night, Bad Blood, Johnny B. Goode, Scat Thing, I Can't Keep From Crying Sometimes, Victim Of Circumstance, I'm Going Home, Choo Choo Mama, Sweet Little Sixteen.

November 18, 1989
U.N. Hungerthon
Benefit Concert
United Nations Plaza
New York, NY

Rock & Roll Music To The World, Victim Of Circumstance, I'm Going Home, Choo Choo Mama.
The performance is broadcast live on KROC-FM New York.

November 20, 1989
Diamond Club
Toronto, Canada

Rock & Roll Music To The World, Hear Me Calling, Good Morning Little School Girl, Slow Blues In C, Let's Shake It Up, Hobbit, Love Like A Man, Saturday Night, Bad Blood (Alvin says, "this is a song written by Mad Dog Lyons"), Going To Chicago, Johnny B. Goode, I Can't Keep From Crying

Sometimes (with a slow instrumental lead-in by Alvin, similar to the recording on the 1st LP!), Victim Of Circumstance, I'm Going Home, Choo Choo Mama, Sweet Little Sixteen.

<u>November 21, 1989</u>
Parkwest
Chicago, Illinois

Rock & Roll Music To The World, Hear Me Calling, Good Morning Little School Girl, Slow Blues In C, Let's Shake It Up, Hobbit, Going To Chicago, Love Like A Man, Saturday Night, Bad Blood, Johnny B. Goode, Classical Thing, I Can't Keep From Crying Sometimes, Victim Of Circumstance, I'm Going Home, Choo Choo Mama.

<u>November 25, 1989</u>
The Palace
Auburn Hills, Michigan

<u>December 1, 1989</u>
Paradiso
Amsterdam, Holland

Rock & Roll Music To The World, Hear Me Calling, Good Morning Little School Girl, Slow Blues In C, Let's Shake It Up, Hobbit, Going To Chicago, Love Like A Man, Saturday Night, Bad Blood, Johnny B. Goode, Scat Thing, I Can't Keep From Crying Sometimes, Victim Of Circumstance, I'm Going Home, Choo Choo Mama.

<u>December 3, 1989</u>
Gent, Belgium

<u>December 4, 1989</u>
Elysee-Montmartre
Paris, France

<u>December 5, 1989</u>
Bern, Switzerland

Rock & Roll Music To The World, Let's Shake It Up, Good Morning Little School Girl, Slow Blues In C, Hear Me Calling, Hobbit, Going To Chicago, Love Like A Man, Saturday Night, Bad Blood, Johnny B. Goode, Classical Thing, I Can't Keep From Crying Sometimes (a superb nearly all-instrumental reduced tempo version with a Leo Lyons bass solo and a Chick Churchill piano solo), Victim Of Circumstance (great extended guitar solo by Alvin), I'm Going Home.

<u>December 6, 1989</u>
Volkshaus
Zurich, Switzerland

Rock & Roll Music To The World, Let's Shake It Up, Good Morning Little School Girl, Slow Blues In C, Hear Me Calling, Hobbit, Going To Chicago, Love Like A Man, Saturday Night, Bad Blood, Johnny B. Goode, Scat Thing, I Can't Keep From Crying, Victim Of Circumstance, I'm Going Home.

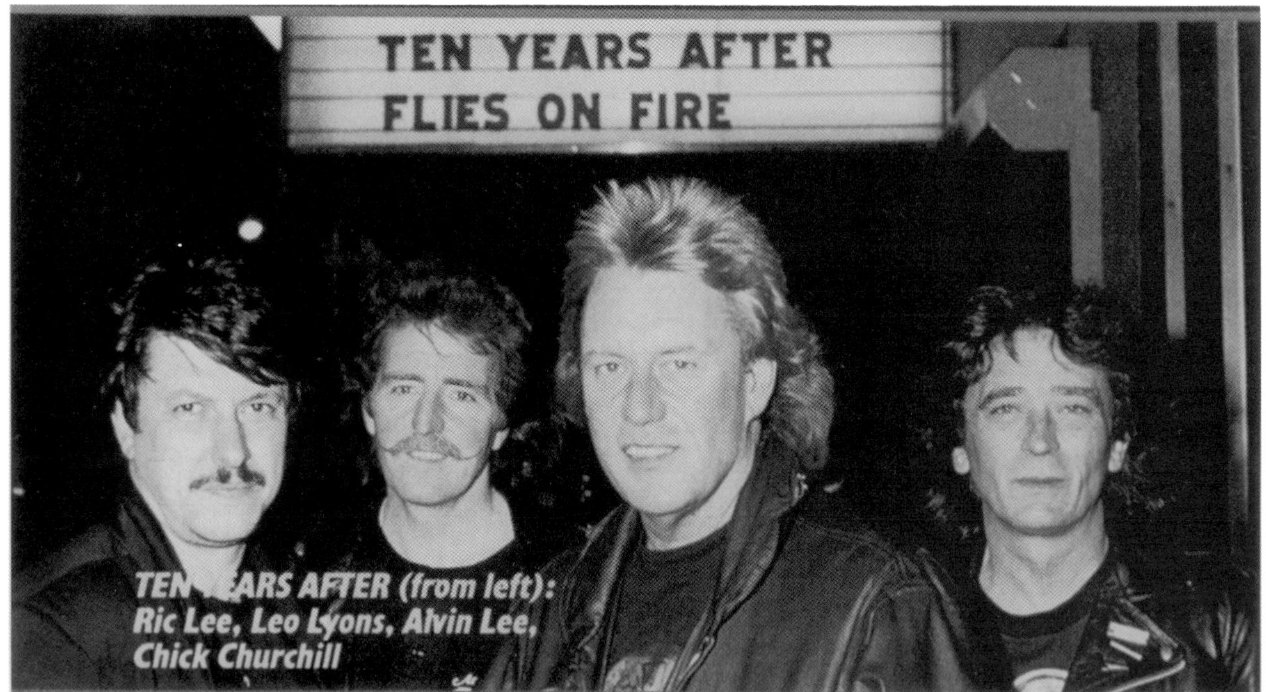

TEN YEARS AFTER (from left): Ric Lee, Leo Lyons, Alvin Lee, Chick Churchill

December 7, 1989
Messe - Kongresszentrum
Stuttgart, Germany

December 8, 1989
Rosengarten - Musensaal
Mannheim, Germany

December 9, 1989
Ford Garage
Saarbrucken, Germany

December 10, 1989
Jurahalle
Neumarkt, Germany

December 11, 1989
Deutches Museum
Munich, Germany

December 13, 1989
Metropol
Berlin, Germany

December 14, 1989
Grugahalle
Essen, Germany

December 15, 1989
CCH Saal 3
Hamburg, Germany

Rock & Roll Music To The World, Going To Chicago, Good Morning Little School Girl, Slow Blues In C, Hear Me Calling, Hobbit, Let's Shake It Up, Love Like A Man, Bad Blood, Johnny B. Goode, Scat Thing, I Can't Keep From Crying Sometimes (with a long guitar lead-in to a great jazzy version of the song!), Victim Of Circumstance, I'm Going Home.

December 16, 1989
Rheingoldhalle
Mainz, Germany

Rock & Roll Music To The World, Going To Chicago, Good Morning Little School Girl, Slow Blues In C, Hear Me Calling, Hobbit, Let's Shake It Up, Outside My Window, Love Like A Man, Bad Blood, Johnny B. Goode, Scat Thing, I Can't Keep From Crying Sometimes, Victim Of Circumstance, Going Home, Choo Choo Mama, Rip It Up.

December 1989
East Berlin, Germany

Ten Years After perform with Uriah Heap to a huge outdoor crowd.

Comment: *part of the Ten Years After performance ("I'm Going Home") is broadcast on TV.*

January 27, 1990
Hammersmith Odeon
London, England

February 27, 1990
Fastnachtfestival
Mainz, Germany

Rock & Roll Music To The World, Going To Chicago, Good Morning Little School Girl, Slow Blues In C, Hobbit, Let's Shake It Up, Love Like A Man, Bad Blood, Johnny B. Goode, Scat Thing, I Can't Keep From Crying Sometimes, Victim Of Circumstance, I'm Going Home.

Comment: *The show is broadcast on German radio, however there are technical problems with the stage monitors during the first four numbers and Alvin is not very pleased. Alvin says, "you may be able to hear us, but we can't - aren't we lucky". As a result, more instrumentals fills are played and Alvin does*

a fierce solo during "Slow Blues In C".

March 3, 1990
Switzerland

March 20, 1990
Posthof
Linz, Austria

Rock & Roll Music To The World, Going To Chicago, Good Morning Little School Girl, Slow Blues In C, Hear Me Calling, Hobbit, Victim Of Circumstance, Outside My Window, Love Like A Man, Bad Blood, Let's Shake It Up, Johnny B. Goode, Scat Thing, I Can't Keep From Crying Sometimes, I'm Going Home, Choo Choo Mama, Sweet Little Sixteen.

March 21, 1990
Volkshaus
Braunau, Austria

March 25, 1990
Switzerland

May 17, 1990
Studio 8
Nottingham, England

Ten Years After perform a show in Alvin's home town. The concert is recorded and subsequently released on home video. The songs as they appear on the video are: Let's Shake It Up, Good Morning Little School Girl, Slow Blues In C, Hobbit, Love Like A Man, Johnny B. Goode, Bad Blood, Victim Of Circumstance, I Can't Keep From Crying Sometimes, I'm Going Home, Sweet Little Sixteen.

June 29, 1990
Waterloo Village, New Jersey

Rock & Roll Music To The World, Let's Shake It Up, Good Morning Little School Girl, Slow Blues In C, Hobbit, Love Like A Man, Victim Of Circumstance, Bad Blood, Johnny B. Goode, Scat Thing, I Can't Keep From Crying Sometimes, I'm Going Home, Choo Choo Mama, Sweet Little Sixteen.

Comment: *Ten Years After return to the U.S. and perform at many of the summer music pavilions. The tour is*

billed as "The Road Warriors" and includes Nazareth and Blackfoot supporting Ten Years After.

July 4, 1990
Great Woods
Mansfield, MA

July 6, 1990
Lake Compounce
Bristol, Connecticut

September 8, 1990
Albatos
Peuerbach, Austria

Partial Set List: Rock & Roll Music To The World, Let's Shake It Up, Good Morning Little School Girl, Slow Blues In C, Hobbit, I Woke Up This Morning, Hear Me Calling/On The Road Again, Love Like A Man.

September 10, 1990
Theater Fabrik
Munich, Germany

Rock & Roll Music To The World, Let's Shake It Up, Good Morning Little School Girl, Slow Blues In C, Hobbit, I Woke Up This Morning, Hear Me Calling/On The Road Again, Love Like A Man, Victim Of Circumstance, Johnny B. Goode, Scat Thing, I Can't Keep From Crying Sometimes, I'm Going Home, Choo Choo Mama, Sweet Little Sixteen.

November 3, 1990
Ca-Zelt
Vienna, Austria

Rock & Roll Music To The World, Let's Shake It Up, Good Morning Little School Girl, Slow Blues In C, Hobbit, Hear Me Calling/On The Road Again, I May Be Wrong But I Won't Be Wrong Always, Love Like A Man, Bad Blood, Victim Of Circumstance, Johnny B. Goode, Scat Thing, I Can't Keep From Crying Sometimes, I'm Going Home, Choo Choo Mama.

November 26, 1990
Music Hall
Hannover, Germany

Rock & Roll Music To The World, Let's Shake It Up, Good Morning Little School Girl, Slow Blues In C, Hobbit, Hear Me Calling/On The Road Again, I Woke Up This Morning,

Love Like A Man, Victim Of Circumstance, Johnny B. Goode, Scat Thing (includes extended guitar riffing with Smoke On The Water, etc.), I Can't Keep From Crying Sometimes, I'm Going Home, Choo Choo Mama, Sweet Little Sixteen.

November 27, 1990
Aladin
Bremen, Germany

November 30, 1990
Volkshaus
Zurich, Switzerland

December 3, 1990
Metropol
Nollendorf Platz
Berlin, Germany

December 7, 1990
Kehl, Germany

April 13, 1991
Volkshaus
Zurich, Switzerland

April 26, 1991
Anti-Atomic Energy Festival
Bratislava, Czechoslovakia

May 3, 1991
Vienna, Austria

May 5, 1991
Timelkam, Austria

Rock & Roll Music To The World, Let's Shake It Up, Good Morning Little School Girl, Slow Blues In C, Hobbit, Bad Blood, Hear Me Calling, Love Like A Man, Johnny B. Goode, Scat Thing, I Can't Keep From Crying Sometimes, I'm Going Home, Choo Choo Mama.

June 14, 1991
Lorsh, Germany

Rock & Roll Music To The World, Let's Shake It Up, Good Morning Little School Girl, Slow Blues In C, Hobbit, Love Like A Man, Hear Me Calling, Victim Of Circumstance, Johnny B. Goode, Scat Thing, I Can't Keep From Crying Sometimes, I'm Going Home, Choo Choo Mama. The concert is broadcast on radio.

June 29, 1991
Bolsward, Holland

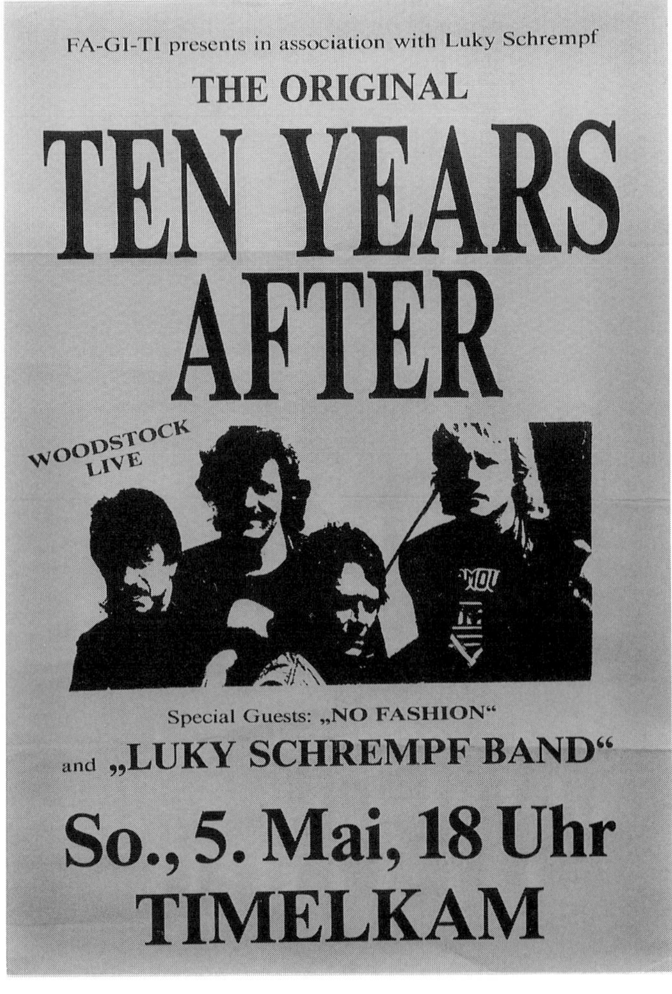

<u>August 9, 1991</u>
Open Air Festival
Nunningen, Switzerland

Rock & Roll Music To The World, Let's Shake It Up, Good Morning Little School Girl, Slow Blues In C, Hobbit, Love Like A Man, Hear Me Calling, "Waltz" (Alvin and the band briefly imitate a German marching song), Victim Of Circumstance, I Woke Up This Morning, Johnny B. Goode, brief instrumental shuffle by Alvin, Scat Thing (includes lightening-speed guitar riffing by Alvin with an extended "Sunshine Of Your Love" segment), I Can't Keep From Crying Sometimes (great "psychedelic" version), I'm Going Home, Choo Choo Mama, Sweet Little Sixteen.

<u>August 17, 1991</u>
Open Air Festival
Nidau, France

Rock & Roll Music To The World, Let's Shake It Up, Good Morning Little School Girl, Slow Blues In C, Hobbit, Love Like A Man, Hear Me Calling/On The Road Again, Victim Of Circumstance, Johnny B. Goode, Scat Thing (with extended "Purple Haze" and "Smoke On The Water" guitar riffs), I Can't Keep From Crying Sometimes, I'm Going Home, Choo Choo Mama, Rip It Up.

<u>November 15, 1991</u>
Rockhaus
Vienna, Austria

Rock & Roll Music To The World, Let's Shake It Up, Good Morning Little School Girl, Slow Blues In C, Hobbit, Love Like A Man, Hear Me Calling, Johnny B. Goode, I Can't Keep From Crying Sometimes, I'm Going Home, Choo Choo Mama, Sweet Little Sixteen.

<u>November 18, 1991</u>
Longhorn
Stuttgart, Germany

Rock & Roll Music To The World, Let's Shake It Up (instrumental only due to sound system problems),

Good Morning Little School Girl, Slow Blues In C, Hobbit, Love Like A Man, Hear Me Calling, Victim Of Circumstance, Johnny B. Goode, Scat Thing (with extended guitar riffs), I Can't Keep From Crying Sometimes, I'm Going Home, Choo Choo Mama.

November 19, 1991
Josefhaus
Weiden, Germany

November 22, 1991
Augsburg, Germany

Rock & Roll Music To The World, Let's Shake It Up, Good Morning Little School Girl, Slow Blues In C, Hobbit, Love Like A Man, Hear Me Calling/On The Road Again, Johnny B. Goode, Scat Thing (extended version), I Can't Keep From Crying Sometimes, I'm Going Home, Choo Choo Mama, Sweet Little Sixteen.

November 25, 1991
Metropol
Nollendorf Platz
Berlin, Germany

November 29, 1991
Elysee Montmartre
Paris, France

Rock & Roll Music To The World, Good Morning Little School Girl, Slow Blues In C, Hobbit, Love Like A Man, Hear Me Calling/On The Road Again, Johnny B. Goode, Scat Thing, I Can't Keep From Crying Sometimes, I'm Going Home, Choo Choo Mama, Sweet Little Sixteen.

Supporting TYA is Johnny Diesel.

December 1991
Augsburg, Germany

December 3, 1991
Vooruit Gaet, Holland

Rock & Roll Music To The World, Good Morning Little School Girl, Slow Blues In C, Hobbit, Love Like A Man, Hear Me Calling, Johnny B. Goode, Instrumental, I Can't

Keep From Crying Sometimes (starts off as slow and jazzy version but Alvin picks up the tempo as the guitar solo builds in intensity), I'm Going Home (a long version with extended riffing: "Be Bop A Lula" & "Rock Around The Clock"), Choo Choo Mama. Due to monitor problems, the first several songs of this show are performed with minimal vocals which results in interesting "instrumental versions".

<u>December 5, 1991</u>
Town & Country Club
London, England

With Wishbone Ash and Man.

The Ten Years After set list is: Rock & Roll Music To The World, Good Morning Little School Girl, Slow Blues In C, Hobbit, Love Like A Man, Hear Me Calling (with "On The Road Again" added in the middle), Johnny B. Goode, Scat Thing, I Can't Keep From Crying Sometimes, Victim Of Circumstance, I'm Going Home, Choo Choo Mama, Sweet Little Sixteen.

Comment:
The second reunion of Ten Years After ended in 1991 after a series of amazing festival appearances in which Alvin Lee, almost 25 years after the start of TYA, is playing better than he ever has.

THE KICK - 1992

Release of the album "Heartland" on Line Records LICD 9.01202 O

The Kick is Leo Lyons on bass, Tony Crooks on lead vocals and guitars & Andy Nye on keyboards and backing vocals. "Heartland" was recorded at Butts Green Studio in Oxfordshire, England. All songs written by Lyons, Nye & Crooks.

The album tracks include: Do You Know The Feeling, This Can't Be Love, She's Got It All, Heartland, Livin' It Up, See You On The T.V., Louise, On The Beach, Don't Fool Around With Love & Working In A Parking Lot.

ALVIN LEE BAND

Alvin Lee (guitar & vocals), Steve Gould (bass), Steve Grant (keyboards) and Alan Young (drums).

April 29, 1992
Koninginnenach
Den Haag, Holland

One Of These Days, Little Bit Of Love (Alvin says,"this is a new song called A Little Bit Of Love goes a long way"), Good Morning Little School Girl, Slow Blues In C, It Don't Come Easy, She's So Cute, Love Like A Man, Johnny B. Goode, Guitar Medley: Scat Thing/Smoke On The Water/Sunshine Of Your Love, Hey Joe, Slow Down, Help Me, I'm Going Home, Choo Choo Mama, Rip It Up.

June 1992
Release of the Alvin Lee CD: "Zoom" Domino 8003-2

The artists who perform on this album include: Alan Young, Steve Grant, Steve Gould, Deena Payne, Clarence Clemons, Richard Newman, ***George Harrison****, Jon Lord, Billy Dixon, Jimmy Johnson and Tim Hinkley.*

The tracks include: A Little Bit Of Love (Alvin Lee 3:45), *Real Life Blues* (Alvin Lee 4:33), *The Price Of This Love* (Alvin Lee 4:04), *Moving The Blues* (Alvin Lee 4:02), *Lost In Love* (Alvin Lee/Steve Gould 4:05), *Wake Up Moma* (Alvin Lee 3:55), *It Don't Come Easy* (Alvin Lee 5:05), *Remember Me* (Alvin Lee 4:35), *Anything For You* (Alvin Lee 4:53), *Jenny Jenny* (Alvin Lee/Steve Gould 4:22), *Use That Power* (Alvin Lee/Tim Hinkley 4:19).

June 28, 1992
Donavinsel
Vienna, Austria

It Don't Come Easy, Good Morning Little School Girl, She's So Cute, Real Life Blues, Medley: Scat Thing/Sunshine Of Your Love/Smoke On The Water, Hey Joe, Johnny B. Goode, Jenny Jenny, Victim Of Circumstance, Help Me, I'm Going Home, Choo Choo Mama, Sweet Little Sixteen, Rip It Up.

August 23, 1992
Open Air Festival
Gampel, Switzerland

October 3, 1992
Burghausen, Germany

Little Bit Of Love, Wake Up Moma, Love Like A Man, Slow Blues In C, Remember Me, It Don't Come Easy, Good Morning Little Schoolgirl, She's So Cute, Real Life Blues, Medley: Scat Thing/ Sunshine Of Your Love/Smoke On The Water/Peter Gunn, Hey Joe, Johnny B. Goode, Jenny Jenny, Victim Of Circumstance, Help Me, I'm Going Home, Choo Choo Mama.

October 4, 1992
Longhorn
Stuttgart, Germany

October 16, 1992
Heide-Volm Planegg
Munich, Germany

October 18, 1992
Rockhaus
Vienna, Austria

October 1992
Bern, Switzerland

April 2, 1993
Salle FMR
Toulouse, France

April 3, 1993
Bataclan
Paris, France

May 19, 1993
Colos-Saal
Aschaffenburg, Germany

Little Bit Of Love, Wake Up Moma, Love Like A Man, Slow Blues In C, I Don't Give A Damn, Long Legs, Good Morning Little Schoolgirl, She's So Cute, The Bluest Blues, Johnny B. Goode, Take It Easy, Jenny Jenny, Medley: Scat Thing/ Sunshine Of Your Love /Smoke On The Water, Help Me, brief instrumental, I'm Going Home, Choo Choo Mama, Rip It Up.

June 25, 1993
Peterlee Blues Festival, England

Wake Up Moma, Love Like A Man, Slow Blues In C, I Don't Give A Damn, Long Legs, Good Morning Little School Girl, She's So Cute, Johnny B. Goode, Jenny Jenny, Victim Of Circumstance Medley: Scat Thing/ Sunshine Of Your Love/Smoke On The Water, Help Me, I'm Going Home, Choo Choo Mama.

Comment: *Richard Newman substitutes for Alan Young on the drums.*

June 26, 1993
St. Wolfgang, Germany

Partial Set List: Wake Up Moma, Slow Blues In C, I Don't Give A Damn, Long Legs, Johnny B. Goode, Jenny Jenny, Help Me, I'm Going Home, Choo Choo Mama, Rip It Up.

July 17, 1993
Augsburg, Germany

Little Bit Of Love, Wake Up Moma, Love

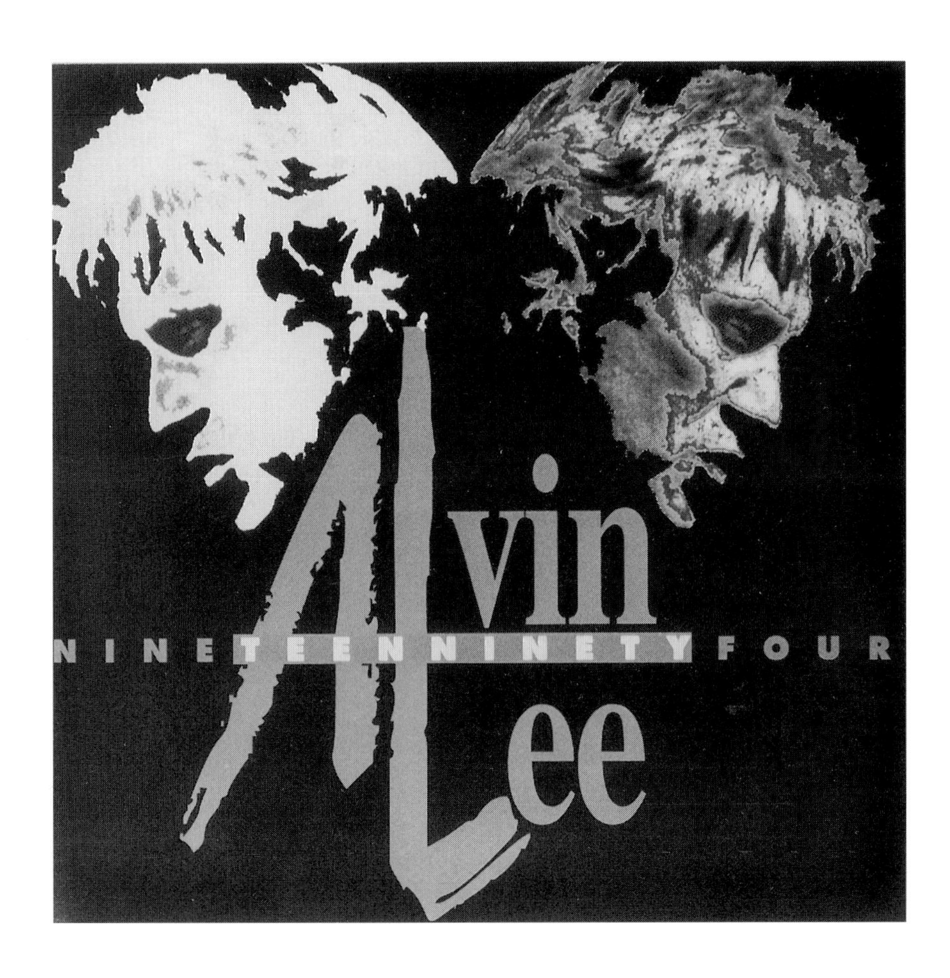

Like A Man, Slow Blues In C, I Don't Give A Damn (Alvin says,"this is a brand new song, we just recorded it, you can't get it yet"), Long Legs, Good Morning Little Schoolgirl, She's So Cute, Johnny B. Goode, Medley: Scat Thing/Sunshine Of Your Love/Smoke On The Water, Help Me, I'm Going Home, Choo Choo Mama, Rip It Up.

<u>August 1993</u>
Beim Festival
Karlsruhe, Germany

Little Bit Of Love, Wake Up Moma, Love Like A Man, Slow Blues In C, I Don't Give A Damn, Long Legs, Good Morning Little Schoolgirl, Johnny B. Goode, Jenny Jenny, Victim Of Circumstance, Scat Thing (with extended riffing), Help Me, I'm Going Home, Choo Choo Mama, Rip It Up.

<u>August 1993</u>
Egliswil,
Switzerland

<u>October 30, 1993</u>
Toulouse, France

<u>November 1993</u>
Release of the Alvin Lee CD: "1994" Magnum CDTB 150

In addition to the Alvin Lee band, guests appearing on the album are ***George Harrison****, Joe Brown, Sam Brown, Deena Payne & Tim Hinkley.*

The tracks include: Keep On Rockin' (Alvin Lee 5:09), *Long Legs* (Alvin Lee 6:16), *I Hear You Knockin'* (King, Bartholomew Francis Day & Hunter 3:40), *Ain't Nobody's Business* (Alvin Lee/Steve Grant 4:11), *The Bluest Blues* (Alvin Lee 7:27), *Boogie All Day* (Alvin Lee 3:52), *My Baby's Come Back to Me* (Alvin Lee 4:58), *Take It Easy* (Alvin Lee 6:24), *Play It Like It Used To Be* (Alvin Lee/Tim Hinkley 4:01), *Give Me Your Love* (Alvin Lee/Steve Gould 5:58), *I Don't Give A Damn* (Alvin Lee 5:46) *and I Want You / She's So Heavy* (Lennon & McCartney 9:52). *This album is released as "I Hear You Rockin" in the U.S. in 1994.*

<u>November 10, 1993</u>
Merkers
Freizeitzentrum,
Germany

Keep On Rockin', Long Legs (Alvin says,"we have a new album and we are going to play it for you tonight"), I Hear You Knockin', Ain't Nobody's Business, Love Like A Man, The Bluest Blues, Good Morning Little School Girl, Take It Easy, Play It Like It Used To Be, I Don't Give A Damn, I Want You (She's So Heavy), I'm Going Home, Choo Choo Mama, Rip It Up.

<u>November 20, 1993</u>
Gartlagehalle
Osnabruck, Germany

<u>December 9, 1993</u>
Melkinegg
Amsterdam, Holland

<u>December 11, 1993</u>
Kasteel Alphen
Ran de Ryn, Holland

Keep On Rockin', Long Legs (Alvin says,"O.K., we've got a lot of new songs to play for you tonight from 1994, this one's called Long Legs"), Ain't Nobody's Business, Slow Blues In C, Good Morning

Little Schoolgirl, I Hear You Knockin', Boogie All Day, Love Like A Man, Take It Easy, Play It Like It Used To Be, I Don't Give A Damn, Johnny B. Goode, I Want You (She's So Heavy), I'm Going Home, Choo Choo Mama, Rip It Up.

LEO LYONS' KICK

"Tough Trip Through Paradise"
KDC Records 10016

The Kick 1994 are: Leo Lyons (bass), Tony Crooks (guitar & vocals), John Willoughby (guitar & backing vocals) and Mark Price (drums).

"Tough Trip Through Paradise" was recorded at Butts Green Studio in England in 1993 & 1994. The tracks include: Feel Good About It, Driving On The Wrong Side, Save Me, Living Legend Of The Blues, Mad Bad And Dangerous, Working In A Parking Lot, Tough Trip Through Paradise, Bad Blood, The Last Picture Show, Big Black 45, Say The Word & Living It Up.

ALVIN LEE BAND

January 22, 1994
Regensburg, Germany

Keep On Rockin', Long Legs, I Hear You Knockin', Ain't Nobody's Business, Slow Blues In C, Love Like A Man, Boogie All Day, My Baby's Come Back To Me, Good Morning Little School Girl, Take It Easy, Play It Like It Used To Be, I Don't Give A Damn, Johnny B. Goode, I Want You (She's So Heavy), Scat Thing, I'm Going Home, Choo Choo Mama, Rip It Up.

January 29, 1994
Planet Rock
Kerava, Finland

Keep On Rockin', Long Legs, I Hear You Knockin', Ain't Nobody's Business, Good Morning Little School Girl, Take It Easy, Slow Blues In C, I Don't Give A Damn, Johnny B. Goode, Love Like A Man, I'm Going Home, Choo Choo Mama.

April 3, 1994
Schulsporthalle
Wintersbach, Germany

April 18, 1994
Baden Baden, Germany

The concert is taped and subsequently broadcast on the "Ohne Filter Extra" TV show.

May 28, 1994
Porrentruy, Switzerland

June 16, 1994
Rockhaus
Vienna, Austria

Keep On Rockin', Little Bit Of Love, Long Legs, I Hear You Knockin', She's So Cute, Johnny B. Goode, Slow Blues In C, I Don't Give A Damn, Good Morning Little School Girl, Help Me, I'm Going Home, Victim Of Circumstance, Choo Choo Mama, Rip It Up.

Comment: *This concert is recorded and several of the*

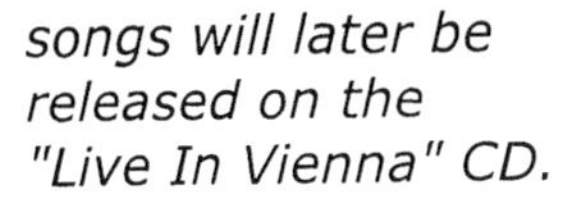

songs will later be released on the "Live In Vienna" CD.

July 30, 1994
Amriswiler, Switzerland

August 26, 1994
Harley-Davidson Rolling Thunder Festival
Munich, Germany

Keep On Rockin', Long Legs, I Hear You Knockin', Hear Me Calling, Good Morning Little School Girl, Take It Easy, Slow Blues In C, I Don't Give A Damn, Johnny B. Goode, Love Like A Man, guitar medley: Sunshine Of Your Love/Smoke On The Water, I'm Going Home, Choo Choo Mama, Rip It Up.

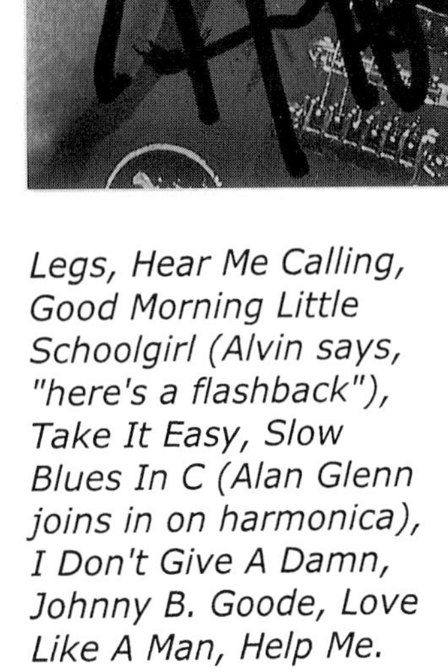

ALVIN LEE with NINE BELOW ZERO

Alvin Lee (guitar & vocals), Gerry McAvoy (bass), Brendan O'Neil (drums) & Alan Glenn (harmonica & guitar).

October 20, 1994
Toad's Place
New Haven, Connecticut

October 21, 1994
Tramp's
New York City, NY

Partial Set List:
Keep On Rockin', Long Legs, Hear Me Calling, Good Morning Little Schoolgirl (Alvin says, "here's a flashback"), Take It Easy, Slow Blues In C (Alan Glenn joins in on harmonica), I Don't Give A Damn, Johnny B. Goode, Love Like A Man, Help Me.

October 22, 1994
Roxy Music Hall
Huntington, NY

October 23, 1994
Club Bene
Sayreville, New Jersey

Keep On Rockin', Long Legs, Hear Me Calling, Good Morning Little Schoolgirl, Take It Easy, Slow Blues In C, I Don't Give A Damn, Johnny B. Goode, Love Like A Man, Classical Thing, I'm Going Home, Choo Choo Mama, Rip It Up.

October 25, 1994
The Strand
Providence, Rhode Island

October 26, 1994
Sting
New Britain, Connecticut

October 28, 1994
Chubby Bear Lounge
Chicago, Illinois

October 29, 1994
Cabooze
Minneapolis, Minnesota

October 30, 1994
Shank Hall
Milwaukee, Wisconsin

October 31, 1994
Pierre's
Ft. Wayne, Indiana

November 3, 1994
Flash Cafe
San Diego, California

November 4, 1994
The Palace
Los Angeles, CA

November 5, 1994
Ventura Theater
California

Nov 6 & 7, 1994
Coach House
San Juan Capistrano, California

November 11, 1994
Jimmy Z's
Everett, Washington

November 12, 1994
Detour Tavern
Renton, Washington

November 13, 1994
Captain Cooke's
Seattle, Washington

November 15, 1994
Great American Music Hall/San Francisco, California

Keep On Rockin', Long Legs, Hear Me Calling, Good Morning Little Schoolgirl, Take It Easy, Slow Blues In C, Jenny Jenny (Alvin brings out Clarence Clemons for a great rockin' version of the song), I Don't Give A Damn, Johnny B. Goode, Silly Thing, Love Like A Man, I'm Going Home, Choo Choo Mama (Clarence Clemons returns for the encores - Alvin says, "the Alvin Lee Big Band...Choo Choo Mama"), Rip It Up.

November 19, 1994
Salle Henri Darras
Marzingarbe, France

THE BREAKERS

"Milan" - Fast Western Records FWCD BR1

The Breakers feature Ric Lee and Ian Ellis of Savoy Brown. Their album "Milan" was recorded at Walnut Tree studios in Berkshire, England.

The tracks include: How Many Times? You're Gonna Miss Me (When I'm Gone), Two Hearts, Time For Leaving, What Does It Take? Young & Ready, How Many Rivers? Make It Last All Night, Not Guilty, Don't You Want My Love? Reconsider Baby, No Sympathy & Crossroads (live).

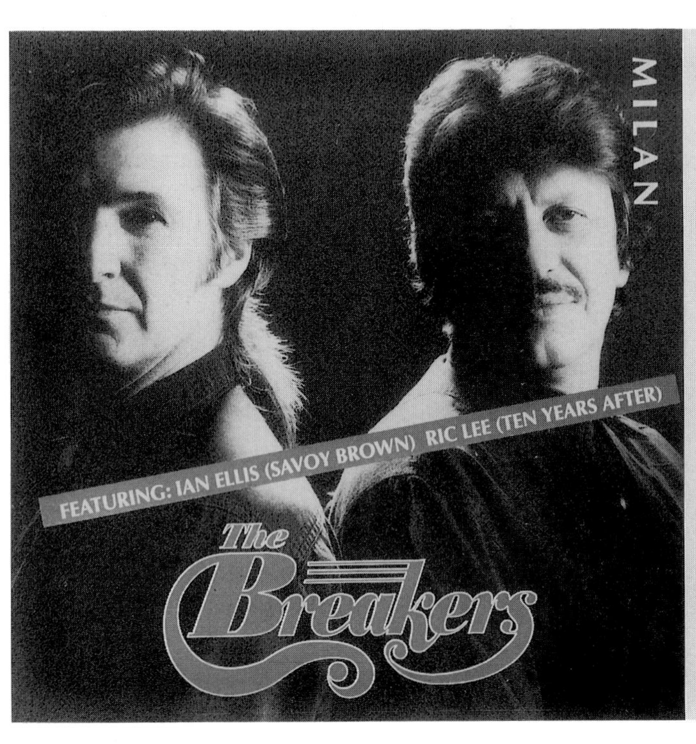

ALVIN LEE BAND

Alvin Lee, Steve Gould, Steve Grant & Alan Young.

January 28, 1995
Switzerland

March 1995
Release of the CD: "Live In Vienna" Castle CSC 7157-2

Recorded live at the Rock House in Vienna on June 16, 1994. The tracks include: Keep On Rockin' (4:14), *Long Legs* (8:19), *I Hear You Knockin'* (3:37), *Hear Me Calling* (5:29), *Love Like A Man* (5:33), *Johnny B. Goode* (2:01), *I Don't Give A Damn* (5:32), *Good Morning Little Schoolgirl* (7:42), *Skooboly Oobly*

Doobob (1:13), *Help Me Baby* (9:50), *Classical Thing* (0:57), *Going Home* (13:26) and *Rip It Up* (3:45).

March 1, 1995
Woodville Halls
Gravesend - Kent, England

March 4, 1995
The Forum
London, England

March 24-25, 1995
Youth Hall
Moscow, Russia

March 31, 1995
Poznan, Poland

April 1, 1995
Wroclaw, Poland

April 2, 1995
Warsaw, Poland

April 15, 1995
Mazingarbe, France

April 17, 1995
Besancon, France

April 18, 1995
Paris, France

April 20, 1995
Reims, France

April 21, 1995
Strasbourg, France

April 22, 1995
Mayenheim, France

May 11, 1995
Theatro del Ateneo
Cerdanyola, Spain

May 13, 1995
Elefante Blanco
Vitoria, Spain

June 4-6, 1995
Ireland

June 8, 1995
Wuppertal, Germany

June 14, 1995
Sportfest
Neudorfl (Burgenland), Austria

June 15, 1995
Bruck-Mar
Tenishalle
Marinsel, Austria

June 16, 1995
Reobnitz
Veranstaltungszelt, Austria

June 17, 1995
Open Air
Sportsplatz
Zurndorf, Austria

June 27-29, 1995
Israel

July 7, 1995
Star Club
Oberhausen, Germany

July 8, 1995
Sandrennbahn
Altrip, Germany

July 13, 1995
Schlacthof
Munich, Germany

July 14, 1995
Staff Rock Club
Hinwil, Switzerland

July 15, 1995
Genf Reithalle
Payern, Switzerland

July 22, 1995
Hangarhalle
Neubiberg, Germany

July 29, 1995
Langoland Festival
Rudkobing, Denmark

August 4, 1995
Festzelt
Gurbru, Switzerland

August 5, 1995
Kalkofen Festival
Warstein, Germany

August 11, 1995
Skanderory, Denmark

August 12, 1995
Flensburgh Festival
Jubeck, Germany

September 30, 1995
Posthof
Linz, Austria

Keep On Rockin', Long Legs, Hear Me Calling, Good Morning Little Schoolgirl, Take It Easy, Slow Blues In C, I Don't Give A Damn, Love Like A Man (with "flamenco" style guitar playing from Alvin), I'm Going Home.

January 10, 1996
Oldenburg, Germany

March 14, 1996
Messehall
Frankfurt, Germany

Partial Set List: Keep On Rockin', Hear Me Calling, Long Legs, Victim Of Circumstance (Clarence Clemons comes onstage and Alvin says,"Ladies and gentlemen we have a special guest tonight from the USA, Clarence Clemmons - the Man!"), Slow Blues In C, Jenny Jenny, Love Like A Man.

April 4, 1996
L'Olympic
Nantes, France

April 5, 1996
La Pleiade
La Riche, France

April 6, 1996
Circuit Buyatti
Le Mans, France

April 7, 1996
Salles des Fetes
Lure, France

BRITISH BLUES BUSTERS

Alvin Lee, Eric Burdon, Micky Moody, Tim Hinkley and Ansley Dunbar.

May 15, 1996
Coach House
San Juan Capistrano, California

Keep On Rockin', Long Legs, Love Like A Man, Johnny B. Goode, Slow Blues In C, I Don't Give A Damn, I'm Going Home, Choo Choo Mama, Rip It Up.

May 16, 1996
The Fillmore
San Francisco, California

May 18, 1996
Ventura Theater, California

Keep On Rockin', Long Legs, Love Like A Man, Slow Blues In C, I Don't Give A Damn, I'm Going Home, Choo Choo Mama, Rip It Up.

May 19, 1996
House Of Blues
West Hollywood, California

Keep On Rockin', Long Legs, Slow Blues In C, I Don't Give A Damn, I'm Going Home, Choo Choo Mama, Rip It Up.

Concert review from HOLLYWOOD REPORTER by John Lappen:

Classic rockers never die, they simply re-form into varying configurations and hit the road, to continue the tour that never ends. The "Best of British Blues" package currently circling the United States contains some interesting names. Highlighted by former Animal's lead growler ***Eric Burdon*** *and ex-Ten Years After fretman Alvin Lee, the band also includes solid drummer Ansley Dunbar (ex-Journey), guitarist Micky Moody (originally with Whitesnake), bassist Boz Burrell (ex-Bad Company) and former Humble Pie keyboardist Tim Hinkley.*

Burdon and the core band minus Lee opened the show, which was divided into two sets. They played a one hour set that featured various blues forms - a Booker T & the MG's cover, some nifty slide work by Moody, a shuffling blues and some funk tossed in for good measure - the songs were'nt anything special, but the

performances were top notch. Burdon's whirling dervish entrance elevated the proceedings a couple levels as the Rock Hall of Famer led the troops through dirty, greasy, rockin' versions of Animals classics such as "Don't Let Me Be Misunderstood", Sam Cooke's "Bring It On Home To Me" and a crazed John Lee Hooker "Boom Boom".

Burdon's singing is as strong as it's been in years, and his constant onstage mugging had bandmates cracking up.

Faster than light gunslinger Lee headlined the second one hour set with signature TYA songs. Best remembered for his career breaking performance of "Going Home" at Woodstock, Lee's set is still built around a lengthy version of the classic boogie tune. He's probably played the song more times than he cares to remember, but he still gives it his all, his blazing leads still fiery enough to drive a crowd bananas. While Burdon's set reminded one of the lads getting together for an all-star pub jam, Lee's performance was heavy on rock star flash and panache; he remains a defining icon of 1970s arena rock.

<u>May 20, 1996</u>
Humphrey's By The Bay
San Diego, California

<u>May 22, 1996</u>
Cain's Ballroom
Tulsa, Oklahoma

<u>May 23, 1996</u>
Deep Ellum
Dallas, Texas

<u>May 24, 1996</u>
Liberty Launch
Austin, Texas

<u>May 25, 1996</u>
River Festival
Pittsburgh, PA

<u>May 26, 1996</u>
Casino
Hampton Beach, New Hampshire

Keep On Rockin', Long Legs, Hear Me Calling, Slow Blues In C (with great solos on hammond organ by Tim Hinkley and on slide guitar by Micky Moody), Classical Thing, I'm Going Home, Choo Choo Mama.

Following Alvin's encores, Eric Burdon came back out and all performed House Of The Rising Sun.

<u>May 28, 1996</u>
"9:30" Club
Washington, DC

<u>May 29, 1996</u>
Harro East
Rochester, New York

<u>May 30, 1996</u>
Seventh House
Pontiac, Michigan

ALVIN LEE BAND

Alvin Lee, Steve Gould (bass) & Alan Young (drums).

<u>June 15, 1996</u>
Tenth Biker's Festival
Udine, Italy

<u>June 22, 1996</u>
Santnerhalle
Wartberg-Krems, Germany

Keep On Rockin', Hear Me Calling, Long Legs, Take It Easy, Slow Blues In C, On The Road Again (instrumental), I Don't Give A Damn, Scat Thing, Love Like A Man, I'm Going Home, Choo Choo Mama.

<u>July 7, 1996</u>
Ljubljana Hippodrom
Slovenia

<u>July 20, 1996</u>
Samsoe Festival
Denmark

August 10, 1996
Friedrich Eberthalle
Ludwigshafen, Germany

August 17, 1996
Citadella de Roses
Spain

September 21, 1996
Uni Halle
Wuppertal, Germany

October 3, 1996
Sonny Boy Club
Treviso, Italy

October 4, 1996
Cap Creces Imola
Bologna, Italy

October 5, 1996
Aurora Theatre
Como, Italy

October 11, 1996
Taverny
Paris, France

October 12, 1996
Blues Rock Festival
Comines, Belgium

October 18, 1996
Waldhaus Konigsee
Thuringen, Germany

October 19, 1996
Stradthalle
Apolda, Germany

October 26, 1996
Starclub
Oberhausen, Germany

Rock & Roll Music To The World, Keep On Rockin', Good Morning Little Schoolgirl, She's So Cute, Victim Of Circumstance, I Don't Give A Damn, Slow Blues In C, I'm Going Home.

March 14, 1997
La Laiterie
Strasbourg, France

March 15, 1997
La Vapeur
Dijon, France

March 20, 1997
Rock House
Vienna, Austria

March 21, 1997
Kulturfabrik
Kufstein, France

March 22, 1997
Posthof
Linz, Austria

March 28, 1997
M J C
Tours, France

March 30, 1997
Salles des Fetes
Concarneau, France

April 19, 1997
Cannes, France

April 30, 1997
Sporthalle
Saarbrucken, Germany

May 2, 1997
Sandweiler, Luxembourg

TYA - 3rd REUNION

In 1997 the members of Ten Years After rejoin for their first ever concerts in South America. They also perform at festivals in Scandinavia and France.

May 21, 1997
Palace
Sao Paulo, Brazil

May 23, 1997
Salao De Artes
Da Reitoria
Porto Allegre, Brazil

Set List: Love Like A Man, Victim Of Circumstance, Rock & Roll Music To The World, Hear Me Calling, Good Morning Little School Girl, You Give Me Loving, Slow Blues In C, Help Me, Johnny B. Goode, I'm Going Home, Choo Choo Mama, Sweet Little Sixteen.

May 24, 1997
Belo Horizonte, Brazil

May 31, 1997
Rock Festival
Esbjerg, Denmark

Rock & Roll Music To The World, Hear Me Calling, Help Me, Slow Blues In C, Good Morning Little School Girl, Love Like A Man, Victim Of Circumstance, Hobbit, Johnny B. Goode, Classical Thing, I'm Going Home, Choo Choo Mama, Sweet Little Sixteen, Rip It Up.

June 14, 1997
Rock Festival
Karlshamm, Sweden

June 28, 1997
Rock Festival
Helsinki, Finland

August 14, 1997
Free Wheels Festival
Clermont, France

June 20, 1998
Faaker See
Karnten, Austria

Ten Years After perform at the Harley Davidson Festival with Bon Jovi.

August 1, 1998
Bilzen, Belgium

Ten Years After perform at the "Jazz Bilzen" Festival near Brussels.

August 14, 1998
Day In The Garden
Bethel, New York

Ten Years After return to the site of the original 1969 ***Woodstock Festival*** *to perform before 14,000 people at the "Day In The Garden" Festival.*

Almost 30 years after their legendary performance on this farmsite, Ten Years After are introduced as ***"The band who rocked the world!"*** *Their set includes: Rock & Roll Music To The World, Hear Me Calling, Love Like A Man, Good Morning Little Schoolgirl, Hobbit, Slow Blues In C, Johnny B. Goode, I Can't Keep From Crying Sometimes, I'm Going Home, Choo Choo Mama and Rip It Up.*

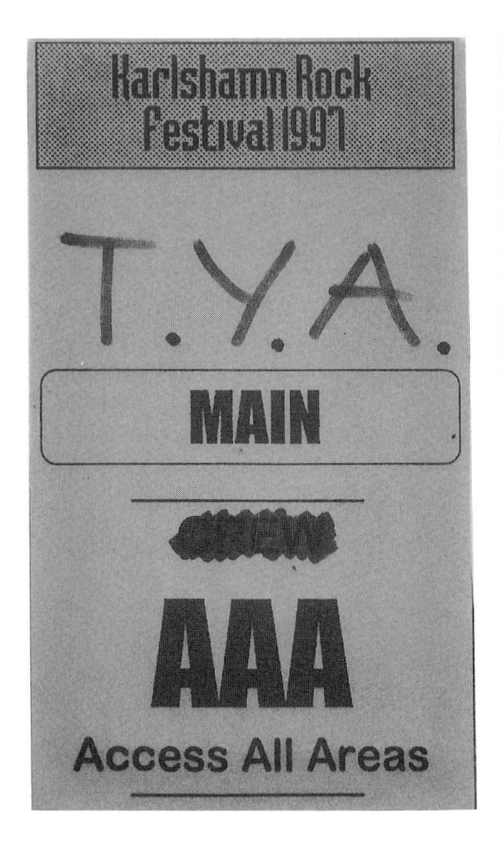

June 11, 1999
"Down By The Laituri " Open Air Festival Turku, Finland

July 6, 1999
Museumplatz Bonn, Germany

July 7, 1999
Serenadenhof Nuremberg, Germany

July 9, 1999
Rolling Thunder Festival Moorenweis, Germany

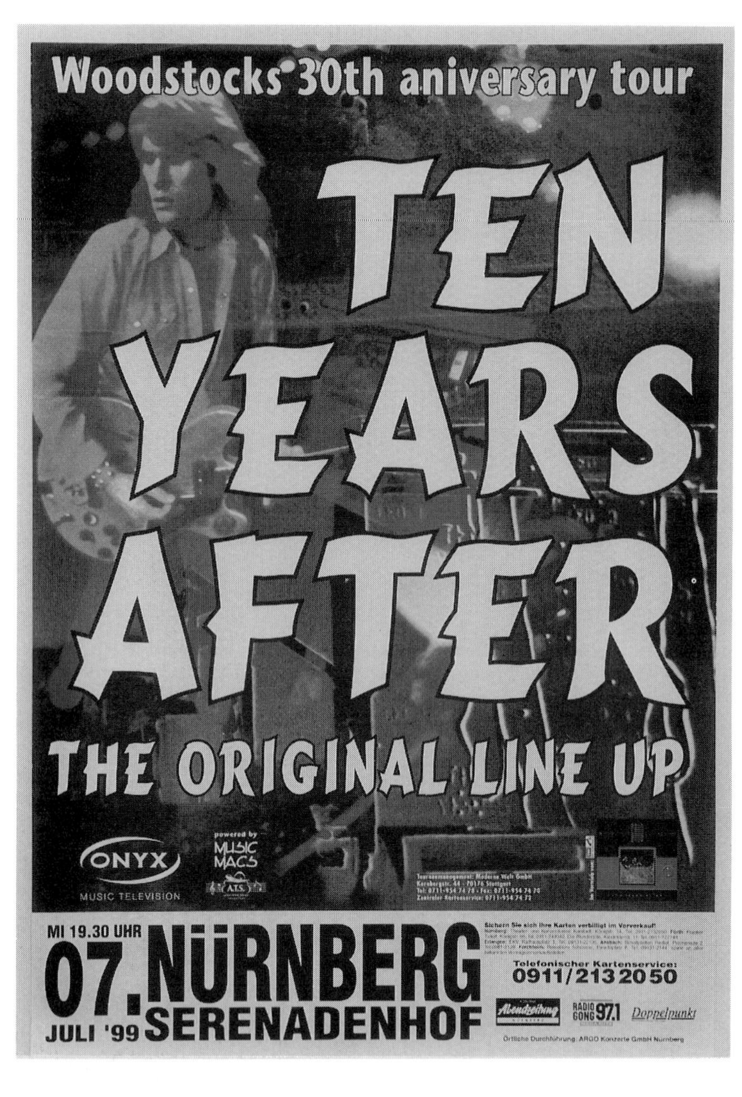

July 10, 1999
Grosse Freiheit
Hamburg, Germany

August 26, 1999
Casino Ballroom
Hampton Beach
New Hampshire

Rock & Roll Music To The World, Hear Me Calling, Love Like A Man, Good Morning Little School Girl, Hobbit, Slow Blues In C, Silly Thing, Johnny B. Goode, Classical Thing, I Woke Up This Morning, Scat Thing, I Can't Keep From Crying Sometimes, I'm Going Home, Choo Choo Mama, Rip It Up.

August 27, 1999
Pineknob
Music Theater
Clarkston, Michigan

August 28, 1999
House of Blues
Chicago, Illinois

September 1, 1999
PNC Arts Center
Holmdel,
New Jersey

With Jethro Tull.

September 2, 1999
Jones Beach
Wantagh, New York

September 4, 1999
House of Blues
Orlando, Florida

Sept 16, 1999
Sun Theatre
Anaheim, CA

Sept 17, 1999
House of Blues
Las Vegas,
Nevada

Sept 18, 1999
Adams County
Fairgrounds
Brighton, CO

Sept 20, 1999
House of Blues
Hollywood, CA

ALVIN LEE BAND

***Steve Gould** on bass and **Alvin Shane** on drums.*

May 12, 2000
Teplice,
Czechoslovakia

May 13, 2000
Zlin,
Czechoslovakia

May 20, 2000
Biker's Festival
Cremona, Italy

May 31, 2000
Reims, France

June 1, 2000
Mulhouse, France

June 2, 2000
Nevers, France

June 3, 2000
Brainans, France

June 7, 2000
Lycabettus Theater
Athens, Greece

June 16 & 18, 2000
Budapest, Hungary

July 29, 2000
Pula,
Slovenia

August 26, 2000
Easy Rider Festival
Egiswil,
Switzerland

August 31, 2000
Esbjerg,
Denmark

September 1, 2000
Open Air Festival
Randers,
Denmark

September 2, 2000
Open Air
Isle of Fehmarn,
Germany

September 3, 2000
Arhus, Denmark

September 6, 2000
Odense, Denmark

September 7, 2000
Copenhagen,
Denmark

Rock & Roll Music To The World, Keep On Rockin', Hear Me Calling, Long Legs, Silly Thing, I'm Writing You A Letter, Take It Easy (with bass & drum solos), Slow Blues In C, Flamenco Thing, I Don't Give A Damn, Johnny B. Goode, Scat Thing, Love Like A Man, Classical Thing, Guitar Medley with: Smoke On The Water, Sunshine Of Your Love & Purple Haze, I'm Going Home.

September 8, 2000
Trondheim,
Norway

Zildjian

ALBUM DISCOGRAPHY

Ten Years After:

TEN YEARS AFTER (1967) LP-Deram DES 18009, CD-Deram 830 532-2
UNDEAD (1968) LP-Deram DES 18016, CD-Deram 820 533-2
STONEDHENGE (1969) LP-Deram DES 18021, CD-Deram 820 534-2
SSSSH (1969) LP-Deram DES 18029, CD-Chrysalis VK 41083
CRICKLEWOOD GREEN (1970) LP-Deram DES 18038, CD-Chrysalis VK 41084
WATT (1970) LP-Deram XDES 18050, CD-Chrysalis VK 41085
A SPACE IN TIME (1971) LP-Columbia KC 30801, CD-Chrysalis F221001
ALVIN LEE & COMPANY (1972) LP-Deram XDES 18064, CD-Deram 820 566-2
ROCK & ROLL MUSIC TO THE WORLD (1972) LP-Columbia KC 31779, CD-Chrysalis VK 41009
RECORDED LIVE (1973) LP-Columbia C2X 32288, CD-Chrysalis VK 41049
POSITIVE VIBRATIONS (1974) LP-Columbia PC 32851, CD-Chrysalis VK 41573
GREATEST HITS (1975) LP-London LC 50008
GOING HOME! (1975) CD-Chrysalis CDP 1C 538-3 21077 2
CLASSIC PERFORMANCES OF TEN YEARS AFTER (1976) LP-Columbia PC 34366
LIVE AT READING '83 (1983) CD-Raw Fruit FRSCD003
ABOUT TIME (1989) LP-Chrysalis 210 180, CD-Chrysalis F221722
LIVE (1990) CD-Code 90 Ninety 3

Selected TYA Collections (several others exist worldwide):

THE LEGENDS OF ROCK (1981) LP-Telefunken-Decca 6.28560 DP (Germany)
HISTORIA DE LA MUSICA ROCK (1982) LP-Decca 9-47 019 (Spain)
THE COLLECTION (1985) LP-Castle/Decca CCSLP 115 (United Kingdom)
AT THEIR PEAK (1987) LP-Pair/Polygram PDL2-1171
PORTFOLIO-A History (1988) LP-Chrysalis CNW 5, CD-Chrysalis CDP 32 1639 2
THE ESSENTIAL TEN YEARS AFTER (1991) CD-Chrysalis F2 21857
ORIGINAL RECORDINGS (1993) CD-See For Miles SEECD 387
THE COLLECTION (1994) CD-Griffin Music GCD-218-2
PURE BLUES (1995) CD-Chrysalis 7243 8 33450 21
SOLID ROCK (1997) CD-Chrysalis 7243 8 21312 29

Chick Churchill:

YOU AND ME (1974) LP Chrysalis CHR 1051

Alvin Lee:

ON THE ROAD TO FREEDOM with Mylon LeFevre (1973) LP Columbia KC 32729
IN FLIGHT (1974) LP Columbia PC 33187, CD Repertoire REP 4702-WP
PUMP IRON (1975) LP Columbia PC 33796, CD Repertoire REP 4703-DG
ROCKET FUEL with Ten Years Later (1977) LP RSO RS13033, CD Repertoire REP 4788
LET IT ROCK (1978) LP Chrysalis CHR 1190, CD Repertoire REP 4704-DG
RIDE ON with Ten Years Later (1979) LP RSO RS13049, CD Repertoire REP 4787
FREE FALL (1980) LP Atlantic SD 19287, CD Repertoire REP 4705-DG
RX5 (1981) LP Atlantic SD 19306, CD Repertoire REP 4706-DG
DETROIT DIESEL (1986) LP 21 Records 7-90517-1, CD-21 Records 290-07-093
ZOOM (1992) CD-Domino 8003-2
I HEAR YOU ROCKIN' (1994) CD-Viceroy VIC8012-2
LIVE IN VIENNA (1994) CD-Castle CSC 7157-2

Ric Lee:

MILAN with The Breakers featuring Ian Ellis (1994) CD Far Western FWCD BR1

Leo Lyons:

TOUGH TRIP THROUGH PARADISE (1992) CD KDC 10016
HEARTLAND (1994) CD Line LICD.01202 0

FILM, TELEVISION & VIDEO APPEARANCES

Ten Years After:

The Butterflies/BBC TV (1967) - Film about teenagers, with TYA live at the Marquee in London.
Top Pop/Danish Television (Feb. 16, 1968) - "I May Be Wrong", "Love Until I Die" & "Spoonful".
Swedish Television (1968) - "Spider In My Web" & "Help Me".
Groovy Show/U.S. Television - Los Angeles (July 10, 1968) - "I Want To Know".
P.O.W./U.S. Television - San Francisco, California (1968) - "Spider In My Web".
Beat Club/German Television (1969) - "Good Morning Little Schoolgirl".
Rehearsals in Germany/a film by Wim Wenders (late 1968) - "I Can't Keep From Crying" and two takes of "I Woke Up This Morning".
Colour Me Pop/U.K. Television (1969) - "A Sad Song", "No Title" & "I'm Going Home".
Montreux Casino/Swiss Television (1969) - "Summertime/Shangtung Cabbage" & "I'm Going Home".
Woodstock/Michael Wadleigh film (Aug. 17, 1969) - the legendary performance of "I'm Going Home".
Groupies/1969 film documentary by Maron (released in 1970) - "Help Me" & "Spoonful".
Dallas Pop Festival (Sept. 1, 1969) Got No Shoes/Got No Blues-Whoopy Cat Home Video - "Spoonfull".
Music Scene/U.S. Television (October 27, 1969) - MPI Home Video - "Bad Scene".
Beat 69/K.B. Hallen-Copenhagen/Danish Television (Dec. 6, 1969) - "I May Be Wrong", "Good Morning Little Schoolgirl", "Scat Thing" & "I Can't Keep From Crying Sometimes".
Trans-Canada Tour (June 1970) - unreleased film - "I Can't Keep from Crying" & "Love Like A Man".
Goose Lake Park/Michigan Rock Festival (August 9, 1970) - unreleased film - "Sweet Little Sixteen".
Isle of Wight (August 30, 1970) - Message To Love/film by Murray Lerner - "I Can't Keep From Crying".
Columbia Records promo film (1971) - "I'd Love To Change The World" performed in recording studio.
Winterland Arena/San Francisco, California (August 4, 1975) - unreleased black & white video of the Ten Years After final tour performance recorded by Bill Graham Presents.
Marquee Club, London (July 1, 1983) - Castle-Hendring Home Video - the Ten Years After reunion performance at the Marquee Club's Silver Jubilee Celebration.
Milan, Italy/RAI Italian TV (July 1988) - "Hear Me Calling", "Love Like A Man" & "Choo Choo Mama".
Berlin, Germany/German Television (December 1989) - Alvin Lee interview and "Going Home" live.
Live Legends/Castle Home Video (May 17, 1990) - Ten Years After concert at Studio 8 in Nottingham.
Frankfurt Jazz Festival/German Television (December 1991) - TYA at the Music Hall in Frankfurt.

Alvin Lee:

Midnight Special/U.S. Television (November 30, 1973) - episode #44 in which Alvin Lee & Mylon LeFevre perform, "Rockin Til The Sun Goes Down", "Carry My Load" & "The World Is Changing".
Rainbow Theater/London, England (March 22, 1974) - unreleased concert film of the Alvin Lee & Company performance featured on the "In Flight" album.
Old Grey Whistle Test/U.K. Television (April 1974) - two songs from the above Alvin Lee & Company Rainbow Theater concert are broadcast (reportedly "Don't Be Cruel" & "Money Honey").
Jukebox/French Television (1974 & 1975) - Freddy Hausser's program airs two Alvin Lee segments.
Midnight Special/U.S. Television (March 21, 1975) - in episode #117 Alvin Lee & Company perform "Somebody's Calling Me", "Time and Space", "Going Through The Door" & "Ride My Train".
Speakeasy/U.S. Television (1975) - Alvin Lee performs "Time and Space" and jams with other guests Al Kooper & Mike Bloomfield on this music & talk show hosted by Woodstock announcer Chip Monck.
Old Grey Whistle Test/U.K.TV (April 1978) - parts of the 4/26 Ten Years Later Paris concert are shown.
Winterland/San Francisco, California (May 19, 1978) - unreleased black & white video of the Ten Years Later concert performance recorded by Bill Graham presents.
Old Grey Whistle Test/U.K. Television (1978) - Ten Years Later perform "Hey Joe".
Rockpalast/German TV (Sept. 13, 1978) - The Ten Years Later concert at the Grugahalle in Essen.
Rockpop/German Television (1979) - Ten Years Later perform "Hey Joe" & "Ain't Nuthin' Shakin".
Gas Tank/U.K. TV (1983) - Alvin Lee appears on the January 15th and February 12th & 26th shows.
Night Of The Guitar/Vol. 1 & 2, PMI Home Video (Nov. 1988) - Alvin performs in the guitar greats tour.
Gottschalk Show/German TV (Oct. 4, 1992) - The Alvin Lee Band performs "A Little Bit Of Love".
Alvin Lee Rockspective/Viceroy Home Video (1993) - Alvin Lee interview, 1975 promos & TYA footage.
Ohne Filter Extra/German TV (April 18, 1994) - The Alvin Lee Band performs an hour long concert.

BIBLIOGRAPHY

Books:

A-Z of Rock Guitarists, Chris Charlesworth (Proteus Publishing Co., 1982)
Barefoot In Babylon, Robert Stephen Spitz (The Viking Press, 1979)
Bill Graham Presents, Bill Graham & Robert Greenfield (Doubleday 1992)
Blues - The British Connection, Bob Brunning (Blandford Press, 1986)
Encyclopedia of Rock Stars, Dafydd Rees & Luke Crampton (DK Publishing, 1996)
The Great Rock Discography, M.C. Strong (Canongate Books Ltd, 1994)
The Illustrated Encyclopedia of Rock, Nick Logan & Bob Woffinden (Harmony, 1977)
Legends of Rock Guitar, Pete Brown & HP Newquist (Hal Leonard, 1997)
Message To Love - The Isle of Wight Festival 1968-70, Brian Hinton (Staples Printers, 1995)
The Midnight Special - Late Night's Original Rock & Roll Show, B.R. Hunter (Pocket Books, 1997)
The Rock 'N' Roll Years (Hamlyn Publishing Group Ltd. & Crescent Books, 1990)
Rock Movers & Shakers, Barry Lazell (with Rees & Crampton), Billboard Publications, 1989

Magazines & Periodicals:

Aquarian Weekly - #84 (1975) & #281 (1979)
Beat Instrumental - 7/68, 10/68, 12/68, 12/69, 6/70, 10/70, 7/71, 7/74 & 12/74
Beetle - January 1974
Best - May 1972 & June 1974
Billboard - 1/18/69
Circus - 7/69, 11/69, 5/70, 9/70, 4/71, 11/71, 1/73, 2/72, 8/73, 3/75 & 7/20/78
Circus Raves - July 1974
Crawdaddy - Vol. 4, No. 1 (1970)
Creem - 7/70, 4/73, 6/75 & 1/87
Disc - 12/6/69, 7/18/70, 9/5/70, 9/25/71, 10/2/71, 3/25/72, 5/13/72, 9/23/72, 3/31/73 & 8/11/73
East Village Other - 3/1/69 & 9/10/69
Goldmine - 9/28/84 & 10/6/89
Guitar Player - October 1971
Guitarist - 4/1/87
Hit Parader - 7/69, 6/70, 7/70, 9/71 & 4/74
History of Rock - Vol. 63 & Vol. 69
International Musician & Recording World - 8/75 & 6/76
Jazz & Pop - May 1970
Kerrang - 1/20/90
Let It Rock - 6/1/75
Los Angeles Free Press - 6/68, 11/68 & 3/69
Melody Maker - 7/1/67, 10/14/67, 11/4/67, 11/11/67, 8/17/68, 12/21/68, 1/25/69, 2/8/69, 6/28/69, 10/4/69, 10/18/69, 5/2/70, 9/5/70, 11/14/70, 2/20/71, 11/6/71, 1/15/72, 4/8/72, 9/16/72, 11/4/72, 4/21/73, 6/23/73, 8/11/73, 8/18/73, 6/22/74, 11/2/74, 3/15/75, 5/8/76 & 5/6/78
New Musical Express - 8/12/67, 11/25/67, 8/31/68, 3/8/69, 5/17/69, 5/24/69, 8/3/69, 5/16/70, 3/13/71, 9/18/71, 9/25/71, 10/30/71, 12/25/71, 4/21/73, 7/7/73, 9/8/73, 3/16/74, 4/20/74, 4/27/74, 11/9/74, 12/14/74, 12/28/74, 4/5/75, 5/17/75 & 9/2/78
Pop - No. 16 (1974)
Record Mirror - 11/30/68, 5/16/70, 2/21/71 & 3/27/71
Replay - 5/1/92
Rock - 9/27/70, 10/25/71 & 3/12/73
Rock & Folk - June 1970 & May 1974
Rock Scene - January 1987
Rolling Stone - 9/6/69, 6/25/70, 2/1/73 & 2/13/75
Seconds - Issue No. 38
Sounds - 10/17/70, 12/26/70, 6/26/71, 8/28/71, 9/18/71, 9/25/71, 10/2/71, 8/19/72, 9/23/72, 4/14/73, 6/23/73, 7/14/73, 10/27/73, 11/3/73, 11/23/73, 2/2/74, 3/23/74, 4/27/74 & 9/7/74
Zoo World - July 1973
Zygote - Vol. 1, No. 2